Praise for DEBBIE MACOMBER'S Dakota books

Dakota Born is "a heartwarming tale
set in a small farming town on the brink of extinction.
Fans are certain to take to the Dakota series as they
would to cotton candy at a state fair."
—*Publishers Weekly*

"*Dakota Born* is a poignant story of the plight of the
modern American farmer and of townspeople pulling
together to make their hometown one they can be
proud of. It is a story of relationships between husband
and wife, lovers, friends and neighbours…an extremely
well-written and touching tale. Ms. Macomber certainly
has a knack for telling the story of small-town life."
—*Romance Communications*

Debbie Macomber "is skilled at creating characters
who work their way into readers' hearts. In this book,
she masterfully moves the story along while
not shortchanging the main plotline."
—*RT Book Reviews* on *Dakota Home*

"Macomber closes [*Dakota Home*] with a cliffhanger,
leaving readers anxiously awaiting the final instalment
to this first-rate series."
—*Publishers Weekly*

"Poignant, moving, compelling,
Always Dakota comes very highly recommended."
—*WordWeaving*

Dear Friends,

I've been looking forward to seeing the Dakota series in print again! And judging by the letters and e-mails I've received over the past few years, so have many of you.

These books are special to me. They reflect the fact that the Dakotas are an important part of my own heritage. My mother was born and raised in Dickinson, North Dakota, and my father came from Ipswich, South Dakota. The Dakotas and the immigrants who settled there shaped my parents' lives and, in turn, shaped mine.

In November 1998, I flew into Minneapolis and met my cousin Shirley Adler. With a rental car and a map, we toured the Dakotas, laughing ourselves sick along the way, sharing childhood memories. I looked up cousins I hadn't seen in more than thirty years and savored some wonderful moments with Aunt Gladys in Dickinson and with Aunt Betty and Uncle Vern in Aberdeen, South Dakota. Uncle Vern has since died, which makes the memories of that visit even more precious. At the time of his death, he and Aunt Betty had been married for seventy-two years!

While I was on this research trip, two writing friends—Judy Baer and Sandy Huseby, both of North Dakota—provided invaluable assistance. They answered countless questions and shared their pride in their state with me. I can only hope I did North Dakota justice.

And I hope you enjoy this story about finding love in a small town.

Debbie Macomber

P.S. I'd be delighted to hear from you! You can reach me at my Web site, www.debbiemacomber.com, or write to me at P.O. Box 1458, Port Orchard, WA 98366.

DEBBIE MACOMBER

Dakota
BORN

MIRA®

MIRA®

Recycling programs
for this product may
not exist in your area.

ISBN-13: 978-0-7783-2960-2

DAKOTA BORN

Copyright © 1999 by Debbie Macomber.

For questions and comments about the quality of this book please contact us
at Customer_eCare@Harlequin.ca.

www.MIRABooks.com

Printed in U.S.A.

Eight

Sarah Stern pulled the pickup truck into the service station and leaped down to pump her own gas. Dennis was outside immediately, eager to help her; he'd removed the handle from the pump before she'd even reached it.

"It's good to see you," he said. The words were casual but his voice said how much he'd missed her.

"You, too."

"You haven't called since the night of the town council meeting," he reminded her, concentrating on his task, eyes focused on the moving numbers of the pump.

Sarah was just as aware of how long it'd been. She'd missed him, needed him, and had tried to be strong. But she couldn't do it anymore. Filling up her father's truck was an excuse to see him, and they both knew it.

"What's wrong?" he asked, standing beside her.

"What makes you think anything's wrong?" His ability to read her thoughts unnerved her a little.

"Because I know you. Because I love you."

"Oh, Dennis, please don't say that." Sarah cursed herself again for being weak, for her inability to stay away from him. She tried, she really did, but some days she got so lonely it was all she could do to keep her sanity. Her quilt business helped, but at night, when she crawled into bed, reality returned to stare her in the face.

She was living under her father's roof. It mortified her that at the age of thirty-four she couldn't seem to make her own way in the world. And here she was, Calla's role model. She'd made so many mistakes through the years. Now, despite her efforts to live a decent and honest life, she was using Dennis. She loved him, but she *couldn't* impose her troubles on him anymore.

"Tell me what's wrong," he urged gently.

Sarah lowered her head. "Calla got a postcard from Willie," she finally said. She hadn't meant to tell him, she really hadn't….

Dennis was quiet for a few moments. He knew without her having to say it how much any contact with her ex-husband upset her.

"It's about time she heard from her dad, isn't it?" he asked in a neutral tone.

"But now she's all excited about seeing him at Christmas."

"Is that what he told her?"

Sarah shrugged to hide the hurt. "Apparently. Calla wouldn't let me read the card. He's in Vegas and the picture's of some fancy hotel, supposedly where he's staying. I couldn't believe how excited she was. She doesn't hear from him for months at a time, he forgets her birthday, doesn't even send her a Christmas gift—and then she's doing cartwheels because he mails her a *postcard*."

"He *is* her father."

Sarah bit her lip. While it was true that Willie had fathered Calla, he'd never shown much interest in her. He hadn't paid the court-ordered child support, nor had he made more than a token effort to keep in touch with his daughter. Every five or six months he sent her a five-dollar bill in an envelope—usually without so much as a note. What irritated Sarah most was how willingly Calla made excuses for him.

"Willie isn't going to pay for her ticket and I can't afford to buy her airfare to Las Vegas or wherever he's living now," Sarah protested. "And even if I could, I wouldn't."

Dennis finished with the pump and led her inside the station, where he rang up the total on the old-fashioned register. "You're afraid Calla's going to accuse you of taking her father away from her."

"You're right—I am." Her daughter's attitude seemed ridiculous to Sarah. "He ignores her, abandons her emotionally and financially and is completely worthless as a father, yet Calla thinks he walks on water."

"That's fairly typical, I'd think." He reached for her hand, holding it between his own. "He's her father. It's obvious she's built Willie up in her mind as this wonderful, caring father figure. She needs to see him that way, otherwise she'd have to deal with the rejection she feels when he ignores her."

Dennis was pretty wise about people, and Sarah knew he'd figured out the reason for Calla's behavior. But that didn't make living with her daughter any easier. She found it almost impossible to say nothing while Calla went on and on about what a fabulous father she had. She talked this way to anyone who'd listen. She'd even taken the postcard to school with her to show the new teacher.

Ironically, Calla's attitude toward Sarah was hostile. When Sarah had recently confronted her about it, Calla had insinuated that the failure of the marriage must have been Sarah's fault. If she'd been a better wife, none of this would have happened. If she'd tried harder, loved him more, they could still be a family. Her daughter simply didn't know the facts, but Sarah couldn't tell Calla about her father's neglect and infidelity; she felt she had no right to place that burden on a fourteen-year-old. Besides, it was *her* problem, *her* history, not Calla's.

"How's it you're so smart?" she asked, squeezing Dennis's hand, grateful for his unflinching support. "You should've been a psychologist." She smiled at him, loving him more than ever.

"If I was so smart, I'd have found a way to convince you to marry me."

"Dennis, don't, please." She closed her eyes, unable to cope with any additional pressure, especially from him. Not when marriage was impossible.

"It's crazy for us to go on like this," he argued. "You know how I feel about you."

"Yes—I know."

"You're thirty-four and I'm twenty-nine. Big deal."

"It isn't only that," she said, resisting the urge to cover her ears. She hadn't come to him to fight, especially when the subject was one they'd already covered so many times. She needed comfort and reassurance, not pressure.

Refusing to discuss it further, she slid a hand inside her hip pocket for her cash and counted out three fives to pay for the gasoline. She put the money on the counter.

Dennis ignored it. "I love you, Sarah."

The best thing to do, she decided, was change the subject. "I went out to see Jeb on Sunday."

"Are you saying you prefer not to talk about us?"

"Yes." Unable to meet his eyes, she looked away.

His sigh revealed both frustration and defeat. "All right," he said. "How's Jeb?"

"Disagreeable as always. I brought him some biscuits and gravy. Made them myself, just the way Mom used to."

"I imagine he scarfed them down fast enough."

Sarah smiled. "Between growls."

Since the farming accident that had claimed his leg, her brother, who'd never enjoyed social situations, had become a real loner. Jeb's entire life now revolved around his bison, and his only social activity occurred when his family and friends made their infrequent trips out to the ranch.

"Did Calla go with you?"

"No." Her daughter was uncomfortable around Jeb, uncertain how to act. Most of the time, Jeb was gruff and unfriendly, even to Sarah and his father. When Calla was there, he tended to ignore all three of them. Every once in a while, her daughter would agree to accompany Sarah on the long drive, but not often. When she did make the trip, Calla spent her time looking at the calves.

"He's going to be all right, you know."

"How can you say that?" Sarah cried. Dennis knew she worried about her brother, knew that everyone did. "It's been three years. I'd hoped—I assumed that…" Her voice trailed off.

"We all did," Dennis said with such gentleness that she raised her eyes to meet his. "Don't let yourself worry so much about him."

"I can't help it."

"Then let *me* help you."

Without realizing it, Dennis made everything so much more difficult. "I can't do that, either."

"Try… Let me take you to dinner Friday night. Just the two of us. We'll give Buffalo Bob's karaoke machine a try."

"I can't sing."

"You can. I've heard you!"

Once more she attempted to change the subject away from the two of them. "Did I tell you I sold another quilt? A lady in Dickinson saw that sunflower quilt I made and phoned and ordered one for herself."

Sarah was passionate about quilts and took real pride in her small business. She bought muslin and colored it with natural dyes, which created subtle tones and interesting, often unusual effects; no two bolts of cloth ended up looking exactly the same. Then she worked out designs, using the traditional patterns as a basis. Her sunflower quilt, for instance, was a variation on the classic "Dresden plate" design. That quilt had taken first place in the State Fair in Minot two years earlier and sold for an incredible one thousand dollars. Her second and third sales came within four months of each other and she'd been selling consistently since. It wasn't enough money to support herself and Calla, but it made a difference.

"Thanks for the dinner invitation, but I'd better not. I have to finish that quilt for my new customer."

"You can't stop sewing long enough to eat dinner?" Dennis asked wryly.

"Dennis, please, I don't want to go through this again."

"Have dinner with me," he said. "Friday night. Please."

"I can't."

"You can sleep with me, but you can't go out with me and—"

"Shh." Embarrassed, she looked around, fearing someone might have heard him.

"And," he went on, "it's perfectly fine to come to me when you need something."

"I shouldn't. I know I shouldn't."

"Don't use me, Sarah. This can't just be on your terms, you know."

She hung her head, not knowing what to say. "All right,

we can go out to dinner," she whispered. She knew he was right; she did use him and when she didn't need him, she avoided him. Dennis deserved better.

"Good, and when we're done eating, we'll drive over to my house and you can have your way with me."

"Dennis!"

"You think I'm joking? It's been July since we…"

"That's all?" It'd seemed much longer.

To her surprise, Dennis burst out laughing. His hug was spontaneous and she found herself smiling.

"We're going to do the town," he insisted. "Kick up our heels and let down our hair. Just the two of us. No more secret meetings. I'm not ashamed to let everyone know you're with me."

The joy evaporated from her. "Dennis, I don't think—"

"Then let me do the thinking. Now, no more arguing. Friday night Calla's working, right? I'll order one of Rachel's pizzas for your dad—and I'll give Calla a good tip for delivering it. Then you and I are going to celebrate the sale of your quilt."

Sarah closed her eyes, allowing herself the luxury of dreaming that a future was possible for her and Dennis, even though she knew it wasn't.

"Lindsay phoned," Leta announced when Gage walked into the house late Thursday afternoon.

Gage managed to hide his reaction beneath a scowl. He'd been waiting to hear from Lindsay ever since the night they'd dug around that old fireplace. If there'd once been a moveable brick, there wasn't one now.

He believed Lindsay when she said she'd seen—or heard—it move. Granted, that was about twenty years ago. He suspected there must've been a mechanism that triggered it someplace on or near the fireplace. He'd checked everywhere he could think, with no success.

"She wants to remind you about Friday."

Gage didn't know why he'd ever agreed to talk to the high-school students. Well, yes, he *did* know. It'd been the only way he could think of to see Lindsay again without being overt about his feelings.

"Are you going to call her back?" his mother asked as she began shucking corn, preparing the evening meal. She was humming softly to herself, and Gage knew she loved all this. He wasn't fooled. His mother and Hassie would like nothing better than to do some matchmaking between him and Lindsay. Gage was willing, although pride demanded that he not let it show. The problem was with Lindsay.

"I don't think there's any reason to return the call," he said.

His mother stopped and smiled at him. "Lindsay's a beautiful woman," she said dreamily.

"What's that got to do with anything?" he muttered. It wasn't as if he hadn't noticed.

"Well," Leta said, "I thought you'd welcome an excuse to talk to her."

"I don't." It was best to maintain this air of disinterest, otherwise his mother would go at the matchmaking full-tilt. She'd be pressuring him to ask Lindsay out; he didn't want to tell her he already had and that Lindsay's answer was no.

"You like her, don't you?" His mother sounded worried.

Maybe he was overdoing the disinterested part. "She's all right."

"Hassie and I think she's wonderful with the kids."

He shrugged, but he shared their opinion.

"Did you know the high-schoolers are publishing the first Buffalo Valley newspaper in ten years? Lindsay drove all the way to Grand Forks yesterday afternoon to have it printed." Leta filled a large pan with water for the corn and started mixing dough for buttermilk biscuits.

"The kids produced the entire newspaper themselves," she went on. "Kevin wrote the piece about the Hansen Grocery being up for sale and he drew the political cartoon."

"I'll look forward to reading it."

"Kevin told me this morning that Lindsay's started a drama club. She approached Joshua McKenna about cleaning out the old theater and using it for a stage play, which I thought was an excellent idea. Don't you?"

A play? What would she think of next? "I suppose she's planning a production of *Les Miserables.*"

"Not a musical," Leta said with a laugh. "A Christmas play. They're going to write it themselves."

The way Lindsay worked, she'd probably persuade all the townsfolk to help her with her project, whether they wanted to or not. Gage could see it already. He'd be spending every evening for weeks down at the theater with a bunch of other guys getting the place fixed up—and he'd do it gladly. "She, uh, certainly has ambitious plans."

"Lindsay Snyder is just what this town needed," his mother said firmly.

Gage could do nothing but agree.

"She's exactly what *you* need, too."

Gage didn't want to continue down this path. "I'll go wash for dinner."

"Don't you think so?"

"About Lindsay? Oh, sure, she's a welcome addition to Buffalo Valley." No argument there. Everyone knew what would have happened without her, what might still happen with the bitter news of low grain prices.

"Gage?"

He turned reluctantly.

"Lindsay's been in Buffalo Valley more than two months now."

He didn't comment.

"Are you going to ask her out or not?"

"You mean…on a date?"

"What else? You're thirty-five and it's long past time you were married. I was hoping—"

Gage held up his hand. "Mother, I love you, but this isn't a subject I'm willing to discuss with you, especially not right now."

Her shoulders lifted as if she were about to say something else, then she stopped herself. "All right. If that's the way you want it."

Gage headed for the stairs as Kevin burst in. "I got a copy of the newspaper!" he said with rare excitement. He waved it in the air like a kid hawking papers on a busy street corner.

"Look here." He carefully smoothed it out across the kitchen table, and his mother pulled out a chair and sat down. Kevin and Gage stood behind her as she opened the paper.

"Who formatted it in this newspaper style?" Gage asked, impressed by the paper's professional appearance.

"Miss Snyder has a laptop she brought into school, and she let Stan Muller type it up."

"He did a good job," Gage said approvingly. "You all did." For the next five minutes, Gage heard another round of Miss Snyder this and Miss Snyder that, until he wanted to shout at his brother to stop.

"Did you hear about Ambrose Kohn?" Kevin asked.

Gage knew the farmer, but only vaguely. He lived in the next county over and owned thirteen thousand acres of prime farmland. The Kohn family had money, and not all of it was tied up in their acreage.

"What about him?" Leta asked before Gage had the opportunity.

"He drove all the way over from Devils Lake to ask Miss Snyder to the Halloween costume party the Elks club is putting on."

Despite his efforts to hide his reaction, Gage's jaw tightened. Then, as casually as he could, he asked, "Did she take him up on his offer?" Still, he was sure Lindsay must've said no to Kohn. Since she'd already turned *him* down, explaining that she didn't plan to get involved with anyone for at least a year, he doubted she'd accept an invitation from Ambrose.

"That's the kicker. She's actually going. Jessica and a couple of the other girls are helping her plan a costume."

Gage couldn't believe his ears. His mother whirled around in her chair, eyes narrowed accusingly. Without saying a word, she told him it should have been Gage taking Lindsay to that dance and not some stranger from another county.

Gage had always thought of himself as a peaceable sort of man, but right then it was all he could do to keep from plowing his fist through the wall.

Speaking to a room full of high-school students, dismantling her fireplace—oh, he was just fine for *those* things. But a date? No, sir. She preferred someone else. Anyone else.

"Gage?"

His mother was studying him. "What?" he snapped.

She flinched at his anger. "Are you going to let Lindsay slip through your fingers like that?"

"Enough, Mom. I—"

"You like Miss Snyder?" Kevin asked, studying Gage.

"Stay out of this," he growled at his younger brother.

"Did you hear?" his mother cried. "Lindsay's dating Ambrose Kohn. Aren't you going to *do* something?"

"Doesn't look like I have much choice in the matter,

now does it?" he said. "Ambrose Kohn has a whole lot more to offer Miss Snyder than I do."

"But if she marries Ambrose, she'll move away and Buffalo Valley needs her." Leta seemed to think Gage was the only hope the community had.

"If she marries Ambrose, she marries Ambrose," he said as though it was of little concern to him.

Kevin glanced from Gage to his mother. "I think it's too soon to know if she's going to marry Mr. Kohn, Mom. This is only their first date."

October 5th

Dear Maddy,

It was so wonderful to get your letter. You're right, homesickness has hit me hard. This isn't like being away at college. Living in Buffalo Valley is an entirely different world. Not that I'm complaining. I've discovered something about myself that I didn't know, something I'd only suspected. I *love* teaching school! The kids are terrific and smart and fun. The best part is they're game for just about anything. As you know, we've had our ups and downs. Their idea of life in the city is what they see on MTV. Can you imagine teaching a room full of teenagers who learned everything they know about sex and intimacy from Madonna?

I'm enclosing the first edition of the Buffalo Valley High School newspaper. I'm so proud of this paper. My students spent hours putting it together: the writing, the political comments, the artwork. Everything.

Take a good look at the political cartoon. That was done by Kevin Betts. Is he good or what? I don't think anyone knows how much his artwork means to him. When I told him I thought it was terrific, he brushed off my compliment, almost as if he was embarrassed. One day after school, I found a drawing he did of his brother standing in a wheat field and it was so damn good it brought tears to my eyes. I was blown away by his talent. Without telling him, I've contacted a number of art schools around the country and inquired about scholarships. Once I get the information, I'm going to approach Gage, his older brother, about having Kevin apply.

Before you ask, yes, Gage is the farmer I mentioned earlier and no, there's nothing romantic going on between us. Absolutely nothing. I knew it was a mistake to tell you about that kiss, but the whole thing was a fluke and won't be repeated. I'm sure he regrets the incident as much as I do. Okay, okay, we did go to dinner, but we went as friends and nothing more. Honest. I can't deal with anything beyond that just yet.

All right, I know you're dying to find out what's been happening with Monte. Well, here goes. He wrote me again last week, and this time he didn't just demand that I come back, he actually said he misses me. Oh, he did add that he thinks I made a terrible mistake. As usual, he's hoping I'll have a change of heart soon. Fat chance of that! He's annoyed that I haven't answered his other letters. Then he had the gall to tell me he won't allow me to blackmail him into marriage. He just doesn't get it.

I threw this letter away just like I did the other two, and you know what? It's easier every time. I wish I could tell you I tossed it without reading it first, but my curiosity got the better of me. Maybe the next one.

Buffalo Bob sends his greetings, by the way. He's been morose all week because of Merrily—his one and only Buffalo Gal. She left, apparently for no reason. From what Hassie told me, Merrily does this once in a while. No one knows why or where she goes. What I suspect is that she has a whole other life she escapes to when she gets bored or restless here. Which is sort of like me at the moment, I guess, only in reverse.

I've lived my entire life in Savannah, and although I've only been in North Dakota a couple of months, it feels as much like home as the South. Don't misunderstand me, I miss everyone. Some days more than others. And everything isn't exactly smooth sailing, either. Some people, like Hassie and Leta Betts, are wonderful and helpful, and then others like Marta Hansen seem to be waiting for me to pack my bags and disappear the way Merrily did. Buffalo Bob told me he's been in town a couple of years now and some folks still treat him like an upstart.

Yes, I will be home for Thanksgiving. We can shop till we drop. Just remember I'm not as flush as I used to be, although the cost of living here is much cheaper than I realized. A bonus, to be sure.

Hassie has proven to be a dear friend and mentor. If I'm not busy with the kids after school, I drop by the pharmacy and visit with her. We have dinner together two or three nights a week. She's witty and insightful, and the only one who knows about Monte. Gage guessed why I took the job, but he doesn't know the details.

Did I mention I started a drama club? Remember Mr. Olsen when we were in high school and how much fun we had doing *Our Town, The Crucible* and *The Music Man?* I'm not ready to try one of the classics—or, heaven forbid, a musical—but I've had some thoughts about what we might do. Tell you later. My first problem was finding someplace to hold the play. The answer seemed obvious. Remember that closed-down theater on Main Street? I asked Joshua McKenna about it—he's the president of the town council—and he told me it actually belongs to a family in Devils Lake. I was able to reach the son of the owner about using it, and he roped me into attending some Halloween party with him in exchange. I agreed, but I don't like it. Laugh if you must, but I have a date with a man named Ambrose.

Oh, yes, you asked about Rachel Fischer's pizza. Who'd believe the best pizza in the world is baked right here in Buffalo Valley? I asked if she'd sell me a jar of her pizza sauce to take home at Thanksgiving so you can taste it for yourself. Expect to be amazed. It's that good, and you know what a pizza connoisseur I am. I'm getting to know Rachel. It feels good to have another woman close to my own age to talk to. I treasure Hassie, but...

Lindsay's letter-writing was interrupted by a rapid pounding on her front door. Mutt and Jeff beat her there, barking madly. She hurried to open it, thinking there might be some kind of emergency. Gage Sinclair stood on her porch looking furious about *something*.

"Gage." She held the door for him and gestured him inside. He marched in, glancing around as if he suspected she had company.

"What's wrong?"

He frowned at her. "I hear you're dating Ambrose Kohn."

"Oh, that. You'd better let me explain." It hadn't occurred to her that Gage might be offended by her agreeing to attend the party with Ambrose. Now, if he'd give her a chance to tell him—

"I'm not here to listen to your reasons. They're fairly obvious."

"Oh?" Lindsay found that comment curious.

"He's got a whole lot more land than I do. Money's what makes the world go round, isn't it?"

That was downright insulting. "You're being ridiculous. Now sit down and—"

"I feel like standing."

"Fine, stand then," she said, doing her best to maintain her own composure. She crossed her arms and waited for him to continue.

"You *refuse* to go out with me—"

"You *refuse* to listen to—"

"Are you mocking me?" he barked.

"You're behaving like a jealous lover."

"Lover?" He laughed sarcastically. "I can't even get you to have a beer with me. Apparently I didn't pass your scrutiny in that department. Oh, I'm worthy enough to work three nights in a row getting your fence repaired. I'm worthy enough to talk to your class for an hour on a Friday afternoon. I'm—"

"Gage…" If he'd only let her explain! "It isn't like that," she began.

"The hell it isn't."

Lindsay slapped her hands against her sides. "You're the most irrational man I've ever known!"

"Me?" he shouted. "I don't know where I stand with you half the time. You practically threw yourself at me—"

"Threw myself at you?" The man was living in a dream world!

"What else am I to think when you kissed me like that?"

Now she was fuming. "You're the one who kissed me!" she reminded him, so angry she could barely speak.

"And you loved it."

"I…I… You *are* jealous."

His head came up. "The hell I am. What I am, in case you haven't noticed, is *mad*."

"You don't have a right to feel anything when it comes to me."

"Be that as it may," he said, his gaze narrowed. "I can't help feeling something for you."

She stood there openmouthed, with no idea how to respond to his confession.

"I thought you were someone special," he said, his voice low and vibrating with emotion. "Now I can see how wrong I was."

His words shouldn't have hurt her, but they did. "I think you should leave," she told him, pointing at her front door. It occurred to her that this wasn't the first time she'd ordered him out of her house.

His hesitation was momentary, and then he stalked out in much the same way he'd entered.

For good measure Lindsay slammed the door after him. The bastard! Then, because she was so furious she needed to vent her emotion, she kicked the bottom corner of the fireplace. She'd never done anything this childish in her life; she'd never been this angry in her life. Not even at Monte. Pain shot up her foot and she cried out, hopping up and down, clutching at her toes.

That was when she saw it.

Lindsay froze. The brick, the one she'd been searching

for all these weeks, had effortlessly slid into view. Apparently, when she kicked the fireplace, she'd struck the mechanism that opened it.

Nine

Friday afternoon, against his better judgment, Gage showed up at the high school, just as he'd promised. He was a man of his word, and that meant he had to follow through, even when he would have preferred to stay as far away from Lindsay Snyder as humanly possible. Early on he'd made a decision to maintain his reserve when it came to the schoolteacher, and he knew others had, too. He'd wavered from that decision—distracted by his emotions—but now he'd become more determined than ever. In a year's time she'd be gone and it was just as well for everyone.

What he'd told her the night before remained true in his mind. She wasn't anyone special. Not anymore, not to him. She could date Ambrose Kohn with his thirteen thousand bottomland acres and his money in the bank and Gage wouldn't give a gnat's ass.

"Hi, Gage." Kevin stepped out of the school and walked toward the pickup. "Miss Snyder asked if you were going to show up this afternoon and I told her you would. I told her you *always* keep your word."

Gage saw the look of relief and suspected his half brother

hadn't been as confident of that as he claimed. It just went to prove how important it was to follow through on his promises—despite his feelings. If he'd made an excuse the way he'd been tempted to, he would've sent Kevin the wrong message. Gage was the closest thing Kevin had to a father figure, and he took his responsibility seriously.

"Can I help you carry something inside?"

"Yeah." Gage lowered the tailgate of his truck. He'd brought along a couple of boxes and frames, an extractor and a smoker, which he planned to demonstrate with during his talk.

Kevin reached for a box. "Miss Snyder said she'd like to talk to you privately for a couple of minutes when you're finished. She wants to know if you can stay."

"I'll tell her I can." He wasn't going to send a teenager to do his talking for him. As far as he was concerned, he had nothing to say to Lindsay Snyder that hadn't been said the night before. Apparently she wanted the last word; he'd give it to her, but that was all she was getting from him.

The class watched as Gage and Kevin walked in with various boxes and pieces of equipment. Lindsay's gaze sought him out, and he met her look with cool indifference.

She took her cue from that, and didn't personally greet him.

"When I first moved to Buffalo Valley," she said, standing in front of the class, "I approached a number of people about coming in and talking about their lives, their interests, their history in Buffalo Valley. We're fortunate to have Kevin's brother, Gage Sinclair, here to talk to us today about beekeeping."

Her introduction was followed by polite applause and plenty of curious stares as he and Kevin carried the equipment to the front of the classroom. He waited until Kevin took his seat. Gage wasn't comfortable talking in front of a group and was especially ill at ease when it was a group of teenagers, even if he *had* known most of them their entire lives.

"I thought I could start by telling you how I got interested in bees." He waited until he saw Lindsay nod before he continued. He cleared his throat. "Anyone in here ever been stung?"

They almost all raised their hands.

"I was, too, plenty of times. The summer I was twelve I got stung by a nasty-tempered bee. Do you know what happens if you don't get the stinger out?" Again his question was followed by several raised hands. "It festers into a boil. I couldn't believe that a stinger so small I could barely see it would do that to my body. It was an unpleasant experience, but it made me curious about wasps and hornets and bees, and I found honeybees fascinating."

"I'd be more afraid of them than curious," Kevin's girl-friend piped up.

"That's because you're a girl," one of the Loomis twins said with a snicker.

Lindsay cast her students a look that quickly silenced them.

"When I was thirteen, I was assigned to write a paper on the subject of my choice. My mother suggested I write about bees, seeing I already knew so much about them."

"When did you start keeping bees?" Amanda Jensen wanted to know.

"About ten years ago," Gage said. "And I'm still learning. The hives are a challenge every single season."

"Even now?"

"Even now," he told them, and went on to explain the different feeding cycles.

"Where did you get your bees? Did you buy them?"

One of the Lammermann boys laughed at Caila Stern's question and she turned around and glared at him.

"Actually, that's an excellent question. There are three ways to get bees, and each has its pros and cons. The first is a nucs or nucleus, and they're generally bought as a three- or five-foot frame. They store an open brood and a laying queen, plus a fair number of bees of all ages." He held up a frame for them to see. "This frame fits inside the box where the hive lives."

"So you can buy the nucs?" Stan Muller asked.

"Yes. You can also get what's known as a package. Bees are sold by the pound, just like something off Hansen's grocery-store shelf. Like the nucs, the package includes a mated, laying queen bee."

"You can actually buy bees," Calla said with a tinge of righteous justification.

Gage went on to explain that this was the method he'd first used himself, and he described a lot of the errors he'd made in those early days.

"You said there were three methods of getting bees," Kevin reminded him.

"The third is swarms. How many of you have seen a bee swarm?"

Only one hand went up. "Personally I never have," Gage confessed. "Most beekeepers don't resort to catching swarms to supplement their hives."

"But why?" Bert Loomis asked. "It sounds like a great way to get bees without having to pay for them."

"It does, but there's always the risk of bringing disease into your hives and that's something all beekeepers want to avoid."

For an hour Gage answered questions and was impressed by the students' interest. When the school bus arrived, he was pleasantly surprised to note the time. He hadn't expected his talk to go this well.

"Thank you, Mr. Sinclair," Lindsay said from the back of the room.

"I brought everyone something to take home," Gage explained opening a box. "There's a small jar of honey…"

"It's really good," Kevin assured his friends. He stood and grabbed his books from the edge of his desk. "Meet you at the truck in half an hour, Gage."

Gage nodded. "I also have these creamy bars made from beeswax. They're used like hand lotion. I brought one for each of the ladies."

He was thanked again as the students filed out of the classroom. Gage stayed behind, taking extra time to gather up the items he'd brought with him.

It wasn't long before he was alone with Lindsay. "I understand you had something you wanted to say," he said stiffly.

"Yes." She stayed at the far end of the room, near the door, as if she, too, were uncomfortable being close to him. Her hands were clenched, shoulders straight, back rigid.

"First of all, I want you to know I appreciate your coming in this afternoon."

"I stick to *my* word."

"I didn't tell you I wouldn't date anyone else," she reminded him, her eyes flashing.

He supposed he had to concede that point, but he was uninterested in furthering the argument. From this day forward, he'd do everything in his power to avoid her. It only made sense. Clearly, she didn't *want* to pursue a relationship; just as clearly, he *shouldn't* pursue one.

"Perhaps it'd be best not to talk about our quarrel."

"I'm more than willing to drop the entire matter." He reached for his equipment again.

"The reason I asked to speak to you," she began in a rush. She hesitated and glanced down at her clenched hands. "I thought you'd like to know I found the hollow brick."

"You did?" Gage said, astounded. "How?" He'd been over every inch of that fireplace.

A chagrined smile came and went. "After you left, I…uh, I kicked the fireplace."

"You *kicked* the fireplace?" he repeated incredulously.

Her expression was sheepish. "You made me so mad, I couldn't stand it. Wherever I hit must've triggered the mechanism because the brick slid out smooth as could be."

"And?" He sincerely hoped she didn't intend to keep him in suspense.

"It was empty."

"Empty," he echoed. He could tell from her voice that she was intensely disappointed. He didn't know what she'd been expecting to find; she hadn't said and he hadn't pried. But finding the brick wasn't idle curiosity on her part.

"I'm sure she moved it."

Gage figured the *she* had to be Gina Snyder. He remembered her well, and she hadn't looked like someone with a deep dark secret she kept buried in a fireplace.

Lindsay gave a small shake of her head as though she regretted having spoken. "Never mind."

Gage lifted the boxes and headed toward the door. This time she didn't stop him, but she followed him outside. Walking ahead of him, she lowered the tailgate on his pickup. Gage slid everything onto the bed.

"Thank you again," she said, and Gage thought he heard a hint of sadness in her voice.

He didn't have anything else to add. He merely nodded in acknowledgment and climbed inside the truck.

"Gage." She walked over to the driver's side of the

vehicle. Eyes cast down, she said, "I wanted you to know I'm sorry our friendship's come to an end, especially over something so silly. If it's any consolation, I had a miserable night. I don't even *want* to go out with Ambrose...."

He tightened his grip on the steering wheel. "Listen, I'm not interested in your date. It's better like this for both of us. I'll stay out of your way and you can stay out of mine. Agreed?"

"What is it with everyone?" she cried. "Why does everyone treat me like this? I came to this town hoping to make a difference, but so far my only real friend is Hassie. Am I really such an outsider? It's like you're all holding your breath waiting for me to pack my bags and leave— even the kids. It drives me crazy. I'm here day after day, and...never mind, you don't want to hear it... You're like everyone else. Fine, you don't want to be my friend because of some terrible wrong I'm supposed to have committed against you. You know what? I don't need friends like you." She turned and hurried back into the school.

Gage watched her leave, astonished at her outburst and half tempted to go after her. But he didn't. She *wasn't* one of them; she didn't understand. Most likely, she never would.

Joanie Wyatt reached deep inside the large-capacity washing machine for Brandon's wet coveralls and placed them inside the dryer. With the heavy October rains, she could no longer use the line to dry their laundry.

The washer still looked new, although the bright enamel sheen had faded a bit. She'd once viewed the beautiful new washer and dryer as the most incredible appliances on the face of the earth. The anniversary gift had added excitement to her sagging marriage, but her joy had been tarnished by Brandon's cruel words.

He seemed to regret that awful night as much as she did. His anger was gone, replaced by depression. Whereas earlier he'd lashed out at her, now his frustration had turned inward. She wanted to help him, but didn't know how, and her inability to reach him left her with a hopeless, desperate feeling.

Joanie would've given anything to be able to return the new appliances. She'd rather beat clothes against a rock than have Brandon worry about meeting the payments, although he'd never actually complained about it. The amount wasn't all that much—a hundred and twenty-five dollars a month—but on top of all their other expenses… Every time she used the washer and dryer now, she felt guilty.

But it wasn't as if she could avoid washing clothes, and Mondays were wash days. That was the schedule her mother had kept and the one Joanie adopted when she got married. The house seemed unnaturally quiet as she hauled the sheets, still warm from the dryer, upstairs to Sage's and Stevie's bedrooms.

She was making the beds when the room started to swim, and she realized she was close to fainting. Eyes shut, she sat on the edge of her daughter's bed, waiting for the dizzy spell to pass.

She drew in several deep breaths and tried to remember if she'd had breakfast with the children. Sage had wanted French toast, Joanie recalled, and she'd prepared half a dozen slices, but now that she thought about it, she realized she hadn't eaten any herself. Her unhappiness had robbed her of appetite this past week. She didn't need to step on a scale to know she'd lost weight, which was probably why she was so tired. Most nights she went to bed soon after the children were asleep.

When the dizziness passed, Joanie resumed the bed-making, but it wasn't long before she felt faint a second time. If this was going to continue, it would take her all day to change the sheets.

Disgusted with herself, she returned downstairs and popped a slice of bread in the toaster, thinking that if she ate something she'd feel better. She added peanut butter to the toast and had just swallowed her first bite when the phone rang.

It was her mother. "Hi, Mom," she said, forcing a note of gladness into her voice. She was trying to hide her unhappiness from her family.

"Hello, sweetheart. I didn't hear from you yesterday." Her mother's tone was slightly accusatory.

They took turns phoning each other on Sundays. Brandon hadn't said anything, but she knew he was looking for ways to cut expenses. "I wrote you, instead," Joanie explained.

"Wrote me a letter?" Her mother sounded puzzled. "Joanie, is everything all right?"

"Everything's fine…. It's just that with wheat and corn prices so low, I was hoping to save a few dollars, that's all."

"But I'll miss talking to you and the kids. Perhaps I should phone *you*."

"No, Mom, that wouldn't be fair. Anyway, it won't be for long. Next year's sure to be better."

"For your sake I hope so." Her mother hesitated, then asked, "Is Brandon treating you well?"

"Mother, of course he is!" She didn't care to explain that her own husband seemed to be blaming her for the low price of corn, the current rainy conditions and just about everything else that was wrong with his world. "I love him—I've always loved him."

"I know. It's just that…" Her mother let the rest fade. "The reason I wanted to talk to you has to do with Thanksgiving."

"That's not for weeks yet."

"It'll be here before you know it."

Joanie suspected that was true; the summer seemed to go so quickly, and now they were halfway through fall.

"Your brother and Kelly are flying in with the kids."

"Jay's coming?" Joanie hadn't seen her older brother in two years. "It'll be wonderful to see Jessie and Eddie."

"It's hard to believe they're twelve and ten," her mother said conversationally. "It seems only yesterday that they were born. I do hope you and Brandon will be here. Your father and I thought this would be a perfect opportunity to have a family portrait taken."

The joy and excitement Joanie had felt for a moment left her. "I'll talk to him, Mom, but I can't make any guarantees."

"Do try. It would be so nice if we could all be together."

"It would be," she agreed. "I'll ask him right away."

"Ask me what?" Brandon said from behind her.

Joanie placed her hand over the mouthpiece and looked at her husband, trying to gauge his mood. "Thanksgiving," she said.

His eyes revealed no emotion.

"I'll talk it over with Brandon and let you know as soon as we decide," she told her mother.

"Will you write or phone me with your answer?"

"I'll write you, Mom."

Brandon was waiting for her when Joanie finished with the phone call. "What's this about writing your mother?"

"It's nothing," she said, dismissing the question rather than explaining why she wasn't phoning the way she normally did.

"We can afford for you to call your family, Joanie."

Inexplicably, her eyes filled with tears.

"You crying?" He frowned as he asked the question.

"No…yes." She plucked a tissue from the box and blew her nose, shocked at this unwarranted display of emotion.

"All right," he said, with an exaggerated sigh. "You do what you want. Write your mother, phone her, it's up to you."

She blew her nose again, wondering if she was coming down with a cold. It wouldn't surprise her with the cold damp weather they'd been having.

"About Thanksgiving?" she said, glancing at her husband, hoping she could convince him to leave the farm long enough to spend the holiday with her family. It would be like a vacation, and they could use the break.

"My brother and his family are flying in," Joanie told him. "I haven't seen him in two years."

"And you want to be with Jay and his family at Thanksgiving," Brandon said. "I'd never keep you and the kids from seeing your brother and your parents."

"Mom and Dad want you there, too."

He shook his head even before he spoke. "I can't leave the farm."

"But Gage said he'd be willing to look after the animals if we wanted to get away for a little while," she said, rushing the words in her eagerness. "We'd only be gone a couple of days."

"Joanie…"

"We could leave early Thursday morning, have dinner with them and then drive home on Friday afternoon. Mom mentioned something about a family portrait or we could leave their place sooner, but I don't think any photography studios would be open Thanksgiving Day." She knew why she was rambling—because the instant she stopped talking, Brandon would tell her no.

"You know how I feel about your parents," he muttered.

The tears were back, frustrating and angering her. "You

don't have a clue how they feel about you! You've never given them a chance."

"If you want to spend Thanksgiving with your family, Joanie, go. I won't stand in your way."

"You'd rather spend Thanksgiving Day alone than be with your family?"

"Tell me, do I have a lot to be thankful for? Not this year."

"You have your health and a wife and children who love you. Isn't that enough?" She knew there was no point in arguing with him; Brandon wasn't going to listen. Smearing the tears across her cheek, she forced herself to stop. "I'll plan on driving to my parents without you then," she said as evenly as her emotions would allow. "We'll leave Thursday morning, like I suggested, and return on Friday."

"There's no reason for you to hurry home."

He might have hit her for the effect those words had on her heart. "Brandon, are you saying…you don't want us to come back?" she challenged. "Because if you are, then you don't need to wait until Thanksgiving for us to leave." If he wanted out of their marriage, the least he could do was be honest enough to tell her.

He took his time answering. "You can leave when you want and you can return when you want. The choice is yours."

The first Friday of November, Lindsay walked into Knight's Pharmacy after school, feeling excited and happy.

"Lindsay," Hassie called to her from the back of the store. "You look like you just won a lottery."

That was the way she felt. She held up a key dangling from a bright red ribbon. "Look what I've got in my hot little hands," she cried, resisting the urge to jump up and down with glee.

"You have the theater key from Ambrose Kohn?"

"Got it." Not without her share of angst and resentment at being manipulated into attending a ridiculous costume party with him. But it had all been worth it.

"You wore the prisoner costume with the ball and chain? You borrowed it from Calla Stern, right?"

"Yes and yes." To Lindsay's way of thinking, if Ambrose was going to make her attend the Halloween party with him, she'd wear a fitting costume. She'd felt trapped—like a prisoner—but had agreed because she badly wanted the use of the old theater for the Christmas play her students were putting on. The kids were in on her scheme and Calla had lent her the Halloween costume her mother had designed for her the year before.

"You slay me, girl," Hassie said with a laugh of sheer delight.

"Rachel's meeting me here, and we're going to take a look inside."

Ambrose had told her the movie house had been closed for ten years and he had no idea what condition the place was in. He'd also let it be known that he was unwilling to commit even one cent to it. Anything she or the high-schoolers did was at their own expense and at their own risk.

"My heavens, it's been years since anyone went in there," Hassie muttered.

"That's what Ambrose said."

"Have you and Rachel got flashlights?"

She nodded. "Plus a kerosene lamp."

"You'll need those and more." With the approach of winter, the days were shorter now, and it was nearly dark by the time school was out. "Let me check my back room," Hassie said, "and see what's there."

A jingle of bells alerted Lindsay to the arrival of her friend. "You got the key?" Rachel asked.

"It's in my hand as we speak," Lindsay told her, holding it aloft. "I picked it up this afternoon at the post office." Ambrose seemed to think she'd abandon him the minute she took possession of the key, so he hadn't brought it to the Halloween party. He'd put it in the mail, instead.

Rachel glanced at her watch. "We'll have to hurry."

Lindsay knew it wouldn't be long before the pizza orders started coming in, and was grateful Rachel had agreed to accompany her. "I know, I know."

Despite what she'd said to Gage a week earlier, she was making friends. Slowly but surely. Since Rachel drove the school bus, she made a stop at the high school every afternoon. Lindsay had gone out of her way to talk to Rachel and was gratified by the fledgling friendship. She admired the young widow and wanted to support her business venture.

Hassie returned with a third flashlight. "I'd come with you girls, but I'm the only one at the store."

"Don't worry, we'll be fine." Lindsay was thrilled that the drama club had been such a success. She was pleasantly surprised by how much talent, ability and initiative her students possessed. The impetus for creating their own production had come after Joshua McKenna's classroom visit. Her students' play revolved around a bleak Christmas in the depths of the Great Depression. Everyone was involved, not only in putting together the script and performing, but in making costumes, set construction and all the other production elements. Everything hinged on being able to use the old theater.

"You ready?" Rachel asked.

"Ready," Lindsay said.

Like giddy schoolgirls, they hurried out of Hassie's and down the street to the boarded-up theater. The door opened easily enough—a good sign, Lindsay decided. The interior was dark and smelled of must and mildew. Cobwebs cluttered the doorway and Lindsay swept them aside with a gloved hand.

Rachel flashed the light about the lobby. "I remember this place from when I was a kid," she whispered, "and it didn't look anything like this." The light shone on a glass counter where popcorn and other snacks had once been sold. Doorways on either side led into the theater itself.

"Why are you whispering?" Lindsay asked, as she moved toward a heavy velvet curtain to the right of the counter.

"I don't know—but it's kind of spooky, don't you think?"

"Nah," Lindsay said, and she meant it. She was entirely focussed on the future and its possibilities.

"This place smells dreadful," Rachel complained.

"Nothing some fresh paint and a few dozen bowls of potpourri won't cure." Lindsay was too excited to let reality dampen her enthusiasm. She imagined the theater as it would look on opening night. The light fixtures would be polished and gleaming; the faded maroon velvet, draped with gold braid, would be cleaned and elegant. She could see the audience, farmers and ranchers from miles around, filling the seats, could hear the applause as the curtain slid open for the opening scene of *Dakota Christmas*.

"We have our work cut out for us," Rachel said with a deep sigh.

"Just you wait. It's going to be fabulous."

Rachel laughed. "You're such an optimist."

Lindsay thought of all the time she'd wasted on a dead-end relationship because she couldn't make herself stop believing that Monte would eventually marry her. "It's a curse," she said, laughing now, refusing to let the memories distract her.

Pushing aside the drape that led to the audience seats,

Lindsay used the handle of her flashlight to sweep away more spider webs. The light revealed rows of velvet-covered seats and her breath caught. They were beautifully preserved, at least those she could see.

"I'll light the kerosene lamp," Rachel offered.

"This is incredible!" Lindsay cried. "I didn't dare hope."

Once the lamp was lit, she saw that her first estimation had been correct. The seats were old, but for the most part in surprisingly good condition. "This place is a piece of history."

"It first opened in the early 1920s," Rachel told her. "At least that's what my mother thought. She remembered it from when she was a kid and recalls her mother talking about watching silent movies there."

"This is just incredible." Lindsay couldn't help repeating herself.

"Rachel? Lindsay?" A male voice called to them from the lobby.

"It's Heath," Rachel said to Lindsay.

Lindsay watched her friend carefully and saw how she struggled to hide the telltale burst of excitement at the sound of Heath's voice. She'd wondered about the two of them—particularly since Heath seemed to be lingering at the café whenever she went in to pick up a pizza—and that had been easily half a dozen times. Now she was convinced something was going on between them.

"In here," Rachel called out.

Heath Quantrill pushed back the entrance curtain and paused in the doorway. "Mark said I'd find you at the theater. I stopped by the café on my way home for a pizza." He glanced at Lindsay. "I realize it's a bit early, but I hoped you'd be open."

"Oh," Rachel said, sounding flustered, "I am open—

well, sort of. I'll be right there—as soon as Lindsay and I are finished in here."

"Take your time," Heath said, joining the two women. "What are you doing, anyway?"

Lindsay explained and he nodded, but made no comment.

"I know it needs a lot of work," she murmured.

"That's an understatement," he said. "But I assume you have plenty of volunteers."

"Yes—I hope so, anyway." She'd talked to Joshua McKenna about giving the theater a face-lift, and he'd promised to discuss it with the town council. Lindsay would need all the volunteers she could get. But her guess was that Gage Sinclair wouldn't be among them. It amazed—and disturbed—her how much she missed him.

She hadn't heard *from* him in weeks, but she'd heard plenty *about* him from a number of sources. Both Hassie and Leta had taken it upon themselves to drop his name into casual conversation as often as possible. Lindsay wasn't fooled. She knew matchmaking when she heard it, and suspected Gage was getting an earful about her, too. But if they were going to establish some kind of friendship, she supposed it would have happened before now. That was her fault as well as his. She might not be Dakota-born like Gage, but she could be just as stubborn.

"My grandmother used to love this theater," Heath said. "I remember hearing stories about it when I was a kid."

"I wonder if your grandmother and mine used to go to the movies here together?" Rachel asked on a wistful note.

"How about your grandfather and my grandmother coming here on a date?"

Rachel laughed. "That would've been something."

"Their grandchildren just might."

Rachel went speechless at the suggestion, and Lindsay

sympathized with her discomfort. From what Hassie had told her, Rachel hadn't dated since her husband's death.

"You'd better get over to the café and work your miracles with the pizzas," Lindsay suggested, hoping to give her a way out. "Otherwise you might lose customers."

"Mark will let me know once the phone starts ringing," Rachel assured her, still flustered.

No sooner had she spoken than her son barreled into the theater. "Mom, Mom," he shouted, then stopped, apparently awestruck. "Hey, this place is cool." He grinned as he gazed around the theater. "Hi, Miss Snyder. Hi, Mr. Quantrill. Hey, you got two orders, Mom. Calla told me to come get you."

"Two orders!" Rachel was jubilant.

"Three," Heath corrected. "Remember mine. I'm going to visit my grandmother this evening and thought I'd bring dinner with me. She'll get a kick out of eating a slice of Buffalo Valley's own pizza."

"When you've got a chance, make me a medium sausage and black olive," Lindsay told her. "I'll be by to pick it up when I'm through here."

A few minutes later, the others had left. Lindsay stayed on for a while, savoring the feel of the place, anticipating its return to glory with the students' production.

She flicked off the lantern and tucked the flashlights in her pockets. Then she locked the door and turned back toward Hassie's. She came to an abrupt standstill when she saw Gage Sinclair.

He was in his pickup, heading down Main Street. The joy that had risen inside her only minutes earlier evaporated. Silently she watched as he pulled into an empty parking space near Buffalo Bob's and climbed out of the truck's cab. He glanced casually around.

Lindsay didn't move when his gaze came to rest on her. She resisted the urge to greet him with a wave. Their eyes held for a long while as if he, too, felt tempted to acknowledge her. Then he slowly turned his back and walked away.

Once more, Lindsay experienced a feeling of unaccountable loss. He would have made a good friend.

Ten

Rachel was genuinely satisfied with the success of her pizza venture. She'd been in operation for only two months, and was already showing a profit. With the disastrous news of low grain prices, she'd been afraid her business wouldn't stand a chance.

It helped that people like Heath Quantrill routinely ordered from her, and Lindsay Snyder, too. Hassie and Sarah had turned into good customers, as well. The second Saturday in November she'd sold a record fifteen pizzas. For the first time since Ken's death, she felt hopeful about the future.

Even with the profit from Buffalo Valley Pizza, Rachel continued to work on Hassie's books two mornings a week. She suspected Hassie was perfectly capable of handling her own accounts, but she enjoyed her time with the older woman. And, of course, the extra income was a help.

Rachel considered Hassie a blessing to the community and, in fact, to the entire county. People went out of their way to shop at Knight's Pharmacy because Hassie dispensed far more than prescription drugs. They were drawn to her because of her optimism; she inspired and encouraged them. They came to her for medical advice, as well, and she wasn't shy about steering folks to a physician when she felt one was needed.

"Rachel." Hassie stepped into the back room where Rachel pored over the ledgers. "I'm afraid I'm feeling a bit under the weather this morning."

Hassie did look pale. "The flu bug got you?" Mark had missed two days of school the week before because of a virus.

"That's what it feels like." She blew her nose with a honking sound that made Rachel smile despite her sympathy. "I'd better follow the advice I've been giving everyone else—go home and take care of myself."

"That sounds wise to me."

"I'll need to close the pharmacy." She coughed from deep inside her chest.

"Oh, Hassie, you sound wretched. Now listen, there's no need to close the store until I have to leave to drive the school bus," Rachel said. She was eager to show her appreciation for all Hassie had done to help her. "I'd be more than happy to stay. People who need prescriptions filled will have to wait, of course, but anything else I can do."

Hassie's look was hesitant, but relieved. "You're sure it wouldn't be too much of a problem?"

"Positive."

"That would be wonderful. I'm expecting a delivery sometime today that has to be signed for. If you can deal with that, I'd be grateful." She brought her hand to her forehead as though to test for a fever. "I'll be fine in no time," she mumbled, obviously wanting to convince herself as much as Rachel.

"Is there anything I can get for you?" Rachel offered, escorting Hassie to the door.

"Not a thing." That was followed by another hacking cough.

"Well, call me if you need anything." Rachel watched her cross the street and then round the corner. She sincerely hoped it *was* just a touch of the flu and not something more serious. Buffalo Valley couldn't afford to lose Hassie Knight. She was the glue that held them together.

Rachel was surprised by the number of customers, considering that this was a weekday morning. By noon she'd waited on more than a dozen people, all of whom asked about Hassie.

There seemed to be a lull following lunch. Rachel had returned to working on the books when the bells above the door chimed, alerting her to a customer's arrival.

She left the back room to find Heath Quantrill. "Heath!" she greeted him delightedly. "Hello." At his insistence, she'd dropped the Mr. Quantrill months ago. Heath had actually become a friend, and she still found that somehow astonishing. At first he'd intimidated her and she'd felt awkward and ill at ease around him, but gradually that had changed. He regularly came in for pizza, and while she knew hers was good, he could probably get equally good pizza at home in Grand Forks. One Friday, soon after she'd opened, they'd talked for an hour over cups of coffee. Calla and Mark had been involved in a Monopoly game, and the phone had remained silent. That was the night he'd first mentioned his brother, and she'd told him about Ken. She understood his pain over Max's death and he seemed to understand hers. So often, especially since her family had moved, Rachel had simply brushed aside talk of her husband, brushed aside others' concern, rather than acknowledge the loss. But Heath empathized with the emptiness she felt, even the anger, because he, too, had been dealing with those emotions since Max's death.

No one needed to tell Rachel that she and Heath Quantrill were about as different as could be. She'd only left the state of North Dakota once, and that had been on her honeymoon. Heath had traveled all over the world. He was rich and sophisticated and could probably have any woman he wanted. A struggling widow with a child to support wasn't going to interest him. Still, Rachel had found him witty and clever, fascinating and, yes, she'd admit it, damned attractive. It probably wasn't a good idea to let herself think of him in those terms, but she couldn't help it.

Recently Lindsay had suggested that something romantic might be developing between them, but Rachel was quick to correct her. It was true he'd made that vague remark about the two of them going to the theater together, the same theater where their grandparents had once sat, but that was all it was: a vague remark.

"Rachel?" he said, obviously surprised. "Where's Hassie?"

"Home, probably in bed. She wasn't feeling well this morning."

"So you're taking her place? I'm glad I came in." He grinned as he said it, and she found herself blushing, wondering whether he really was pleased to see her there. "I don't suppose I could talk you into fixing me one of Hassie's sodas?" he asked.

She looked away. "Sure." She suspected Heath had come to talk to Hassie, that he wanted some of the sensible advice Hassie served along with her famous sodas. Rachel also knew that Hassie and his grandmother, Lily Quantrill, were good friends.

"How about a strawberry soda?" Heath suggested.

"Coming right up." She reached for a glass and an ice-cream scoop.

"I don't know Hassie all that well, and I've often wondered about her," Heath commented absently.

"How do you mean?" Rachel glanced up from her task, her eyes meeting his.

"Well, for one thing, why does she have an American flag by the picture of her son? I've never heard anyone mention him."

Rachel's hand stilled. "That's Vaughn. He was killed in Vietnam. Some people say Hassie changed after that. I was only a few months old at the time and I don't remember him, but my parents do. They say he was a good kid. My dad's views about the war changed after Vaughn was killed. Hassie keeps his picture out and the flag the Army gave her when they laid Vaughn to rest because she wants people to remember his sacrifice."

"She doesn't talk about him, does she?"

"It's been nearly thirty years and it's still painful for her."

Heath nodded but didn't touch the soda when she placed it on the counter. "Besides my grandmother, the only person I've talked to about Max is you."

"If it wasn't for Hassie, I don't know what I would have done that first year after Ken died. Without her, I think I probably would've moved to Arizona with my parents. It does help to have someone listen."

"I thank you for that," Heath told her. "I was so mad at Max for dying and yet it makes perfect sense that he'd swerve to avoid hitting a deer. That's just the type of person Max was."

The burning tears that filled her eyes were as unexpected as they were unwelcome. She knew his brother had been killed on the highway, but hadn't heard any of the details. She blinked in an effort to hold back her emotion, not wanting to embarrass herself in front of Heath.

He reached across the counter and stroked the side of her face. His touch was gentle, so gentle. Rachel closed her eyes and immediately the tears began to fall.

"I'm sorry," he whispered. "I shouldn't be talking like this now."

"No, no, it's fine. Usually I don't react like this. I'm sorry, I…" She didn't bother to finish what she'd been about to say.

Walking away from the counter, she grabbed a box of tissues from the shelf and opened it. She turned to discover Heath directly behind her.

"I shouldn't have brought up Max," he said, staring down at her. "Especially since it reminds you of Ken."

"No…no, it isn't that, really," she said, a little breathless. He was close, closer than he'd ever been before, and her heart began to race.

He slid his arms around her. Rachel rested her hands on his chest and was amazed to discover that his heart was beating as fast as hers. Slowly—feeling confused and uncertain—she raised her eyes to his. Rachel knew she should pull away, end the embrace; at the same time, she hoped he'd kiss her.

It seemed that, along with all his other talents, Heath Quantrill was a mind reader. After the slightest hesitation, he lowered his mouth to hers.

At the approach of his lips, Rachel had the distinct feeling that if she allowed this to happen, if Heath actually kissed her, everything between them would change. Still, she didn't stop him. She hadn't dated since Ken's death. The thought of another relationship hadn't even occurred to her. And now…there was Heath.

Parting her lips, she stood on the tips of her toes, straining toward him. The kiss was tender, and as she'd known it would be, devastating.

He released her, and his look told her he was as confused and unsure as she was.

"I...I..."

He didn't let her finish. Instead, he kissed her again, and she responded with a greed that left her weak—and astonished. Her arms wound their way around his neck and she leaned against him. She felt his hands in her hair, his fingers tangling in its length.

When she dared to meet his eyes, she found them wide and bewildered.

"I know what you're thinking," she whispered.

"I doubt it," he returned with a short, abrupt laugh. "Because if you did your face would be beet-red."

Rachel's cheeks instantly filled with heat. "I—I'm sure you didn't expect this to happen."

"I didn't plan to kiss you when I came in here, if that's what you mean, but I'm not sorry about it." His eyes narrowed. "Are you?"

She had trouble meeting his gaze, but told him with a small shake of her head that she wasn't.

Hugging her again, he sighed. "Good. This is a surprise, but a pleasant one. I'm thirty-one and long past the age of pretending. Let's always be honest with each other, Rachel."

"Yes," she whispered, her voice still quavering from the effects of their kiss.

"This is a beginning for us."

She nodded, uncertain what he meant, but not needing clarification. Not then, not when his arms were warm and secure around her. If Ken's death had taught her anything, it was that the future held no guarantees.

* * *

As soon as Leta Betts heard that Hassie Knight had come down with the flu, she took a chicken from the freezer and made a big pot of her chicken noodle soup. Leta often worried about Hassie, who was well into her seventies. Over the last year, she'd noticed that Hassie's energy seemed to be slipping, and that concerned her. The soup was an excuse to visit her friend.

Gage was busy tinkering with some farm equipment when she found him. "Hassie's got a bad case of the flu," she explained.

"She's tough. You don't need to worry about Hassie," Gage said, glancing up from the tractor. His hands were smudged with grease. His task, whatever it was, seemed to be frustrating him.

"I was hoping you could drive me into town?" she asked.

Gage straightened and wiped the grease from his hands on a mechanic's pink rag. "Kevin can't do it?"

"He's busy at the school."

She noticed Gage's frown at her mention of school and knew he was thinking about Lindsay Snyder again. He'd been doing that a lot. Gage might be able to fool other people and even himself, but she knew him far too well. He was interested in Lindsay Snyder, and whatever had happened between them had thrown him for a loop.

"I won't be finished here for a couple of hours," he finally said.

"I'll be ready when you are."

Two hours later, Gage came into the house, took a quick shower, then drove the car around. During the thirty-mile drive into town, Leta had plenty of time to think, not that it did her much good. She wished she knew of some way to help Gage resolve his feelings about

Lindsay, but suspected any interference on her part wouldn't be welcome.

That matter was still on her mind when she arrived at Hassie's. Her friend, dressed in pajamas and robe, looked delighted to receive company. She opened the door and welcomed her inside.

"I'm telling you, Leta, I wasn't cut out for a life of leisure." A half-empty box of tissues and a glass of orange juice stood on the coffee table.

"I brought you some of my homemade chicken noodle soup." She took the quart jar out of the basket and carried it to the kitchen. Then she returned to the living room and settled herself in the chair across from Hassie. Reaching for her knitting—an afghan for Lindsay—Leta began the comforting and familiar motions.

Hassie sat on the sofa and leaned against a pillow, her feet propped on the ottoman. "I've had three days to do nothing but think—trust me, daytime television just isn't what it used to be."

Leta lowered her knitting and eyed her friend. "Financial worries?"

Hassie shook her head. "Nothing that stressful. I was wondering about Lindsay and Gage. What's happened to those two, anyway?"

Leta snorted. "I wish I knew." She paused. "I've been thinking about them, too. I think he likes her…."

"Well, I can tell you she's interested in him."

Leta nodded. "I hope so."

There was silence for a while, punctuated only by the chiming of the grandfather clock in the hallway.

"She's wonderful with the teens," Leta said, yanking on her skein of yarn. Kevin had never enjoyed school more. Lindsay kept all the kids busy with all kinds of projects.

Leta didn't worry as much about her son and Jessica, since both of them were so involved in the newspaper and now the Christmas play.

"I wonder if we can persuade Lindsay to stay on after this year," Hassie murmured. "She's a good teacher." There was a pause. "So was Eloise."

"But she was old and tired."

Hassie nodded. "Like us," she muttered.

That comment wasn't typical of her friend, and Leta frowned. Hassie's optimism was usually invincible; she must really be feeling poorly.

"You don't know what happened between Lindsay and Gage?" Leta asked, more to distract her.

"No," Hassie said. "I wish to hell I did. Have you thought about asking him?"

"No, I don't dare."

"Well." Hassie gave a deep sigh. "They obviously had some sort of disagreement."

"Because of her date with Ambrose Kohn, I think."

"Gage knows it was a set-up, right? That the only reason Lindsay agreed to attend the Elks Halloween party with him was so she could use the theater?"

"I told him, or tried to, but he wasn't in the best of moods at the time." As Leta remembered it, Gage had nearly bitten her head off.

"I suspect Lindsay never explained."

"Oh, she probably tried, but knowing my son, he didn't give her the chance."

"Men!" Hassie made a tsking sound. "And now we have another worry."

"What?" Leta murmured, almost afraid to ask.

"Lindsay's flying home for Thanksgiving."

"She's coming back, isn't she?"

Hassie nodded. "It would surprise me if she didn't."

"Then what's the problem?"

"Well…" Hassie paused, as if weighing her words. "Lindsay accepted the job here in Buffalo Valley for a specific reason. She didn't say I couldn't tell other people, but I know she hasn't mentioned it to anyone else."

"And you don't want to betray her confidence," Leta finished for her.

"You see my dilemma?"

"I wouldn't want you to come right out and tell me." Leta did, of course, but couldn't ask that of her friend.

A slow smile appeared on the older woman's lips. "Perhaps you could guess."

"I take it there's a man involved?"

"Very much so."

"He was married, and when she learned he had a wife she instantly broke off the relationship. Then she moved here so he'd have no way of finding her?"

Hassie shook her head.

"He was gay?"

"No."

"Diseased?"

Hassie rolled her eyes. "No."

"Mentally deranged." Leta had it. "She caught him wearing women's underwear."

"Oh, Leta! For the love of heaven, no."

"Heaven," she repeated slowly, certain that her friend was giving her a clue. "He was a priest."

Hassie slumped back in her chair. "Not even close."

Setting her knitting aside, Leta stood up and started pacing. She'd already covered the more obvious reasons. Then it dawned on her, and she wondered why it'd taken her so long to guess the truth. "Lindsay's pregnant, isn't she? The baby's father refused to marry her."

Hassie's eyes looked as if they were about to fall out of her head. "*Part* of that's true."

"Part. Lindsay's pregnant." Gage must know, too. That explained his attitude. My goodness, it wasn't as if Lindsay was going to be able to hide her secret much longer.

"No!" Hassie cried, clearly exasperated.

"Then what?" Leta had lost her patience, as well.

"The *second* part of what you said."

Leta frowned, not remembering.

"She was pregnant and the man…"

"The man…?"

"Refused…"

Leta remembered. "Refused to marry her!"

"Yes." Hassie's expression implied that Leta should have come up with the answer a lot faster than she had.

"She wants to get married?" This was better than she'd dared hope. "She wants a husband—but that's wonderful, just wonderful!" Leta's heart pounded with excitement.

"She loves him," Hassie murmured, frowning.

"Gage?" Things were looking brighter by the minute.

"No, the man in Savannah. He says he loves her, too, but he's gun-shy."

"He had his chance," Leta insisted sternly.

Hassie laughed out loud. "You're right, he did. I'd be very happy if Lindsay decided to settle down in Buffalo Valley."

"So would I," Leta said and reclaimed her chair. She picked up her knitting, her needles flying, keeping pace with her thoughts. "You say Lindsay's going home for Thanksgiving?"

Hassie nodded. "She'll be seeing this other guy."

"She'll need a ride to the airport, won't she?" Leta said casually, tugging on the yarn.

"Yes…"

"I think I know just the person to drive her."

It took Hassie a moment to catch her drift, but once she had, a slow smile spread across her face. "You're a clever woman, Leta Betts."

Leta grinned, too. "So it's been said."

"You're coming back, aren't you?" Calla Stern followed Lindsay out to her living room, hauling Lindsay's carry-on bag. She'd come for detailed dog-watching instructions. It was Wednesday afternoon, and Lindsay was catching the red-eye out of Grand Forks, and then a connecting flight in Minneapolis, arriving in Savannah early Thanksgiving morning. Not only was the plane ticket more affordable this way, it worked best with her teaching schedule.

"I'll be back," Lindsay promised as she set the large bag down next to the front door. As if she'd abandon her dogs! Kevin and Leta Betts had volunteered to drive her into Grand Forks, a ninety-minute ride. Leta said she had some last-minute shopping for Thanksgiving dinner and Kevin, bless his heart, had volunteered to drive.

"We still have the play, you know," Calla reminded her.

"Calla, I'm coming back."

"Sometimes people say things and then change their minds."

Lindsay was certain this was a painful lesson the girl had learned from her father. "That's true," she agreed, "but I'm not going to change my mind."

Lindsay could see from the look on the girl's face that she still didn't believe her. "All right, this might help. See?" She held out a small silver coin suspended from a delicate chain. It was her favorite necklace and one she wore almost every day. "My father gave this to me when I graduated from high school."

"It was treasure found on a sunken ship," Calla said. "Isn't that the coin you showed us the day Mr. Quantrill came to talk to the class?"

"It is." Lindsay was pleased that Calla remembered. "The *Atocha* sank off the Florida Keys in 1622 and was discovered in 1975. This piece of silver is more than three hundred years old." She slipped off the necklace and placed it in Calla's palm. "You can keep this safe for me until I get back."

"You're letting me baby-sit your necklace *and* your dogs?"

"I am," Lindsay said, smiling at the term.

Calla nodded, her eyes huge. "You'll be back."

"Isn't that what I've been telling you all afternoon?"

Lindsay was still feeling good an hour later as she waited for Leta and Kevin. She wondered about Gage. She hadn't seen him in weeks—not since that Friday when he'd driven into town and gone to Buffalo Bob's.

A light snow had started shortly after Calla left, and Lindsay stood at the window looking out. The snow, falling steadily now, looked misty in the headlights as a vehicle turned onto her street. Because of the weather and the unfamiliar roads to the airport, Lindsay was particularly grateful for Leta's offer of a ride. Warm and cozy inside her home, she found the pristine landscape beautiful. It wasn't the first snowfall of the season and plenty of people had gone out of their way to warn her that it wouldn't be the last. Sarah Stern, for one. Lindsay wished Calla's mother could be a friend, but she'd subtly rejected every gesture Lindsay had made toward friendship. Hassie said Sarah was a hard person to get to know, fiercely protective of her family, especially her brother. She didn't make room in her life for many friends.

The headlights slowed as they neared her house. A large, dark car pulled over and parked at the curb. Lindsay reached for her coat and opened the door, ready to leave. The crisp wind stung her face and brought tears to her eyes.

Taking the largest of her bags, she lowered her head until she heard the crunch of footsteps approaching the house. When she glanced up, she discovered it wasn't Kevin who'd come, but his brother.

"Gage?" Lindsay blinked in surprise.

"Do you have a problem with me driving you into Grand Forks?" he asked stiffly.

"No…no, it's just that I was expecting Kevin."

"He didn't come and neither did my mother." The tautness was back in his voice.

"That's fine…."

He took the bag she held and carried it to the trunk of the car, then returned for the rest of her luggage while she murmured her goodbyes to the dogs and locked the house. Within minutes, they were on their way to Grand Forks.

Gage sat not more than two feet from her. Neither spoke. After ten minutes, he finally broke the silence. "I want you to know I'm only doing this because I didn't want Kevin out on these roads," he explained.

"I already guessed as much."

He made no further comment.

Another ten minutes passed before she found the courage to speak again. "However it happened, I'm sorry. I didn't mean to inconvenience anyone."

"It isn't an inconvenience."

"I could have driven myself."

"No, you couldn't," he snapped, and his attitude angered her so much she said nothing more.

"I'm sure your family's anxious to see you," Gage said out of the blue, almost as if they were back on friendly terms.

"Yes, and I'm looking forward to seeing them."

He frowned; her answer didn't appear to satisfy him. She gazed out at the road. The landscape was shockingly bright as the falling snow started to accumulate.

"Anyone else you're anxious to see?" he asked.

The question held a hint of contempt, which she didn't understand. "Maddy, of course."

"No one else?"

Oh, now she understood. "You mean…Monte?"

"You didn't mention his name before," Gage told her. He stared straight ahead, his concentration on the road. But Lindsay wasn't fooled. Gage wanted to know what would happen once she saw Monte again. It was a question she'd asked herself a thousand times.

"I doubt I'll be able to avoid him," she said as matter-of-factly as she could. Monte had written to say he intended to talk to her when she got home. His letters had been full of anger. He'd been furious that she refused to write him. Thankfully he hadn't tried to reach her by phone, and she suspected he hadn't asked her family for her unlisted number, knowing she'd requested that it not be given out. The school didn't have a phone, and the only way to get her at work was through the district office.

"You still in love with him?"

"Why do you care?"

"I don't," he was quick to assure her. "Just curious, is all."

"Well, don't be. It's none of your business."

He chuckled at that. "A little defensive, don't you think?"

"Me? You're the one who leaps to conclusions."

Gage didn't respond, and the silence grew oppressive. But Lindsay held her ground, refusing to apologize.

It wasn't long before city lights appeared in the distance. "That's Grand Forks," Gage told her. "The airport's north of town."

"We're almost there, then?"

"Another fifteen minutes."

When they reached the airport, Lindsay expected Gage to drop her off and head home. Instead, he parked the car, then carried both bags into the small terminal for her. He stood back while she checked in at the airline counter and received her boarding pass.

"You don't need to wait with me," she told him, thinking he'd want to leave.

"I know, but I thought I would."

They sat next to each other like silent strangers while they waited for her flight to be announced. The terminal wasn't big, and it seemed half of Grand Forks was either coming or going on this same evening.

When her flight was called, Lindsay got quickly to her feet. "That's me," she told him.

Gage stood, too.

She swung the strap of her purse over her shoulder. "I appreciate the ride," she said. "Thank you…"

He acknowledged her words with a nod. "Happy Thanksgiving, Lindsay."

"You, too." Her reluctance to leave came as a surprise, but she tried not to let it show. With her purse and her carry-on bag secure in her hands, she turned to line up with the others boarding the same flight.

"Lindsay." His voice sounded desperate, and she turned back, wondering what she'd forgotten.

Gage gripped her by the shoulders, his eyes as intense as she'd ever seen them. Then, abruptly, he kissed her—and she returned the kiss. Lindsay understood that Gage was saying with his kiss what he hadn't been able to tell her earlier. That he was sorry.

He broke away from her just as suddenly. "Come back, Lindsay," he said, his eyes burning into hers. "Come back."

Eleven

*Minutes for the November 24th meeting of the
Buffalo Valley Town Council*

As recorded by Hassie Knight, Secretary and Treasurer, duly elected.

The meeting was opened by council president Joshua McKenna with the Pledge of Allegiance to the American flag. Council members attending included: Joshua McKenna, Dennis Urlacher, Jacob Hansen, Gage Sinclair, Heath Quantrill and Hassie Knight. Marta Hansen and Buffalo Bob Carr were present as observers.

In regard to old business, Jacob Hansen announced that Hansen's Grocery was officially for sale and will permanently close on September first if a buyer can't be found.

A heated discussion followed, but despite pleas from town council members, the Hansens were firm in their decision. A number of ideas were brought forth as possible ways to prevent the closing of Buffalo Valley's one and only grocery store, but at Gage Sinclair's suggestion, the talk was shelved until a later date.

Also under old business, Jacob Hansen brought up the subject of searching out a high-school teacher for next September. Discussion followed. Gage Sinclair agreed it would be prudent to do so, in order to ensure that the high school will not be left in the same position as last summer. Joshua McKenna has agreed to contact the district school office and put in this request.

Under new business, Joshua McKenna commended everyone for their efforts regarding the clean-up and renovation of the theater for the high-school play. The council agreed to pay for lighting and to cover heating costs for the month without taking it from the school budget.

Gage Sinclair suggested that a portion of the proceeds from the sale of snack foods during performances be used to pay the extra expenses and the rest be allocated to the school budget. Heath Quantrill seconded and the motion was passed.

On Veterans' Day, Hassie Knight and Joshua McKenna placed flags on the headstones of those fallen in foreign wars.

The meeting adjourned at one o'clock.

Respectfully submitted,
Hassie Knight

Thanksgiving morning, Joanie Wyatt woke with a queasy stomach. Brandon was already up, feeding and tending the animals, and she could hear the children stirring upstairs. Sage and Stevie were both eager to spend the holiday with their grandparents and cousins. Joanie had hoped to be on the road before dawn, but if this dizziness and nausea continued, she might have to cancel her plans. For the children's sake, she hoped not. For her sake, as well.

She needed to get away from the farm and, sadly, from her own husband. Undoubtedly he needed a break from her, too. How could two people who obviously loved each other let their marriage deteriorate to this point? It was easy to blame Brandon, but Joanie knew she was also at fault.

"I thought you'd have left by now," Brandon said when he stepped into the kitchen and found her still in her pajamas. His cheeks were red with cold and he rubbed his hands together briskly.

"I was hoping to leave early, but it didn't work out that way."

"The kids are packed and ready to go."

"I know," she said irritably. He sounded as though he *wanted* to be rid of them. "I'm feeling a little queasy this morning," she muttered as she heard the children bounding down the stairs.

"There's a flu bug going around," Brandon commented casually. "Hassie came down with it last week."

"I think I'll make an appointment with Dr. Baker in Grand Forks when I get back," Joanie said, as she poured them each a freshly brewed mug of coffee.

"Why see a doctor when it's just the flu? There isn't anything he can do, is there?"

Joanie tensed at the suggestion that she'd spend money frivolously. "I haven't been feeling well for a while. Why are you so angry?" She hadn't had a physical since Stevie was born, and lately there'd been the dizzy spells, the lack of appetite, the depression.

Her husband sat down at the kitchen table and stared

blankly into space. "If we could put off any extra expense just now, I'd appreciate it."

"But we have health insurance and—"

"No, we don't," he said, cutting her off.

"We don't have health insurance?" Joanie repeated, stunned at the news.

"I missed a few payments and it got cancelled," Brandon said, his voice defensive.

He hadn't even told her. "But how could you let our health insurance lapse? What if something happened to one of the kids or I needed an operation or—"

"I feel enough of a failure without you ramming it down my throat. It was either that or the electric bill. I didn't mean for it to happen. Dammit, Joanie, I can't work any harder than I already am."

Joanie didn't need to be reminded that the payments on the washer and dryer stretched their budget to the limit. Those payments might not be much but she knew it was money that should have gone toward the four-hundred-dollar a month health insurance premiums.

Before she could comment, Brandon left the house.

"Mom?" Sage stood in the doorway leading into the kitchen. "Are you and Daddy fighting again?" she asked in a small voice.

Joanie held her arms open to her daughter and tried to hide the hurt she felt by comforting her child.

"Why is Daddy so mad all the time?" Sage pressed.

"He isn't angry with us," Joanie said, hoping to reassure her.

"I wish Daddy would come to Grandma and Grandpa's with us," Sage whispered, her arms tight around Joanie's neck.

"I wish he would, too."

Brandon didn't return to the house before Joanie left. The kids raced into the barn to kiss him goodbye and then piled into the car. Joanie waited, leaning against the steering wheel. If he wasn't going to come to her, she'd leave without another word. She wouldn't seek him out.

In a festive mood, the children sang and chatted excitedly on the trip to Fargo. Joanie was silent for most of the drive, brooding on her fears and problems, still hurt by Brandon's behavior that morning. When they arrived at her parents' house, Peg and Leon Bouchard greeted them with huge hugs and shouts of joy.

Joanie's father carried in the suitcases while her mother ushered her into the kitchen, happy and flustered with all her children and grandchildren home. She reviewed the menu for Joanie's benefit. The house was redolent with mouth-watering scents: roasting turkey, sage-and-onion stuffing. A variety of homemade pies—mincemeat, pumpkin and apple—lined the countertops, along with a number of festive serving bowls waiting to be filled.

"Jay, Kelly and the kids are off seeing Dan Jefferson and his family," her mother said conversationally. "You remember Dan, don't you? He was good friends with your brother in high school."

"Of course I remember Dan. How is he?" Joanie helped herself to a crescent roll, eating for the first time that day. Whatever had been wrong with her stomach earlier seemed to have disappeared, and she was grateful. She opened a can of black olives and placed them inside a small crystal dish, then reached for a jar of pickles she'd brought from the farm. Last year's crop had yielded several dozen jars, and they were exceptionally good.

"How are you?" her mother asked, crouching in front of the open refrigerator to remove a gelatin salad.

"I'm fine."

There must have been something in her voice because her mother paused in her task and turned to look at Joanie. "How are you *really?*"

Unwilling to discuss the details of her unhappiness, Joanie shrugged.

"You look like you've lost weight." Peg set the salad on the counter and studied her daughter closely. "Weight you can ill afford to lose, I might add."

"I'm fine. Mother, please, let's not get into this now." Everything about the way she'd been feeling was beginning to add up in her mind, and she didn't want to think about it. Not today when she was surrounded by family.

"I wondered if Brandon would come," her mother muttered, frowning.

"It hurt us financially when the grain prices came in so low. Things are hard for him just now."

Her mother reached across the table to touch her cheek. "You never were very good at hiding things from me. What's wrong, Joanie? Why are you so unhappy?"

"I'm happy. It's just that I haven't been feeling well lately," she confessed with some reluctance.

"Have you seen a doctor?"

Joanie dropped her gaze. "We don't have any health insurance."

"No health insurance?" she cried. "That does it! I'm taking you to see a doctor myself, first thing tomorrow morning. Dr. Carson is open, I'm almost sure of it, and if he's not, then I'll find someone who is."

Joanie closed her eyes. "Mother, please don't. I'm fine, really."

"I knew something was wrong the minute I saw you."

Joanie was warmed by her mother's love and concern—

and suddenly her growing worry seemed to overwhelm her. She'd been so lonely the last while, bearing her fears and regrets by herself. "If you must know, I think I might be pregnant." It didn't seem likely, since they'd only made love a few times. Besides, Joanie was on the Pill—well, admittedly she'd gotten lax in the past few months. She and Brandon made love so infrequently it barely mattered if she took the pills or not, she'd assumed. It was the stress, she'd told herself repeatedly. Stress and worry had interfered with her monthly cycle.

As Peg tried to reassure her, Sage and Stevie's laughter could be heard from the other room. Her father was wonderful with the children, and Joanie wished Brandon paid that kind of attention to them. All he did was work.

Late fall and winter was usually a slack time, but Brandon was putting in as many hours now as he had during harvest.

Thanksgiving day with her family was wonderful, full of laughter and shared family stories. Joanie tried not to think about Brandon home alone. It'd been his choice to stay behind, and in fact he'd seemed happy enough to be sending her and the children away.

After the big turkey dinner, with her mother's special dressing and Joanie and Jay's favorite cranberry salad, Joanie took a two-hour nap in her old bedroom, sleeping in her childhood bed. The kids were content playing with their cousins. They fell asleep in front of the television at ten that night.

On Friday, the appointment with the photographer wasn't scheduled until the afternoon. True to her word, Peg Bouchard scheduled an appointment for Joanie with Dr. Carson, a longtime family friend, that morning. He'd known Joanie most of her life.

While her mother sat in the waiting room, Dr. Carson gave her a physical and asked her a number of questions. He had his nurse draw blood, collected a urine sample, and after several minutes, escorted her into his private office to talk.

"Did you know you're pregnant, Joanie?"

"I suspected as much," she murmured. "I'm on the Pill, but—"

"How faithful have you been about taking it?"

She sighed and looked down at her hands, letting her hair fall forward to hide the emotion in her face. "I guess I missed more often than I realized," she whispered.

"This pregnancy isn't welcome?"

His words jolted her, and Joanie broke into huge sobs. She could only imagine what Brandon would say when she told him. Without health insurance they'd have to carry the full brunt of the medical expenses on their own. Problems with her second pregnancy had resulted in a cesarean birth, so having a midwife deliver the child at home was no longer an option. A hospital stay would cost thousands of dollars, far beyond what they could afford.

Brandon would blame her for letting this happen. She was the one who'd been careless with the birth control pills. A pregnancy now would only confirm his feelings of failure.

Dr. Carson handed her a tissue. "Would you like me to get your mother for you?"

Weeping uncontrollably, Joanie nodded.

When Peg entered the room, Joanie looked at her mother and sobbed. "Oh, Mom, I don't know what I'm going to do."

"What is it, Joanie? *Are* you pregnant?"

She nodded, barely able to speak.

"Sweetheart, that's wonderful news!"

"Brandon won't think so—he doesn't want another baby."

"Joanie, give him a chance. Once you tell him—"

"No." Joanie was adamant. "I'm not telling him. I don't even want him to know until I decide what I'm going to do about this marriage. Oh, Mom, I'm so confused."

On the Friday after Thanksgiving, Lindsay and Maddy did their part to ensure that this was the biggest shopping day of the year. Exhausted, Lindsay sat in her friend's living room, her legs stretched out and her feet on the coffee table.

Together they'd hit the mall in the predawn hours, hoping to catch the early-shopper bargains, and hadn't stopped until late afternoon. Lindsay had bought enough to require an additional suitcase to take all her purchases—including some new sweaters, underwear, books and videos—back to Buffalo Valley.

"I can't deal with these crowds anymore," Lindsay complained. "I'm just not used to so many people in the same place."

Maddy giggled. "Four months in North Dakota, and I hardly recognize you anymore. Where's the super shopper who used to drag me from store to store?"

"Most of the buying I do these days is out of a catalog, and believe it or not, that's the way I like it." Lindsay had been born and raised in Savannah and had always loved the South, but after two days away from Buffalo Valley, she found herself thinking about her life there and all the people she'd met.

Most often it was Gage who wandered, uninvited and unwelcome, into her mind. Again and again she found herself obsessing about their kiss at the Grand Forks airport. She had to know what it meant.

Maddy sank into the chair across from her, a soda in her

hand. "I've missed you, Lindsay. It doesn't seem right with you living so far away."

"I've missed you, too. You, and a few of the more modern conveniences."

"You mean like your choice of fast food?"

"No—well, yes, I *have* missed pulling up to a drive-in window and ordering my favorite bean burrito, but I was thinking more along the lines of real luxuries like a hair-dresser and a dry cleaner's. And a bookstore…"

"Those aren't luxuries."

"They are in Buffalo Valley."

Maddy laughed. "Tell me more about your…chat with Monte."

True to his word, Monte had shown up at her parents' door early Thanksgiving morning. He wanted to talk to Lindsay. At least, that was what he'd said; when it came right down to it, though, he'd wanted to argue with her. Rather than cause any unpleasantness, Lindsay had agreed to see him. That had been her first mistake.

Their meeting hadn't gone well. Monte was angry, and no matter what she said, he refused to believe she was serious about breaking off their relationship. Even now, four months after her move, he insisted that the entire undertaking was a desperate ploy to entice him to marry her. Again and again he'd insisted he wasn't going to let her manipulate him into proposing, no matter what she said or did.

"I never realized what a colossal ego Monte has," Lindsay said, reaching for the bowl of chocolate-covered pretzels.

"Everyone else saw it," Maddy was unkind enough to point out.

"Oh, thanks for telling me," Lindsay said humorously.

A few months ago, Lindsay might have taken offense

at her friend's honesty. But not now. "I know it sounds ridiculous, considering how much I wanted to marry him, but I'm actually embarrassed that I was so crazy about Monte."

Grinning broadly, Maddy nodded, as if she knew a delicious secret and was keeping it to herself.

"What's that look about?" Lindsay demanded.

Maddy sat up and took a pretzel herself. "It's very interesting, what you just said."

Lindsay gestured for her to continue.

"You're truly over Monte," Maddy announced. "Already you're distancing yourself from him emotionally. You used to look at him through rose-colored glasses. You might have seen his faults, but you ignored them because you'd convinced yourself you were in love with him."

"I *was* in love with him," Lindsay said. "You know what part of our conversation bothered me the most?" she asked, shaking her head. "When I suggested he start dating other women, he accused me of being devious." He'd said he wasn't seeing anyone else because he refused to believe she actually wanted to end their relationship. The only reason she wanted him to see other women, he claimed, was so she could prove she no longer cared; it was all part of her marriage ploy.

Lindsay had laughed outright, calling his reasoning outrageous. Her attitude had angered him even more, and he'd left soon after that. Lindsay wasn't sure whether to laugh or cry as she recounted their visit.

"I wondered how long it would take for you to see the light."

"Longer than it should have," Lindsay confessed. "Now, enough about me and Monte." She noted how Maddy had cleverly avoided talking about herself. "What's going on with you? You've hardly said a word about yourself and practically nothing about your job." It used to be that Maddy talked endlessly about the cases she handled, although, naturally, she never mentioned names or identified the people she worked with.

Maddy wouldn't meet her eyes.

"Maddy?" she coaxed.

"All my life I've wanted to help others," Maddy began in a low voice.

"That's why you're such a good social worker. You have a very big heart, Madeline Washburn."

To Lindsay's amazement, tears welled in her friend's eyes. "I'm burning out. My supervisor warned me about this. It was one of the reasons she told me to take my vacation last summer. She recognized the signs and hoped I'd look after myself before I crashed and burned."

"But it was too late, wasn't it?"

Maddy hugged a pillow to her stomach and nodded. "I woke up one morning a few weeks ago and realized I don't want to do this anymore. I feel *empty*. I've given away so much of myself, I no longer know who I am." She stared into the distance, her eyes devoid of emotion. "That sounds crazy, but…"

"It doesn't," Lindsay was quick to tell her. "I understand."

"How can you, when I don't understand it myself?"

She knew Maddy was right; as a friend, Lindsay could sympathize, but she hadn't experienced these feelings herself, so she couldn't truly understand. Lindsay got up and went across the room to give her a hug. "If there's anything I can do—"

"There isn't," Maddy said. "I'll work it out in time."

"But shouldn't you let someone help you?" Lindsay asked. "You're willing to leap into the fray for everyone else, but you won't share your own troubles…."

Maddy nodded. "I know. Don't worry, though, I'll be fine." She gave Lindsay what looked like a forced smile. "I'm not going to ruin the few days we have together by thrashing over my problems."

"Why not? You've listened to mine."

"Then tell me about Gage Sinclair," Maddy suggested, deftly changing the subject. "You've talked about practically everyone in Buffalo Valley but him. Has anything changed?"

Lindsay did what she could to sidestep the question. "How could it? We're barely on speaking terms."

"But let me tell you—sparks fly whenever you two are anywhere near each other. I could see that the day you met, in July."

"Don't be ridiculous," Lindsay interrupted. She didn't want to think about Gage. She'd tried, unsuccessfully, to put him out of her mind all weekend. So many questions remained unanswered. Most important, she was still unsure of herself and her own feelings.

"You know," Maddy said, "when you first told me you were taking that teaching job in North Dakota, I thought it was a bit drastic, but after four months I can see a real difference in you. I don't mind telling you I'm envious."

"Envious? I have to drive an hour for a haircut."

"I'm serious, Lindsay."

"Then pull up your stakes and do the same thing," she said, only half joking.

Maddy's gaze held hers. "Don't be shocked if I do exactly that."

The rest of Lindsay's time in Savannah passed far too quickly. Her parents were busy with their grandchildren, and the only private time Lindsay had with her mother was early Sunday morning, when she drove her to the airport.

"You seem different," her mother said as she parked the car close to the terminal.

"Different?" Lindsay repeated, smiling to herself. Maddy had said the same thing. It made her wonder if she really *had* changed from the woman who'd left Savannah only a few months ago.

"You're moving back home, aren't you?" her mother pressed. "After the school year, I mean. You won't actually consider settling in Buffalo Valley, will you?"

"My intention is to teach one year, and that's all. Then I'll come home." But Buffalo Valley felt like home, too. Yes, she missed Savannah, her friends and family here, but Buffalo Valley offered its own satisfactions.

"You'll fly back for Christmas?"

"I can't, Mom." They'd already discussed this. "Not with the school play and the price of airfare…"

"Your father and I'll pay for your ticket."

"I just can't, Mom. If possible, I'll visit again during spring break, around Easter time."

Her mother hugged her close before Lindsay entered the terminal. "I feel like I'm losing you," Kathleen Snyder whispered, and her voice broke. "If it was up to me, Monte would be strung by his thumbs for being so damned obstinate."

"That's the amazing part, Mom," Lindsay said. "I think Monte might have done me one of the biggest favors of my life."

Father Damian McGrath was the visiting priest who celebrated Mass twice a month at St. Paul's, the old Catholic church in Buffalo Valley. He'd immigrated from Ireland just before World War II and was well past the age of retirement.

For the first time, Lindsay would be attending Mass

there, accompanying Gage and his family and joining them for dinner afterward. He knew that Lindsay's father had been raised Catholic, but her mother was a staunch Baptist and had brought her daughters up Baptist, too. Lindsay had told him she felt quite ecumenical, since she'd sometimes accompanied her Grandpa Snyder to Mass in Savannah, as well.

Because of a shortage of priests and the area's declining population, St. Paul's had ceased to be a functioning parish. In his generosity, Father McGrath visited the community the first and third Sunday of each month to celebrate Mass and then usually stayed for dinner with a local family.

Gage's mother had invited both Father McGrath and Lindsay. She'd been cooking for two days, preparing an elaborate dinner, as if it were the Pope himself who was paying them a visit.

Gage didn't understand all the fuss, but his mother had repeatedly told him it wasn't for him to understand. All she asked was that he be a gracious host.

Gage wasn't sure if he should be pleased about seeing Lindsay again or not. She'd been back in Buffalo Valley a week and he had yet to speak to her or she to him. Which was just as well. When they did meet, she'd probably ask why he'd kissed her, and Gage didn't know what to say. It had been spontaneous. If he'd stopped to think about it, he'd never have done it.

He knew one thing. He'd felt a whole lot easier when he found out she was back. Rachel Fischer and Mark had driven Lindsay's car into Grand Forks to meet her return flight; Heath Quantrill had apparently suggested it. That was fine by Gage. He liked Rachel, and for a man with money in his pocket, Heath wasn't half-bad.

Dressed in his Sunday best, Gage watched his mother

flutter nervously about the kitchen. He didn't know why, since everything seemed ready. The dining-room table was set with their best china and a crisply ironed linen tablecloth and napkins. He hadn't seen those since the previous Christmas.

"Hurry, or we'll be late for church," Leta ordered. His mother's excitement remained at a high pitch, and Gage was forced to listen to her chatter the entire drive into town. He was more amused than annoyed, however, realizing she derived genuine pleasure from this event.

During Mass, Lindsay sat across the aisle from him. He couldn't help being aware of her and knew from the surreptitious looks she sent in his direction that she was conscious of him, too.

Following Mass, the small caravan of cars returned to the farm. His mother immediately ushered Father McGrath inside and out of the cold, biting wind.

"Gage," his mother called to him over her shoulder. "Help Lindsay into the house, would you?" Twelve inches of compact snow covered the ground. Gage opened Lindsay's car door and held out his arm.

"It's good to see you, Gage," she said, gazing up at him. He found it difficult to meet her eyes, but managed. "Did you have a nice Thanksgiving?" she asked.

"Fine, and you?" he returned politely. His warm breath made small clouds as he spoke.

"Very nice." She slid out of the driver's seat, her feet sinking a bit in the snow. Gage shut her door, and she tucked her hand in the crook of his arm. As they hurried toward the house, he felt her stiffness, sensed the emotional distance she placed between them.

No sooner was everyone inside, than his mother, with Lindsay's help, started carrying serving dishes to the dining-room table. They only ate there on special occasions and holidays; having Father McGrath over was most definitely a special occasion.

Leta did a good job of managing the conversation, asking Lindsay about her trip to Savannah. Gage listened carefully to her answers and admired the way she skillfully avoided any mention of Monte.

"You're Anton and Gina's granddaughter?" Father McGrath asked, apparently making the connection for the first time.

"Yes," Lindsay answered. "You knew my grandparents?"

"Very well. Very well, indeed. Your grandmother was a brave woman."

"Lindsay's living in her grandparents' old house," Gage commented.

"What do you mean about my grandmother being brave?" Lindsay asked, leaning forward.

"I admired her deeply," the priest continued.

"I did, too, but I didn't know her very well," Lindsay said. "Were you close to her?"

He shook his head, obviously intending to say nothing more.

"But you called her brave," Lindsay reminded him.

"For overcoming her unhappiness." His answer was vague.

Gage watched as Lindsay grew still. "My grandmother was unhappy?"

Her remark seemed to take the old priest by surprise. "It was a long time ago, child, and best forgotten."

"But I don't *want* to forget. I want to know everything there is to know about her."

"It all took place during the war years… So many young men died."

"Did my grandmother lose someone?" Lindsay's voice was intense.

"Lose someone? You mean a young man?" The priest shook his head. "No, no. Well, not exactly."

After that, Father McGrath turned the conversation to other matters, despite Lindsay's attempts to ask him about her grandmother.

When dinner was finished, Leta and Father McGrath lingered over coffee talking quietly, while Kevin sat there looking bored. Gage took advantage of the opportunity to lean toward Lindsay. "Do you think Father McGrath might know something about that brick?" he whispered. "The hollow brick in your fireplace?"

Her eyes widened and she pressed her finger to her lips. "No one knows about that but you and me."

"All right, I won't say any more."

Eager to escape the conversation, which consisted mostly of stories about people who'd once lived in Buffalo Valley, Gage got up to leave the table. "I'm going out to check some equipment in the barn," he said. "If you'll excuse me?"

"I'll go with you," Lindsay volunteered.

"Me, too," Kevin said with unmistakable relief.

His mother must have signaled Kevin not to join them because he sat back down with a shrug. "Never mind, I'll go with Gage another time."

Fully dressed in their winter coats, Gage and Lindsay left the house, Tramp following on their heels. She buried her hands deep inside her pockets and had wrapped a muffler around her neck. A matching knit hat covered her head. Only her eyes were visible, and that was enough, possibly too much for Gage. She was watching him a little too intently, and he found it unnerving. Lindsay was only passing through Buffalo Valley—and his life. He didn't *want* to feel anything for her, but the attraction grew more intense with each meeting.

"I take it you don't want to talk about your grandmother," he said abruptly, leading the way to the rear of the small apple orchard where he kept his bees.

"Why'd you kiss me?" she asked, ignoring his question.

If he had the answer to that, he would've been in town thirty minutes after she returned. Instead he'd waited, attempting to sort out his feelings before they talked again.

"Well?" she demanded.

"I don't know." At least he was honest, whether she wanted to hear it or not.

"That's not good enough."

"Fine. If you have a theory, I'd be pleased to hear it."

"You didn't *plan* to kiss me?"

"Hell, no!"

"But you wanted me to come back to Buffalo Valley. You said so."

"Yes." He couldn't very well deny it.

"Why did you care, one way or the other?" Her voice was softer now.

"The school…"

"This has nothing to do with the school." Her irritation was back.

"What do you want from me?" Gage muttered.

"The truth."

He scoffed. "You don't want the truth. You can't deal with the truth."

"The hell I can't."

It seemed to him that she asked everything and offered nothing. "What are *you* looking for?" he shouted. "For me to lay my heart on the line—is that it? Sorry, you're too damn fickle for that. You love someone else, remember? Monte what's-his-face."

His words were followed by a shocked silence. Then, "You're the most stubborn, unreasonable man I've ever met. Even more than Monte," she muttered under her breath.

"Me?" Never in all his life had he met a more exasperating woman. "I'm not going to let you jerk me around, Lindsay, nor will I let you use me. You say you want to get over your old boyfriend so you don't want a relationship— fine, then don't give me come-hither looks. And don't expect everything to be on *your* terms. You want me to help dig up some old secret about your grandmother. No way. Leave me out of this."

"*Come-hither looks?* How can you say such a thing?" she asked tightly.

Before he could answer, she turned to run back to the house. Gage started after her, but he really didn't know what he'd do if he actually caught up with her.

"Lindsay," he called, wanting her to stop before she fell. "Lindsay, it isn't safe—"

He was too late. She stumbled in the hard snow, staggered a couple of steps and fell forward, catching herself with her hands.

He was at her side instantly. Before he could stop himself, he'd pulled her into his arms and he was hugging her and telling her how sorry he was.

His arms were around her and hers around him. Their breath rose like mist as they knelt in the snow clinging to each other with a desperation he'd never felt before.

"I kissed you because it's all I can think about," he confessed.

"Don't you know?" she said, staring up at him, her eyes huge and so very blue. As blue as cornflowers in spring. "Kissing you is all I can think about, too."

Twelve

The conversation with Father McGrath had raised questions Lindsay couldn't leave unanswered. He'd told her Gina Snyder had been brave and that she'd been unhappy. But why? And about what? Lindsay had to believe Father McGrath knew more than he was telling. She suspected that whatever he'd left unsaid had to be linked to what she'd seen as a child.

Her memories of that summer's night remained vivid in her mind. The tears that streaked her grandmother's face had glistened in the moonlight. She'd wept as she held her treasure—whatever it was—before hiding it inside that hollow brick. It was gone now and Lindsay couldn't help wondering if her grandmother had found another hiding place. She'd looked everywhere she could think of and found nothing. But Lindsay knew she couldn't rest until she'd uncovered all she could.

With school and rehearsals for the play, plus the renovation of the theater, Lindsay didn't have a lot of time to dwell on it. She was gratified by the way everyone in town had mobilized to help the high school and to work on the theater.

Hassie organized people, requesting their assistance and scheduling tasks. She'd talked Joshua into taking care of the lights, Gage and Dennis into doing carpentry chores, Sarah into repairing and cleaning the curtains. And so on… People in Buffalo Valley did not say no to Hassie. Lindsay had frequent meetings with her to discuss the theater's progress, and one day, when the opportunity presented itself, she asked about her Grandma Gina. Hassie hadn't lived in Buffalo Valley during the war years, but suggested Lindsay contact Lily Quantrill, a longtime friend of Gina's. At Hassie's request, Heath had kindly approached his grandmother, who'd agreed to talk to Lindsay that weekend.

Luckily—despite his earlier assertions about wanting nothing to do with her search—Gage was willing to help her. He arrived early Saturday morning to drive her into Grand Forks.

"I made us a thermos of coffee for the drive," Lindsay said, when she opened her front door. Although they'd talked since Sunday, planning this excursion into the city, Lindsay felt shy around him. She could hardly believe the things she'd said and done. He'd shouted that she was fickle, that he wasn't willing to lay his heart on the line for her—so she'd handed him hers. They'd held each other in the snow, kissed until she thought she'd melt, then returned to the house, holding hands.

His mother had immediately noticed the change in their attitudes toward each other and all but crowed with delight.

Lindsay didn't know where their relationship was leading, but after much reflection decided it wasn't necessary to be sure of the future. Her relationship with Monte had made her cautious and somewhat insecure about her own judgment. For now, she liked spending time with Gage, enjoying his wit and his friendship, and was grateful for his help in deciphering her grandmother's secret.

"You talked to Lily Quantrill?" Gage asked.

"Last night," Lindsay said. "I told her to expect us about ten this morning."

Gage glanced at his watch. "Then we'd better leave now."

"I'm ready." She reached for her coat, muffler, gloves and hat. She hadn't appreciated what it meant to be cold—really cold—until she'd moved to Buffalo Valley. She'd bought an insulated coat and boots through the Land's End catalog; everything else had been given to her. So far, anyway, she was well equipped to deal with snow and cold.

"I thought we'd go out for lunch when we're finished," Gage said as he helped her to his truck cab.

"That would be a real treat." She needed to be back for rehearsals at three that afternoon. She was also scheduled to meet with Sarah Stern to discuss costumes and props. Sarah had been in to talk to the class on Friday and had brought a recently completed quilt, as well as some books that showed different quilt patterns; she'd also brought examples of the natural dyes she used. The students were enthralled, as was Lindsay. Sarah had graciously agreed to let them use one of her quilts in the Christmas production.

Lindsay found Gage studying her, and he looked so damned sexy it was all she could do to keep from kissing him. She laughed and Gage glanced in her direction. "What's so funny?"

"Nothing." She shook her head. "I'm happy, that's all."

"I am, too," he said with a grin.

"I'm excited about this morning," Lindsay admitted. "This is the first real chance I've had to learn anything new about my grandmother. My dad just doesn't know any of this history."

"Well…I hope Mrs. Quantrill can answer your questions."

"So do I."

As promised, Lily Quantrill was waiting for them in her suite on the top floor of the retirement center. She sat regally in her wheelchair, a crocheted blanket over her lap. Her hands, gnarled and veined, rested on the arms of the chair.

"You want to ask me about your grandmother?" Lily asked, before Lindsay had a chance to sit down. Clearly this woman wasn't one to waste time on idle chatter.

"Yes," Lindsay said, "if you don't mind telling me about her."

"You wouldn't be here if I did," the older woman muttered. "Now, what do you want to ask?"

"How well did you know her?"

"We grew up together, and I considered her one of my dearest and closest friends." She gestured imperiously. "Sit down, sit down."

"Could you tell me about the war years?" Lindsay asked as she perched on a small, elegant couch. Gage sat stiffly beside her, obviously uncomfortable on such a feminine piece of furniture.

The old woman paused and looked quickly from Lindsay to Gage, then back to Lindsay. "You know about that, do you?"

"No," Lindsay responded, then regretted her honesty. If she pretended she knew, she might learn something that Lily Quantrill would otherwise be unwilling to tell her. "I was hoping you'd explain…"

Mrs. Quantrill paused, apparently choosing her words carefully. "Did you know she was in love with Jerome Sinclair?"

"My grandfather?" Gage said, his shock causing him to sit even straighter.

"I assumed that's why you're here," Lily snapped.

"I didn't know," Gage said unnecessarily. His gaze sought out Lindsay's. "They were never married."

"There's a very good reason for that, if you'll give me a chance to continue." Lily Quantrill spoke in a softer voice as she began her story. "Gina Colby was smitten with Jerome from the time she was in junior high. In seventh grade, she told me she planned on marrying him one day. I remember I laughed and asked her if Jerome knew about that." She smiled at the memory, lost for a few moments in an era long past. "Gina told me Jerome loved her, too, only he didn't know it yet. Can you imagine? But I'll tell you what. She was right." Lily shook her head. "We were all so young at the time. Jerome was a couple of years older than Gina and me. He was a tall, skinny kid, but none of us had much to eat back then.

"That was during the dust bowl years, during the Great Depression, and we were all so poor we didn't have two nickels to rub together. People today don't understand what it was like to live in those times."

"I'm sure that's true," Lindsay said, not wanting to get sidetracked. "You said there was a good reason my Grandma Gina didn't marry Gage's grandfather."

"There was." She paused, and a sadness entered her eyes. "Gina thought he was dead."

Gage reached for Lindsay's hand and held it tightly. "My grandfather was captured by the Japanese in 1943 and kept in a POW camp for two years," he said hoarsely.

"All Gina learned was that Jerome was missing in action. We both knew what that meant. She grieved for him something fierce and even took sick for a time. Her mother was beside herself, not knowing how to help her. She was afraid Gina might die from her grief."

"How long was it before she married my grandfather?"

Lily closed her eyes for a moment. "Maybe six months. Maybe even a year. Anton had been exempted from the war for medical reasons. He farmed with his father and that was his contribution to the war effort. He'd always loved Gina and pursued her for months before she agreed to see him. She seemed like a new woman after she married Anton Snyder."

"Then the war ended and my grandfather returned to Buffalo Valley," Gage said without emotion.

Lily nodded. "By that time, Brian had been born— Lindsay's dad—and Gina and Anton had settled down on the farm. Anton had taken over from his father, and the two of them made a good life for themselves."

"Did she and Jerome ever talk about it?" Lindsay asked. She could imagine her grandmother's shock at discovering he was alive. Her shock and his pain. It hurt to think of what they must have endured, loving each other all those years and then pulled apart by war.

"They must've sorted everything out...eventually. Whatever was said remained between the two of them, but I know the early months were difficult for them both. Gina had no way of finding out that Jerome had survived. The Japanese hadn't released his name. It'd been over two years, and he'd already been through one hell only to return home to another."

"That must be why Father McGrath called her brave," Lindsay said, thinking aloud. "She was married to my grandfather, and yet all those years she loved another man."

"I believe Gina always held a special place in her heart for Jerome, but he was the love of her youth. As a woman, an adult, the man she genuinely loved was Anton, always Anton. She pledged her life to him and her heart, and she stood true to her vows. The years proved that."

"But Gina and Jerome—they still lived in the same place!"

A faraway look came over Lily Quantrill. "I suppose

that sounds strange to you young people, but those days weren't like times now, when vows mean nothing. Gina was married to Anton and bore his sons. While it might seem hard to believe, both Jerome and Gina lived in this community, raised their children, went on with their lives. They didn't have any choice."

"What about my grandfather?" Gage asked, leaning forward with his elbows on his knees. "Was he happy?"

"It's difficult to say, but I think so. It wasn't easy for him when he came home. He was bitter when he found Gina married, but he didn't hold it against her." She paused, shaking her head. "The war had been hard on him. He'd never been much of a talker, but he grew even quieter afterward. He eventually married your grandmother Molly, and it's my belief that he found his own peace…and eventually, happiness."

Gage and Lindsay left ten minutes later, declining coffee. On the drive into Grand Forks, they had talked and laughed, but now both were silent.

"She loved your grandfather," Lindsay finally whispered. "I know she did."

"In her own way."

Lindsay stared down at her hands, weighing her thoughts. "I…I don't suppose it would do any harm to tell you now."

"Tell me what?"

"How I knew about the brick." She hesitated, recalling that long-ago promise. She'd told her grandmother she wouldn't tell and had kept her word all these years.

"Lindsay?"

"I…promised her."

"What?"

"I promised I wouldn't tell, but it was your grandfather… You have a right to know."

Gage reached for her hand. "It's fine. It doesn't matter."

She nodded, grateful for his understanding. "She loved him, Gage, more than we'll ever know. For years she wept for him. I'm sure what Mrs. Quantrill said about her loving my grandfather was true, but her heart belonged to her first love. I'm absolutely certain of it."

Inexplicable tears filled her eyes and she glanced away, not wanting Gage to see. But he must have noticed because he pulled into a vacant lot and shut off the engine.

"Lindsay." Her name was the gentlest of whispers.

She turned to him then, and he took her in his arms and held her close.

They clung tightly together, as if holding on to each other now would make up for what their grandparents had lost half a century ago. They didn't speak. They didn't need to.

Joanie waited until Saturday night, when the children were asleep, before she approached Brandon.

The television blared out the laugh track of a situation comedy as she carried her husband a mug of coffee. He sat in the living room, shoeless feet propped up on the coffee table.

"Can we talk?" she asked, sitting on the edge of his chair.

He looked away from the television with obvious reluctance. "About what?"

She reached for the remote control and turned off the television. "This is serious, Brandon."

"All right," he said, dropping his feet to the floor, tensing. He straightened, his shoulders as stiff and unbending as his stubbornness.

"I need to ask you something."

"If it's about Christmas—"

"This has nothing to do with Christmas." Her husband

had already made it plain that it would be a meager holiday season. Each of the children would get one gift. He and Joanie wouldn't exchange gifts at all, not with each other. Not with anyone. Joanie wouldn't be doing the normal holiday baking, either. This Christmas there was nothing to celebrate, as far as Brandon was concerned.

"I want to preface what I'm about to say," she said, inhaling a deep breath and holding it for a couple of seconds, "because—well, because I don't want you to respond with anger."

His eyes narrowed suspiciously. "In other words, I'm not going to like whatever you've got to say?"

She couldn't deny the truth of that.

"Just say it!"

"I think…" Joanie was afraid he'd never agree, but for the sake of their marriage, for the sake of their family, she had to try. "I think we should sell the farm."

Once she'd made the suggestion, she closed her eyes, anticipating his backlash. She didn't have to wait long.

Brandon was out of his chair in seconds, pacing the floor. "This farmland's been in my family for a hundred years!"

"I know that, Brandon."

"You're asking me to sell my heritage, my son's heritage."

"I'm just asking you to consider it. To look for alternatives. You're killing yourself working as many hours as you do. We don't have a life. You're constantly worried about money. You might want to continue like this, but I don't. The stress is making me ill. I'm already anemic."

Her husband sank back into his chair and pressed the heels of his hands against his eyes.

"The small farmer hasn't got a chance anymore," she told him. "Not in today's market."

"Farming is all I know, Joanie."

The pain in his voice was nearly her undoing. But she forced herself to go on. "You can learn something else, something less demanding and stressful."

He frowned, and she could see his doubt and his fear.

"My dad said if you were willing, he might be able to get you into the pipefitters' union. He knows the apprenticeship coordinator."

"You talked to your parents about this?" His voice throbbed with hurt.

"Is that so unforgivable?"

"It might surprise you, Joanie, but I do have my pride."

"Don't let your pride destroy our lives!"

Brandon didn't answer. The muscles in his jaw quivered and he broke eye contact and looked away.

"You think I've…betrayed you by talking to my mom and dad," she said, her voice barely above a whisper, "but I've done everything I know to save this marriage."

Her husband said nothing. Then he muttered, "Your parents were right. We should never have married."

"I'll let *you* tell Sage and Stevie they were a mistake," she cried, fighting back anger. This wasn't the first time he'd hurled these accusations at her, and she was tired of them.

"That's not what I mean," Brandon shouted.

"In other words, the *kids* weren't a mistake. I was."

"Not you. *Us*. We were nothing but one big mistake waiting to happen. I should've known better than to bring you here to the farm. You don't understand what it means to be a farm wife. I should have listened to my instincts."

She should be used to hearing it by now; still his words cut deep. "Then your answer is no. You refuse to consider selling the farm."

"My answer is *hell, no*."

She nodded, not even disappointed, since this was exactly

what she'd expected. Unwilling to prolong the agony, she left the living room and retreated into their bedroom.

The suitcases were stored in the back of the closet, and she dragged out the largest one and started emptying her dresser drawers. She hadn't wanted to come to Brandon with threats or hysteria. Had he agreed to consider selling the farm, she would have told him her reason for asking. But the knowledge that another baby was on the way would only add to his burdens. For now, the pregnancy was her secret. She wouldn't be accused of manipulating him with that.

"What the hell is this?" Brandon demanded when he found her. "You're leaving me?"

Without emotion, Joanie looked at her husband. "Don't tell me you're surprised. From everything you've said and done in the last few weeks, it seems this is what you want."

He stood there, silent. Pride kept him from denying her words or asking her to stay, she realized, her heart breaking. It wasn't supposed to end like this. She loved Brandon, had always loved him, had planned to grow old with him.

"I know you think you've failed us, Brandon, but that's not true. You're trying to cope with circumstances that have become impossible. We can't go on like this. I was hoping we might be able to try again, but I can see that isn't going to happen."

"Because I refuse to sell the farm?" he asked bitterly.

"It was the only thing I could think of that would give us a chance. I'm sorry it's come to this."

He sat on the edge of the bed. "Do you plan on taking the kids?"

She nodded.

"I guess that's for the best," he said, sounding resigned.

"I haven't told them. I thought we could do that together in the morning."

He agreed. "I assume you're moving in with your parents?"

"No. Mom and Dad have a rental that's vacant and they said the kids and I could live there for the time being."

"How long have you been planning this?" he asked.

"It isn't what I want, it never was, but we can't go on as we are now, destroying each other little by little. It's obvious you don't love me anymore."

"I bought you that damned washer and dryer, didn't I?"

Joanie held her head high. "Yes, you did get me the washer and dryer, and you've resented doing it every minute since. Do you honestly think I could enjoy using them after the things you've said? If I could've found a way, I would have returned them both."

Brandon watched her silently. Suddenly he stood and walked to the door, but before leaving the room, he turned back. "I suppose you're expecting me to beg you to stay."

"No."

"This is your choice, remember that."

She nodded.

"I didn't ask you to go."

"No, you drove me to it," she said, not immune to bitterness herself. This was hard. She'd anticipated Brandon's anger, but was stunned by his pain.

"I'm not coming after you, Joanie," he said tonelessly.

"I don't expect you to, Brandon."

"Just remember you're the one who wants out of this marriage."

"I want a *marriage,* and what we have isn't that."

"I've got a signed wedding license that states otherwise. If you want to end our marriage, there's nothing I can do. But let's get something settled right now."

She closed her suitcase and secured the lock. He

waited until she'd straightened and was looking at him before he spoke.

"Once you walk out that door, don't think I'm going to follow."

"Okay."

"I mean it, Joanie."

She didn't doubt him.

He shoved his hands in his pockets. "I'll send you what I can financially."

Tears burned her eyes and it took the full force of her determination to keep them at bay. "I'd appreciate whatever you can do to help."

"How do you plan to support yourself?" he asked. "Will you be getting a job?"

She nodded. "I talked to a friend of my mother's when I was home at Thanksgiving…. She said if things don't work out here, she'd hire me."

Cold, hard anger flashed from his eyes. "How many people have you discussed this with? How long have you been planning it, anyway? You didn't answer me before."

She stared at him. "Does it matter?" she finally asked.

"I guess not," he said in a defeated voice.

"That's what I thought." She slid the suitcase off the bed and set it next to the others. "I'll make sure the children keep in touch."

He nodded. "Just remember this was your decision."

"I'll remember."

"I'll sleep on the couch tonight." With those words, he hurried from the room. The lump in her throat made breathing nearly impossible.

It was over.

After she'd left with the children in the morning, she wouldn't see Brandon again. Not unless it was in court.

* * *

Rachel had looked forward to this evening all week. Mark was spending the night at Lindsay's while she went to dinner with Heath. The one unfortunate aspect of her pizza success was that it tied up her weekends. Since he was in town three days a week, Heath suggested they go out for dinner on a Wednesday.

During the last three months, Rachel had felt she was beginning to know Heath. He'd waited a long time to ask her out; he'd become her friend first, and she was grateful for his patience. He was the kind of man who knew what he wanted—and knew exactly how to get it. And if *she* was what he wanted… Well, she had to feel flattered.

Over Thanksgiving, he'd invited her to meet his grandmother, and Rachel had spent an enjoyable afternoon at the older woman's home. Lily remembered not only Rachel's parents, but her grandparents and had told her several stories she'd never heard before.

Rachel had loved watching Heath with his grandmother and enjoyed the conversational play between them. Lily Quantrill was as prickly as a cactus, and Heath always managed to say just the right thing to rile her. Rachel had teased him about it afterward and he'd told her how much he loved his grandmother. It was obvious to her that Lily Quantrill treasured her grandson, too. Rachel suspected these two were more alike than either one realized.

Tonight's dinner was important, a turning point for them. Rachel wasn't sure how she knew this, but she had the distinct feeling that it was much more than a routine date. Meeting his grandmother had been the first step, and apparently she'd passed muster.

Rachel's dress had cost a small fortune, and she'd spent copious amounts of time on her hair and makeup. When she dropped Mark off, Lindsay had assured her she looked fabulous. Rachel hoped that was true. It'd been years, at least fifteen years, since she'd gone out on a date, and despite knowing Heath and feeling comfortable with him, she was nervous.

The doorbell chimed and she leaped off the sofa, her heart pounding. She forced herself to be calm as she walked to the front door.

"Hello, Rachel," Heath said, stepping inside. He'd stamped the snow off his boots and brushed off his coat as he stood on the porch waiting for her. The December wind howled outside, and she could see that it was snowing more heavily now.

"You got your Christmas tree up early," he said, glancing around the house. He seemed to approve.

"Mark wanted the tree up last weekend. I don't know how I managed to put him off as long as I did."

Heath returned his attention to Rachel, and his gaze softened. "You look lovely."

"Thank you. You do, too."

Heath grinned, and Rachel swore it was the most wonderful smile she'd ever seen. "I don't think I've ever been called lovely before."

"You know what I meant," she said, blushing.

He helped her on with her coat, and his hands lingered at her shoulders. When his lips touched the side of her neck, Rachel closed her eyes as the shivers raced down her spine. He turned her in his arms and she didn't resist when his mouth sought hers. His kiss was light and gentle. And brief—he pulled away almost immediately.

"We'd better go," he murmured, his breath a little unsteady.

She nodded.

"I made a reservation at Mulligan's in Devils Lake."

It was by far the best restaurant in the area. Getting there entailed a fairly long drive, but if Heath didn't mind, she certainly wasn't going to object.

"Mark's with Lindsay, so it doesn't matter what time I get back."

"Is she keeping him for the night?"

"Yes." Rachel flicked off all but a few lights. "He was really excited, especially since he's got a minor role in the play. He gets to practice his lines with the director."

"The play's next week?"

"Thursday to Saturday. It should be wonderful— everyone's worked so hard." One way or another, the entire community was involved in this play. Her job had been publicity—sending press releases to radio stations and local newspapers. She'd heard that people from as far away as the Canadian border were planning to attend.

Heath handed her into his car, then raced around the front. "Damn, it's cold," he muttered as he slipped into the driver's seat.

She didn't think now was the time to remind him that it was going to get much colder come January. Officially it wasn't even winter yet. He hadn't lived in North Dakota in some years and must have forgotten about the weather.

Rachel had never eaten at Mulligan's and was pleased to discover that the restaurant's glowing reviews had been accurate. They both ordered steak and shared a bottle of red wine. She found their conversation equally delightful. He told her about his travels and she was fascinated by the places he'd been and the things he'd seen and done. She could have listened to him forever.

"Lindsay told me how much the high-school kids enjoyed it when you came to talk," she said when the conversation moved closer to home.

He smiled. "It was fun for me, too. Originally I was going to discuss banking, checking accounts and so on, but we got sidetracked and one thing led to another. Soon I was talking about my travels. Luckily I'd thought to bring along some foreign money and a few other mementos."

According to Lindsay, Heath had enthralled the high-school students. He'd brought not only an English pound, French francs and more, but an Italian goblet dating from the 1600s, an Egyptian flag and a petrified branch from the Alps. Each article had a story behind it and these stories had led to one of the liveliest afternoons of the school year. Lindsay said the kids had begged to have him return.

The restaurant was getting ready to close when Heath finally suggested they leave. They hurried through the cold to his car and quickly got inside.

"Oh, Heath, I had such a wonderful evening."

"I did, too," he said, smiling at her.

Warm and happy, Rachel leaned her head against the back of the seat and sighed. "You sure know how to make a girl happy, don't you?"

"I try."

She laughed softly at his response.

When they arrived in Buffalo Valley and he'd parked in front of her house, Heath said, "Are you going to invite me in for coffee?"

"Do you want me to?"

"That would be nice."

"Then consider yourself invited."

Like the gentleman he was, Heath helped Rachel out of the car. He followed her into the kitchen and watched her prepare a pot of coffee.

"It isn't really coffee that interests me," he told her.

"Oh?"

"It's you."

"Oh, Heath…"

He led her back to the living room and pulled her into his lap as he sat on the sofa. Rachel slid her arms around his neck and kissed him. She felt a tenderness growing inside her because of the things Heath made her feel. Because of his gentleness and his kindness and his interesting stories. Because of his kisses…

He kissed her again, more urgently than before. "I never guessed it would be like this with you," he whispered. He angled his head and dropped a succession of kisses along her throat until she moaned softly. He made a small sound of his own, then quickly joined their mouths again.

Rachel felt weak with desire. Her head was clouded with wine and kisses.

"You chose a very beautiful dress," he murmured before another lengthy kiss. "I just wish it wasn't one with a zipper down the back."

She heard the hissing sound as it opened and maneuvered her arms so that he was able to loosen the bodice. His hands found her breasts and she moaned as he rubbed his thumbs over her nipples, which responded immediately.

"I've been all over the world," Heath told her between soul-searing kisses. "And all along you've been right here."

He said the most romantic things.

"We're going to make love, Rachel—"

Her eyes flew open. "Now?"

"Tonight." He sounded so confident, so sure of himself.

"Heath." She placed her hands on either side of his face and looked down at him. "I'm not ready for that to happen. Not yet."

His eyes revealed his confusion. "What do you mean? I thought—"

"I didn't realize what you thought and if I had, I would've set you straight. It's too soon."

"But you had Mark spend the night with Lindsay."

"That wasn't because I was planning to sleep with you!"

"You don't expect me to drive all the way to Grand Forks tonight, do you?" His words were light, teasing, but there was an underlying disappointment.

"No."

"Good." His face relaxed.

"Buffalo Bob will appreciate the business."

He frowned, as though he didn't quite believe her.

"Heath, I don't know where you got the impression that I'd be willing to jump into bed with you on our first date, but you've been misinformed."

He stared at her.

"What's the matter, hasn't a woman ever turned you down before?" she asked softly, making a joke of it.

"As a matter of fact, no." He removed her from his lap and stood up, still looking bewildered. "I don't understand." He rammed his fingers through his hair. "We kiss, and I feel like I'm about to explode while you sit there, all calm and collected."

"I like your kisses, too, but I'm not about to do something I'll regret later. I have a reputation to consider, and maybe it's a bit old-fashioned in this day and age, but I do have certain values."

He paced back and forth but didn't speak.

"I'm genuinely sorry if I misled you," she said.

"You haven't misled me," he growled. "I got your message loud and clear. You're looking for a man who's more of a saint than I'll ever be. Good luck to you, Rachel. I hope you find him—but he isn't me."

Thirteen

Gage escorted his mother into the old theater and had to admit he was impressed with the changes. His own contribution had been an earlier part of the whole process, when it looked as if Lindsay—and Hassie—were asking the impossible. The task of renovating the boarded-up movie house had seemed hopeless, but the job was done. He admired Lindsay's grit and determination. Before he knew how it'd happened, he was doing carpentry and plastering, and after that he'd found himself painting walls and washing light fixtures along with just about everyone else. Once again, the community had come together for a common goal because of Lindsay. First the school, then the theater… Even Jacob and Marta Hansen had contributed—without their usual long list of complaints.

The old theater had responded graciously to the attention and, looking around, he saw hints of its former glory. Now a Christmas tree stood where there'd once been a player organ, and someone—Gage suspected Lindsay—had strung evergreen boughs around the huge room.

"Oh, look, Gage," Leta said, nodding to the left. "The Hunters are here."

Gage recognized a number of people he hadn't seen in a long time. Word had spread quickly about this Christmas play. Farmers and ranchers from various neighboring towns had come and brought their families. There were so few entertainment opportunities available to the region these days.

"It does my heart good to see all these people," his mother added.

Every seat was filled, and if Lindsay hadn't reserved the first few rows for the parents and families of the high-school class, Gage figured he'd be lucky to find two seats together.

He ushered his mother to their fifth-row seats, then sat down himself. He didn't like to think about what would happen at the end of the school year. He knew he wanted Lindsay to stay, but he didn't count on it.

She'd brought energy and hope when she'd moved to Buffalo Valley. Her enthusiasm had affected the entire community. Here it was, the end of a year that had been filled with bad news, and people were laughing and talking. There was a sense of festivity, of excitement. Instead of concentrating on what they lacked, people, himself included, were grateful for what they had. He would never be a rich man by the world's standards. Yet he had everything he needed to be happy, and he thanked the new schoolteacher for reminding him of that.

Lindsay was responsible for a lot of the good things that were taking place in Buffalo Valley. Kevin actually looked forward to classes, and Gage was well aware that his brother's renewed enthusiasm for school could largely be attributed to Lindsay. Not since grade school had Kevin shown such eagerness to learn.

But it was more than that. Kevin talked more freely to Gage now, and had even shown him a few of his art projects. The boy had talent and had beamed with pride when Gage said so.

Having members of the town come in as guest speakers every Friday afternoon had inspired pride in each of these visitors. Joshua McKenna walked a little taller these days, since it was his talk about Dakota history that had inspired the play. Much of the furniture for the set had come from his store and he'd helped with the lighting, as well. One of Sarah's quilts was used in the play, too, and an old blanket chest of Hassie's.

Lindsay had motivated the people of Buffalo Valley to show this generosity, this pride in who they were. She'd given them a way to recapture a spirit of community—and of Christmas. Maybe not all of them would admit that, but Gage knew it to be true.

He supposed he'd fallen in love with her that first day he'd met her, last summer. Try as he might, he'd been unable to forget her. When she'd accepted the job and moved to Buffalo Valley he'd tried to ignore her, knowing, as he had at their first meeting, that she could become someone important in his life.

What they'd learned about their grandparents had brought them closer. Gage felt a genuine kinship with Lindsay, and an appreciation for the sacrifices his grandfather had made. Lindsay seemed confident that her grandmother had always loved Jerome Sinclair; by the same token, Gage knew his grandfather had loved Gina Snyder with an equal passion. He wouldn't have stayed out of her life otherwise.

"I can hardly wait," Leta said, after she'd settled into her seat. "Oh, I hope nothing goes wrong." Gage couldn't remember his mother being this nervous about anything— not even dinner with Father McGrath. Kevin didn't have an actual role in the play, but he'd designed and painted the scenery, spending long afternoons on the project, and he was the assistant stage manager, or "ASM" as he told them importantly.

Gage read the program and noted that Buffalo Bob had taken advantage of the promotional opportunity with a full-page advertisement—including a ten-percent off coupon. He'd sponsored the printing of both the program and the posters, which had been designed by Rachel Fischer and hung in three different counties.

Many families would make use of the dinner coupon. Gage suspected Buffalo Bob would do more business in the next three nights than at any other time since he'd opened his doors.

Chalk another one up for Lindsay. Hiring her had been a boon to their town's economy.

"Look," his mother said proudly, pointing to Kevin's name in the program. All twelve members of the high school, plus a handful of younger students, were listed. Lindsay had also made sure that everyone who'd worked on getting the theater ready had received an acknowledgment.

The chatter lowered to an excited hush as the curtain parted and Lindsay stepped center stage. The lights were in her eyes; Gage could tell from the way she squinted. She was nervous and struggling to hide it, holding a small white card in a death grip, her gaze nervously darting around the full auditorium. Gage liked to think she was seeking him out and he smiled at her, trying to lend her confidence.

But when she spoke, her voice was strong and sure. "Good evening, everyone," she said. "I want to welcome each of you to our Christmas play. I'm happy to announce that we're sold out for the first night. The box office just informed me there's standing room only."

Enthusiastic applause followed.

When she left the stage, Gage was gratified by the cheers and loud clapping. She deserved it.

The play was everything he'd known it would be. Lindsay's students had taken incidents from their grandparents' lives and built a play around their hardships and triumphs. People had made memorable Christmas celebrations out of very little in those days—some homemade gifts and decorations, a community carol-singing service, dinner with family and friends.

It was fascinating to watch these kids play their own grandparents. The Loomis twins had talents Gage would never have guessed. People had been complaining about them for years, but Lindsay had found a way to channel their boisterous energy into a creative endeavor. Rachel Fischer's son, Mark, did a good job, too, in his small role as the youngest son of a desperate farmer. Gage glanced around, surprised to find Rachel sitting with Hassie. Heath Quantrill was nowhere to be seen. No one had said anything to Gage, but he'd thought there was some romantic interest between those two. Well, maybe Heath couldn't make it tonight; maybe he'd see the play tomorrow.

When it was over, the actors, holding hands, took two curtain calls, their faces flushed with pleasure at the overwhelming response to their efforts. As the audience filed out of the theater, Milly Spencer played Christmas carols on her flute.

Once outside, Gage saw several people heading for Buffalo Bob's, and wondered if he'd had the foresight to hire additional help. He'd been running the place without Merrily, telling everyone who asked that she'd be back sooner or later. In Gage's opinion, the person he was really trying to convince was himself.

Both Gage and Leta had been invited to Lindsay's house for a cast party following the play. His mother had baked several batches of Christmas cookies, and Gage had volunteered to mix a punch—two versions, one for the kids, the other for adults.

Hassie had gone ahead to open the house and put the dogs in the back bedroom, and by the time his mother had finished visiting with people, Gage saw that the students were closing down the theater.

Gage arrived only a couple of minutes before Lindsay. He hadn't even taken his coat off yet when she walked into the house. She went directly to him. He wished they could be alone for a few minutes, but since that wasn't possible, he reached for her hand.

"You did a wonderful job. Everyone did."

Her smile was big enough to drown in. She stood on the tips of her toes and kissed him, happiness radiating from her. "I'm so *proud* of everyone. The kids were wonderful and it felt as if, for the first time, the whole community was behind me."

"You have a right to be proud. Include yourself in this, Lindsay—you did some fabulous work here."

Christmas music played softly. The high-school class congregated in one corner, their parents in another. Excited, the students chatted nonstop, reliving the play scene by scene, recounting their mistakes, and giggling at the way they'd managed to pull the whole thing off.

In the kitchen, Gage prepared the Christmas punch—with rum and without—then returned to the living room, where he stood back and listened. Before long, Hassie, his mother and Lindsay carried in plates of holiday goodies and set them about the room.

He was astonished at the speed with which the food disappeared. The kids descended on his mother's fancy Christmas cookies and Hassie's popcorn balls and Lindsay's cheese and crackers as if they'd only just discovered food. Sipping his drink—the rum version—he shook his head in amazement.

The students and their parents left en masse an hour later, and both Hassie and his mother were suddenly absent, leaving him with Lindsay.

"Alone at last," he said, pulling her into his embrace. She didn't object and slid her hands up his chest, linking her fingers behind his neck. He knew she was exhausted and he should leave, too, but he couldn't make himself go. Not yet.

"This has been an incredible night, one of the best of my entire life." Her eyes sparkled like jewels.

Not kissing her then would have been impossible. She sighed and leaned her head against his shoulder.

"You're coming for Christmas?" His mother had told him only yesterday that she planned to invite Lindsay to the farmhouse for the day. Until then, he'd assumed she'd be flying home.

"I'll be there."

"Good." He kissed the bridge of her nose. "So will I."

She closed her eyes and sighed. "I have a wonderful surprise."

"For me?"

"No." She giggled softly.

"Then who?"

"Kevin."

"Tell me," he ordered.

Her beautiful eyes met his. "I shouldn't, but this is too good to keep to myself. I had Kevin research art schools and asked him if he could choose any two, which ones would he pick. He told me, but said it was a wasted effort because there's no way on earth he could ever attend."

"There isn't."

"Oh, ye of little faith," Lindsay said, kissing him again. "I wrote to each school and told them about Kevin and included samples of his work."

Gage went still, dread working through him.

"They've both sent me letters full of praise for his talent and included applications, plus scholarship information. Gage, there's a very good possibility Kevin could get a scholarship."

Gage said nothing.

"Isn't that wonderful?" Her expressive eyes registered her surprise at his lack of response.

"No. Kevin's a farmer, not an artist."

"But…"

"I don't mean to discourage you, Lindsay, but this is an area that's none of your concern. Kevin's attending agricultural college, and that's it. I can't afford to send him—"

"There might very well be a scholarship, and—"

"Lindsay, please, I don't want to argue. Not tonight. We'll talk about it another day. Tell Kevin, if you must, but keep in mind that it won't make any difference." Unwilling to end their evening on a sour note, Gage kissed her one last time, then hurried across the street to pick up his mother who was over at Hassie's.

"Is Uncle Jeb coming for Christmas dinner?" Calla demanded, standing just inside the kitchen.

Sarah Stern slid the turkey back into the oven and closed the door. It was the first time her daughter had spoken to her all day. "I hope so. Dennis is driving out to get him."

"Dennis? Don't tell me you invited *him*."

Sarah ignored that. "Your uncle Jeb will be here if Dennis has anything to say about it. He told me he's not taking no for an answer."

"I don't want Dennis here." Calla marched into the living room, then slouched down in the overstuffed chair and crossed her arms rebelliously.

"Calla, please! It's Christmas."

Her daughter stubbornly refused to look at her. "If it wasn't for you, I'd be with my father right now."

"But you're not. You're here with your grandfather and me."

Calla snickered as if to say that was a pretty poor substitute. It hurt that her daughter refused to open her Christmas gifts. Sarah had tried everything, but Calla had insisted the only gift she wanted was a plane ticket to visit her father. The argument had begun the day Willie's Las Vegas postcard arrived.

"Is Dennis playing pinochle, too?"

"Yes." Sarah knew she sounded defensive, but that was the way Calla made her feel. As soon as everyone arrived, her father was sure to suggest a game of pinochle. He'd taught Calla how to play when she was ten and she'd caught on to the game's strategy right away.

"Did you invite him for dinner or did Grandpa?"

"Why do you care?"

The surly look was back. "Because." Then without a pause, she added, "You're sleeping with him, aren't you?"

"Calla!"

"You think I don't know, but I do and so does everyone else." Her glare was full of contempt. "You're disgusting."

Sarah had taken all she could from her daughter. She marched into the living room and stood there, hands on her hips. "Listen here, little girl, what goes on between me and

Dennis Urlacher is none of your damned business." She heaved in a deep breath. "Furthermore, you will not say or do anything to embarrass us. Do you understand me?"

Calla met her gaze defiantly. "Did you sleep with other men, too?"

Sarah thought she was going to be sick.

"Is that why my daddy divorced you?"

The ugliness of her daughter's accusations closed Sarah's throat. Her hand ached with the impulse to slap Calla's face and demand an apology. The girl had no way of knowing that Willie was the one who'd engaged in countless affairs. No way of knowing that he'd destroyed Sarah's self-esteem, crippled her financially and then deserted her and their child.

"What's going on?" Joshua McKenna asked, as he walked into the house, his arms loaded down with firewood. He set the logs by the fireplace, then stood between mother and daughter. This kind of confrontation was familiar enough, to Sarah's shame, that her father automatically took on the role of buffer.

"Nothing, Dad," Sarah whispered. She retreated into the kitchen. As she left, she felt Calla's eyes following her, her resentment and bitterness burning holes in Sarah's back.

"Nothing's happening, Grandpa," Calla said, refusing to allow Sarah the last word.

Jeb and Dennis arrived shortly after that. Sarah didn't know what Dennis had threatened, but whatever he'd said had worked. It was the first time Jeb had been to Buffalo Valley in months. Her brother had lost part of his leg in a farming accident three years earlier. Now, the only obvious physical evidence was a slight limp. The psychological damage had been far worse.

Sarah ached for her brother, who was younger by five

years, and wished she knew how to help him, how to bring him back into the world. Ever since he'd returned from the hospital, Jeb had lived a secluded life. He'd broken off a promising relationship with a woman from Devils Lake and refused to see most of his friends. Getting him to join in family functions was difficult, if not impossible.

"Merry Christmas, Jeb," Sarah said, affectionately kissing her brother's cheek. He looked good, his color healthy. She was pleased to see that he wore the shirt she'd sewed him, a thick one of wool plaid. Despite the loss of his leg, Jeb worked his buffalo herd and lived by himself on a huge spread fifty miles outside of town. He wasn't as surly now as he'd been right after the accident, but he wasn't the same man, either. "I'm glad you decided to join us," she told him.

Jeb scowled, then smiled. "How long until dinner?"

"An hour." Sarah knew why he asked. As soon as he could, he'd make his excuses and head back to his ranch.

"There's time for a game of pinochle before we eat," her father called out from the living room.

"Can I play?" Calla asked, revealing the first sign of enthusiasm she'd shown all day.

"Don't you want to help your mother with dinner?"

Calla laughed as if the question amused her. "No."

"I'll get the cards," Joshua volunteered. "Jeb, you know where the card table is, don't you?"

Jeb made his way to the hallway closet.

"I can play, can't I?" Calla repeated, smiling sweetly at her grandfather.

"Of course you can," Dennis told her before Joshua could respond.

Calla bristled. "I wasn't asking you."

"Calla," Sarah warned, her voice low.

Her daughter cast her an insolent look.

"What's the matter with her?" Dennis asked, staying behind in the kitchen.

Sarah sighed and tried to act as if it didn't matter what Calla said or did. "You don't want to know."

"How'd she like the silver bangle I got her?"

Embarrassed, Sarah lowered her eyes. "She didn't open it, but I love my gold necklace. You shouldn't have spent so much."

"I wanted to spend a lot more."

Sarah knew he was saying he wanted to buy her a wedding band, but she let the comment pass, not wanting to argue on Christmas Day.

"I'm real happy with the sweater you knit me."

"Leta helped. I'll have you know my entry into heaven was in serious jeopardy with that pattern."

Dennis laughed and Sarah noticed her daughter watching them from the living room. Dennis did, too.

"Is she still upset about not spending the holidays with her father?" he asked.

Sarah nodded, the hurt inside her expanding. She'd tried so hard to be a good mother. But today, if Joshua hadn't come into the house when he did, Sarah might actually have slapped Calla's face. She'd never thought herself capable of such a thing. But these days her daughter seemed to bring out the worst in her.

"Did she open her Christmas gift from you?" Dennis asked.

"No," Sarah said, with a forced smile, "but it's her loss." Sarah had sewn Calla a vest, which had taken weeks. Her daughter had seen a similar one in a catalog and drooled over it for the longest time. She'd gone as far as to cut out the photograph and tape it to the bathroom mirror, knowing it was far too expensive to order. The vest alone cost nearly as much as a return ticket to Las Vegas. Out of love for her daughter, Sarah had designed and made an almost identical vest, complete with the delicate needlework. The fact that Calla refused to open her gift hurt more than Sarah wanted anyone to know.

"Thanks for bringing Jeb," she told Dennis.

His fingertips gently touched her face. Sarah placed her hand over his, closing her eyes, needing his comfort, hungry for his love. When she looked up, she found that Calla's expression had turned openly hostile.

"If Dennis is playing cards, then I'm not." She flopped back into her chair.

Both Jeb and her father paused in their task of setting out the card table and four folding chairs. Everyone seemed to be waiting for Dennis to respond.

"I don't need to play," Dennis said with a shrug, willing to step aside in order to appease Calla.

"The hell you won't," Sarah cried, refusing to let her daughter insult Dennis.

"It's a better game with four players," Joshua commented, sitting down on one of the folding chairs. He reached for the deck and shuffled the pack. "But we can play with three, if that's what Calla wants."

Calla frowned, clearly torn. "I bet Dennis wants to stay in the kitchen with my mother," she said, challenging him to defy her.

"Actually, I think Sarah's got everything under control," Dennis said, and joined the other two men.

Calla glared at him so hard that—as he later told Sarah—if looks could kill, he'd be a dead man.

The three men quickly became involved in a boisterous game of cards. Sarah kept herself busy putting the finishing touches to the dining-room table. The next time she glanced up, Calla was sitting, eyes shut, earphones on, as she listened to her iPod. It must've been set at its highest volume, because Sarah could hear the music from across the room.

When the men finished the game, dinner was ready. Still talking about the card game, Dennis, Jeb and her father gathered around the table. Ignoring them, Calla stayed where she was.

"Leave her be," Sarah said, knowing her daughter would try to ruin the meal if she was forced to join them for dinner.

"No," Jeb surprised her by saying. He walked over to where Calla sat and pulled out her earphones.

"Hey!" Calla straightened and scowled at her uncle, daring him to say something else.

He merely said, "Dinner's ready."

"I'm not hungry."

"That's too bad, because I've come all the way into town for this dinner. If I have to be there, then so do you."

"Do I have to eat?"

"Every bite," Jeb said, not quite managing to hold back a grin. "Even the Brussels sprouts."

Calla wrinkled her nose, but Sarah could see that her daughter was as sick of her own bad mood as everyone else.

"After we help your mother with the dishes, we'll play another game of pinochle and you can be my partner. We'll beat the socks off Dennis and your grandpa."

Calla seemed about to disagree, but then she gave what looked like an almost-smile and nodded. "Okay. Just as long as you and I are a team."

"You got it, kid," Jeb told her, and placed his hand on her shoulder. Sarah was grateful. They all sat down together and bowed their heads as Joshua said the blessing.

Perhaps later, Calla would open her gifts and appreciate her mother's love, and the effort she'd made. At Calla's age, Sarah had been just as insolent, just as unkind to her parents, just as uncompromising. What Sarah feared most of all was that her daughter would make the same painful mistakes she had.

The house had never seemed so empty. Christmas morning, Brandon woke and stared up at the ceiling for long minutes before he found the energy to climb out of bed.

The Christmas decorations Joanie had placed around the house were still there, but earlier, in a fit of rage, he'd taken the Christmas tree and thrown it out the front door. That was what he thought of Christmas. It might have been a stupid, futile action, but he'd felt better afterward. For a few minutes, anyway…

The phone rang around ten, and thinking it might be Joanie and the kids, he rushed to answer it. Instead, it was his parents in Arizona. He hadn't told them he and Joanie had separated; he figured he'd wait until after the holidays. No need to ruin their Christmas.

With a small deception, he was able to get off the telephone, promising to call back later. What he hadn't said was how *much* later.

Opening the refrigerator, he examined the meager contents, reached for a slice of bologna and ate it standing up. When he'd finished, he wandered outside to the barn where the animals were impatiently waiting for him.

"Hold on," he told Princess, as he grabbed the milking stool. He could sell the milk now that there was only him to feed. The eggs, too. He wouldn't eat more than half a dozen in a week. As it was, he'd fed the extra eggs and milk to the pigs rather than take it into town. He grimaced; the pigs had been eating luxuriously because he didn't want to face his friends with the truth.

Some people were probably aware of his split with Joanie. The schoolteacher over in Bellmont might've heard—or guessed. He'd written a letter telling her that he and Joanie were withdrawing Sage and Stevie from school. He'd put it in the mail, hoping she wouldn't receive it until after the Christmas holidays.

The message light on the machine was blinking when he came back into the house. It was Sage, wishing him a merry Christmas and asking him to phone her and Stevie at Grandpa Bouchard's house.

Brandon hesitated, but not for long. He missed his children and damn it to hell, he missed Joanie, too. But leaving had been her choice. It wasn't what *he'd* wanted.

The phone rang three times. Just his luck, Joanie was the one who answered.

"It's Brandon," he said, doing his level best not to convey what he was feeling.

"I...know."

"Sage phoned." She probably knew that, as well.

"I told her you were probably out with Princess."

His hand squeezed the telephone receiver hard. "I was."

An unnatural silence flowed between them.

"How are you?" Joanie asked after a minute.

"All right." He wouldn't lie and tell her he was jumping with joy to have her out of his life, but he wouldn't let her know how emotionally devastated he felt, either.

"Me, too."

"Are you in your dad's rental house?"

"Not yet." She didn't elaborate, and Brandon speculated that she hadn't moved in because she'd been waiting for him to rush after her and beg her to come home. It'd be a cold day in hell before he did that. A very cold day.

"What are you doing about furniture?" he asked, letting

her know she shouldn't expect him any time soon. She could take what she wanted from the farmhouse since he wasn't going to be needing it. Not all of it, anyway.

"I have a few things already. The kids and I don't need much."

"Fine."

"Do you want to see an attorney, or should I?" she asked, her voice so low he had trouble hearing her.

"We'll both have to sooner or later." She was going to go ahead with the divorce.

"I was thinking—if you don't mind—that we could wait a while."

He wasn't sure what had prompted this suggestion and guessed she might be having second thoughts. "How long?"

"Until June—maybe July—when the kids are out of school."

He tried to make it seem as if he didn't care one way or the other. "Whatever."

"Stevie wants to talk to you. Merry Christmas, Brandon." Her voice cracked, and she sounded close to tears. He resisted the urge to call her back, tell her how miserable he was, plead with her to give their marriage another chance. Even before the thought had finished going through his mind, his son was on the line.

"Hello, Daddy."

"How's the Stevie-boy?"

"Okay. Grandpa and I built a birdhouse, and he said we could make a toolbox next."

Joanie's father had always been good with the children. In some ways, better than Brandon himself. He didn't have the patience Leon did.

"Did you know we're moving into the house across the street from Grandma and Grandpa?"

"That's what your mother told me." His in-laws owned a number of rental properties, and Brandon hadn't been sure where Joanie would be living. At least she'd be near her parents. She was going to need their support for a while.

"Sage wants to talk now."

"Merry Christmas, Stevie."

"Merry Christmas, Daddy."

Brandon's throat thickened, and he had difficulty talking when his daughter got on the phone. "Hi, honey."

"Hi, Daddy." Sage sounded sad, her voice lifeless.

"How's my little girl?" Brandon asked, forcing himself to act cheerful. "Are you having a good Christmas?"

"It's okay. Do you miss us?"

"Of course I do."

"Do you miss Mommy, too?"

"Yes, sweetheart, I do." He couldn't lie, not to Sage, who seemed to know his heart.

"Mommy misses you, too. She cries a lot."

"You give her a big hug when you see her crying, all right?"

Sage whimpered softly. "I don't want you and Mommy to get a divorce. You told me you wouldn't. You said you loved Mommy, remember?"

Brandon couldn't bear the pain he heard in his daughter's voice. "I do love your mother and I love you."

"Then why are you getting a divorce?"

He wanted to tell her that question was one she should ask her mother, but resisted being petty. "Sometimes even people who love each other can't live together."

"That's what Mommy said, but I don't understand it." Sage was sobbing openly now.

Her misery was killing him. "Let me talk to your mother," he told her. He leaned his shoulder against the wall and rubbed his eyes, trying to figure out what had gone wrong with his marriage.

A moment later, Joanie was back on the line. "Sage seems to be having problems dealing with the separation," he said, his eyes tightly shut.

"Yes…I think she's afraid she'll never see you again."

"Are you planning to keep my children away from me, too?" he snarled, lashing out at her for leaving him, for destroying their family. "Don't even try it, Joanie."

She didn't answer for a long time, her breathing soft and shaky. "Maybe it would be a good idea if we did see an attorney right away," she suggested.

"Do whatever the hell you want," he shouted, and slammed down the receiver. "Merry Christmas, Joanie," he said in a low, bitter voice. "And a happy new year."

Fourteen

Christmas Day turned out to be a disaster for Lindsay. She didn't want to argue with Gage and she knew he hadn't wanted that, either, and yet they'd let it happen. Despite their best efforts, they fought over the issue of Kevin's attending art school. Each had strong feelings about what was right, and before they could stop themselves, they were embroiled in an argument that threatened to destroy their relationship.

"What's my brother going to do with an art degree?" Gage challenged her after she'd excitedly told Kevin the news. She'd waited until after dinner, when they'd all gathered in the living room for coffee and dessert.

"There are any number of ways Kevin might use his talent," Lindsay said, angered that Gage wouldn't drop the subject. Kevin sat silently across from them. "A scholarship to art school—it's a gift. You don't refuse a gift."

Hassie came into the room, carrying the coffeepot. Leta followed with a tray holding the sugar bowl and a pitcher of cream.

"Do we have to discuss this now?" Hassie asked, glancing from one to the other.

"Not at all," Lindsay said, eager to move on to a different topic.

"My brother owns this land. This is his inheritance, his *heritage,* and he isn't going to turn his back on it."

"But he loves art." Lindsay knew that Kevin had talent; the boy was passionate about art and she refused to discount his talent or his desire.

"I didn't say he couldn't draw if that's what he wants," Gage snapped. "But as far as I'm concerned, art school is a waste of time and effort. He should be taking business and agricultural classes, not art. We can find the money for agricultural college because that's an investment in his future. Art school isn't." Gage set his coffee aside and strolled over to the window, gazing out at acre after acre of snow-covered fields, his hands deep in his pants pockets. "We just can't afford it," he said with finality.

"But if Kevin gets a scholarship, money won't be an issue," she said.

"There are other issues besides money. There's Kevin's responsibility to his family, to this farm, to—"

"But what about his responsibility to his talent?" Lindsay asked.

Gage turned to glare at her. "You aren't from North Dakota. You don't know."

"I know plenty," Lindsay had thrown back at him, resenting his words. She struggled not to say more, not to escalate their disagreement. Despite what Gage said, she *was* part of the Buffalo Valley community. Her family's roots went as deep into the soil of this land as his. She felt offended that any time she disagreed with him, Gage would bring up the fact that she'd come from Savannah. She *wasn't* a stranger. She lived and worked in Buffalo Valley, same as he did. She might not be Dakota-born, but that didn't make her understand hardships and trouble any the less.

"Children, please," Leta said, sitting down with her coffee. "We can decide all these things later. Not today. It's Christmas."

For a moment, she thought Gage would be willing to let it go, but then he looked at his brother. "Kevin, this is your life. What do you want?"

Poor Kevin stared at them, his face stricken.

"You can't put him on the spot like this," Lindsay cried. "It isn't fair!"

"He needs to decide," Gage said coldly. "Once you understand that my brother knows his duty, maybe you'll stop filling his head with this nonsense."

"Nonsense?"

"Okay, okay," Gage said, and held up one palm. "Maybe that wasn't the right word, but you need to face reality here." He glanced at his brother. "Tell her, Kevin."

The boy gazed straight ahead, his eyes unwavering. "This land is my inheritance. I'll be a farmer, just like Gage said."

Gage's expression was so smug, Lindsay stood up and walked into the kitchen before she could say something that would make matters even worse. Other than their polite farewells later in the day, Gage and Lindsay didn't speak again.

The Saturday following Christmas, Lindsay talked to Maddy for a full hour by phone. She'd been worried about her best friend, who was rarely home before eight or nine at night. So much of herself, her very heart, went into her work with Social Services and the volunteer projects that were so important to her. Lindsay could see the trouble as clearly as Maddy had seen *her* problems with Monte.

Maddy cared, perhaps too much. She genuinely wanted to help. The families she worked with were so needy and desperate that when someone as giving and generous as Maddy stepped into their lives, they drained her. She told Lindsay about a case she'd been working on recently, involving a mother with three daughters. The situation was one of abuse, both emotional and physical, and Maddy was under tremendous stress trying to decide if the girls should be taken out of the family home and placed in foster care. Her fear was that once the girls, especially the oldest girl, were away from their mother, they'd run away and end up on the streets. Maddy was getting no cooperation from the mother and very little from the daughters.

Lindsay listened and asked questions and sympathized until her friend changed the subject—to Gage and the disastrous Christmas dinner.

"So you and Gage had another argument," Maddy said, sounding amused.

Lindsay didn't want to talk about herself, but Maddy so rarely shared her own troubles that she felt obliged. "It seems all we do is fight," she murmured.

"Which, in my opinion, is a lot healthier than the relationship you had with Monte."

Lindsay didn't quite see it that way. "If you say so."

"Speaking of good ol' Monte, what was in that large package he mailed you for Christmas? I ran into him at the post office, you know."

"A cashmere sweater." It'd probably cost a hundred times more than the crystal apple-shaped paperweight Gage had given her, along with a small letter opener that had belonged to his grandfather. She would treasure both, and stuff Monte's sweater in the back of her closet.

"Did you send Monte a gift?"

"Just a Christmas card." There'd been no letter in the package, no insulting note or blackmail or accusations. It appeared Monte was finally getting the message. Her leaving Savannah wasn't a ploy, a game or a trick to persuade him to marry her. It was real—her real life.

"You'll patch things up with Gage."

Lindsay hoped that was true, for Kevin's sake, and for her own.

She and Maddy always exchanged books for Christmas, and they spent some time discussing the titles they'd chosen. Maddy had sent her a history of American theater; she'd sent Maddy a photographic guide to the Dakotas. Once they'd finished their conversation and hung up, the afternoon dragged for Lindsay. She was ready for school to start, ready to end the holidays—and ready to end this squabble with Gage. One of them had to make the first gesture toward reconciliation.

When the doorbell chimed late in the afternoon, Lindsay immediately thought of Gage. If he ventured into town, it was almost always on a Saturday. Mutt and Jeff raced her to the door, barking furiously.

Leta Betts stood at the door, bundled up against the winter cold, a wicker basket over one arm.

"Leta," she said, genuinely glad to see Gage's mother. "Come in, please."

The older woman stomped the snow off her boots and loosened her scarf before she entered the house.

"I was just putting on a pot of tea. Would you like some?" Lindsay asked.

"I would love a cup," Leta told her and after pulling off her boots and coat, followed Lindsay into the kitchen. She set the basket on the countertop. "I brought you a dozen eggs."

"Leta, how thoughtful."

"I have a lot to thank you for, Lindsay," she said in a solemn tone. "Including what you've done for Kevin." She paused. "It was brave of you to confront Gage like that."

"I should have waited. Christmas Day wasn't the best time for us to…exchange our views." She wouldn't drag Kevin's mother into the controversy, but wished she knew her thoughts.

Carrying the pot of tea and two cups to the table, she sat across from Leta.

"I'm afraid my son can be too stubborn at times. Gage takes his family responsibilities very seriously. He wants what's best for Kevin. He's tried to prepare his brother for life as a farmer. Kevin's always been slated to take over the farm—and it's what Gage has been waiting for all these years."

"Taking over the farm? You mean Gage is leaving Buffalo Valley?"

Leta stared down at the steaming cup of tea. "He'll stay nearby, I imagine, since he'll need to work closely with Kevin over the next few years. But there's a section of good farmland for sale south of here, not far from Devils Lake. Gage has had his eye on it for some time now. He's never said anything, but I know he'd dearly love to buy it."

Lindsay cradled the teacup, the heat seeping into her palms. He hadn't even left Buffalo Valley, and already she felt a sense of loss. She realized that so much of what she felt for the town was connected to her feelings for Gage. Although they often disagreed, that only seemed to heighten their attraction.

"It was always understood that when the time came, Kevin would assume the farming operation and Gage would move on. He's been counting on it for a number of years."

"But isn't that rather selfish?" She didn't mean to insult Gage, but was genuinely curious. Sometimes she simply didn't understand what made people think or act the way they did. Over the past few months, she'd faced attitudes that seemed completely illogical to her. Why should Kevin be a farmer if that wasn't what he wanted? Why wouldn't Sarah marry Dennis when it was obvious to everyone that they were in love? And why did people in this town treat her like an outsider?

"Selfish? Gage?" Leta repeated. "The last word I'd use to describe Gage is *selfish*. I don't know what I would've done without him during the last twelve years. He always intended to farm his own land. Then John died, and our property was mortgaged to the hilt. Gage ran the farm after that, and he's worked it to support us all. When Kevin takes over, he'll be getting land that's nearly free of debt, thanks to Gage.

"It's long past time Gage had his own life. I don't fault him for that, and you shouldn't, either." Her hands nervously pushed wisps of hair from her face. "Kevin has a lot of years to pursue his dream, while Gage has put his entire life on hold waiting for his brother to take responsibility for the farm. It might sound a bit ridiculous to put it in these terms—but it's Gage's turn. Kevin knows this and accepts his duty the same way Gage did twelve years ago."

Lindsay had her answer. "In other words, it would help if I stopped encouraging Kevin to think about art school."

Leta averted her gaze. Her fingers smoothed the fringed edge of the placemat. "Plain speaking? Yes, it would help. I love my sons and I want what's best for both of them. In a situation like this, I feel I need the wisdom of Solomon."

Lindsay felt an oppressive sense of disappointment. She'd seen for herself the look in Kevin's eyes when she'd mentioned the art schools and the possibility of a scholarship. Talent shouldn't be a source of pain to one so young.

But she also understood what Leta had told her. Gage had sacrificed years of his life in order to support Kevin and his mother. He'd carried that burden long enough.

"I hope you don't mind me stopping by like this," Leta said anxiously as she sipped her tea. "But I thought you should know."

"Yes," Lindsay whispered. "I should."

"One last thing," the older woman said. "Be patient with Gage. He can be thickheaded at times, but his heart is big."

Earlier, Lindsay had decided that one of them would need to make an overture toward reconciliation. This relationship was important to her. Gage was important to her. He was a complex man and she was only beginning to know him. So that probably meant the first move was up to her....

Leta and Lindsay talked a few minutes longer about various people's plan for New Year's Eve. Almost everyone—including Gage—seemed to be going to Buffalo Bob's. Tony Lammermann, Joe and Mark's dad, played the fiddle, and Bob had coaxed him into playing for a dance that night. Leta and Hassie were getting together for dinner, but probably wouldn't stay up until midnight. She invited Lindsay to join them if she had no other plans.

When they'd finished their tea, Lindsay, with the able assistance of Mutt and Jeff, escorted Leta to the door. Standing at the window, she watched her friend walk toward Hansen's Grocery. Her head full of their conversation, she turned her attention to housekeeping. She started by taking down and packing away the Christmas decorations. She didn't have many; her apartment back home had been too small. Not only that, she'd had to be judicious when she moved and had left a lot behind. What she did have was precious to her.

After carefully wrapping the decorations, she stored them in cardboard boxes, which she carried to the back bedroom, the room her grandmother had once used for sewing. The closet was narrow, and when she lifted the box to set it on the shelf above the rail, the corner ripped out a section of wallpaper.

"Damn," she muttered as she pushed the box into place.

Turning on the light, she investigated the tear, disgusted with herself for being careless. But when she looked more closely, Lindsay realized that the space behind the wallpaper was empty. Someone had purposely papered over a hole in the wall. She suddenly went still. Someone had covered a space where the plaster had been cut away—perhaps to hide something. She hurried to find her flashlight.

When she returned she was breathing hard. Hands shaking, she shone the light into the dark space—and illuminated a cigar box. Even before she reached for it, Lindsay knew that this box was what her grandmother had placed inside the fireplace brick all those years ago.

Since taking over the ownership of the 3 OF A KIND, Buffalo Bob had learned one important lesson about tending bar. Folks wanted to be greeted by a smiling, friendly face. His customers came in for cold beer and warm conversation.

Some wanted a willing ear to listen to their troubles, their sorry lot in life, their cheating wives, the unfairness of it all. But under no circumstances did his customers want to hear his own litany of problems.

Until recently, Buffalo Bob's problems were few. He was financially sound, thanks to the Christmas play. For three nights in a row, he'd had lots of customers. The good business had continued throughout the Christmas season; in fact, he'd kept his decorations up, although they were looking a little limp now. Bob was definitely satisfied with life. Even during these hard times he'd showed his biggest profit to date. This year he'd actually be in the black, if he conveniently forgot to pay himself wages.

His concerns had nothing to do with money and everything to do with Merrily. She'd been away a long time now, and Buffalo Bob was beginning to believe she wouldn't be back.

A week before Christmas, he'd gotten a card from her. She hadn't told him where she was, but the smudged postmark said California. The sun shone in California even in the dead of winter. If Merrily was sunning herself on some beach, it wasn't likely she'd be in any hurry to get back to him in North Dakota.

Dammit all, he missed her.

"What're you looking so down in the mouth about?" Dennis Urlacher asked, stepping into the bar.

"Not much," Buffalo Bob told him. He'd been restocking the bar, his thoughts distracted. He knew without asking what Dennis usually ordered and placed a cold bottle of beer on the counter.

"Want to see a menu?" Bob was hoping to increase his food sales and had made up a special appetizer menu that catered to his bar customers.

"No, thanks." Dennis took a swig of beer.

"So, how was your Christmas?" Buffalo Bob asked. His own had been miserable without Merrily, even though he'd never given a rat's ass about the holiday before.

"It was all right," Dennis answered without much enthusiasm.

"You spent it with Joshua McKenna and his family?"

"I did."

"You have people in the area, don't you?"

"My parents," Dennis said, taking another swig of beer. "They weren't pleased that I stayed in town."

"Frankly, you don't look that happy about it yourself." Buffalo Bob was getting fairly good at identifying a customer's mood.

"I got a problem with a teenager."

Buffalo Bob retreated a step and raised both hands. "Hey, man, I thought you were smarter than that. Teenage girls are jailbait."

"It's not what you're suggesting," Dennis snapped

"Whew." Buffalo Bob was genuinely relieved. "Thought you had a thing going with Sarah?"

"I do."

"Sarah's got a teenage daughter, doesn't she?" Buffalo Bob asked, thinking out loud. Yeah, that had to be it. Sarah's kid was the problem.

"Calla isn't exactly fond of me," Dennis muttered. "And that's putting it mildly."

He didn't need to say more. Bob got the picture. If it weren't for Calla, Dennis and Sarah would probably be married by now.

"Maybe you ought to spend some time with the kid," Buffalo Bob said, trying to be helpful. "Try to make friends with her."

Dennis laughed. "And risk getting my head bit off? She doesn't want me hanging around, doesn't want anything to do with me. One postcard from her good-for-nothing father and she's convinced her parents are about to remarry. That's what she wants."

"Which naturally paints you as the bad guy."

Dennis answered with a nod, then stared off into space. "The thing is, I want to marry Sarah, want us to have kids ourselves."

It went without saying that as long as the teenage daughter put up a fuss, it wasn't going to happen. Buffalo Bob didn't envy Dennis, but then he had woman problems of his own.

Dennis left soon afterward, and Brandon Wyatt walked into the bar. He looked like hell.

"A beer, right?" He pointed both index fingers in the farmer's direction.

Brandon nodded, and Bob set a cold, frosty bottle on the counter. If and when Brandon wanted to talk, Buffalo Bob would be ready with a willing ear. From the way the farmer slouched on that stool, huddled over his beer, Bob could tell he was hurting.

"Have a nice Christmas?" he asked casually.

Brandon glanced up, irritation on his face. "Just great."

Okay, so Brandon wasn't in a talking mood; Bob could deal with that. He made himself scarce, disappearing into the back room to unload cases of beer. A few minutes later, he heard another customer enter.

Poking his head around the corner, he saw it was Gage Sinclair. "Be with you in a minute," he called out. Gage, he knew, was sweet on the new schoolteacher. Buffalo Bob had seen the chalk on the blackboard soon after Lindsay Snyder arrived in town. Oh, yeah, Gage was interested. They'd gotten off to a slow start but seemed to be making up for lost time.

When he'd finished in the storeroom, Buffalo Bob headed out front. "You want a beer?" he asked.

"Sure. I'll have a draft."

Bob paused, wondering if he was seeing things. Gage Sinclair had that same down-in-the-mouth expression as Dennis Urlacher and Brandon Wyatt. What the hell was happening?

Gage slouched on a stool, a space down from his neighbor. They were ignoring each other—and Bob wasn't about to wade into conversation with either one of them. His best bet was to shut up.

He set a glass of beer on the counter and Gage nodded his thanks. Turning away, Buffalo Bob was about to pour them each a small bowl of peanuts when Brandon finally spoke.

"Joanie left."

Bob hesitated, uncertain whether the comment was meant for him or Gage. "Left?" he asked.

"Moved out, lock, stock and barrel."

"Joanie?" Gage repeated, sounding incredulous.

Buffalo Bob was equally shocked. He didn't know Brandon's wife well, but he liked her. The day she'd sung with the karaoke machine had been one of the most enjoyable afternoons he'd had in a long time. Soon afterward, she'd come into the bar and asked him to recommend a bottle of wine for their anniversary dinner. That didn't sound like someone who was planning to divorce her husband.

Buffalo Bob didn't often have people asking his advice on matters such as this, and it'd made him feel good. Joanie had a contagious laugh and a bright spirit. Merrily had said she'd like to know her better, but then neither she nor Bob had seen Joanie again, other than to pass her on the sidewalk.

"What about the kids?" Gage asked before Buffalo Bob had a chance.

"They went with her." Brandon stared straight ahead, looking at the wall as if there was something really important written there instead of a neon sign advertising the brand of beer he drank.

"I'm sorry to hear that," Gage said.

"Yeah."

His wife had left him and taken his family with her, and

all Brandon Wyatt had to say was "Yeah"? Buffalo Bob didn't get it. "She's coming back, isn't she?" he asked urgently.

Frowning, Brandon took a swallow of beer. "I doubt it."

One glance told Bob it hadn't been easy for Brandon to deal with this. "I'm real sorry."

"It's my own damn fault," Brandon said, showing emotion for the first time. His voice vibrated with anger. "I should've known better than to get involved with a city girl."

Gage didn't say anything, but Buffalo Bob could see that Brandon's words had affected him. If ever Buffalo Bob had seen a city girl, it was Lindsay Snyder. It'd be a pity if Gage called a halt to the relationship for such a flimsy reason. Well, Bob considered it flimsy. People could adapt to all kinds of circumstances; he knew that as well as anyone.

"What do you mean by city girl?" Buffalo Bob asked, figuring that whatever Brandon said would tell Gage that Lindsay was different. She hadn't complained once, not that he knew of, at any rate. The lack of shopping malls or fancy restaurants didn't seem to bother her. Nor had he witnessed any evidence of big-city attitude. Without her, Buffalo Valley would have been a ghost town inside of five years, and they all knew it.

"Joanie was born and raised in Fargo."

"Fargo isn't exactly the big city," Buffalo Bob commented.

"How long has it been since *you* were in Fargo?" Brandon asked, his voice hard. "She never knew what it meant to be a farmer's wife, never had a farmer's mentality. It's not her fault," he added, "she just didn't know."

"That's why she left?" Gage asked.

"She left because I wouldn't sell the farm."

Neither man spoke much after that. No more talk was needed. Gage and Brandon both understood that the life-blood of the family was in the land. Without it, they lost their purpose, their identity. It wasn't that Brandon *wouldn't* sell the land that had been in his family for three generations. He couldn't. Without the farm, he wouldn't know who or what he was.

By the time Buffalo Bob closed down for the night, he was tired and worn-out. People had been in and out of the 3 OF A KIND all evening, and they all had their troubles. His own seemed twice as heavy after he'd listened to those of his friends. Hell of a way to start the new year. Didn't bode too well for his party, either.

After locking the place, he crawled into bed, but tired though he was, he couldn't sleep. That was when he heard the first sound, coming from downstairs. Someone had broken in and was creeping around. He lay there quietly, listening, hoping it was merely the building creaking and groaning as it settled. A few minutes later, he knew for sure that he had an intruder. As quietly as possible, he pulled on his pants and reached for the baseball bat he kept in the corner of his room for just such an eventuality.

From the direction of the sounds, it seemed that whoever was there had gone into his office. That was where he kept the cash. He hurried down the stairs in bare feet. Then, staying in the shadows, he edged his way toward the office and peeked inside. The moonlight showed him a flash of dark hair.

With a growl, he stepped into the room and threw on the light switch.

A woman's startled cry followed.

Buffalo Bob took one look and dropped the baseball bat. "Merrily!" Not another second passed before she was in his arms.

"You scared the living daylights out of me," she cried, looping her thin arms around his neck. His sense of excitement and happiness was so great, he lifted her right off the ground.

"I didn't want to wake you," she whispered.

She'd still had a key to the front door and had let herself in. She'd gone into his office, searching for the key to her old room. Buffalo Bob didn't care if she *had* been after his cash box. He would've cheerfully given her every cent.

"Glad to see me, are you?" she asked, her expression changing as she smiled down on him. She bent her head and gave him a kiss so potent it nearly buckled his knees. He knew without a doubt that she'd missed him as much as he'd missed her.

"You back for good this time?" he asked, when he had the breath to form the question.

Her smile was the most beautiful thing he'd seen in months. "Probably not," she told him, "but I promise you'll be glad I'm here for however long I stay."

Buffalo Bob groaned, then carried her straight into his bedroom. From now on, she'd be sleeping there with him. That was where she belonged.

Gage was over at Brandon Wyatt's farm when Lindsay phoned the first Friday of the New Year. His mother handed him the message when he walked in the door. He stared at it a long time, not knowing what to think. Brandon's warning about getting involved with a city girl had struck a nerve with him. As attracted as he was to Lindsay—and much as he admired what she'd done for the town—he knew she didn't really understand their ways. But all the warnings in the world couldn't keep him from thinking about her and what her kisses did to him. They'd reached the point where kissing was no longer enough. More and more he thought about what it would be like to make love to Lindsay, to hold her in his arms, sleep with her beside him. To love her the way a man was meant to love a woman.

"Are you going to call her back?" Leta asked when he didn't instantly head toward the phone.

In the past week, Gage had thought about calling her. Would have, if he hadn't run into Brandon Wyatt at Bob's that day, just before New Year's. His neighbor was in a world of pain and Gage realized that if he did seek out Lindsay, he'd be courting the same kind of troubles. Gage had tried to talk Brandon into attending the party at Buffalo Bob's with him, but in the end had gone by himself and left early. Lindsay, it turned out, had dinner with Leta and Hassie. No "Auld Lang Syne" or midnight kisses for Lindsay, then—or for him. Or Brandon, either…

Today, Gage had stopped by the Wyatt farm and been shocked at the condition of the house. Dishes were piled high in the sink, the kitchen countertops were littered with discarded mail and old newspapers. Piles of dirty clothes were heaped on the washer and dryer. Worst of all, Brandon was in a perpetually depressed state. He was managing his farm chores—which were fewer in winter, anyway—but other than that he seemed to be barely functioning.

Gage's visit had done little to assuage his fears about getting involved with Lindsay.

"Did she say what she wanted?" he asked his mother.

That simple question took an inordinate amount of time to answer. "Wouldn't you like to find out for yourself?"

Although he hadn't said anything about Brandon and Joanie's problems, his mother seemed aware of the doubts Gage was experiencing. Without another word, he grabbed his hat again and headed back out the door. Driving into town to see Lindsay was either the smartest move he'd ever made, or the dumbest.

Gage thought about what he'd say when she looked at him with her big blue eyes. He hoped to remain calm and dispassionate. Let her do the talking. But he knew that was too much to expect. He'd missed her, missed their conversations, their kisses.

It was snowing when he arrived on her doorstep. He stood under the porch light, rang the doorbell and waited for the inevitable barking. Lindsay answered almost immediately, dogs at her side, as if she'd been anticipating his arrival. He wouldn't put it past his mother to have called ahead and informed her that he was on his way.

"Gage, come in." Her eyes told him how pleased she was to see him and he suspected his own expression mirrored hers. She looked good to him, so good...

"I'm glad you're here," she said simply.

"I am, too." He wasn't so proud he couldn't admit the truth. Lindsay took a step toward him and at the same moment he moved toward her. It seemed an eternity since he'd last held her, and their kiss was explosive. It always seemed to be like that, this powerful need that erupted every time they touched. If the kissing was this spectacular, he could only imagine how their lovemaking would be. After two or three kisses, Gage had to force himself to stop. It wasn't easy. He brushed his thumb over her moist lips while he struggled to end it there. They had to talk; he sensed that this would be either the beginning or the end for them.

"I debated a long time before calling you," she said as she led him to the sofa.

He sat down and refused her offer of something warm to drink.

She left the room and returned with what looked like a wooden cigar box. "I found it, Gage—what my grandmother hid inside the fireplace."

She went on to tell him about finding a hole in the closet wall. Carefully, as if it were of great value, she lifted the lid and removed a gold locket. "It's a picture of your grandfather and my grandmother when they were teenagers," she said breathlessly. She handed it to him.

Gage laid the locket on his palm and studied it. The oval was plain, unadorned, and had a small clasp on the right side. He opened it. As she'd said, there were two small black-and-white photographs of a man and a woman. He'd never seen a picture of his grandfather at this age, but he knew in an instant that this was Jerome Sinclair. The eyes were honest, without guile, the jaw square and stubborn. Gage had inherited both.

The woman's picture showed a blond woman with a delicate, clear-eyed beauty. Gage saw how much Lindsay resembled her grandmother and knew in his heart that his grandfather had indeed loved Regina Snyder.

"I never knew she was so beautiful," Lindsay said when he lifted his eyes to meet hers.

Gage smiled; she didn't see the resemblance, but he did. "So you found it," he said, knowing how gratified she must be.

"There's more," she said. Opening the box again, she retrieved a small envelope yellow with age. "Read this and tell me what you think."

Gage carefully took the letter from her, the paper brittle, the ink faded. Careful not to tear the sheet, he unfolded it and read.

January 10, 1943
My dearest Gina,
I only have a few minutes, and pray this letter will reach you. Your last letter took three weeks to find

me and I know how worried you must be. I love you,
Gina. Please don't worry. We'll be married as soon
as I can arrange it. Everything will work out.

Yours always,
Jerome

"So…what do you think?" Lindsay asked, her eyes
pleading with him.

"They were in love." He'd known that earlier, after
talking to Lily Quantrill. He didn't need a letter written
nearly sixty years ago to tell him that their grandparents
had shared a deep and abiding affection.

"You don't see it?" She seemed to beseech him to
notice the same things she did or to interpret them in the
same way.

"What am I supposed to see?"

"Gage," she began, her voice trembling with emotion.
"Obviously, I can't read what my grandmother wrote
Jerome—the letter he said took three weeks to reach him—
but from his response can't you tell how desperate she was?
Can't you guess why?"

He frowned, unwilling to speculate. "What do *you*
think it said?"

"My grandmother was pregnant."

"I don't believe that!"

"Read between the lines."

"You have no proof and even if you did, what difference does it make?"

"What *difference* does it make?" she cried, as though she
couldn't understand why he'd ask anything so outlandish.

Gage was sorry he'd come. He didn't want to know
this, didn't want to pry into his grandfather's life. "You
have no proof of it," he said again. "Lindsay, listen, some-

times it's better to leave things alone. Whatever happened was a long time ago."

"You're wrong. I do have proof," she whispered, and reached inside the cigar box again. "This is a letter from an adoption agency telling my grandmother about the placement of the child she relinquished."

Fifteen

Lindsay could tell from the stricken look on his face that her discovery had come as a shock to Gage. It had shocked her, too. Frowning, he sat and stared at the letter from the adoption agency for several minutes.

Lindsay had read the letters enclosed within the cigar box so many times she'd practically memorized them. The one from the agency was straightforward, written over fifty years earlier by an empathetic supervisor to a grieving young woman.

> September 30, 1944
> Dear Regina,
> I have your letters here before me. I appreciate your concern and love for your daughter. As you know, it isn't our practice to let mothers who've relinquished their children know the details of the child's adoption. However, I'm willing to make an exception in your case, with the clear understanding that this is all the information I can and will give you. You must not ask again.

Your daughter was adopted by a good family; of that you can rest assured. Her parents are educated and respected, her father a noted physician. As you requested, she will be raised Catholic and, in fact, has an uncle who is a priest. She has already been baptized.

I realize that giving up your daughter was a difficult decision, but as we have discussed on many occasions, it was in the best interests of both the child and, I believe, you. You have your whole life ahead of you. Bury the memory of your daughter and the lost soldier you loved deep within your heart. Hold them there through the years. But begin your new life with a sense of hope and a willingness to love again. Be strong. God bless you.

Sincerely,

Mrs. Merline Hopfinger, Supervisor

Dickinson Adoption Agency

"She never told anyone about the baby." Lindsay was fairly confident of this. Certainly, Lily Quantrill didn't know; neither did Hassie. Granted, she wasn't part of the Buffalo Valley community until after the war, but she and Gina had become friends. If Gina was going to tell anyone, it would probably have been Hassie. No, Lindsay was sure that Gina hadn't divulged her secret, even to her closest friends.

Gage disagreed with a shake of his head. "You have no way of knowing that."

"You're right, but I don't think she ever did." Lindsay was convinced her grandmother's silence had little to do with guilt or the shame of being an unwed mother. She was protecting the memory of Jerome Sinclair, the man she'd believed dead. And she was doing as Mrs. Hopfinger had suggested and holding tight to the memory of the daughter whose heartbeat she'd once shared.

"Do you remember what Lily Quantrill said?" Gage asked, as if the thought had suddenly come to him. "She mentioned that your grandmother was sick for a time after she got the news that my grandfather was missing in action."

"I remember."

Gage's look was pensive. "I wonder if that was when she went away to have the baby."

Lindsay knew it must have been. Her grandmother had probably hidden the pregnancy as long as she could. When it was no longer possible, she'd left Buffalo Valley, her heart broken, her very will to live taken from her.

"The baby was born sometime in August," Lindsay said with certainty.

Gage handed back the agency letter. "What makes you say that? The letter doesn't give any indication of the child's birthday."

"I know." In the dead of night, Lindsay had found her grandmother weeping for the child she would never hold, grieving for the child she would never know. That had been in August and Lindsay now believed she'd seen her grandmother reliving the birth of the child she'd given up for adoption, mourning her all over again….

"How do you know?" Gage demanded.

"Camp was the last week of July—I went for years. So my family was here in Buffalo Valley in August. It was definitely August."

Gage glanced at the cigar box. "This is pretty incredible information, but I don't intend on breaking their secret, do you?"

Lindsay had only recently made her decision. Unsure at first, she'd reviewed the contents of the box a dozen times. Then she'd called Gage. Now she knew what she needed to do.

"I want to find her."

"Her? The child?" Gage shook his head, resolutely dismissing the suggestion.

"Yes," she said calmly. "Whoever she is, she has a right to know about her birth parents."

His mouth thinned and he continued shaking his head. "Lindsay, no."

"No?"

"First of all, adoption records are closed."

"I don't need any records. The letter gives me enough information to find her. At least I hope it does." It probably wouldn't be easy, but it could be done. She'd hoped Gage would be willing to help her, would find the importance of this task as compelling as she did.

He was silent, then stood and walked to the other side of the room, as though to put distance between them. His absolute rejection of her plan disappointed Lindsay more than she'd expected it would.

"I'm not going to pry into her life," she rushed to explain, responding to his objections before he had a chance to speak then.

"No, you plan to force your way in, uninvited and unwanted. And for what possible reason? What's done is done. All this happened nearly sixty years ago. What possible good could come out of invading her privacy?"

"She has a right to know her parents loved her," Lindsay said as persuasively as she could.

"Don't do this," he pleaded softly.

"What about the gold locket and the letters? If you were an adopted child, wouldn't you want those?"

"No, I wouldn't." The words were flat. Unyielding.

His jaw was hard and his eyes cold in a way she hadn't seen before. Shaking his head, he added, "Brandon said it last week—and again today. I took his warning with a grain of salt, knowing he's bitter and miserable over Joanie and the kids being gone."

Now it was Lindsay's turn to feel confused. "What's Brandon Wyatt got to do with any of this?"

"You don't understand us…."

"*Us?* What the hell is that supposed to mean?" She hated it when he said things like this.

He held her look. "You aren't one of us."

"Are you saying I'm an outsider?" she asked angrily.

"You mean well, Lindsay, but you don't understand. People here believe that other folks should be allowed to make their own choices and live by them. We're independent. Self-reliant. We don't interfere in other people's lives—or want ours interfered with. That's what you don't understand." He walked toward the door, pausing to reach for his coat. "Don't do this, Lindsay. Leave the woman alone. She didn't ask for anyone to intrude in her life. She has a right to her privacy."

"I'm not going to invade her life—I'm giving her a gift."

He glared at her. "Gift." He spat out the word. "You talk about a scholarship for Kevin and call that a gift, too. Don't you see? Can't you understand? You insist on giving people gifts they don't need or want."

Lindsay opened her mouth to argue, but he wouldn't let her.

"Your grandmother *chose* to keep her daughter a secret," he said earnestly. "If for no other reason, honor her wishes."

"I'll…think about it," she promised.

"That's all I can ask." He moved to open the door.

"Gage," she said, stopping him. She didn't want him to

leave, not like this, not when so much remained unspoken. "I think we should talk some more about Kevin and the scholarship."

His back was ramrod straight. She felt a sudden fear of losing him. She could feel it, see it. He was pulling away from her, emotionally as well as physically.

"I understand about duty and responsibility, and that Kevin's future is already planned for him—but I also believe strongly that he should apply for the scholarships. If he's rejected, then nothing's lost, and if he's accepted, well, we can all cross that bridge when we get to it. If he *is* accepted, he'll never doubt his talent. He'll know that if circumstances were different, he could have pursued art had he wanted. And still might if the future allows."

"You encouraged him to fill out the applications?"

She nodded.

"Kevin agreed?"

"He wasn't sure… Yes, he agreed after I talked to him." Heart sinking, she clasped her hands in front of her. Gage looked past her, but she didn't miss the expression on his face. He thought she'd betrayed him. That had never been her intention, never entered her mind. "I…felt you should know," she said, rubbing her palms together. "That's all…"

"You do what you feel is best, and so will I." He turned toward the door.

"Gage!" she cried, stopping him again. "If I were adopted, I'd want to know about my birth parents."

He said nothing.

"I wouldn't interfere in her life."

"Are you looking for my approval? Because if you are, I'm not giving it. Like I said, you do what you feel is necessary and so will I."

"But you won't help me find her?"

"I want nothing to do with this."

She took a step toward him. "I'm going to do some research this weekend. I figured if I found the name of a physician who practiced during that time—a man who was Catholic and had a brother or brother-in-law who was a priest—then I might be able to locate her. I was hoping we could work together."

"Perhaps you didn't hear me the first time. I said I want nothing to do with this. Can I make it any plainer than that?"

Lindsay felt numb. "No, I guess you can't," she managed, her voice barely a whisper.

Gage opened the door and this time she didn't stop him.

Heath Quantrill hadn't talked to Rachel Fischer since the night of their dinner date a month earlier. In retrospect, he realized he'd made a mistake in rushing her.

The women he knew, and there had been plenty over the years, had a more sophisticated and liberal view of life and sex. Often they were the ones who'd aggressively pursued him, eager to take him to their beds. Sometimes he forgot he was back in North Dakota, where the mere suggestion of physical pleasure made women like Rachel blush. She'd lived her entire life in Buffalo Valley, had married right out of high school and settled into a role she'd never questioned. It'd been years since he'd had to charm a woman into his bed—not that he wasn't up to the challenge.

Rachel's sexual experience was probably limited to her marriage. He was sure she had much to learn, and he looked forward to teaching her. He was vaguely aware that his attitude might be a bit arrogant, but it didn't concern him much. Women tended to like confidence in a man— judging by his observations, anyway.

He'd been a fool to believe she was like the other women

he'd known. Although it'd been difficult, he'd purposely stayed away and allowed enough time to pass for her wounded sensibilities to heal. Now, with Christmas over and the holidays behind them, he'd try again. He'd advance a little more slowly, though.

Her January payment on the pizza oven was due, and when she brought it to the bank, Heath planned to use the opportunity to make amends. Subtly, of course. He'd be contrite, but not excessively so. He knew what he wanted— and he wanted Rachel, in his bed. Rachel was a woman who needed to be seduced. Persuaded. Courted. If he hadn't been so distracted by her, he would have recognized it.

All day, every time the bank door opened, Heath looked up, hoping it was Rachel.

But the entire day passed and still no Rachel. Before this, she'd always been prompt with her payment. Then, just as the bank was ready to close, a breathless Mark raced inside.

"Hello, Mr. Quantrill." The ten-year-old's cheeks and nose were rosy red from the cold. His flyaway hair stood straight up with static electricity from his knit cap, which he'd yanked off when he entered the bank. "My mom asked me to give you this." He removed his glove with his teeth, then reached into his coat pocket and withdrew a crumpled check.

Instead of bringing the payment herself, Rachel had thwarted him and sent the boy.

"It's the money for the pizza oven," Mark explained when Heath didn't immediately accept the check.

The paper felt cold against his warm fingers. "Thank her for me," Heath said.

Mark nodded. "I gotta go, Mom needs me to help at the house." He pushed the knit hat back on his head and pulled on his glove. "See you next month, Mr. Quantrill."

"Right," he muttered. So that was the way it would be.

A few minutes later, Heath locked up, but instead of heading straight back to Grand Forks, he wandered over to Buffalo Bob's. He wanted to think and didn't know of a better place than the 3 OF A KIND.

"How're ya doin'?" Bob greeted him.

"Great," Heath mumbled, "just great."

Buffalo Bob paused and stared in Heath's direction. "Don't tell me *you* got women troubles, too."

Heath slid onto a stool. "What do you mean?"

"Seems to be afflicting every man in town." He held up a beer and Heath shook his head. Buffalo Bob reached for the coffeepot and poured him a mug, instead. Heath had found it to be the best coffee around. Bob served real coffee and not some watered-down version. Or, God forbid, that flavored stuff. After living in Europe, Heath had developed a connoisseur's taste for coffee. In his opinion, most folks in North Dakota served coffee weak enough to resemble tea.

"Take Brandon Wyatt," Buffalo Bob said as he set the mug down on the bar. "I suppose you already heard he and the missus split?"

"Brandon and Joanie?" Heath hadn't heard, and the news depressed him.

"Don't know what went wrong," Buffalo Bob added. "All Brandon said was he should've known better than to marry a city girl."

Heath shook his head and cupped the mug with both hands, his elbows on the bar. "That's a real shame."

"Dennis Urlacher was in recently, all miserable about him and Sarah. Apparently he's having trouble with that teenage daughter of hers. From what he said, it looks like the girl wants her parents to get back together."

"Any chance of that?"

Buffalo Bob shrugged. "I doubt it, seeing they've been divorced for years, but I wouldn't know." He poured a coffee for himself. "You got the look, too, Mr. Quantrill."

"Me?" Heath didn't want to discuss his personal affairs, not with Bob or with anyone. Others might, but he wasn't in the mood to talk about his mistakes. He'd drifted in here for some privacy, a chance to think. "It's nothing," he murmured.

"I thought you and Rachel Fischer were hitting it off."

"Not really." He took one last sip of coffee, put the mug down and left a dollar on the counter. "Guess I'm ready for the drive now."

Buffalo Bob seemed surprised by his abrupt decision to leave. "Good to see you," he said, scooping up the mug and the money. "Come by anytime."

"Thanks, I will." Heath was halfway out the door when he heard a woman's giggle. Glancing over his shoulder, he saw Buffalo Bob and Merrily engaged in a kiss that looked as if it was never going to end. For an instant, he experienced a pang of envy. If he hadn't been so stupid, Rachel might be kissing him like that right now. Instead, he was slinking out of town, defeated, and wishing like hell for a second chance.

Sunday afternoon, Heath made his weekly trek to visit his grandmother at the retirement center. He found her asleep in her wheelchair, head to one side, eyes closed.

As quietly as he could, he made his way into her suite and set the small bouquet of flowers on top of the television.

"Don't put those there," she snapped, fully awake and alert in a split second. She looked at him suspiciously. "When did you get here?"

"Hours ago," he fibbed.

He could tell she was amused by the hint of a smile that tilted one side of her mouth. "You're late."

"Thank you for the flowers, Heath," he said with humorous sarcasm as he handed her the bouquet. "My, what a thoughtful grandson I have."

"What are you doing bringing an old woman flowers, anyway? It's a waste of good money. You should be giving those to Rachel Fischer."

He must have made a revealing gesture, because she caught on right away that there was a problem between him and Rachel.

"You *are* seeing Rachel, aren't you?"

"Not recently," he said, taking a seat some distance from her. If she found out what he'd done, she might decide to beat him over the head with those flowers.

"Why not?"

His grandmother had always been one to get straight to the point. It was a characteristic they shared. "I didn't come here to discuss my personal life with you."

"Then what the hell good are you?"

"I beg your pardon?"

"How old are you now? Don't you think it's time you got married?"

"I will. All in good time." He leaned back and spread his arms across the back of the couch.

"In good time," she scoffed. "Who's to say how much time any of us has? Max always said he had lots of time, too, and now he's gone."

Heath tried not to think about his brother and how sorely Max was missed by both his grandmother and him.

"You've been frittering away your life for years. Climbing mountains, living like a Bohemian. I blame your parents for this. I told them that sparing the rod spoiled the child."

"Grandma," Heath said, struggling to curtail a laugh. "I received my share of the rod."

"Not near enough for someone as stubborn as you. I should've taken the paddle to you myself."

At that, he laughed outright. His grandmother was all bark, and he knew it.

She wheeled around to face him. "Tell me what happened with the widow."

He hesitated, then figured he deserved whatever criticism she gave him. "I tried to rush her into bed."

Lily Quantrill made a disapproving sound, but she didn't explode the way he'd figured she would. He could tell by her scowl that she considered him a fool, and frankly, Heath agreed with her.

"What's the outlook now?" she demanded.

"Not good, I'm afraid."

Her gaze narrowed. "You giving up on her?"

"No." He'd never been a quitter in his life and wasn't about to start now.

"You going to marry her?"

"Too soon to tell."

Lily snickered. "So, you wanted to bed her, did you?"

"Yes, but…" He hesitated, thinking better of enlightening his grandmother about the morals and values of modern days. She might take exception.

"But what?" she asked. "I like her, you like her. My grandparents met when her father went to a marriage broker. It was good enough for them. They were married sixty-eight years. Should I call Rachel, get this matter straightened out once and for all?"

Appalled, Heath was on his feet. "Don't you dare do that! I'll take care of it myself."

"Apologize to her."

He sighed. "If that's what it takes."

"And remember, wed before bed—it's worked that way

for hundreds of years. Must be a reason for it, don't you think?" Muttering under her breath, she wheeled over with the flowers and returned them to him. "Do something quick. I want to see you married before I leave this world, and I'm not as young as I look."

Joanie delayed phoning Brandon until afternoon. She couldn't put it off any longer, otherwise the kids would be rushing in the door from school. It was a task she dreaded, but she had no choice. There were a number of things they needed to discuss.

That morning, as soon as the children had left, she sat down and in an organized and methodical way wrote out a list of items to discuss with her husband. All day that list had accompanied her from room to room.

So far, every contact between them had left her shaken and emotionally drained. Brandon didn't make it easy on her, but despite that, she had to call. Now.

The baby stirred as she sat at the kitchen table and reached for the old-fashioned phone. Joanie placed her hand over her swollen abdomen, loving this child already. Poor, sweet baby. He had no idea what was happening to his family.

Earlier in the month, an ultrasound had revealed the likely sex of her unborn child. The health clinic had ordered the procedure when Joanie experienced some minor complications. Luckily, she'd qualified for free health care. Had he known, Brandon would have bristled at the thought of anyone in his family receiving charity. In the weeks since leaving him, she'd become accustomed to accepting the kindness of others. Her parents, in particular, had been wonderful, but she didn't want to depend on them any more than she already did.

Brandon had sent her a check for January and, last Wednesday, one for February, a week early. But it wasn't nearly enough to meet their living expenses, even with the nominal rent she paid. Her parents had urged her to tell her husband about the pregnancy, and twice now she'd tried, and both times had failed. When they did talk, it was by phone and he always sounded so angry and bitter, and despite her resolve to inform him about the baby, she found she just couldn't.

Joanie picked up the receiver. She missed her home and her friends, and being part of Buffalo Valley. But mostly she missed the life she'd once shared with her husband. For a while now, she'd been plagued with doubts. Alone in bed at night, she couldn't help wondering if she'd done the right thing.

Two months ago, the answer had seemed much clearer than it did now, as she tried to deal with her children's pain and her own.

Before she lost her nerve entirely, she dialed the familiar number. Brandon answered just before the answering machine came on.

"Hello, Brandon," she said, placing her finger on the list in front of her, trying to maintain her emotional balance.

"Is something wrong with the kids?" he demanded in the surly voice she'd grown to expect from him.

"They're doing fine." Her words were followed by a tense, awkward silence, which she eventually broke. "But I did want to talk to you about them."

"All right."

She sighed inwardly and forged ahead. "They want to know if they can come home for spring vacation."

There was no hesitation. "This is their home. *They're* welcome any time."

But not her. He didn't say it, but Joanie didn't need it spelled out. "My dad said he'd be willing to drop them off."

"Your dad. Not you?"

Joanie closed her eyes and forced herself to continue. "I can't. I've got a job. I work weekends."

"You working in a bank?"

"No—it's just part-time." She didn't want to tell him she stood on her feet for an eight-hour shift four days a week in a convenience store. It was the only work she could find, and what little income she received helped put groceries on the table.

"I'll be waiting for the kids the second week of March then." His voice softened perceptibly, and she knew he looked forward to spending time with his children.

"While he's there, would it be all right if Dad picked up a few things for me?" she asked, rushing the question in order to get it out before he hung up.

"Such as?"

"I've got two or three boxes of old clothes in the attic."

"What do you want clothes from the attic for?"

Now was the time to tell him, to casually mention that those old clothes were maternity outfits she'd tucked away after Stevie's birth. "I...need them, is all."

"For your part-time job?"

"Yes." It was the truth, and it wasn't.

"I'll bring them down for him."

"Thank you."

He sighed, as if tired of the ugliness between them. "We're so polite with each other."

Joanie didn't respond. At least politeness was preferable to bitter silence or angry accusations.

"You seen your big-city attorney yet?" he asked, an edge of pain evident in his voice.

"No."

"You've got a job now, you can afford it. Then you can nail me to the wall financially. You wanted me to sell the farm. Well, a divorce is certainly one way to get me off the land."

Joanie rested her elbow on the table and leaned her forehead against her palm. "I haven't talked to an attorney, but I'll let you know when I've made an appointment."

"You do that."

Silence, but Joanie refused to let it continue. "I had Sage at the dentist last week," she told him, "and he thinks she's going to need braces."

His response was full of sarcasm. "Like I can afford braces."

"I thought I should tell you." She wished now that she hadn't. It wasn't something they needed to worry about immediately. Not until she was twelve or thirteen, according to the dentist.

"Anything else on your list?"

He knew her so well. They hadn't spent all those years together for nothing. "No," she whispered. "That's everything." Except...*I'm pregnant.* She couldn't make herself say it.

Neither of them said goodbye or disconnected the line.

"I appreciate that you're having the children write me every week," he murmured.

"They enjoy your letters, too." Each Tuesday, two letters arrived, one addressed to Sage and the other to Stevie. Sage kept hers in a shoe box in her bedroom. At night when she went to tuck her daughter into bed, Joanie often found Sage reading over her letters, one by one. Brandon's letters to his son ended up all over the house. Joanie gathered them up for him, but Stevie didn't seem to care one way or the other. At least outwardly.

"Goodbye, Brandon," she finally said.

"Before you go, tell me one thing." He hesitated and seemed to be formulating his question. "Tell me, Joanie," he blurted out, "are you happy?"

She didn't know how to answer him. The truth was more complex than that. She'd been miserable when she left, but instead of diminishing, that misery had only increased. Oh, there'd been a short blissful period of a week or so after she'd moved to Fargo with the children. A week during which everything seemed better. The tension was gone, she'd taken action, it'd felt right. But that reprieve hadn't lasted. The doubts and troubles returned; the pain had never gone away, for her or the children. And there was this new baby to worry about....

"Is that such a difficult question to answer?"

"Apparently it is," she told him. "No, I'm not happy. I never wanted to do this, never thought it would come to this."

"It's so hard on you because you love me, right?" The sarcasm was back in full force.

"Believe it or not, I do love you, Brandon."

"Well, you have a strange way of showing it. I'll look for the kids next month. Goodbye, Joanie."

"Goodbye, Brandon." Gently she set the receiver back and dropped her face in her hands, struggling to control her grief and her fears.

The children would be home from school soon and she didn't want them to find her upset. It unsettled them. So she pretended everything was fine.

She wondered if anything would ever be fine again.

Sixteen

The first week of February, it seemed as if spring would never come, and winter pressed down on Lindsay, heavy and bitter cold. The wind hissed and howled across stark, barren land, the white fields almost featureless. The town looked bleaker than ever in the gray light of winter, with dirty drifts of snow at the side of the roads.

With spring apparently far off, Lindsay's students had grown listless and bored with their studies. What little enthusiasm she'd been able to muster was forced and hardly seemed worth the effort. It didn't help that she felt oppressed by personal problems, too. She hadn't yet made a decision about searching for Gina's child—and wasn't sure how to go about it, anyway. Hire a detective? She'd barely seen Gage all month, and when they were together their behavior toward each other was guarded. She longed to end the strain between them, but couldn't. Not without making painful compromises.

As was her habit, Lindsay stopped at Hassie's after school almost every day. This first Monday of February, she felt in particular need of her friend's wisdom and advice.

"I feel sorry for the kids," Lindsay admitted, sipping her tea. Sorry for herself, too, but she didn't mention that. "They don't have much of a social life. In a normal high school, there'd be dances and sporting events. But Friday nights for these kids means partying in some remote field, drinking beer out of a can and listening to the radio."

Sighing, she rested her elbows on the counter.

"That sounds about right," Hassie said, fussing with her own cup of tea. She poured in a teaspoon of Gage's honey and drew lazy circles with her spoon.

"My favorite dance of the year was the Sweetheart Ball every Valentine's Day." Lindsay's memories of high school were pleasant ones and she remembered fondly all the energy invested in finding the perfect dress, the fun of double-dating with Maddy, the happy, carefree experiences they'd shared.

Hassie grinned, as if Lindsay had said something of real importance. "So, what's stopping you?" she asked.

"Stopping me?"

"From throwing a dance. You put on that Christmas play, didn't you?"

Well, yes, but she'd had a theater, which would be used again at graduation. "Putting on a dance sounds like a fine idea, but—where?"

Hassie glowered at her. "Use your head, girl. There's plenty of empty buildings around here. A high-school dance wouldn't require nearly as much fuss as fixing up that old movie house."

"We could have a dinner to go along with the dance." She was starting to feel excited about this. "The year Maddy and I were seniors, it was the in thing to rent limos and dine at ultra-expensive restaurants. The two of us thought it was silly to waste our money like that, so we decided to come up with something really wonderful, something *different*."

"What did you do?"

Although her lips were sore and cracked from the dry and the cold, Lindsay grinned. "We had dinner in Forsyth Park. Five couples got together and our parents brought out their best china and linens for us. A few of the younger brothers served as waiters, and the ten families supplied a fabulous dinner. Right there in the middle of the park, we showed up in our tuxedos and fancy dresses and acted as if we were dining at the White House. It was the talk of the school."

"Do that here," Hassie suggested. "I've got a pretty lace tablecloth I'd be willing to let you borrow. You might be able to strike a deal with Buffalo Bob on the food and probably the music. You could have dinner there and follow it up with a dance somewhere else. You know, it'll be the first formal dance for those kids. You're right. They need that experience. It'll be good for them."

"But the girls can't afford gowns any more than the boys can buy suits."

"They can borrow them. Most of 'em will fit into a discarded suit of their father's. Vaughn wore his dad's suit when he graduated from high school. Folks around here have been making do for a long time. Leave it to your students and don't be surprised by what they come up with."

Suddenly they seemed to have a plan. One that was both thrilling and—more important—possible. Already she felt immeasurably better. "We can do this!"

"You're darn tootin' we can. A dance is just what this community needs."

"But it's for the high-school kids," Lindsay said.

"You'll need chaperons, won't you? You can't have a Sweetheart Dance without chaperons."

"You're right."

"Ask Gage," Hassie suggested, her eyes twinkling.

Lindsay had given up trying to hide her feelings for Gage. Hassie knew, and she encouraged the romance, what little of it there was these days. Lindsay and Gage disagreed about some fundamental issues—Kevin's applying for the scholarships and the wisdom of Lindsay's searching for their grandparents' illegitimate child. Even so, Lindsay felt drawn to Gage; she respected and liked him and maybe more… Mostly, she wished things could be different, but didn't know how to go about changing them.

"You'll have to get working on it," Hassie said, "especially if you want to do this any time close to Valentine's Day."

"I'll get started tonight." Her enthusiasm high, she decided they'd hold the dance the Saturday after Valentine's—which gave her less than two weeks. Before she left, Lindsay kissed Hassie on the cheek.

"What was that for?"

"Because you're brilliant."

Hassie laughed outright. "Hey, tell the town council that, if you would. I'm getting too old and tired to be fighting with them." Her smile brightened her eyes and added color to her cheeks.

Two days later, Lindsay had made the arrangements for the first Buffalo Valley High School Sweetheart Dinner and Dance. She talked to Rachel Fischer, who offered to let them use her parents' old restaurant for the dance itself. The place was virtually empty of tables and chairs, but had heat and electricity—an advantage when funds and time were in short supply.

Buffalo Bob took to the idea immediately. He made up a special menu and offered it at a rock-bottom price. He also agreed to let the teens use his stereo system for the dance, although he insisted on setting it up and dismantling it himself.

To her delight, Heath Quantrill volunteered to be a chaperon without her having to ask. Hassie did, too, but she'd let it be known that she was rarely up past ten and would probably leave early. The one person she had yet to ask was Gage.

"Everyone in town's talking about the Sweetheart Dance," Hassie teased her the next time Lindsay dropped by Knight's Pharmacy. "You work faster than the U.S. Army Corps of Engineers when you put your mind to something."

Lindsay smiled. Since that Monday afternoon conversation with Hassie, the winter doldrums had all but vanished. "It was a terrific suggestion."

"It was," Hassie agreed, "and I take full credit." She paused, then asked tentatively, "Gage *is* coming, right?"

"I…I haven't asked him yet."

"I've got Leta's refill on her blood pressure medication. You could always drive that out to her and, while you're there, casually mention to Gage that you need another chaperon."

"I could," Lindsay said, more than willing to participate in a bit of minor subterfuge.

She left for the farm soon afterward. The afternoon was cold and crisp and, as she drove, Lindsay lost sense of time and distance. All that gave her perspective were fence lines and telephone poles. Out here, away from town, Lindsay felt a peace, a stillness. There was a beauty in this white emptiness that she was only beginning to appreciate.

When she arrived at the farm, Leta greeted her as if it'd been months since they'd last spoken. Trying not to be obvious, Lindsay looked around for Gage.

"He's working in the barn," Leta told her with a knowing smile. "I'm sure he'd like to talk to you."

Lindsay wasn't convinced of that, but sought him out anyway. When she walked into the barn, she saw him bent over the tractor, tinkering with the engine, his hands greasy and a pink rag tucked in his hip pocket. He couldn't have been more different from Monte. This was a man who used his hands, a man who knew the meaning of hard work. Real work. She hadn't known him long, and yet she'd seen his soul. She'd read his heart. She'd heard him speak of lying in a field with his eyes closed, listening to the grass sigh. Felt his love for the land as he scooped up the dry earth and let the wind carry it. They shared a bond, the secret of their grandparents' love and the daughter that love had created. They shared other things, too, not as easily defined.

And that shattering attraction between them…

She must have watched him for at least a minute before he became aware of her presence.

Gage glanced over his shoulder and their eyes met. "Lindsay." The way he spoke her name was soft and yearning, and she saw the longing in his eyes before he could disguise it. He looked away, straightened, then set aside the wrench. He pulled out the rag and wiped his hands clean.

"I dropped off your mother's blood pressure medication," she said, turning to point back at the house.

"I heard about the dance."

She remained just inside the barn, uncertain. "I came to ask a favor," she finally said.

He nodded.

"I could use an extra chaperon."

"Just let me know what time and I'll be there."

"Thank you." With a quick smile, Lindsay started to turn away.

"Lindsay." He walked toward her, and when he reached her, he sighed. "I—"

"Shh." Lindsay touched her finger to his lips. "You don't need to say it," she whispered.

He frowned. "What?"

"You want to tell me you missed me—I know because I feel the same way. But you're not sure how to say it."

"You're wrong. I do know how to say it." He settled his mouth over hers. His kiss was tender and as smooth as velvet.

"Oh, Gage," she whispered, her hands on his face, loving the feel of his skin against her fingertips.

"I'm filthy," he moaned. "I don't dare touch you."

"I dare…"

His mouth trembled when she kissed him with all the pent-up longing of these past few weeks. He groaned as she deepened the kiss, parting her lips. Her arms went around him then, but he kept his hands at his sides to avoid smearing engine grease on her coat. Lindsay wouldn't have cared if he had.

They kissed again and she closed her eyes as hard as she could, wanting to block out the immutable reality of their differences. When she opened them again, Gage had backed her against the barn door and his upper body was pressed against hers, his mouth exploring the side of her throat.

"We're crazy," he whispered huskily. "This is crazy."

"Then so be it. Just don't stop."

"I don't think I could if I wanted to, only I've got to wash my hands. This is torture."

He lifted his head to pull away, but Lindsay wouldn't let him. "Torture, you say?" She released a slow, sexy laugh. "I like the sound of that." Wrapping her fingers around the metal clasps of his coveralls, she dragged him back to her. Before he could protest, she'd covered his mouth with her own, kissing him with an open-mouthed aggression that left him groaning.

"Lindsay, please…"

"Do you want to show me your hayloft?" she teased, not nearly as in control as she led him to believe.

The sound of footsteps alerted them both that someone was entering the barn. They broke apart an instant before Kevin strolled in.

The boy stopped midstride and, embarrassed, glanced from one to the other. "I didn't mean—I…"

"Don't worry, you didn't interrupt anything." Gage's eyes found hers as if to say *more's the pity*.

"I saw Miss Snyder's car and—"

"It's all right, Kevin. I came to ask your brother if he wouldn't mind chaperoning the dance."

"Oh."

"Do you have any objection to my being there?" Gage asked.

"No, sure, that's fine by me. I, uh, guess I'll be heading back to the house, then."

"Good idea," Gage said.

Kevin paused at the door. "Mom asked me to tell you it won't be long until dinner and Lindsay's invited if she wants to stay."

"Tell Mom to put an extra plate at the table. We'll be inside in a few minutes."

Kevin nodded, looking distinctly relieved to make his escape. As soon as he was gone, Lindsay sagged against the side of the barn.

"Before we go inside, there's something I need to ask you," Gage said.

"Anything." She straightened away from the wall, her hands clasped behind her. She knew that the tenderness and the passion that had passed between them was gone.

"Did you find her?"

Lindsay knew who he meant. "Not yet. But I've decided to hire an on-line search company that specializes in cases like this. I'll look on my own, too, on the Internet. If I do find her, I'm not even sure I'll contact her. I want to give it more thought."

Gage nodded.

She gave a slight shrug. "Despite what you said, though, I can't help feeling she'd want to know about her birth parents. If she doesn't, I'll make no further effort to get in touch with her."

He shook his head. "It's not that simple. Once she knows, she can't go back to not knowing. You will have changed her life, Lindsay. And think about this—what if no one ever told her she was adopted?" He raised his hands in defeat. "Never mind, we've been through all that. I'd hoped you'd have a change of heart, but I can see you haven't."

"Can't you understand?"

"No." He gazed down at his hands. "I just hope you know what you're doing."

Rachel knew before Heath arrived at the dance that he'd volunteered to be a chaperon. She also knew why. He'd never hidden his intentions. He wanted her to be his lover.

The knowledge didn't boost her self-esteem or flatter her ego. In fact, his interest had quite the opposite effect. Oh, she'd briefly been excited by his attention, but she'd done a lot of thinking since the night of their dinner date, and realized a relationship between them couldn't possibly work. They'd been drawn together by their shared losses.

But that was all they had in common. Heath was rich and worldly, and she was neither. The physical attraction they shared would wane in time and there would be nothing but regrets. Her marriage had been solid and strong; she knew that physical love was only one small facet of a relationship. She had a son to raise and an example to set. Plain and simply put, she wasn't interested in what Heath had to offer.

Heath, however, saw her attitude as a challenge and refused to give up.

Saturday, the night of the dance, Rachel stood in her pizza kitchen with Sarah Stern, who was taking over for her later in the evening. As soon as the high-school kids finished dinner at Buffalo Bob's, they were coming to Rachel's empty restaurant for the dance. At midnight she'd serve pizza, and then the kids would head home.

For two days, groups of teens had been in and out, decorating the large room that had once been her parents' restaurant. Balloons, crepe paper and big red hearts filled every nook and cranny.

"Are you about done there?" Sarah asked, while Rachel put the finishing touches on a pepperoni pizza.

"Soon."

"The kids'll be here any time."

"I know, I know."

"Heath, too."

As if Rachel needed reminding. Her friend was fond of stating the obvious. "Did Calla like her dress?" she asked, in an attempt to change the subject.

Sarah crossed her long legs and sighed. "I think she must have. She wore it."

"You talked her out of wearing the vest you made?"

"It took some persuasive arguments," Sarah muttered. She shook her head. "She wouldn't even open it Christmas

Day, and when she did finally unwrap her gifts, she put it on and hasn't taken it off since."

Rachel laughed, enjoying the retelling of the story. Calla was certainly a handful and she hoped that when Mark entered his teenage years she'd have as much patience with him as Sarah did with Calla.

"Are you and Dennis stopping by later on?" Rachel asked, knowing that several other parents had told Lindsay they intended to visit at some point during the evening. She dipped her hands into the large bowl of grated cheese, scooped it up and sprinkled it over the pizza's surface.

"Dennis?" Sarah's laugh was answer enough. "He's got two left feet. Besides, Calla would have a hissy fit if Dennis showed up with me. She doesn't want *me* there, let alone Dennis."

Rachel didn't envy her friend. "Calla's still having trouble accepting him, I take it?"

"I'm afraid so." Sarah gathered her arms around her middle, as if warding off a chill.

"Give her time," Rachel suggested. Finished now with the pizza, she placed it on the wire rack of the pizza oven and pushed the button. Ten minutes later the pizza would slide out the other end, perfect and ready to eat.

"Where are you planning to change your clothes?" Sarah asked, glancing around.

"Actually," Rachel said, wiping her hands down the front of her white apron. "I was thinking of skipping out. Lindsay's got more than enough chaperons."

Slowly Sarah shook her head. "Sorry, I won't let you do that."

"Sarah, how can you dictate to me when you won't be there yourself?"

"But I have a good reason. This dance is for Calla, not

for me." She pointed directly at Rachel. "You, on the other hand, are acting like a coward."

"Oh, please. All I'm doing is avoiding another needless confrontation with Heath Quantrill."

"At least you're honest enough to admit it."

"Of course I'm honest. Why shouldn't I be?"

"In my humble opinion, you should give him another chance."

"Why? He's looking for one thing and I'm looking for another."

"I wouldn't be so sure of that." Sarah wasn't going to let up on this, and Rachel realized that she'd actually *wanted* someone to persuade her. "Now go change," Sarah ordered. "As soon as the pizza's ready I'll deliver it to Dad and then I'll be back."

"Oh, all right."

In spite of what she'd said to Sarah, she really didn't mind; in truth, she'd been looking forward to it. Her dress, on loan from Hassie, hung in the restroom around the corner from the kitchen. The 1950s gown was a full-length full-skirted black dress with a scoop neck and long sleeves. It had the elegance of simplicity.

By the time Rachel had finished with her hair, pulling one side up and pinning it back, Sarah was waiting with the pizza in her hand, about to walk out the door. Her smile said she approved.

"The kids are here."

Rachel could hear a wild song from some rock group she didn't recognize. The kids had sorted through Buffalo Bob's collection of CDs and brought along some of their own.

"How's it going?" She knew the dance portion of the evening had given Lindsay some worry. Never having attended a school dance before, the kids were likely to feel awkward. Lindsay had wanted suggestions for icebreakers, but Rachel didn't have any.

"At this point," Sarah said with a soft laugh, "all they're doing is staring at one another."

"Oh, dear."

"Get out there," Sarah said. "By the way, you look gorgeous. I almost feel sorry for Heath."

"Heath, nothing."

"Don't be so hard-nosed. Everyone's entitled to one mistake."

Rachel knew she shouldn't have told Sarah what had happened on their dinner date. But at the time, she'd needed someone to share her indignation and outrage.

When she finally did step out of the kitchen, she saw that her friend's assessment of the dance was accurate. The boys, with Heath and Gage, stood on one side of the room and the girls, dressed in their fancy formal gowns, stood on the other, joined by Lindsay and Hassie.

The boys stared down at their shoes. The girls gazed hopefully, dreamily, at the boys, hoping one of them would find the courage to cross the great chasm.

Eventually one of them did, and to her dismay, Heath Quantrill headed directly toward her.

"Would you care to dance?" he asked, and confidently held out his hand. The song was a lovely slow number, Neil Young's *Harvest Moon*.

Everyone watched and waited. The girls gazed upon her with wide-eyed envy and the boys marveled at Heath's bravery. Rachel knew she dare not refuse.

With her heart in her throat, she reluctantly placed her hand in Heath's. Together they stepped toward the middle of the freshly polished floor, beneath the crepe paper streamers. A large cut-out of Cupid with his arrow aimed directly at them glowed silver in the dimmed lights.

Heath slipped his arm around her waist and she laid her hand on his shoulder. She held herself as stiffly as she could, unyielding against his gentle pressure. She refused to meet his eyes.

"Relax," he whispered. "We have an audience."

"I don't enjoy being the center of attention," she returned from between clenched teeth.

Thankfully they weren't the only ones on the floor for long. Within a few moments, Kevin Betts joined them with Jessica Mayer. Soon after that, one of the Loomis twins—Larry, Rachel guessed—asked Calla Snyder to dance.

Sarah had designed and sewn Calla's dress—and it was stunning. The girl, whose normal wardrobe consisted of combat boots, black denim jeans and plaid flannel shirts, was transformed into a young beauty. Rachel wasn't the only one who noticed, either. Both of the Loomis twins buzzed around her, and Calla fairly glowed with all the attention. Some girls wore dresses that had been in their families for years, gowns their mothers or grandmothers had worn. Some were fancy, others not. There had been a lot of old trunks opened and closets cleaned in the time before the dance, and a lot of lending and sharing had taken place.

Stan Muller, the youngest of the boys, asked Amanda Jensen to dance. Amanda was a year older and a full foot taller. The difference didn't appear to bother Stan, and Amanda smiled down on him with adoring eyes.

"See, it's not so bad, is it?" Heath whispered as another song began.

Without her being aware of it, he'd brought her closer into his arms as their bodies swayed rhythmically to the mellow sounds of the seventies hit, *Close to You*. His jaw rested against her temple, creating a comfortable intimacy that lulled her into closing her eyes. Had he attempted conversation, she wouldn't have felt that way. But his silence and the music had accomplished what words could never have achieved.

When this second dance ended, she dropped her arms and backed away.

"I made a mistake rushing you, Rachel," he told her, holding on to her hand, tugging her to the side of the room as a new song started playing. Something fast and raucous. "Give me another chance."

His words were full of sincerity; so were his eyes. She hesitated, unsure even now that it would be wise. But Heath refused to release her hand until he had his answer.

"All right," she said. If he hadn't looked so damn earnest, she would have refused. If this was a ploy, Rachel promised herself, Heath Quantrill would rue the day.

Without another word, she turned and walked back to her kitchen.

The dance was over, and everyone had left for home except Lindsay and Gage. He surveyed the room; the balloons that hadn't been broken clung to the ceiling. Pink, red and white crepe paper, twisted into streamers, sagged pitifully, dangling down so far they nearly touched the floor.

"You want to clean up now?" he asked. Lindsay looked as wilted as the streamers. She'd worked hard to put this evening together and now that it was over, she seemed ready to collapse.

"Not tonight, Gage. I'm too tired." Lindsay sat with her feet propped up on a chair. Her shoes had disappeared hours earlier and every now and then she leaned forward to massage her nylon-covered toes.

"Too tired," she repeated, her lashes fluttering open only long enough to glance at him. "And my feet hurt."

He chuckled to himself. "Let me walk you home."

"That would be nice."

He put his arm about her waist and helped her off the chair.

"One more dance first," she whispered, sliding her arms around his neck and gazing up at him.

"I thought your feet hurt."

"Not anymore."

"Buffalo Bob already picked up his stereo equipment."

"But I hear music. Don't you?"

"Are you sure no one spiked the punch bowl?" he teased.

"Positive," she insisted, and looked up at him dreamily. "You don't hear the music?"

He didn't until he placed his arms around her and brought her close. Then it was definitely there, pure melody that flowed between them. Eyes shut, Gage led her gently around the room, their bodies moving in perfect unison to the music in their hearts.

"Oh, Gage, it was a wonderful evening, wasn't it?"

"Perfect." An evening that her students—and everyone else in town—would long remember.

Kissing Lindsay seemed perfectly natural just then. Their lips met, and he knew that she understood and wanted this, too. He felt almost overpowered by the warmth and emotion that swept through him.

The kissing was good, better even than he remembered, and that seemed impossible. He kissed her again and again until he couldn't bear it any longer. He pulled her close against him, close enough so that she'd know exactly what their kissing was doing to him.

"I…think it's time we went home," she whispered, gazing into his eyes.

"I do, too."

"Will you come with me?"

Gage hesitated. "If I do, are you prepared for what will happen?"

She smiled. "Are you suggesting what I think you're suggesting?"

He smiled back, entranced by the happiness in her eyes. "Are you?" he asked again.

"Oh, yes." She kissed him and reached for his hand. "Come on," she said, leading him toward the door, stopping to retrieve her shoes from under a chair and collect her coat.

Gage smiled. He pulled her back into his arms and they kissed once more before they turned out the lights and locked the door.

The night was clear and the moon nearly full, its light streaming down on the main street of Buffalo Valley. The cold was crisp and they breathed out wisps of fog.

Buffalo Bob's neon sign glowed in the dark. The only other lights Gage recognized were Lindsay's porch light and another that seemed to come from Hassie's house.

"Looks like Hassie's still up," he commented, hooking his arm about her waist.

"Can't be Hassie," Lindsay said, and glanced down the street.

"I thought she left hours ago."

"She did. I don't think she was feeling well." She stared into the distance. "You know, it *is* her place."

Gage had vaguely thought something was wrong when Hassie first arrived, but she hadn't said anything and left early.

"Maybe we should check to make sure she's all right," Lindsay said.

"Just to be on the safe side," he agreed.

Lindsay's arm tightened around Gage's as they approached Hassie's home. It stood on a corner lot, a two-story structure with a wide front porch and a single gable directly above it.

They walked up the steps and Gage rang the doorbell. When Hassie didn't respond, he rang again.

"Maybe she just forgot to turn off the lights," Lindsay suggested.

"Maybe." But Gage was doubtful. Forgetting anything didn't sound like the Hassie he knew.

Walking away from the door, he peered into the living-room window. He saw her then, dressed in her robe and slippers, collapsed on the carpet.

"She's lying on the floor," he said, and when he tried to open the door, he found it locked.

Lindsay went to look through the window herself. "Gage, Gage—she's not moving!"

Seventeen

Saturday, a week after finding Hassie, Lindsay sat in the straight-backed chair next to the hospital bed where she slept. She'd spent as much time as possible at the Grand Forks Hospital, doing what she could to make Hassie comfortable. Her friend had suffered a heart attack, and if it hadn't been for her and Gage, Hassie would surely have died.

"How's she doing?" Leta whispered, quietly slipping inside the room.

Lindsay caught a glimpse of Kevin by the door.

"Better, I think," Lindsay whispered back.

Leta brought out framed photographs of Hassie's son and husband and set them on the small table beside the bed. Lindsay knew Hassie had requested them, as well as a few other personal things. When she'd finished, Leta pulled a second chair close to Hassie. "Thank God she survived."

"Yes," Lindsay said. Like everyone else in town, she was both grateful and relieved. So much of Buffalo Valley, past and present, had been shaped by Hassie Knight. If it hadn't been for her encouragement, Lindsay would never have accepted the teaching position, never fallen in love with Gage, never ended the treadmill relationship with Monte. Because of Hassie, Lindsay's life had found purpose. She was making a difference to this community. And in moving to Buffalo Valley, she'd uncovered the heritage she'd never known—and learned her grandmother's secret.

"The doctors suggested bypass surgery," Lindsay murmured. Leta knew that, but it gave Lindsay comfort to repeat the information. It helped to remind her that there was hope for her friend. This wasn't necessarily the end of Hassie's life, although Lindsay hadn't been able to convince her of that. So far, Hassie had steadfastly refused to agree to the operation.

"You've talked to her about it again?"

Lindsay nodded. "No matter what the doctors say, she seems to believe she's as good as dead. I asked her how she felt yesterday, and she told me not to buy her any green bananas."

Leta shook her head, and couldn't quite suppress a smile. "That sounds just like Hassie."

"She needs the surgery, but she's frightened."

Typical of Hassie, the old woman worried about her store and the effect its temporary closing would have on the community. Lindsay had assured her that prescriptions were being handled by the pharmacy in Devils Lake. In addition, Rachel kept the drugstore open several hours every day, closing only when she had to drive the school bus.

"Give her time and she'll agree," Leta assured her. "Right now, she's in pain and still a bit disoriented. That old fighting spirit will kick in any time."

"I never could see her as a quitter," Lindsay whispered.

"You two talking about me again?" Hassie shifted her head to look at them. Her white hair was matted down on one side, her face thin and ashen. The eyes that had once been so clear and direct were clouded by the effects of medication and her lack of will.

Lindsay stood and gently took Hassie's frail hand between her own. She'd lost her grandmother Gina without ever really knowing her and couldn't bear the thought of losing Hassie, who'd become such a dear and trusted friend.

"What are you still doing here?" Hassie demanded, frowning at Lindsay.

"I want to be here."

Hassie closed her eyes and when she opened them, looked past Lindsay and straight to Leta. "They want to put me in a rest home—said I had to be stronger for the surgery. I told them no to both, but they won't listen to me and Valerie… My own daughter signed the papers."

Hassie's daughter lived in Hawaii and was desperately worried about her mother. She planned to visit in a few weeks' time and called her mother daily. Lindsay had spoken to Valerie twice.

"I've been here a week…" Hassie's voice faded and she paused as if to gather her strength. "I'd rather die than live in one of those old folks' homes."

Leta moved to the other side of the bed and patted her hand. "You're weak. Your body's had a terrible shock and needs time to recover before it's strong enough to deal with the trauma of surgery."

"You sound like one of those highfalutin doctors."

"Okay, so you have to rest in a nursing home for a couple of weeks. It's not the end of the world. Once you're ready, you'll have the surgery and after that, you'll be able to move back home where you belong."

"I told those doctors they can forget all about the surgery, and I'm telling you the same thing."

Lindsay knew that without the bypass operation, Hassie's chances of recovery were greatly lessened. She wanted to argue, insist that her friend listen to reason, but knew it would do no good. Hassie had already made up her mind.

"I'm not going into any nursing home," she muttered. "Why won't anyone listen to me?"

"It's for the best," Leta murmured, glancing at Lindsay for help.

Lindsay had gone over the same arguments a dozen times to no avail.

"You want me dead?" Hassie asked querulously. "Once people go into a nursing home, they don't leave until they die."

"That's not true," Leta argued. "It's the best place for you to regain your strength."

"You keep sounding like one of those doctors." Hassie closed her eyes as if the strain of arguing had drained her of strength. "I thought you were my friend."

"I've been your friend for forty years," Leta said calmly, her expression pained. "And that's not going to change. Now quit being a stubborn old lady. Valerie's already signed the papers and you don't have any choice."

"Why is it I have a heart attack and all of a sudden people think I don't have a brain in my head? I used to make my own decisions. You just wait, Leta Betts, your turn is coming." She closed her eyes again and turned her head away.

Leta and Lindsay stood at her bedside, and soon it became evident from Hassie's deep, even breathing that she'd fallen asleep.

Kevin knocked softly at the door and peeked inside.

"I have to go," Leta whispered. "Are you staying much longer?"

"A while." Lindsay didn't want to leave on such a distressing note.

Leta hugged her quickly, reached for her purse and with obvious reluctance slipped from the room as quietly as she'd entered. Once she was gone, Lindsay returned to her chair and opened a book she'd been wanting to read for a long time. Although the novel had been highly recommended, she struggled to keep her concentration on the page.

Lindsay understood her friend's fears. The nursing home was intended to be a short-term solution but the very thought of it terrified Hassie. Medicare wouldn't continue to pay the high hospital rates, and Hassie was far too weak and fragile to go home, even if a caregiver could be found. The only option left was the nursing home.

Hassie woke again in the middle of the afternoon. She blinked when she saw the photographs and lingered on the picture of Vaughn, the son she'd lost in Vietnam thirty years earlier. It was several minutes before she looked at Lindsay.

"He was the most courageous boy I ever knew," Hassie whispered. A tear rolled from the corner of her eye and fell on the pillow. "I suppose you agree with Valerie."

Lindsay hesitated, then nodded. Hassie's daughter, like everyone else, wanted what was best for her.

"Thank God Valerie has the sense enough not to rush home for a deathbed scene."

"Would you stop!" Despite the seriousness of Hassie's condition, Lindsay smiled.

Hassie reached for Lindsay's hand and gripped it with surprising strength. "I'm a frightened old woman who doesn't want to spend her last days as a burden to others."

"You'd never be a burden—your whole life has been a blessing to everyone who knows you."

Tears filled Hassie's eyes. "Everyone seems to know what's best for me. Lindsay, I don't think I can abide this nursing home. They might as well just let me die right here and now."

"Hassie, please, don't talk like that."

Her friend offered her a watery smile, then stretched out a hand for the photograph of her son dressed in his Army uniform. "All these years, I thought of Vaughn as heroic and brave, which he was. His lieutenant wrote me and told me he'd never seen anyone display the kind of courage my son did."

Tears streamed from her eyes, and Lindsay handed Hassie a tissue.

"What I didn't understand," she whispered, dabbing her eyes, "is that sometimes it requires as much courage to live as it does to die."

Snow fell during the first and second weeks of March, and then everyone was talking about Easter and the upcoming spring break. Each afternoon, as soon as school let out, Kevin Betts routinely stopped at the small post office on his way home. It was early yet, Miss Snyder had told him, to be expecting any kind of response from the art schools in Chicago and San Francisco. Nevertheless, each and every day, he went to the post office. Hoping.

"What will you do if you get a scholarship?" Jessica asked him one afternoon.

"Nothing." He shrugged as he said it, as if the chances of that happening were too remote to consider.

Kevin knew Jessica wanted him to stay in Buffalo Valley, just like his mother and Gage did. The only person who understood was Miss Snyder. This new teacher, a stranger, an outsider, was the only person who believed in his talent, who encouraged him to dream. In the past seven months, it'd been Miss Snyder who'd taught him to believe in himself.

Until she'd arrived, Kevin had kept his sketches private. Every now and then, he'd draw something simple, like a flower, to impress a girl. Jessica liked to draw, too, and that was one of the reasons he liked her, but even Jessica didn't really know how important his art was to him. Not the way Miss Snyder did.

Soon after school started, she'd seen his sketchbook. It was a fluke that it'd even happened. Normally he didn't bring his drawings to school. He'd been working on a sketch of Gage during a study period when Miss Snyder happened upon him. He'd slapped the covers shut but it was too late.

Miss Snyder had seen the book, and asked to look at it. The decision to let her see it hadn't been easy, but after a few uncomfortable moments, Kevin had agreed. Even now he wasn't sure what had prompted him to let the new teacher look at his drawings—examine his soul. He hadn't allowed anyone else, not even his mother or Jessica, to see all his work.

Miss Snyder had turned to his most recent picture. Kevin had drawn Gage, walking waist-high in the wheat fields, the grain full and ripe. Gage, dressed in his coveralls and hat. Vast fields stretched beyond the scope of the picture. Kevin knew that to someone like Miss Snyder, a wheat field was of little significance. He'd heard people call the land in North Dakota flat, boring. In his drawing Kevin had wanted to show the beauty, the specialness, of this prairie field and the man who stood in the center of it.

His half brother's passion was farming, and Kevin had tried again and again to capture Gage's look of pride, a look that said he was proud to be an American farmer, proud of who he was and what he did. To love this man was to love the sweeping land of the prairie.

Kevin was proud of that picture in the same way Gage was proud of the work he did. He'd revealed Gage's heart, and in the process exposed his own.

When Miss Snyder had glanced up from the penciled sketch, there'd been tears in her eyes.

Luckily, it was only the two of them in the classroom, since he'd stayed late to finish the sketch. The tears had embarrassed her and she blinked them away, not wanting him to see. But he had, and she'd won him over that afternoon, just like she'd eventually won over every other student.

That same day she'd looked at some of his other work, too, but had repeatedly gone back to that first sketch. Soon afterward, she'd talked to him about a scholarship to art school.

Kevin had tried to tell her it wouldn't do any good, that there wasn't any money for college. Even with a scholarship covering his expenses, he couldn't leave the farm, or his mother. He had responsibilities. Family obligations. Gage had carried the responsibility of the farm for too long. Gage needed a life apart from Kevin and their mother, his own land to farm. He'd never said a word in complaint, but Kevin knew that Gage longed for his freedom. He'd come home from the Army and then college, ready to start his own life, and then Kevin's dad had died and Gage had put all his own dreams on hold. Kevin couldn't ask him to do that any longer.

"You won't leave me, will you?" Jessica asked, pulling Kevin out of his thoughts. She was gazing at him anxiously, and Kevin took her hand.

"You're wearing the necklace I gave you for Christmas, aren't you?"

"Yes, but that doesn't mean you won't leave Buffalo Valley."

"You're right," he said. "Maybe I will…." He enjoyed

teasing her, because they both knew that he would live and die in this valley. Like his father had. Like his mother and his half brother would.

"Kevin, be serious!"

"I'm not going anywhere, so don't worry about it." But saying the words created a small ache in his heart. Even if he did get a scholarship and by some miracle was able to accept it, he'd never fit into life in the big city. Wouldn't even want to. If it was anything like the world he'd seen on TV, he'd be completely and utterly lost.

Jessica had gotten clingy lately, ever since she'd learned about his applying for the scholarships. He didn't mind so much. It was understood that they'd get married when the time was right. Understood by Jessica, anyway. She talked about it a lot. Kevin didn't feel ready for marriage, but he didn't tell her that. It would mean a fight or tears—and probably both.

"I thought I'd pick up the mail," he said, parking outside the post office. He didn't know why he bothered to check. Even if he did get that scholarship, he'd be forced to give it back. Gage was right, though. Miss Snyder, too. He didn't have to go to class to learn how to draw; he'd been doing it all his life. Just because he ran the family farm didn't mean he couldn't keep his art. He could have the best of both worlds. At least that was what he told himself.

The envelope was the only one inside the box. Even without taking it out, he could see the words—San Francisco Art Institute.

"You got a reply," Jessica said in a low voice, then more excitedly. "Look, Kevin, look!"

Kevin thought his heart had stopped.

"Aren't you going to open it?"

He took out the letter and stared at his name. He stared so long that Jessica tried to grab it from his hand.

"I'll open it for you."

"No." His fingers tightened on the envelope.

"Then *open* it."

He shook his head.

"You aren't going to read what it says?" Jessica sounded as if she didn't believe him.

"I can't see any reason to," he said, and stuffed it inside his backpack. Really, what was the purpose? Nothing the Institute said would change a single fact.

Besides, the letter was from the San Francisco Art Institute. He was actually more interested in the School of the Art Institute in Chicago, which was the highest-rated fine-arts school in the United States. He might as well aim high. Miss Snyder had told him that, and so he had. Dreams were cheap.

Kevin drove Jessica home, then headed down the long driveway that led to the road. When he reached the end of her driveway, he had a choice. Left took him back to Buffalo Valley and right led him toward home.

He turned left. Away from home and the farm, and toward town. He went in search of Miss Snyder. His first stop was the school, where she lingered most afternoons now that Knight's Pharmacy was temporarily closed.

Since the school door was unlocked, he went inside and saw her sitting at her desk. Not wanting to interrupt her reading, he waited for her to notice him.

It didn't take her long to glance up.

"A letter arrived from the San Francisco Art Institute," he said, walking toward her.

"And?" She stood, bracing her hands against the edge of her desk.

He looked away, calling himself the coward he was. "I didn't open it."

"Any particular reason?"

He nodded. "I couldn't." He unzipped the side pocket of his book bag and pulled it out. "You do it."

"Me?" She frowned at the letter. "You picked the San Francisco school, remember?"

That was true. Miss Snyder had printed out a list of the ten best art schools in the United States and asked him to do the research on each school and choose two. After Chicago, he'd picked San Francisco because he'd never seen the ocean.

"You open it," he said again, holding it out to her. She had the right, he decided, seeing that it was Miss Snyder who'd spent all that time helping him fill out the applications and submitting a portfolio and the necessary forms. Financial aid was available, but he'd need much more than that. Since they were aiming high, they had requested a full scholarship and a small stipend for living expenses.

Miss Snyder dragged in a deep breath, then tore into the envelope and extracted a single sheet of paper.

Kevin tensed and watched her face. Then, because he shouldn't care this damn much, he turned away and walked to the back of the schoolroom. He'd spent the entire twelve years of his education in this one room, and for someone like him, it was hard to believe there were other classrooms, other schools.

Miss Snyder didn't say anything for so long that he couldn't stand the suspense any longer and whirled around. "What did the letter say?" he demanded hoarsely. That was when he saw the tears in her eyes.

It must be bad. Real bad.

"They want to offer you a full ride."

The words hit him like a powerful punch. He sank into Larry Loomis's chair and waited for the shock to leave him.

"Aren't you going to say anything?" Miss Snyder asked.

"I...I don't know what to say. I mean—that's great, I guess."

"Great?" she repeated. "That's the understatement of the year. Oh, Kevin, don't you realize what this means? You're brilliant! One day your work will hang—" She stopped herself abruptly.

"The farmer artist," he said, forcing a brightness into his voice.

"Right."

They both knew, without saying it, that the scholarship meant nothing. Not for him.

For the first time in almost three months, Brandon Wyatt woke with a sense of anticipation. This afternoon Joanie's father would be bringing Sage and Stevie to spend spring break with him.

He dressed, brewed a pot of coffee and glanced about the house, seeing it with fresh eyes. The television played while he washed the dishes. He had it on most of the time now, needing the noise in order to feel comfortable. A silent house drove him crazy faster than anything, especially in the evenings. His own thoughts were dark and chaotic, so he often sought a distraction. Any distraction. Reruns, talk shows, even music videos, none of which he understood or appreciated.

In years past, he'd enjoyed evenings. Joanie would sit with him, her needlepoint in her lap as they chatted about the day. Only Joanie wasn't there anymore. Funny how they'd given up their habit of making time for each other. They used to share the worst and best of each day, usually over a cup of coffee. But somewhere, somehow, they'd gotten out of that routine. He had to stop and think, now, to remember when their having coffee together in the evenings had stopped, and couldn't. Probably during the last year.

In the weeks before she'd packed up and walked out on him, they hadn't talked much at all. It seemed that whenever he opened his mouth, he said something that angered her—and vice versa. After a while she gave up fighting with him and simply left him to his own devices. He'd sulked in front of the television most nights while she worked on her crafts in the kitchen. After months of that, he should've been accustomed to spending time by himself, but he wasn't.

Since Joanie had left, Brandon had felt desperately lonely. So lonely that twice now he'd ventured into town. He'd sat and cried in his beer at Buffalo Bob's but didn't feel any better afterward. The house seemed ten times emptier when he returned.

Gage Sinclair had taken to stopping by the farm now and again. Brandon could see what was happening with his neighbor and the schoolteacher. He didn't pry and ask a lot of questions, but it was fairly obvious to him that Gage had fallen for her. As subtly as he could, Brandon tried to warn him off.

When he'd finished with the dishes, Brandon dragged out the vacuum cleaner for the first time since Joanie's departure. He hadn't realized how heavy and difficult it was, then remembered that this old vacuum had been his mother's. Seemed to work well enough, though. Joanie had never complained about it, but she'd had plenty to say about the washer.

While he was thinking of it, he dumped his dirty clothes into the machine and set the controls. When he closed the lid, he ran his hand over the smooth enamel surface. Involuntarily, Joanie's happy face the day of their anniversary flashed into his mind.

The image vanished far too soon, and for an instant he wanted to jerk it back, hold on to it. Remember.

But it was gone, the same way everything seemed to be gone.

When Leon Bouchard's car pulled into the yard, at two that afternoon, Brandon had the house in decent shape. No one looking inside would guess what a pigsty it'd been just hours earlier.

Sage was the first one out of the car.

"Daddy, Daddy!" She ran up the back steps and into his waiting arms. Brandon caught his daughter and lifted her high. She threw her small arms around his neck and hugged him tight.

Stevie followed and Brandon crouched to give his son a hug. Sage was still clutching him, and when he glanced up he noticed that Leon had walked to the house.

"How you doing, Leon?" He straightened and gently set his daughter down, then held out his hand. He wanted his father-in-law to know he didn't have any hard feelings. If anything, Leon and Peggy had been right. They'd been against the marriage. Perhaps if Joanie had listened to her parents, she'd be happier, married to that rich guy who owned the appliance store.

"Good to see you, Brandon."

"Dad, can I call Billy?" Stevie asked, tugging on Brandon's sleeve.

He nodded. Stevie hadn't been in the door two minutes and he already wanted to connect with his friends. "Sure."

"I'm going up to my room, okay?" Sage asked.

"Fine." Brandon placed his hands in his hip pockets.

"Would you like something to eat or drink before you head out?" he asked Leon. He knew the invitation lacked welcome, and the truth was he'd prefer to see Joanie's father leave quickly. This was Brandon's time with his children.

"No, thanks, I'll be going right away."

"Thanks for driving the kids. I appreciate it." That part was sincere.

"Joanie said something about some boxes of clothes? She said they'd be ready for me."

Brandon had forgotten all about that. "They're still in the attic," he said, "but it won't take me a minute to get them for you."

He left his father-in-law standing in the kitchen and ran up the stairs, taking them two at a time. The entrance to the attic was inside the closet in Sage's bedroom. He found his daughter sitting on her bed with her favorite Barbie doll.

She looked up in surprise when he came into the room. "I need to get some stuff for your mother," he said, opening the closet door. He pulled down the latch in the ceiling and the stairs unfolded. Climbing up two or three steps, he remembered he needed a flashlight.

"Sage," he called.

"Here, Daddy."

He glanced down and saw his eight-year-old daughter standing there with the flashlight. In the dim light she reminded him so much of Joanie that he paused and stared at her. It was something about her posture and the trusting way she smiled up at him.

"The flashlight, Daddy? Isn't that what you need?"

He nodded and swallowed past the lump in his throat. The urgency he'd experienced only moments earlier had faded. He climbed down and took the flashlight from his daughter's hand.

Squatting, Brandon met Sage's eyes.

"Have you missed me, cupcake?"

She nodded. "Mommy's missed you, too."

"I miss Mommy." He wouldn't say that to anyone but Sage. He hugged her, fighting within himself. It'd been easy to blame Joanie for leaving him. She was the one who'd wanted out of the marriage; she was the one who'd left. The choice she'd given him had seemed straightforward: either sell the farm or end the marriage.

But in that moment, Brandon recognized that nothing was as simple or as straightforward as he'd tried to make it. Joanie was hurting. He was, too. This wasn't what he wanted.

"Brandon?" Leon Bouchard came up the stairs.

"In here," he called.

"Do you need help?"

"I've got it." Reluctantly he released Sage and with weighted feet climbed the stairs leading to the attic. Joanie, who was wonderfully organized, had the boxes stacked and labeled. He'd never paid much attention to what she'd stored up here and couldn't imagine what she wanted with it now. Ah, yes, work clothes. She had a job now, was back in the work world. He sorted through the boxes until he found two that weren't labelled "baby clothes" or marked with the kids' names. He hadn't a clue what her system was or what she meant by "P Clothes." Probably party clothes. He frowned at the thought.

He dragged the first box to the steps and started down.

"Here," Leon said, standing below him. "Hand them to me."

Working together, they had the two boxes down in a matter of minutes. Leon carried one out to his car and Brandon followed with the second.

After setting them in the trunk, Leon closed the lid.

"I'll be heading home now," he announced. "Tell the kids goodbye for me."

"I will." Brandon stepped away from the car, his hands in his pockets as he watched his father-in-law start the engine, back up just enough to turn the vehicle around and then drive off.

Brandon had never felt a bond with Joanie's parents, and in fact, over the years had avoided contact with them. But if he'd had the power just then, he would have called Leon back. For all his grumbling about his in-laws, all his complaints and suspicions, he realized he liked Joanie's father.

Stevie was waiting for him in the kitchen when he returned. "Did Grandpa leave already?"

"He had to get home."

His son accepted the explanation. "I'm hungry."

"There's peanut butter and jelly. Make yourself a sandwich."

"Okay." Stevie was easily satisfied. He peeled off two slices of bread and laid them on the counter. "Mommy doesn't eat peanut butter anymore."

Interesting, seeing that it was one of her favorite foods. "Why not?"

"I heard her tell Grandma she has to watch her diet."

Involuntarily, Brandon bristled. So Joanie wanted to lose weight, probably because she was hoping to get noticed by her new boss. He didn't remember where she said she was working, but her previous experience had been in a bank, so it made sense that was where she'd look now. She probably had her eye on some rich banker like Heath Quantrill. Out with the old and in with the new. One thing was certain—she was never going to get rich married to him.

Stevie smeared a thick layer of grape jelly on top of an

equally thick layer of peanut butter. "Mommy thinks she's getting fat."

Women were habitually dieting. All women. Joanie no more needed to lose weight than he did.

"Her clothes don't fit her anymore."

"Your mother's clothes don't fit her?"

Stevie nodded.

Perhaps Joanie had been using food as an emotional escape, a comfort to get her through this difficult time. But he couldn't imagine her eating so much in three months that her clothes would no longer fit. That didn't make sense.

"I'm sure she'll lose the weight."

Stevie nodded. "That's what Grandma said, too."

"Grandma?"

"They didn't know I was listening."

"Oh."

"Grandma said it's all Jason's fault."

Brandon tensed. So Joanie was dating someone named Jason. Apparently he was rich enough to take her to fancy restaurants, to wine and dine her. Work clothes, nothing; she'd wanted her party dresses for her nights on the town with Jason.

His jaw tightened as the jealousy burned through him. The least she could do was wait until the divorce was final before she started dating again!

Eighteen

Lindsay hadn't heard anything yet from the on-line search agency, so she logged on to the Internet to search for herself. It proved to be a marvelous research tool.

She still wasn't sure this was the right thing to do. For one thing, Gage had worked so hard to convince her to change her mind. For another, she wasn't confident of the reception she'd receive.

Yet, much as she wanted to push the entire matter to the back of her mind, it refused to stay there.

Day after day, she thought about the search and wondered what, if anything, the investigator had found. One afternoon in late March, when Lindsay arrived home from school, she decided she couldn't wait another minute. She had to know, if only to satisfy her own curiosity.

The first thing she did was review all the facts she had, which she'd listed for the on-line investigator. Sex of the child, the approximate month and year of birth, plus the name of the adoption agency. In addition, she knew that the child had been adopted by a Catholic family in which the father was a physician. He also had a brother or brother-in-law who was a priest.

Lindsay was deep into her own Internet search and had located the names of all physicians practicing within the state during World War II. She printed that out and decided to break for dinner. Reading over the accumulated information, she paced the kitchen as the microwave cooked her frozen entrée. She was just about to sit down when the phone rang.

Groaning, she grabbed the receiver and held it between her ear and shoulder as she carried a steaming cardboard dish of low-fat low-sodium low-taste pasta to the table.

"Lindsay, it's good to hear your voice."

Monte.

Lindsay carefully lowered the carton to the place mat. Since Christmas she'd heard from him only sporadically. Most days he was far removed from her thoughts.

"I've been trying to reach you for hours," he said, his voice urgent.

"How did you get my phone number?" she demanded.

"Oh…I have my ways."

Lindsay could imagine. Most likely her uncle had gotten it from her mother and passed it on, intentionally or not.

"Aren't you going to ask me why I phoned?" he asked.

"You've been hurt? You're ill?" He was one of those men who always seemed to need a lot of sympathy when they were injured or sick.

"No, no, nothing like that," he said, then inhaled as though to calm himself. "I can't tell you how frustrating it is to dial your number and get nothing but a busy signal."

"I was on the Internet," she explained. "Was this so important you couldn't call back later?"

"Yes," he nearly shouted. "You can't know how difficult this decision was to make. And now that I've made it, I can't think of anything else."

"What decision?" While she had no idea what he was talking about, Lindsay understood his impatience. She'd only begun her research into the long-ago adoption and now begrudged every minute she couldn't spend on the project. A sense of excitement and purpose had filled her. She had to find this woman who was her aunt, had to let her know that her birth parents had loved her. And she wanted to give her the locket and the letters that rightfully belonged to her. "What decision?" she asked again, a little more irritably.

"I suspect the best way is to just say this," Monte began. "Lindsay, I made a terrible mistake when I let you out of my life. I love you, I've always loved you. I want us to get married."

His words sucked the breath straight from her lungs. Not long ago, she would have given anything to hear this. Now it was too late. "Monte, please, don't do this."

"Hear me out, that's all I ask," he pleaded. "Last summer when you left, I believed you were moving to Buffalo Gulch to—"

"Buffalo Valley," she corrected.

"Yes, whatever. I believed it was a gimmick, a way of trapping me into marrying you when I wasn't ready to commit."

This was old news to Lindsay. "I told you before I left that wasn't the case."

"I know that now, but—"

"You don't know it, or you wouldn't be phoning me," she told him, amazed at how unemotional she felt. She'd agonized over this decision—to leave him, leave Georgia—but once it was made, she'd known it was the right thing to do.

"Is there still a chance for us, Lindsay?"

"A chance?" He really didn't understand. It was over, completely and totally over. Furthermore, she knew through the grapevine—mostly from Maddy—that Monte hadn't lost any time looking for her replacement. He'd dated several women in the months she'd been gone.

"I didn't know what I had in you," he said with the same frantic edge in his voice. "You wanted marriage—"

"And you didn't. We've been through all this."

She heard him take a deep breath. "If marriage is what it takes to keep you in my life, then so be it."

"This is a serious proposal?"

He paused. "Yes," he finally said, his voice stiff.

Laughing probably wasn't the most delicate or diplomatic response, but she couldn't help herself. "Monte, forgive me for being so insensitive, but no woman wants to spend the rest of her life with a man who grits his teeth and offers to marry her. You make it sound like…like being tied to a stake."

"I can't lose you!"

"You already did, seven months ago."

He argued with her some more, insisting she loved him.

This time she interrupted him. "Monte, I did love you, and I still have feelings for you—but not like I used to."

"You could learn to love me again, couldn't you?" he pleaded.

"Oh, Monte, can't you see it's too late?"

"No," he said. "It can't be."

"I don't mean to be cruel, but that's the only way you're going to hear me. *It's over.*" Lindsay had come too far in the past seven months to feel any victory. She wasn't interested in vengeance or reprisals. She wanted nothing from Monte now. If anything, his proposal embarrassed her.

"You said you'd be back after a year. At least promise you'll give me another chance once you're home."

"Monte, please…"

"You are moving back to Savannah, aren't you?" He made it sound like she'd be crazy not to.

"I…haven't made up my mind yet." For one thing, she hadn't been offered a contract, although she hoped she would be.

"You can't mean to say you'd actually choose to live in Buffalo Gulch—"

"Buffalo Valley," she snapped. "By the way, it happens to be a perfectly wonderful town with good and decent people."

"Buffalo Valley. Sorry," he said, sounding genuinely remorseful.

She exhaled a deep sigh, surprised by her quick temper.

"I should have remembered." His voice lowered and he continued, "Don't give up on me, Lindsay, please. I didn't know how much I was going to miss you, didn't know how bleak my life would feel without you in it. I want us to get married, I was sincere about that, and if you still want, we could have a baby. I'm not opposed to a family, you know that."

"Monte, I don't think—"

"Don't say anything else. Wait until you're home."

What he didn't understand was that Lindsay thought of Buffalo Valley as her home now.

Later in the week, Lindsay logged back on to the Internet. Finding the information about physicians had been relatively easy, but only a couple of the Catholic churches had Web sites. The on-line investigator had probably been to all the same sites, but Lindsay was impatient now. Between phone calls and the Internet, she'd been able to compile three lists of names. Then she'd compared those lists but found they had nothing in common, nothing to link them. Disheartened, she wondered about giving up the search.

The next afternoon, everything changed—she received an e-mail from the on-line agency. They had a name.

The girl had been called Angela and she'd been adopted on August 29, 1943, by Dr. LeRoy Farley and his wife, Eugenia. Stark County records showed a birth certificate listing Dr. Farley and his wife as the parents.

Confirmation came via a baptismal certificate, signed by—and this was the clincher—Father Milton Farley.

In addition, Lindsay was provided with a copy of the Stark County court records, a certificate of marriage for Angela Farley and Gary Kirkpatrick, filed in 1964.

Now she had a married name. It seemed too much to ask that Angela Kirkpatrick would live her entire life in or around Bismarck—but she had. The agency e-mailed her the Kirkpatricks' address.

Once she had all this information, a sense of unreality came over her. Until then, this child—Gina's daughter— hadn't seemed quite real. A character in a sad story. The subject of a complicated search. Now, however, she not only had a name, but a family, a husband and perhaps children. She had a history. Angela Kirkpatrick was Lindsay's aunt, and as such a part of her own life.

She knew then that she had to find Angela and talk to her.

Kevin drove with the window down and the cold wind buffeting his face until he lost feeling in his cheeks and had trouble seeing the road. The wicked cold brought stinging tears to his eyes and blurred his vision.

He'd told his mother and Gage that he was going over

to Jessica's, and when he left the farm that had been his intention. But as he neared the turnoff, he realized he wasn't going to stop at his girlfriend's house.

He just kept driving until he could no longer see the road and the lump in his throat wouldn't let him swallow. He pulled off to the side, close to the ditch, and sat with his hands clenching the steering wheel. After a while he closed his eyes, trying to control the frustration and disappointment. He reminded himself that even as a farmer he could be an artist. It brought no comfort or solace.

His mother knew something wasn't right and had tried to get him to talk. He had nothing to say. Not to her and not to Gage. Neither of them understood. Even Jessica didn't get it. Everyone he loved and trusted was trying to force him into something he could never be. His family, his girlfriend—they all assumed they knew what was best for him.

Every morning, he looked at the letter from the San Francisco Art Institute and it reminded him what a selfish bastard he was. He wanted the chance to be the kind of artist he knew he could be, but that meant Gage wouldn't be able to do what *he* wanted. So, art school just wasn't going to happen. Obligation, duty, responsibility—they all worked against him. He owed Gage. His mother had pointed that out every day for weeks, as if she thought he was about to sell the farm out from under them.

The farm was supposed to be this wonderful blessing; to Kevin it was more like a curse. That winter, Miss Snyder had the entire high-school class read the Melville novel, *Billy Budd*. Lately Kevin had begun to feel that he, too, had a noose around his neck, strangling his creativity and his joy.

Some days, like today, he didn't know if life was worth living.

* * *

"Gage, have you seen Kevin?" his mother asked around nine o'clock.

Gage sat in his study, going over a mountain of paper-work. "Not since dinner," he murmured, unconcerned. His younger brother had been brooding for days. Damned if Gage knew what was wrong with him. He suspected Kevin fancied himself some temperamental artist and that gave him the right to subject the entire family to his moods. Come to think of it, though, Kevin *had* been more morose than usual.

An hour later, his mother came into the study. She looked tense and worried. "I thought he said he was driving over to Jessica's."

"That's what I heard him say." Gage had a vague rec-ollection of his brother asking for the truck keys in order to visit his girlfriend.

"Jessica phoned and asked why Kevin didn't show up. She hasn't seen him all night. They were supposed to study for a test together."

"Maybe he went over to see the Loomis twins."

His mother shook her head. "Not according to Jessica. She's talked to everyone in the class, and no one's seen Kevin."

Not knowing what to think, Gage set his pen aside. "There's no need for alarm. I'm sure he's perfectly fine."

"My son's missing—and all you can say is not to worry! Anything might have happened. He could be lying in a ditch bleeding to death, for all you know."

"Have you talked to Lindsay?" he asked.

A look of relief washed over her face. "No, that's probably where he is. Time must have gotten away from him. He just didn't realize." She reached for the phone and Gage crossed his arms and listened to her side of the conversation.

It soon became apparent that Lindsay didn't have any news of Kevin, either. "She hasn't seen him."

Gage knew one thing; he fully intended to give his kid brother hell for worrying their mother like this.

"I think we should phone the police," Leta said frantically.

"I'm sure he's all right," Gage insisted again, "although he won't be once I get my hands on him."

The phone rang just then, and Gage nearly yanked it off the desk in his eagerness to answer.

"Hello."

"Is this Mr. Betts?"

"No—I'm Gage Sinclair."

"Can I speak to Mr. Betts? This is in regard to his son, Kevin Betts."

Gage stiffened and avoided meeting his mother's eyes. "Who's calling, please?"

"The Rugby Police."

"Rugby?" It seemed impossible that Kevin would have driven that far, but obviously he had. Gage couldn't think of a single reason why. Rugby was a hundred miles west of Buffalo Valley, and the geographical center of North America.

"We have Kevin here at the police station."

"For what?" Gage demanded. A list of possibilities raced through his mind, but no scenario seemed acceptable.

"Can I speak to his father?" the office asked.

"I'm sorry, he's dead. You can speak to me. I'm Kevin's half brother."

"Gage, what is it?" His mother was close to ripping the phone from his hand.

He cupped the mouthpiece. "Kevin's with the Rugby police."

"What?"

"If you'll give me a chance to find out, I'll let you know," he snapped.

"We found him outside of town," the police officer continued. "He'd run out of gas."

"That isn't a crime, is it?"

"No," the officer continued. Then he hesitated. "Is Kevin undergoing some personal problems at the moment?"

"What damn business is that of yours?" Gage asked angrily, taking a dislike to this form of questioning.

"I suggest you come and pick Kevin up."

"Has he been drinking?" Gage asked.

Leta gasped and placed her hand over her mouth.

"To the best of my knowledge he hasn't."

"Drugs?"

A predictable gasp followed from Leta.

"No. Perhaps it'd be best if you talked to the doctor yourself."

"Doctor?" No one had said anything about Kevin needing a doctor.

April 4th

Dear Mrs. Kirkpatrick,

You don't know me, but in many ways I feel like I know you. My name is Lindsay Snyder, and I believe you're my aunt.

I hope you'll give me the opportunity to explain. Many years ago, when visiting my grandmother, I came upon her late at night. She was weeping and she held something in her hand. I was only ten at the time and I didn't understand what had made her so sad. In retrospect, I realize the night I found my grandmother crying was your birthday, August tenth.

My grandmother's name was Regina Snyder, originally Colby, and I'm sorry to tell you she died many years ago. I believe what she held in her hand that night was a gold locket with her picture and that of your father. His name was Jerome Sinclair and he was a soldier during the Second World War.

From letters and other things I've found recently, I know they were deeply in love, but your father was sent to the war in the Pacific. Shortly thereafter, Gina (my grandmother) discovered she was pregnant with you. She was able to write and tell Jerome, but before he could arrange for them to marry, he was declared missing in action.

Believing him to be dead, my grandmother spent some time in a home for unwed mothers and signed the adoption papers for you shortly after you were born. Not until the end of the war did anyone learn that Jerome Sinclair had survived and been interned in a Japanese POW camp for nearly two years.

How I discovered the above information is a remarkable story of its own, and one I would love to tell you. I have in my possession the gold locket and a few letters that I feel are rightly yours. It would give me great pleasure to give them to you.

I'm going to be in the Bismarck area this weekend and will stop by your home. If you're not interested in receiving the items that belonged to your birth parents, then you need not answer the door. But if you do wish to meet me—and I sincerely hope that's the case—I look forward to the opportunity to know you.

I don't mean to intrude on your life. I understand and respect your need for privacy. Rest assured that I have told no one (other than one man, the grandson of Jerome Sinclair) the details I've unearthed. I will leave that option completely up to you.

Thank you for your time and consideration.

Sincerely,
Lindsay Snyder

Joanie's feet hurt from an eight-hour shift at the convenience store and the ache in the small of her back refused to go away. This pregnancy hadn't been an easy one; the physical strain coupled with the emotional stress of the separation was almost more than she could bear.

The children had come home from their spring break in high spirits. Unfortunately, that hadn't lasted long. Sage grew quiet and somber whenever anyone mentioned Brandon, and even Stevie, who'd accepted the upheaval in their lives with barely a murmur, broke into tears one night shortly after his return.

"I don't want you and Daddy to get a divorce," he'd wailed into her arms, clinging to her.

Joanie had held her son and wept, too. Soon Sage joined them and they'd all wept together, holding on to each other.

"How'd the doctor's appointment go?" her mother asked, when Joanie came by to pick up the kids after work.

"I didn't go."

"But, Joanie—"

"I got out of the store late and traffic was heavy." She hadn't had the energy to battle her way across town to the free clinic. All she wanted was to get home and soak in a hot tub.

"Did you reschedule?" her mother pressed.

Joanie shook her head. "But I will, I promise."

Her mother walked them to the door and stopped Joanie

just as she was ready to leave. "I'm worried about you, sweetheart."

"I'm fine, Mom." She'd never realized a separation from Brandon would be this heart-wrenching for her and the children. At the time, it had seemed the only option, the only reasonable decision. She no longer knew if what she'd done was right.

"You look wretched."

Joanie tried to smile. "You don't know how long eight hours is unless you spend it on your feet."

Her mother didn't crack a smile.

"Thanks for watching the kids."

"Joanie." Once again her mother delayed her. She hesitated and reached out a hand to touch Joanie's shoulder. "Brandon phoned."

Joanie paused at the sound of her husband's name.

"I only talked to him for a minute. He phoned for the kids."

Since their return from spring break, Brandon had made a point of calling the children once or twice a week in addition to his weekly letters. But he avoided all contact with Joanie. They hadn't said a word to each other in at least a month.

"He says he misses his family," her mother told her.

"We miss him, too," Joanie said, not wanting to get trapped in this kind of conversation with her mother. Not tonight. "Are you telling me you want me to go back to him? Because if you are—"

"Joanie, don't be so defensive. I'm not suggesting anything. Go home, you're tired."

Joanie wanted to weep with frustration and despair. She walked across the street where Sage and Stevie waited for her.

"What's for dinner?" Stevie wanted to know when she unlocked the front door. "Can we have chili and cornbread?"

"I don't make it nearly as well as your father," Joanie said. She hadn't realized Brandon knew anything about cooking, but the kids had raved about his chili and corn-bread from the minute they got home. He must have found the recipe in one of her cookbooks.

"Ask him how to make it," Sage suggested.

"I will," she promised, "the next time we talk."

Stevie sat down in front of the cupboard and sorted through their dinner options. On the days she worked, they generally ate something that came out of a box or a can. She used to avoid feeding her family anything she hadn't cooked herself, but her standards had lowered considerably.

"Daddy phoned this afternoon," Sage said, sitting at the kitchen table.

"That's what your grandmother said."

Stevie handed her a can of stew, then reached inside the refrigerator for the premade biscuit dough. Her son enjoyed slamming the cardboard tube against the kitchen counter and hearing it explode.

It seemed to take Joanie forever to get their simple dinner on the table. By the time the kids were down for the night, her ankles had swollen drastically and she was so tired she could barely keep her eyes open.

Missing the doctor's appointment hadn't been smart. She'd phone first thing in the morning and reschedule. She was sitting on the sofa with her feet propped up and her hands against her stomach. She leaned her head back and let her eyes drift shut. Her problem, she decided, was that she actually felt jealous of her own children.

They'd talked to Brandon and she hadn't. Not that she and her husband seemed capable of a civil conversation anymore. Lately, he seemed to go out of his way to avoid her altogether. That was what she wanted, or so she'd thought at one time.

Perhaps it was because she was so tired or because she felt unsure of her future and the choices she'd made. Whatever the reason, Joanie walked over to the phone and dialed the Buffalo Valley number.

Brandon took his time answering.

"Hello, Brandon. It's Joanie."

His silence told her he wasn't pleased to hear from her.

"I wanted—the kids keep raving about your chili. I thought you might be willing to share your recipe." It was a flimsy excuse and it sounded even flimsier once she'd actually said the words.

"My chili recipe?"

"The kids—"

"I heard what you said," he snapped. "I'm just having trouble making sense of it."

"I can see this was a mistake. I'm sorry, Brandon, I won't bother you again." She was about to replace the receiver when he called her name.

"I'll answer your question if you answer mine."

"All right," she whispered.

"Who's Jason?"

Her eyes flew open. "Who told you about Jason?"

"Ah," he said, sounding almost friendly now. "You didn't know I was that well-informed, did you?"

"No…"

"According to Stevie, you're on a diet to impress your new boyfriend."

"You interrogated your children about my activities?"

"No," he said coldly. "Stevie volunteered the information."

"And you believe I'm actually seeing some other man." The idea was so ludicrous, she laughed out loud.

"What's so damn funny?"

"You don't have a clue, do you?" Her laughter mingled with tears. "Not a clue."

"Apparently not."

The sobs came in earnest now. "I couldn't get a date if I wanted to."

"Then who the hell's Jason?"

"Jason," she cried, laughing, weeping, hiccuping, feeling miserable and unloved, "is your unborn son. For your information, Brandon, I'm seven months pregnant."

Nineteen

"You had to do it, didn't you?" Gage shouted at Lindsay as he jumped out of his pickup. He slammed the truck door and stalked across the street to Lindsay's house, where she'd just parked. Apparently he'd been waiting for her, and from the way he stormed toward her, he wasn't in the best of moods.

Lindsay had already received one verbal harangue that day and wasn't sure she was up to dealing with another. She raised her hand to stop him. "Can you tell me what's wrong without yelling at me?" she asked.

"You mean you don't know?"

"So you found out about me contacting Angela Kirkpatrick." She should have anticipated this type of reaction from him. He'd been against it from the first.

"Who the hell is Angela Kirkpatrick?"

"Maybe you'd better come inside," she said, resigning herself to his anger. At least if he yelled at her it would be in the privacy of her own home.

She led the way into her house and flopped down on the sofa, feeling discouraged and disheartened.

"Angela Kirkpatrick?" he reminded her, firmly shutting the front door.

"She's…our aunt."

Gage momentarily turned his back on her. "So you went ahead and found her?" he said, shaking his head in disgust.

Lindsay braved a nod. "Only…there was a screwup." The best she could figure was that she'd put the wrong zip code on the letter. In any event, Angela hadn't gotten it.

"She didn't want to be found, did she?" His tone unmistakably said *I told you so.*

Lindsay stared down at her hands. "I did write her, but she claims she never got the letter."

"You couldn't leave well enough alone, could you?"

"No, I couldn't," she told him boldly. Given the opportunity she'd contact Angela again.

He went silent for a moment. "You'd better tell me what happened."

Lindsay wadded up a fresh tissue. "Like I said, I wrote her a letter and told her about my connection with her and about finding the locket and the letters. I remembered what you said about invading her privacy, so I gave her the option of not meeting me if she preferred."

"Apparently you didn't remember very well."

Lindsay winced at the harshness of his words. "She answered the door and Gage, she has your eyes." Lindsay paused as she recalled the surge of emotion she'd felt when she saw Angela Kirkpatrick. It had taken restraint not to hug her and tell her how thrilled she was to meet her. Thank heavens she hadn't.

"That was the first thing I noticed about you—what incredible eyes you have."

Gage ceased his pacing and glared at her in the same disquieting way Angela Kirkpatrick had.

Kevin. This town can't afford to lose our young people, and you encouraged both."

"But the scholarship—"

"He can't do it, and now I'm the one who has to tell him that. Thank you very much, Lindsay Snyder."

She felt the blood drain from her face.

"I know you came here with the best of intentions, but you don't know us, you don't know our ways and you certainly don't know me and my brother. So kindly stay the hell out of our lives."

He slammed out of the house with such force, the living-room windows shook. For a long time, Lindsay didn't move. Even breathing was an effort. She'd say one thing for Gage Sinclair—his timing was impeccable.

After her confrontation with Angela Kirkpatrick, she'd been convinced she couldn't feel any worse, but Gage had proved her wrong.

Brandon sat in the roadside café outside Fargo and nursed his coffee while he waited for Joanie. He hadn't seen his wife in four months and he wasn't sure what he'd feel once he did. Pride had carried him the first few weeks after she'd left, but eventually he'd found it damn poor company. He wanted his family back and prayed that this meeting would help bridge their differences.

When Brandon learned Joanie was pregnant, he'd been furious. Not that she was going to have a baby, but that she'd kept the pregnancy a secret from him. He'd thought about it a lot since she'd blurted out the news and figured it must have happened the night of their anniversary.

During the same conversation, he'd questioned her about being on the Pill. She'd started sobbing and admitted she hadn't been as faithful about taking it as she should have been.

Obviously.

Brandon loved Sage and Stevie and certainly didn't object to adding to their family, but what they had now wasn't a cohesive unit. This separation had taught him a great deal about himself, and about Joanie, too. He was sure that living apart wasn't what she wanted, either. He'd heard the pain in her voice. Sage and Stevie had repeatedly told him how unhappy their mother was.

A car door slammed in the parking lot and Brandon glanced out the window. A trim but obviously pregnant woman battled against the wind as she made her way toward the restaurant. Brandon didn't need to look twice to recognize Joanie. He felt his chest tighten with dread; he couldn't predict the outcome of this meeting, didn't know if they could arrive at any agreement. He dragged a deep breath through his lungs as she entered the café.

Brandon immediately saw the toll the past four months had taken on her. She remained as beautiful as ever, but he saw the strain in her eyes. From her awkward movements, he could tell the pregnancy hadn't been an easy one. Little wonder. The first two had been hard on her health, as well, but he'd always been there for her. Not this time. Maybe not even after today.

Once inside, Joanie walked over to his booth. "Hello, Brandon."

He stood, nodding, stiff with politeness. "Joanie." Motioning toward the seat on the opposite side of the booth, he invited her to sit down. "Thank you for agreeing to meet with me."

"I know you're angry—I should have told you about the baby."

"Why didn't you?"

"Is it important?" she asked, her voice small and shaky.

"I happen to think so," he returned, trying to hide his frustration.

The waitress approached their table and glanced doubtfully between the two of them, a coffeepot in her hand. She refilled Brandon's mug; Joanie shook her head.

Joanie waited until the waitress had left before she spoke. "I always intended to tell you… I'm sorry. You had the right to know."

He couldn't live with Joanie all those years and not know the way she reasoned. "It's because of the health insurance, isn't it?" he asked.

She gazed down at the table. "That was part of it. And if you're going to be angry with me for keeping secrets, keep in mind that you didn't tell me our health insurance had lapsed."

Brandon didn't find those facts comparable to a pregnancy, but he hadn't driven all this way to argue with his wife.

"All right," he said, doing his best to stay calm. "Blaming each other isn't going to solve anything. You're going to have a baby."

"That doesn't change the situation."

"The hell it doesn't." His voice had grown louder, and two or three people turned around and stared at him. "I might have my faults—all right, I'll admit it, I can be a real bastard—but there's one thing you can't fault me on. I love my children."

"It just happens to be their mother you don't love."

The agony he heard in her wrenched his heart. "Joanie, no…"

She reached for the paper napkin and dabbed her eyes and he could see she was angry with herself for letting the emotion get to her.

"You were the one who said if I left, you weren't

coming after me, remember? For all you cared, the kids and I could leave, and it wouldn't make a bit of difference to you. Your family was about to walk out, and the most important thing to you was letting me know that once I left, I was on my own."

He had said that. Not exactly in those words, but close. "I had a few lessons to learn," he murmured. "If you want me to say it, I will. I should've fought like hell to keep you and the kids, but I'm willing to fight now. I've learned my lesson."

"So have I," she surprised him by saying. "I thought… Nothing's working out the way I thought it would. The kids miss you and they're hurting. I'm miserable."

He jumped on it. "Does that mean you'd be willing to move back?"

Joanie dabbed her eyes again and offered him a trembling smile. "I've dreamed about you asking me to come home."

"I've missed you, baby, you and the kids. Nothing's right without you."

"Don't say any more," she pleaded, shaking her head.

She was so pale, and he knew she was emotionally and physically stretched to the limit. He reached across the table for her hand, linking her fingers with his, squeezing tightly so she'd know how he felt.

The tears came in earnest then. "I can't move back, Brandon. I can't."

Her rejection hit him hard, too hard to disguise its impact or to keep the hurt from his voice. "Why not?"

Joanie glanced out the window rather than meet his gaze. "Nothing's changed except that you know I'm pregnant."

"I love you, Joanie, and I love Sage and Stevie and baby Jason or Janey. Don't take my children away from me." He'd never thought he'd beg, but he'd learned how lonely life could get when a man was too proud to fight

REQUEST YOUR FREE BOOKS!

2 FREE NOVELS
FROM THE ROMANCE COLLECTION
PLUS 2 FREE GIFTS!

YES! Please send me 2 FREE novels from the Romance Collection and my 2 FREE gifts (gifts are worth about $10). After receiving them, if I don't wish to receive any more books, I can return the shipping statement marked "cancel." If I don't cancel, I will receive 4 brand-new novels every month and be billed just $5.74 per book in the U.S. or $6.24 per book in Canada. That's a saving of at least 28% off the cover price. It's quite a bargain! Shipping and handling is just 50¢ per book in the U.S. and 75¢ per book in Canada.* I understand that accepting the 2 free books and gifts places me under no obligation to buy anything. I can always return a shipment and cancel at any time. Even if I never buy another book, the two free books and gifts are mine to keep forever.

194 MDN E4LY   394 MDN E4MC

Name	(PLEASE PRINT)
Address	Apt. #
City	State/Prov. Zip/Postal Code

Signature (if under 18, a parent or guardian must sign)

Mail to **The Reader Service:**
IN U.S.A.: P.O. Box 1867, Buffalo, NY 14240-1867
IN CANADA: P.O. Box 609, Fort Erie, Ontario L2A 5X3

Not valid for current subscribers to the Romance Collection
or the Romance/Suspense Collection.

Want to try two free books from another line?
Call 1-800-873-8635 or visit www.morefreebooks.com.

* Terms and prices subject to change without notice. Prices do not include applicable taxes. N.Y. residents add applicable sales tax. Canadian residents will be charged applicable provincial taxes and GST. Offer not valid in Quebec. This offer is limited to one order per household. All orders subject to approval. Credit or debit balances in a customer's account(s) may be offset by any other outstanding balance owed by or to the customer. Please allow 4 to 6 weeks for delivery. Offer available while quantities last.

Your Privacy: Harlequin Books is committed to protecting your privacy. Our Privacy Policy is available online at www.eHarlequin.com or upon request from the Reader Service. From time to time we make our lists of customers available to reputable third parties who may have a product or service of interest to you. If you would prefer we not share your name and address, please check here. ☐

Help us get it right—We strive for accurate, respectful and relevant communications. To clarify or modify your communication preferences, visit us at www.ReaderService.com/consumerschoice.

MROM10

Prologue

Ten-year-old Lindsay Snyder woke rigid with fear. For a moment, she didn't know where she was. The room was as dark as coal and hot, terribly hot. Then she realized she wasn't home in Savannah where the air conditioner cooled the worst of the summer heat. She tried not to be afraid, but she was.

The ghost stories she'd heard at camp that summer returned to haunt her. A sudden chill raced down her spine as she recalled the tale of Crazy Man Charlie who was said to tear out people's eyes...before he murdered them. Somehow, Crazy Man Charlie had found her. Everyone else must be dead. Everyone but her. The dream remained vague, and she tried to remember the details and couldn't.

Slowly she sat up in the darkness, prepared to confront whatever danger awaited her. As she did, she remembered she was at her grandparents' house with her parents and two sisters. They'd arrived that evening after driving for what seemed like days and days to North Dakota.

Her eyes had begun to adjust to the night, and Lindsay climbed out of the makeshift bed in her grandma's sewing

room. She tiptoed past her two sleeping sisters and down the hallway to the kitchen for a glass of water.

A sound came from the living room and she froze at the thought of meeting Crazy Man Charlie face-to-face. Holding her breath, she flattened herself against the refrigerator door.

Then Lindsay saw her Grandma Gina, silhouetted in the moonlight that streamed through the big window. The heavy curtains were pulled open and her grandma stood by the brick fireplace, head bent. Lindsay would have rushed to her for a hug and told her all about the crazy man and how scared she'd been, but she didn't know her Grandma Gina as well as she did her Grandma Dorothy. So she stayed in the kitchen, waiting for her grandmother to notice her.

Except her grandma hadn't heard Lindsay and didn't know she was there. Lindsay could see that her grandmother held something in her hand, but she couldn't tell what it was. Grandma Gina moved closer to the fireplace, but it wasn't light enough for Lindsay to see what she was doing.

Lindsay's eyes widened as her grandmother leaned forward and touched the fireplace. A sort of scraping sound followed and a brick slid out. It was a hiding place! A secret hiding place.

Fascinated, Lindsay watched as her grandmother slipped whatever she held in her hand inside the opening. The brick made the same sound as it went back into place.

"Grandma?"

Her hand over her heart, Grandma Gina whirled around. "Good heavens, child! You frightened me."

Lindsay hurried into the living room and toward the fireplace, but she couldn't figure out which brick her grandmother had moved.

"What are you doing up?"

Lindsay looked away from the fireplace. "I had a dream about Crazy Man Charlie."

"Who?"

"I heard stories about him at summer camp." She ran her fingers along the fireplace, trying to work out which brick had moved. "What did you hide in here, Grandma?"

"It's nothing, child."

"But I saw the brick move."

Her grandmother shook her head. "It was…just a trick of the moonlight."

"But, Grandma, I *saw*."

Her grandmother crouched down, meeting her eyes. "The stories frightened you."

Her wrinkled face was marked with the streaks of tears that glistened in the moonlight. "Grandma, are you crying?"

"No…no," her grandmother insisted. "Why would I be crying?"

"But that's what it looks like." Lindsay raised her hand to her grandmother's cheek and brushed her fingertips tentatively against the soft skin.

Her grandmother tried to smile, but her lower lip quivered.

"Are you sad?" Lindsay asked.

"A little," she whispered, and hugged Lindsay close, so close she could feel the beating of her grandma's heart.

"I'll draw you a picture, and then you won't be sad anymore."

"You sweet, sweet child. Now let me take you back to bed."

"I'm thirsty."

She released Lindsay and led her into the kitchen, where she took a glass from the cupboard and filled it with water.

Her grandma had let the tap run and the water was nice and cold. Lindsay gulped it down, then put the glass on the

counter. "What did you hide in the fireplace?" she asked again. She didn't understand why Grandma Gina was pretending like this.

Her grandmother gently stroked the hair from her face. "You didn't see anything."

"But I did." Walking over to the fireplace, Lindsay tried really hard to find the spot her grandmother had touched. She pushed and prodded at various bricks, but nothing moved.

Her grandmother joined her. "Lindsay, look at me."

Lindsay turned around.

Her grandmother crouched down again. The tears were back in her eyes and she hugged Lindsay tightly. "What you saw is our secret, all right?"

Lindsay nodded.

"But I want you to forget all about it."

Lindsay didn't know if she could.

Her grandmother held Lindsay's face in both hands and stared at her intently. "Promise me you'll never tell anyone what you saw."

"All right, Grandma, I won't tell anyone. I promise."

"Good." She kissed Lindsay's cheek. "Now let me tuck you back into bed."

One

"**W**e're doomed," Jacob Hansen said in sepulchral tones. He marched into the room, shaking his grizzled head.

"You might as well board up the entire town right now." Marta Hansen followed her husband into the dining room at Buffalo Bob's 3 OF A KIND. With the energy that so often accompanies righteousness, she plunked herself down at the table with the other members of the Buffalo Valley town council.

Joshua McKenna figured this kind of pessimism pretty much ensured that they wouldn't accomplish anything. Not that he blamed the couple. For nearly twenty years the Hansens, along with everyone else in Buffalo Valley, had watched the once-thriving farm community deteriorate, until now the town was barely holding on. The theater had closed first, and then the beauty shop and the florist and the hardware store… It hurt most when the catalog store pulled up stakes—that had been six years ago—and then the Morningside Café, the one decent restaurant in town, had closed for good.

Even now, Joshua missed Melissa's cooking. She'd

baked biscuits that were so light and fluffy they practically floated into your mouth. Joshua got hungry just thinking about those biscuits.

Businesses survived as long as they could on their continually diminishing returns—until they were driven to financial ruin and finally forced to close up shop. Families drifted away and farmland changed ownership, the bigger farms buying up the smaller ones. Large or small, everyone struggled these days with low agricultural prices. He had to hand it to the farmers, though. They were smart, and getting smarter all the time. Over the years, agricultural research and hardier strains had made it possible to urge a larger yield out of the land. Where an acre would once produce a hundred bushels, it was now possible to harvest almost twice that. Somehow, a lot of the farmers had managed to keep going—because they believed in their heritage and because they trusted in the future, hoping they'd eventually get a fair price for their crops. Since they stayed, a few of the businesses in town clung, too.

Joshua's was one of them, although he'd certainly been struggling for the last while. He sold used goods and antiques, and did repairs; in that area, at least, business was steady. It was his gift, he supposed, to be able to fix things. With money tight, people did whatever they could to avoid buying something new. He just wished his talent extended to fixing lives and rearranging circumstances. If it had, he'd start with his own family. Heaven knew his son needed help. His daughter and granddaughter, too. He didn't like to think about the changes in their lives during the past few years, and he hated the helpless feeling that came over him whenever he did.

His wife, Marjorie, had always dealt with the children, but she'd been gone ten years now. He often wondered if she'd recognize Buffalo Valley these days and wished he had her wisdom in dealing with its problems. She would've

been shocked to learn he'd been elected president of the town council. A position he hadn't sought, but one he'd assumed by default when Bill Wilson had to close his gas station and move to Fargo.

"We're doomed this time," Marta repeated, daring anyone to argue with her.

"This town's survived all these years. We'll hold on now." Hassie Knight, who owned Knight's Pharmacy, said emphatically.

Hassie was a born optimist and the one person in town who was sure to see even this situation in a positive light. If anyone could come up with a solution, it'd be Hassie, God bless her.

Like him, Hassie had experienced her share of grief. She'd buried her son, who'd been killed in Vietnam nearly thirty years ago, and not long afterward, had lost her husband. Carl Knight had died from complications of diabetes, but Hassie had always maintained that the real cause of death was a broken heart. Her daughter lived in Hawaii, and Joshua knew Valerie would like nothing better than to have her mother retire nearby. Thankfully, Hassie had resisted Valerie's efforts. The old woman was long past the age of retirement, but she did much more than fill prescriptions. Hassie was the closest thing the community had to a doctor, and folks from miles around came to her for medical advice. Yes, Hassie Knight was a popular woman, all right. It didn't hurt any that she served the best sodas he'd ever tasted. The old-fashioned kind from the fountain in the corner of her store. Chocolate sodas and good advice—those were her specialties.

"We've hung on for so many years, we're already dead and don't even have the sense to know it," Marta said caustically as she crossed her arms over her hefty bosom.

"Will you stop!" Joshua pounded the gavel on the tabletop with so much force, the ice in the water glasses danced. He sat back down and motioned to Hassie. "Would you take roll call?"

Hassie Knight's bones creaked audibly as she stood.

"Roll call? Now that's gonna be useful," Marta Hansen muttered. "That's like what's-his-name, that emperor, fiddling while Rome burned."

She was obviously mighty pleased with her classical allusion. Must've been on *Jeopardy* last night, Joshua thought.

"Nero. The emperor was Nero," he couldn't resist adding. Still, he hated to admit it, but Marta was right. Roll call was a waste of time; all they had to do was look around the table to know who was present and who wasn't. Hassie, the Hansens, Dennis Urlacher and him. Absent: Gage Sinclair and Heath Quantrill. Joshua stopped Hassie before she had a chance to start.

"Fine, we'll dispense with the usual formalities and get on with the meeting."

"Thank God *someone* in this town is willing to listen to reason," Marta said, glaring across the table at Hassie.

It was only natural that the town pessimist and the town optimist would be in constant opposition. "You and Jacob have as much to gain or lose as the rest of us," Hassie snapped. "A positive mental attitude would help."

"I'm positive," Jacob said with a nod. "Positive that Buffalo Valley is as dead as Eloise Patten."

"If she was going to up and die unexpected like that, the least she could've done was tell someone she wasn't well," Marta said in her usual righteous manner.

"That's the most ridiculous thing you've ever said—which is *really* saying something." Hassie's face reddened,

and Joshua could see she was having difficulty restraining her temper. The truth was, the Hansens exasperated him, too. How they'd managed to run the grocery during these hard times when they had such a negative outlook toward life was beyond him. Still, he was grateful their store had survived. Joshua didn't know what would happen if they ever decided to leave Buffalo Valley.

"All right, all right." Joshua wiped his brow with a stained white handkerchief. "We'll move on to new business."

With obvious reluctance, Hassie reclaimed her seat.

"We all know why we're here," Jacob said. "The school needs a teacher."

"Does anyone mind if I sit in?" Buffalo Bob asked, pulling out a chair before anyone could object.

Marta and Jacob glanced at each other and seemed to understand that if they raised a fuss, Hassie would make a point of asking Marta to leave, since she wasn't officially a member of the town council. Joshua suspected the only reason she attended the meetings was to advise Jacob on how to vote.

"We'd welcome your help," Joshua assured Bob.

Without a word Dennis Urlacher, who owned the Cenex Gas Station, shoved his chair aside to make room for him. Bob Carr was an ex-biker who'd settled in the town a couple of years earlier after winning the bar, grill and small hotel in a poker game. He'd immediately rechristened himself Buffalo Bob.

Joshua looked down at his notes. "As you all know, Eloise Patten is gone."

"She's more than gone," Marta Hansen interrupted. "She's dead!"

"Marta!" Joshua had taken about all he could from her. "The point is we don't have a teacher."

"Hire one." Buffalo Bob leaned back on two legs of his chair, as if he figured they were all overreacting to this crisis.

"No one's going to want to teach in a town that's dying," Jacob grumbled, shaking his head. "Besides, I never did think much of dividing up the schools. Bussing our grade-schoolers over to Bellmont and then having them send their high-schoolers to us was a piss-poor idea, if you ask me."

"We already did ask you," Joshua barked, no longer making any attempt to control his impatience. "It won't do any good to rehash what's already been decided and acted upon. Bussing the children has worked for the last four years, and would continue to do so if Eloise hadn't passed on the way she did."

"Eloise should've retired years ago," Marta complained under her breath.

"Well, thank God she didn't," Joshua said. "We owe her a lot." Eloise Patten had been a godsend to this community, and if no one else said it, he would. The schoolteacher had been the one to suggest splitting up the elementary and high-school students between the two towns. The Hansens' attitude was typical of the thinking that was detrimental to such progressive ideas. The small farming communities, or what remained of them, needed to rely on each other. It was either that or lose everything. If Buffalo Valley was going to survive when so many towns on the prairie hadn't, they had to learn to work together.

"We've got to find us a new teacher, is all." Dennis could be counted on to cut to the chase—to state the basic, unadorned facts. He owned and operated the only gas station left in town and wasn't much of a talker. When he did speak, it was generally worth listening to.

Joshua knew that his daughter, Sarah, and Dennis had some kind of romance going between them, despite the

decided efforts of his daughter to keep it a secret. Joshua didn't understand why she felt it was so all-fired important nobody know about this relationship. After her disastrous marriage, Joshua would've welcomed Dennis into the family. He suspected that Sarah's reluctance to marry Dennis had to do with her daughter, Calla, who was fourteen. A difficult age—as he remembered well.

"We could throw in living quarters, couldn't we?" Buffalo Bob was saying. "For the teacher?"

"Good idea." Joshua pointed the gavel at the hotel owner. "There's two or three empty houses close to the school."

"Nobody's going to want to live in those old places," Marta insisted. "They're full of mice and God knows what else."

"We can always clean one up."

The others nodded.

"In case no one's noticed, there's a teacher shortage in this state." This came from Jacob, and as if on cue, Marta nodded.

"We could always advertise," Hassie began tentatively.

"Advertise? We don't have that kind of money," Marta said in a sharp voice.

"If we don't advertise, what exactly *do* you suggest?" Joshua asked.

Jacob and Marta looked at each other. Jacob got heavily to his feet and leaned forward, bracing his hands on the edge of the table. "I think it's time we all admitted the truth. Buffalo Valley is doomed and there's not a damn thing we can do about it." Marta nodded again, a satisfied expression on her face.

His announcement was met with an immediate outburst from both Hassie and Buffalo Bob.

"Just a minute here!" Buffalo Bob shouted.

"I raised two children in this town," Hassie cried, "and

buried one. I'm not going to let Buffalo Valley die if it's the last thing I do. Any one of you who—"

"...invested my entire inheritance in this bar and grill," Buffalo Bob shouted in order to be heard above Hassie.

Joshua slammed the gavel down. "No one said anything about giving up."

"No teacher's gonna want to move here." Marta apparently felt obliged to remind them of this.

"We'll find a teacher." Joshua refused to let the Hansens' pessimism influence the meeting any longer.

"Look around you," Jacob Hansen said, gesturing at the greasy window that faced the main street.

Joshua didn't need to look; he confronted the evidence every day when he opened his shop. The boarded-up businesses. The cracked sidewalks, with weeds sprouting up through the cracks. The litter on the streets. Whatever community pride there'd once been had long since died.

"We aren't going to let the school close," Joshua stated emphatically.

"I second that!" Hassie said. A deep sense of relief showed on her face, and the determination in her voice matched Joshua's. He had lived his entire life in this place and he'd do whatever he could to save it. Come hell or high water, they'd find a teacher before school started up again at the end of August.

"I'll believe it when I see it," Jacob Hansen said just loudly enough for them all to hear.

"Well, then—prepare to believe," Joshua said grandly.

There was more life in Buffalo Valley than either of the Hansens suspected, and Joshua was going to prove it.

Lindsay Snyder felt the anger churning in her stomach, anger at her own foolishness as much as anything. With her

dogs sound asleep at her feet, she sat at her kitchen table and wrote in the pages of her journal. Whenever she was upset, she described her feelings; it helped her clarify them, helped her analyze what had happened and why. This time, though, she already knew the answers.

When she finished, she set the leather-bound book aside and stared sightlessly out her apartment window. But it wasn't the landscape she saw; it was her future.

Monte was never going to marry her.

She should have recognized it two years ago, and hadn't. She realized it was because she so desperately wanted to be his wife, wanted to have a family with him. She loved him, and wasn't marriage supposed to be the natural outcome of loving a man? But she'd allowed herself to see what she'd *hoped* to see. She'd allowed herself to believe she could convince him.

Monte hadn't lied to her, hadn't misled her. From the beginning, he'd told her he wasn't interested in marriage. He loved her, he said, but his divorce several years earlier had devastated him and he'd vowed not to repeat the experience. He'd never indicated in any way that he might change his mind. Lindsay knew there was only one person to blame for her unhappiness—and it wasn't Monte.

Soon—maybe six months—after their relationship had begun, she'd left him because he'd been adamant on the subject of marriage. He'd persuaded her to come back and she had, foolishly believing that eventually he'd change his mind and see things the way she did.

It hadn't happened.

The phone rang and Lindsay glanced at the caller ID, relieved and at the same time depressed to see that it wasn't his number.

"Hello," she mumbled into the phone.

"It's Maddy."

"I know."

"Hey, it's a beautiful summer afternoon and you sound like you've just lost your best friend. However, I know that can't be the case, 'cause I'm your best friend."

Lindsay sighed, wondering why Maddy had to seem so carefree and happy when her own world was falling apart. "Nothing's wrong. Let me amend that. Nothing's wrong that hasn't been wrong for the past two years."

"Ah, then this has to do with Monte. What happened?"

"Nothing." That much was true. "Monte and I went out to dinner last night and took a romantic ride in a horse-drawn carriage around Chippewa Square. The magnolias were blooming and Maddy…it was perfect. Until—"

"Until what?"

Lindsay squeezed her eyes shut because even saying the words caused her pain. "Until I made the mistake of mentioning the *future*. The way he reacted, you'd think that was a dirty word. The next thing I knew, he was angry with me and we were arguing. And then I saw what I should have recognized all along—Monte is never going to marry me."

At first Maddy said nothing. "Are you breaking it off?"

"Yes…I already did. It's over, Maddy."

"You don't sound absolutely certain of that."

"No, I mean it this time. Nothing he says is going to convince me to change my mind. I refuse to do this to myself any more."

"He told you from the very beginning that he wasn't going to get married again."

"I know, I know."

"I'm surprised you haven't moved in with him. I know that's what he wants."

But Lindsay realized now that even if she had, there still wouldn't have been any commitment, any permanence. She'd actually considered living with him, and felt only relief that she hadn't gone through with it. His feelings wouldn't have changed—and her own anguish would've been that much worse.

"So you broke it off for good?"

"It's over, Maddy. It's time I opened my eyes and faced reality. I refuse to put my life on hold any longer."

"Way to go!" Then Maddy sobered. "I know it's hard, but…"

While in high school, they'd frequently had sleepovers and lain awake talking about the men they'd marry. It'd all seemed so simple back then, and here they were, both nearly thirty and not a husband in sight.

"Remember when we were teenagers?" Lindsay couldn't keep from thinking about all those silly school-girl dreams.

Maddy snorted inelegantly. "We were what you'd call romantic idiots."

Lindsay shrugged wordlessly. It wasn't as though either of them thought marriage was essential to a woman's existence. But they both craved the closeness of a good marriage and the joys of having children. Maddy, at least, had an excuse. As a social worker for the state of Georgia, she worked long hours, looking out for the welfare of others. Almost all the overtime she put in was voluntary. Several nights a week, after work, she taught parenting classes for Project Family, a community-based organization. In addition, she mentored several troubled teenagers. Maddy wanted to save the world and she had a heart big enough to do it.

Lindsay had no such ambition. Following her high-

school graduation, she'd gone to college at the University of Georgia and roomed with Maddy for four years. Her degree was in French—a lot of good that had done her— with a minor in education. After graduation, she'd drifted from one job to another. The closest she'd come to using her French had been a summer job at the perfume counter in an upscale department store.

There'd been a few opportunities to employ her language skills—teaching conversational French to tourists, translating business documents—but nothing that felt right. Then, almost four years ago, the woman who worked in the accounting office of her uncle Mike's huge furniture store in Savannah had gotten sick and Lindsay had filled in. When Mrs. Hudson hadn't returned, Lindsay had taken over permanently.

"One day my prince will come." Maddy's voice sang its way through the telephone line. "And so will yours…"

After college, both girls had been twenty-three, and it seemed as if they had all the time in the world to find their soul mates. Now, seven years later, Lindsay had given up counting the number of weddings in which she and Maddy had served as bridesmaids. Ten, possibly more, so many that it had become a joke between them. Periodically Maddy would suggest a joint yard sale just to get rid of all the pastel satin dresses. Maybe their luck would finally change, she'd say with a laugh.

Then, a little more than two years ago, Lindsay's luck did change. Monte Turner had come to work as a salesman for her uncle. The minute they were introduced, Lindsay had fallen for him. Within a month she'd broken off her relationship with Chuck Endicott, which had never been more than a casual involvement. She hadn't dated anyone but Monte since.

She'd loved Monte, still did, but a two-year relationship had proved that he didn't want the same things out of life as she did. He wasn't interested in children, and the word *commitment* sent him running for cover. Lindsay had spent her entire life dreaming of both.

"Listen," Maddy said excitedly. "My boss insisted I take two weeks off. She's afraid I'm going to burn out if I don't get away. So, as of next Friday, I'm on vacation."

"Vacation." Lindsay couldn't help being envious.

"Come with me," Maddy urged. "You need to escape as much as I do."

Lindsay was tempted.

"If you're serious about breaking it off with Monte, then make it quick and clean. Dragging it out isn't going to do either of you any good."

Maddy was right and Lindsay instinctively knew it. "Where do you want to go? Europe?" Two weeks in Paris sounded heavenly.

"I can't afford that," Maddy said. Social workers were notoriously underpaid.

"What about a couple of weeks on St. Simons Island?" As one of the Golden Isles off the Georgia coast, St. Simons was a prime resort location.

"Paris is cheaper, for heaven's sake!"

Lindsay didn't exactly have money to spare, either. "Okay, where do you suggest?"

"How about a driving vacation? There's so many places in this country I've never seen."

That sounded good to Lindsay. Away was away, wherever they ventured. Their destination mattered little to her. Maddy had recently bought a new car and they could share expenses.

"I've always wanted to see Yellowstone Park," Maddy said.

"It's fabulous," Lindsay told her.

"You've been?"

"As a kid. You know my dad's from North Dakota—he was born and raised there. We drove out to see the old homestead a couple of times while I was growing up. Yellowstone Park isn't that far—at least I don't think it is. I must have been about ten the last time we went."

"I liked your grandfather," Maddie said quietly.

Three years ago, soon after the death of Lindsay's grandmother, Grandpa Snyder had grown disoriented and it was no longer safe for him to live alone. There was no longer any family left in the area, either Colbys—Gina's people—or Snyders. So Lindsay's parents had moved her grandfather from Buffalo Valley to a retirement center in Savannah, where he'd remained until his death the previous year. Lindsay had treasured that time with him, brief though it was. Because North Dakota was so far from Georgia and their visits infrequent, she'd barely known her Grandma and Grandpa Snyder.

At first her grandfather had painfully missed the Red River Valley. He'd spoken endlessly of his life there. Lindsay remembered that he'd called the land blessed, but then said living in North Dakota was like wrestling with an angel. You had to fight it before you found the blessing. He described seeing double rainbows after a fierce rainfall, and wild winter snowstorms that turned the sky as gray as gunmetal. He'd talked about the incredible sunsets, the heavens glowing orange and pink and red as far as the eye could see.

"I'd like to stop in Buffalo Valley," Lindsay said.

"Buffalo Valley?"

"In North Dakota. It's where my dad was raised."

"Sure. Let's do that."

"My grandparents' house is still there. It's never sold."

"The ol' homestead?"

"No," Lindsay said. "My grandparents sold the farm back in the early seventies and moved into town." Lindsay wasn't sure why their house hadn't sold. "From what I understand, the place has been listed with a reputable real estate company all this time." There had been talk of an estate sale, but Lindsay didn't know what had come of it.

"Then it's probably a good idea if we check it out," Maddy said.

Lindsay knew her uncle wouldn't mind her taking a vacation, and her family would be pleased when she told them her plans. Despite herself, she wondered what Monte would think.

She didn't have long to wait.

After four days, during which they'd pretended to ignore each other, Monte showed up at her office. Lindsay had known that eventually he would, and she'd been dreading the conversation all week. Again, her dread was mixed with an odd sense of longing.

"You're going where?" Monte demanded, obviously annoyed that he'd heard of her plans from someone else.

By now Lindsay was nearly starved for the sight of him and focused her attention on a roguish curl that fell across his forehead.

"On vacation," she told him as she moved about the compact room. It would be impossible to sit at her desk and not give herself away. She *wanted* him to react to her news, and at the same time recognized that she shouldn't.

He closed the door and leaned against it. "Isn't this a little extreme?"

"What?" She glanced over her shoulder as she slid a file into the four-drawer cabinet.

"I heard you and Maddy are driving across the country. Two women alone—it's not safe, Lindsay. If you're angry with me, fine. Be angry. But we both know you'll get over it soon enough. I already have. We had an argument. We've had them in the past and probably will again. Let's put it behind us and move on. But don't do anything stupid."

"I am over it," she assured him sweetly.

"Lindsay…"

"Our relationship is finished, Monte. I meant what I said."

"If that's what you want, fine," he responded, as if their relationship was of little importance to him. "Why don't you wait till I can take some time off and I'll go with you? This vacation with Maddy could be dangerous."

"We're capable, confident women. But thank you for your concern."

He hesitated. Lindsay continued filing.

"I really am sorry about Friday night." His voice was gentle. "We were both upset."

"I'm not upset." She turned her back on him and slipped an invoice into the appropriate file.

"You know how I feel about you."

He did love her; in her heart of hearts she believed that. She would never have stayed with him this long otherwise. Seeing him now, so handsome, his expression so caring, she found it hard to think of her life without him. "Marry me, Monte," she pleaded before she could stop herself.

His eyes filled with regret.

As soon as she'd said the words, she wanted to grab them back. She'd done it again, tried to change a situation that couldn't be changed. Sorrow washed over her and she shook her head hopelessly.

"You're going without me?" he murmured.

"Without you." That was the only way she could think clearly. The only way she could teach her heart to forget him.

"When are you leaving?" he asked in a resigned voice.

"Saturday morning."

Monte buried his hands deep inside his pants pockets. "Two weeks?"

She nodded.

"Will you phone me? At least give me that much. Just a quick call so I'll know you're all right."

Lindsay shook her head again. "Please, don't make this any more difficult than it already is." She couldn't. Talking to him would be too painful, too risky.

"I'll miss you," Monte said quietly. He hesitated before he turned and walked out the door.

It was after ten once Gage Sinclair had parked the tractor and finished cleaning his equipment. He'd been in the field from dawn to dusk cutting alfalfa, and he was weary to the bone. Funny how a man could work until he was so damned tired he could fall into bed without removing his boots, yet still experience the exhilaration that comes with pride.

As he walked toward the house, he saw his mother sitting on the porch, her fingers busy with her latest knitting project, probably another sweater for him. Generally she was in bed by this time, since she was up before dawn, feeding and caring for the animals and the garden. With the hottest part of summer almost upon them, it made sense to finish chores in the cool of the morning.

He'd been looking for Kevin, but his younger brother— half brother, actually—was nowhere to be seen. It was too damn hot to be holed up inside the house, and he couldn't hear the television or what teenagers called music these days.

The boy was an object of frustration to Gage. In another

few years, Kevin would be taking over the farm. Naturally Gage would be around to guide and advise him, but the land belonged to Kevin and he would have to assume his responsibilities.

Gage had been fifteen when his mother remarried after ten years as a widow, and eighteen when the boy had been born. John Betts had died when Kevin was five, so Gage had been more father than brother to the seventeen-year-old.

Leta set aside her knitting and stood as he approached the house. Gage realized she'd been waiting for him. "Hassie phoned about the council meeting," she told him, confirming his suspicion.

Gage made no comment.

"Don't you want to know what happened?"

"I figure you're going to tell me." Gage stepped onto the porch, but tired as he was, resisted sitting down for fear that once he did, he wouldn't want to get up.

His mother's brief shrug told him he'd made a wise decision in avoiding the council meeting. If Joshua McKenna wanted to hold an emergency meeting and have him there, he'd need to schedule one when Gage wasn't in the middle of cutting alfalfa.

"Before you tell me, I had a thought about what to do once school starts," he said. With Eloise gone, it was unlikely the high school would be in operation. Unrealistic and selfish though it might be, he wished the teacher had held on one last year, until Kevin was finished.

"I know what you're going to say."

Not surprised, Gage merely glanced at her. After all, they'd had this conversation before.

"You want me to home-school him," his mother continued.

"It's for the best."

"Fiddlesticks! It's his senior year. I know Kevin will be taking over the farm, but he's entitled to a decent high-school education—and some college if we can afford it. I was thinking we could send him to finish high school in Fargo. He could live with your uncle Jim and aunt Mary Lou."

"We'll have to see." He considered his brother spoiled as it was. Letting Kevin spend the next nine months in the city, being coddled by relatives, wasn't the way to prepare him for his life as a farmer. "You didn't mention that to him, did you?"

"No." But she hesitated, as if there was more and whatever it was, he wouldn't want to hear.

"What else?"

"Kevin took the truck again without telling me where he was going."

Despite his earlier decision, Gage gave in and sank down on the top porch step. "Should be fairly obvious where he went, don't you think?"

"Jessica's," his mother sighed.

His teenage brother was in love for the first time. Knowing it was his duty, Gage had assumed the unenviable task of explaining a man's responsibility when it came to protecting a woman from pregnancy—and these days, protecting both of them from disease. Their mother wasn't likely to hand the teenager a condom. Gage had.

At the time, Kevin had been angry and belligerent, but he'd taken the condom. Gage wasn't fooled. Hell, it wasn't *that* long ago that he'd been seventeen himself.

All summer, whenever he could, Kevin slipped away in order to be with his true love. No doubt, Jessica's parents were as concerned about the relationship as Gage was. And about the school situation.

If the high school closed for good, Gage suspected most

families would ship their teens off to live with relatives. Some would end up being home-schooled, but Gage knew his mother was right. With Kevin, it wouldn't work. The boy was still too undisciplined to learn without the structure of classes, exams and deadlines. He preferred to spend his time drawing—or with his girlfriend.

"Hassie's going to contact the teacher's union about getting a replacement," Leta told him. "That's what they decided at the meeting." His mother had the utmost confidence in the pharmacy owner, her closest friend. Gage's respect for Hassie was high, but she wasn't a miracle worker. It was nearly July and school was scheduled to start again toward the end of August. He hated to be a pessimist, but it simply wasn't going to happen. Not at this late date. No doubt a teacher would be found eventually, but in the meantime they had no choice but to close the school.

"You have to have faith," Leta told him, as if simply believing would make everything turn out right.

Gage nodded.

"The good Lord knows what He's doing."

"If that's the case, then I wonder if He's been paying attention to the price of grain?"

"Gage!"

He wasn't going to argue with his own mother, but if the good Lord had any intention of finding a high-school teacher for Buffalo Valley High School, He'd better start working fast. Besides, if Gage was going to indulge in a bit of wishful thinking, he might as well add his own requirements. *Send a teacher,* he mused, gazing at the heavens, *but not just any teacher.* He wanted someone young and pretty and single. Someone smart *and* loving. Someone who liked kids and animals. *Send a woman just for me.*

He nearly laughed out loud. Talk about an imagination.

He attributed the prayer, if it could be called that, to weariness, and to the fact that his little brother had probably lost his virginity that summer. No, more than that—to the fact that his brother had found someone to love, and he hadn't.

Two

Sarah Stern waited until her father had fallen asleep in front of the television set, snoring loudly enough to wake the dead. Calla, her teenage daughter, had shut herself in her room and was listening to music. Restless and worried, Sarah phoned Dennis, then paced the kitchen until she saw his headlights in the distance.

Hugging her arms about her waist, she slipped silently out of the house and ran through the open yard. When he saw her, Dennis leaned across the cab and opened the passenger door and Sarah climbed inside. "Thanks for coming," she whispered.

"Thanks for calling."

As soon as the door closed and the dome light went out, Sarah was in his arms. Despite everything she'd promised herself, she let her mouth meet his. Their lips were touching, twisting, turning, the kiss greedy. Intense. When they finished, Sarah's shoulders were heaving.

Dennis leaned his head back and his chest expanded with a deep sigh. "I needed that."

Sarah didn't want to admit it, but she had, too.

"What happened at the meeting this afternoon?" she asked. Her father had barely said a word all evening, and Sarah didn't know what to think. When she'd asked, he'd put her off, as if to suggest she shouldn't worry about matters that weren't her concern. Only she *was* concerned, and rightly so. If a teacher wasn't hired soon, Sarah would be forced to home-school Calla. If that happened, it was unlikely either of them would survive the school year. At fourteen, her daughter was a handful, and she had a mouth on her that wouldn't quit.

Like mother, like daughter. Sarah supposed this was what she got for giving her own parents so much grief as a teenager.

"We're going to find another teacher," Dennis assured her.

Those were the exact words her father had said. With no explanation, no details.

"Where?" Sarah asked point-blank. "You're going to find a teacher *where?*"

Dennis shrugged as they drove away from the house.

"You don't know, do you?"

"We aren't going to close the school. I promise." He pulled off to the side of the road and turned off the engine. He reached for her, weaving his fingers into her hair and dragging her mouth to his. It was like this when they'd been apart for any time, this explosive need that threatened to burst into spontaneous combustion with the first few kisses. His mouth was demanding and persuasive, and Sarah answered his need and echoed it with her own.

Burying her face in his shoulder, she struggled to keep her mind on the reason for her call. "It sounds as if all the council did was argue. Did anyone suggest a concrete plan?"

"No. Well…not exactly. Except Hassie's going to make some calls."

"That's fine, but it's no guarantee of anything." Exactly what Sarah had feared. "There happen to be very few available and qualified teachers in this area. Is a teacher supposed to drop from the sky or something?"

Dennis said nothing, then murmured, "Honey, don't worry."

Sarah hated it when men, especially men she loved and trusted, placated her like this. It was bad enough that her father didn't recognize the seriousness of her concerns, but Dennis didn't seem to appreciate it, either. The future of the entire town was at stake, and for some reason both her father and Dennis seemed to think everything would take care of itself.

"Hassie's talking to the teacher's union about getting someone here before school starts."

Sarah groaned; she couldn't help it. All anyone seemed to be doing was *talking*. "Don't any of you realize school is scheduled to start in six weeks?"

"A teacher will turn up before then."

Sarah brushed her long hair away from her shoulder, and resisted the urge to bury her face in his shoulder again. "I wish to hell at least one person on the council would be realistic."

"Your dad—"

"My dad thought everyone would want to play pinochle at my mother's wake." In a crisis, Joshua McKenna was useless. That he was president of the town council gave her no confidence whatsoever. "It's as though this entire community wants to pretend there's nothing wrong, and that somehow things will get fixed by themselves."

Dennis said nothing, which wasn't unusual. He sat with his hands clutching the steering wheel. They'd known each other so long, Sarah could tell what he was thinking. He

hated arguments. And evenings when they met, fighting was the last thing either of them was interested in.

"I'm sorry," Sarah whispered, and ran her palm down the length of his arm. She'd much rather kiss than argue, but she was justifiably worried about Calla's future. And her own... She didn't want to leave Buffalo Valley. This was home, and she felt safe here. Safe from the outside world, the doubts and fears. Safe from the mistakes she'd made the one and only time she'd ventured beyond this valley.

Dennis placed his arm around her shoulder and she rested her head against his side. It felt good to be with him, protected. Sheltered. She shouldn't feel this way, shouldn't allow herself the luxury of depending on Dennis, but she was afraid—for Calla and herself. Back when she was eighteen, Sarah couldn't wait to leave Buffalo Valley and find her own way in the world. She'd moved to Minneapolis and found a job paying minimum wage in a fabric store. A second job as cashier in an all-night service station had helped pay the rent. It was there, late one night, that she'd met Willie Stern.

He was a crazy kind of guy—impulsive, unpredictable—and she'd fallen for him hard. Within a month, they were living together and not much after that Sarah was pregnant. The only person she'd told was her younger brother, and Jeb had driven to Minneapolis and insisted Willie marry her. If it hadn't been for her brother, Sarah was convinced Willie would have left her high and dry. Perhaps that would have been for the best.

Later, after Calla was born, Willie didn't want her working. Sarah had learned about quilting from her mother and from her experience in the fabric store. She'd started making quilts and selling them out of their apartment. Willie never did understand why anyone would pay her for them, but he didn't

complain about the extra money. In addition to his part-time job as a shoe salesman, he played back-up guitar in a couple of bar bands—initially part of his appeal for Sarah—and his earnings were erratic.

It didn't take long for her marriage to fall apart—and for her husband to bring them to the edge of bankruptcy. Sarah saw an attorney when she learned Willie had gotten another woman pregnant. Beaten down, discouraged and with a four-year-old daughter in tow, Sarah had returned to Buffalo Valley, to her childhood home. She still lived with her father. She'd continued to make quilts and was passionate about the work she did. Her love for the creative process of blending textures and color, adapting traditional patterns and forming her own designs, had grown over the years. So had her talent, if not her income.

She rarely heard from Willie these days, and that was how she preferred it.

Dennis ran his index finger down the side of her face and coaxed her mouth open with his. "It's been a while," he whispered, his hand cupping her breast.

"I know." She hadn't called him in six weeks. It was cruel of her to rely on him, to reach out to him with her concerns, when she didn't believe they had a future, but Dennis Urlacher was her greatest weakness. As often as she told herself it was necessary to break free, she couldn't seem to do it.

"Why did you wait so long?" he asked.

Sarah didn't want to answer and hung her head, wishing now that she'd resisted the urge to call him. He'd come without the least hesitation. Any time, night or day, she could phone and he'd drop whatever he was doing and come to her. It'd been that way for nearly two years.

She was no good for Dennis. There were things he

didn't know about her. Things she couldn't tell him or anyone, not even her father or Jeb. Things not even Calla knew. She and Dennis should never have become involved, should never have crossed the physical barrier. He was five years younger, and her brother's best friend.

She'd known for a long time how he felt about her, and discouraged him, rejected his efforts to date her. For a number of years she was able to ignore her own growing attraction to him. Then Jeb had nearly been killed in a farming accident and while her brother lay in a hospital fighting for his life, Dennis had joined the family in their vigil. He'd been there, so strong and confident, so reassuring.

That was when she'd lowered her guard and they'd become lovers. After that, it was impossible to go back. Impossible to pretend she had no feelings for him, and impossible to deny their physical need for each other.

And yet she insisted their relationship remain private. Not because she was ashamed of Dennis, but because she was ashamed of herself.

Sometimes Sarah suspected her father knew about her and Dennis, but if so, he never said a word. Calla was completely oblivious, and for that Sarah was grateful. Jeb had always known, but the subject of Dennis and her had never been discussed.

Dennis wove his hands into her thick, dark hair and angled her face to his. He kissed her again, slow and deep. "Come home with me." His voice was slurred with longing.

"No…"

He didn't argue with her, didn't try to persuade her; instead, he kissed her until she moaned softly and turned more fully in his arms, wrapping herself in his embrace.

After a while Dennis lifted his head and held her gaze. His love shone on her, poured over her like sunshine. It'd

been six weeks since they were last together. Six weeks filled with long, lonely nights in which she'd hungered for him and denied them both. Even now, if she insisted, he'd release her and drive away without a word.

Unable to refuse herself or him, she raised her fingertips to the pulse in his neck and smiled softly back. Dennis's brown eyes darkened with desire.

Their kisses took on a renewed urgency then, and when his tongue found hers, she welcomed it; at the same time she wanted to weep in abject frustration.

It was going to happen, the way it always did, because she was too weak to tell him no. Too weak to deny herself his love. And too weak to tell him the truth.

"Are you going to sleep your life away?" Lindsay chided as she set a plastic cup of steaming coffee on Maddy's nightstand.

Her friend rolled over and stared up at Lindsay through half-closed eyes. "What time is it?" she mumbled. She sat up slowly and reached for the coffee.

"It's eight o'clock," Lindsay told her. Sitting on the bed opposite Maddy's, she crossed her legs and sipped her own coffee. They'd arrived in Minneapolis the day before, and after finding a motel, had gone straight to the Mall of America. Savannah had its share of shopping malls, but nothing that compared to the four-hundred plus stores and amusement park inside this one. After they'd checked out the stores, they'd screamed their way through a couple of the more spectacular rides, visited Camp Snoopy and bought souvenirs for their nieces and nephews. Their excursion had ended with dinner and a movie, and all without leaving the massive mall.

"It's eight already? Can't be," Maddy protested.

"Sure is." Lindsay had always liked mornings—even as a teenager. It was a trait she didn't share with her best friend. Maddy woke up one brain cell at a time, as her mother always said. But she had far more energy in the evenings than Lindsay did. Maybe it was in their genes, she thought, since she was descended from farmers—on her dad's side, anyway—and Maddy from city folk.

"Will we make Buffalo Valley today?" Maddy asked, finally tossing aside the bedspread and heading toward the bathroom.

"We will if you get a move on." Her own bags were not only packed but loaded in the car. She'd awakened at six and sat out in the morning sunshine by the motel pool, drinking a first cup of coffee and mulling over the things her grandfather had told her about North Dakota and Buffalo Valley. When he'd arrived in Savannah, he'd been confused and unhappy. In time, he'd adjusted somewhat but it seemed to help to talk about home, and Lindsay had been a willing listener.

Her grandfather had spoken endlessly of fertile land and abundant crops, showed her photographs of a land with a huge expanse of sky above it and fields that stretched to the far horizon. What Lindsay remembered most were his stories of blizzards and his descriptions of the wind. He'd told her more than once that nowhere else in the lower forty-eight states did the wind blow as strong or as fierce as it did in the Dakotas.

He'd said it wasn't uncommon for the wind to roar at forty miles an hour for a day or longer, and that it could turn soggy ground into dust in a matter of hours. Lindsay didn't understand what could make a person stay in such a place, but her grandfather had loved his home as intensely as he had his family.

While Maddy dressed, Lindsay studied the maps. By her calculations, they should arrive in Buffalo Valley by late afternoon. From Minneapolis they'd drive toward Fargo, and take Highway 29 to Grand Forks, get onto Highway 2 and go as far as Devils Lake, then head north from there.

As she refolded the maps, she glanced at the telephone.

"Don't you dare!" Maddy said, framed in the bathroom doorway, the handle of her toothbrush sticking out of her mouth.

"What?"

"You were thinking of calling Monte."

Lindsay didn't admit or deny it, but that was exactly what she'd had in mind. Cutting him out of her life was a hundred times more difficult than she'd imagined it would be. He'd been an important part of her everyday life, and she felt lost without him. If it was this difficult now, she could only imagine how much harder it would be once she returned to Savannah.

"You ready to leave?" Maddy asked, as if Lindsay had been the one holding them up.

"Ready." While Lindsay wore leggings and an over-sized T-shirt, Maddy had dressed in a bright yellow shorts outfit that emphasized her long legs and sleek build. They'd often been mistaken for sisters because Lindsay was tall and blond, too.

By eight-thirty they were on the road, music blaring. They sang along—to Janis Joplin, the Stones, early Dylan. Old songs but good ones. And good traveling music.

They ate a late lunch outside Grand Forks, then made their way west to Devils Lake. As far as Lindsay could tell, they were about an hour from Buffalo Valley. The minute they drove north toward her father's boyhood home,

Lindsay grew quiet. All she could see from the road, in either direction, was field after field of wheat, moving with the wind, rippling like waves on the sea.

The temperature had soared; it was close to a hundred degrees, and the Bronco's air-conditioning system blowing at full speed couldn't keep the heat completely at bay. Lindsay didn't mind; in fact, she loved it. Loved the bright intensity of the sun. Loved the sight of wheat fields and this land where her grandparents had forged a good life. She was conscious of gazing upon her own heritage, and with it came a keen sense—an intuition, almost—that North Dakota would help her discover the woman she really was.

"Dad said we should check in with Hassie Knight when we reach town," Lindsay mentioned. A John Mellencamp CD ended, and they turned off the music.

"Hassie," Maddy repeated. "What an unusual name."

Lindsay didn't remember meeting Hassie, but that wasn't so odd, since the last time she'd visited Buffalo Valley she'd only been ten. "She runs the town's pharmacy and is apparently something of an institution," Lindsay told her. "The pharmacy's the old-fashioned kind with a soda fountain."

"I haven't seen one of those in years," Maddy said.

"Me, either." Lindsay's comment was absentminded, her thoughts suddenly distracted by Monte and their impasse. "Hassie has the key to my grandparents' house. I told Dad I'd check it out while we're here."

They rode in silence, until Maddy said, "You're thinking about him again, aren't you?"

Lindsay stared out the window at the wheat fields. "Yes. I'm worried about what'll happen once I get home. If I was at the store now, he'd be making excuses to come into accounting, chipping away at my resolve, and before I knew it, everything would be back the way it was."

Maddy sighed. "You've heard me say this before, so bear with me. Either you accept the fact that Monte's never going to marry you and go on as you were or you break off the relationship entirely. I know you *have* broken up with him, but I also know you want to take him back. Don't. Because you'll never get what you need from him."

"You make it sound so simple," Lindsay protested.

"It *is* simple," Maddy countered, "but that doesn't mean it's easy."

"How can I avoid him?" Lindsay cried out in frustration. "We work in the same place. It's impossible not to see him every day." It wasn't likely her uncle would fire his best salesman over what he considered a lovers' spat. Nor would she want him to. Still, it made for an uncomfortable situation all around. Naturally she could look for work elsewhere, but she enjoyed her job and there were benefits in working for her uncle that she didn't want to relinquish.

"That isn't the real problem though, is it?" Maddy asked.

Briefly Lindsay closed her eyes. "No. I...I've broken up with Monte once before—a year and a half ago, remember?— and I'm afraid the same thing's going to happen again. I told myself it was over and I meant it. I insisted that nothing he could say or do, short of arriving with a wedding license, would make me change my mind."

"He wore you down then and you're afraid he'll do it again."

Lindsay nodded. Monte had pleaded with her, sent her cards, gifts, flowers, courted her. He wanted to maintain their relationship, but he wanted it on his terms. And he liked things just the way they'd always been. No change and no commitment. No formality and no promises.

"What's wrong with me, Maddy?" Lindsay wailed. "Am I really so weak?"

"No." Maddy's response was emphatic.

"Then why am I stuck in a relationship that makes me this miserable?"

Maddy studied the road. "I'm a social worker, not a counselor, but I'm also your friend. It's like I said, either you accept what Monte's willing to offer, or you get out of the relationship. And stay out."

"I don't know if I can," she murmured. Monte had already made it clear. He didn't intend to lose her, nor would he give her what *she* wanted. "He genuinely cares about me, and he knows I care for him, too."

"I realize all that," Maddy concurred, "but he's using you. You're convenient, fun and you love him. He needs that. He needs *you.*"

"But not enough to marry me and have children with me." She continually had to remind herself of that. She envied her sisters their families. Whenever she spent time with her nieces and nephews, she came away with a hollow feeling deep inside. A longing for children of her own.

Maddy's look was sympathetic.

"I'm watching the best years of my life go down the drain," Lindsay said. "I want children. I really do." That was the crux of the matter. With her thirtieth birthday fast approaching, Lindsay was beginning to feel a sense of urgency, a desire to anchor her life with a husband and family.

"Well, then, the only way you'll ever be free of him is to stick to your guns. You've broken it off. Don't change your mind, and don't let him change it for you."

They drove in silence for ten or fifteen minutes, each caught up in her own thoughts. The plains continued, mile after mile of flat golden land, with an occasional farmhouse in the distance. Lindsay remembered her grandfather telling her that what he missed most about life on the farm

was the solitude. And the silence. It was all the people crowding in around him at the retirement center that had made the adjustment so difficult. She hadn't really understood what he'd meant until now, as she gazed at these acres of wheat, rippling lightly in the hot wind. They hadn't seen another car in some time and hadn't yet seen anyone in the fields.

As they approached Buffalo Valley, Lindsay noted with surprise that the highway didn't go through town anymore, the way it had in years past. A sign from the main thoroughfare pointed in the direction of Buffalo Valley, which was located off the road. Maddy slowed the car and made the right-hand turn.

Before Lindsay left Savannah, her parents had warned her that Buffalo Valley had changed, but nothing could have prepared her for the shock.

"My goodness," she whispered as they drove down the main street. There were potholes in the road and the pavement was badly cracked. A number of the stores were boarded up. The large plastic sign for the catalog store was torn, and half of it was missing. The windows were smudged and dirty. The movie theater, with its sign advertising twenty-five cent popcorn, had obviously been vandalized. At the end of the road, the gas station with its old-fashioned rounded pumps looked like it belonged on a postcard from the 1950s. It appeared to be in use; they'd seen another one on their way into town, and that was boarded up.

The most prominent business was Buffalo Bob's 3 OF A KIND Bar & Grill & Hotel.

"At least there's a place we can spend the night," Maddy said with what sounded like relief.

The only brick building in town was the bank, which

still seemed to be in operation. The grocery was next to that, and something called the "Old Country Store," which sold antiques and such. A sign in the window boasted that there wasn't anything Joshua McKenna couldn't repair.

"That must be the pharmacy," Maddy said as she parked the Bronco on the side of the street. Compared to the other businesses, the drugstore looked clean and fresh. Painted white, it stood out like a beacon in the center of town. Two large pots of flowering red geraniums bloomed by the door.

Knight's Pharmacy was exactly as her dad had recounted, with matching white benches below the large windows. The only thing that had faded was the semicircle of gold lettering on the glass. A large sign propped against the corner of one window read TEACHER WANTED.

"I don't know about you," Lindsay said, "but I could use a nice tall vanilla ice-cream soda."

"I could use something," Maddy agreed, and followed her inside.

Despite its bare wooden floors and old-fashioned hanging lights, the store was a full-service pharmacy selling a little of everything—shampoo and toiletries, postcards and souvenirs, boxed candy, hardware items and such novelties as colorful glass angels with little suction cups to place in a window.

"Can I help you?" an older woman called from the back of the store. The actual pharmacy was in the rear, built up six or eight inches so the proprietor could keep an eye on anyone who entered.

"Hassie Knight?" Lindsay asked the old woman, who was tall and spare, dressed in a cotton shirtwaist dress. Her wiry silver hair was neatly tucked behind her ears.

The woman nodded. "Who might you be?"

"Lindsay Snyder…"

"Gina's granddaughter!"

Hassie hurried out from behind the counter and held out her arms as if greeting long-lost family. "Your father phoned and told me you were planning to drop by. My, oh my, let me take a good look at you."

Before Lindsay could object, she was wrapped in a warm embrace. "This is my friend Maddy...."

"Pleased to meet you, Maddy." Hassie hugged her, too.

"Oh, my, it's certainly good to see you. Set yourself down at the counter and let me make you the best soda in two hundred miles." She led them to the far side of the pharmacy. Not needing a second invitation, Lindsay and Maddy slid onto the stools. The mahogany counter was polished to a fine sheen. Lindsay had never seen another counter like it—except in old movies.

"I have the key to the house, but I hope you're not planning to spend the night there," Hassie said as she scooped vanilla ice cream into tall, narrow glasses.

"Oh, no. Dad told me we'd need to find other accommodation."

"Buffalo Bob will fix you up," Hassie assured them both. "Now, don't let his appearance give you any worry. He's gentle as can be."

Lindsay and Maddy shared a suspicious glance.

Hassie set the two soda glasses on the counter. "Drink up," she urged, giving them each a glass of ice water, as well.

"How many people live in Buffalo Valley these days?" Maddy asked, between long sips.

Hassie hesitated for a moment. "Thirty years ago we had around five hundred or so, counting the farmers and their families. Saturday evenings, this town was bustling."

"And now?"

Hassie shrugged. "Less than half that, I'd guess. Closer

to two hundred would be more like it. The last twenty years have been hard on farmers. Real hard."

Lindsay nodded. "I see you're looking for a teacher," she said next, motioning toward the sign in the window.

Hassie perked up right away. "Either of you interested?"

"Sorry," Maddy said, raising one hand. "I've already got a job."

"What's it pay?" Lindsay didn't know why she bothered to ask. Curiosity, she supposed. Her dad had told her the town was dying and she shouldn't expect much. Nevertheless, she'd been surprised when they arrived; Buffalo Valley was a sad little town not unlike several others they'd passed that day, but her impressions of it, based on twenty-year-old memories, were still so vivid. Reality hadn't quite penetrated yet or displaced the earlier image that lived in her mind. At one time, Buffalo Valley had been the picture of small-town America, with a flag flying high above the post office and banners across Main Street. The summer her family had come to visit, Lindsay remembered that the high school had won the state football championship and proudly announced it with a huge banner strung between the pharmacy and the grocery store across the street.

"You applying for the job?" Excitement flashed in Hassie's blue eyes.

"No, no." Lindsay laughed and shook her head.

"We're in real need of a high-school teacher," the pharmacist said, leaning her elbows on the counter. "As you might've noticed, we've fallen upon hard times here."

Lindsay had noticed.

"You have a minor in education, don't you?" Maddy reminded her.

Lindsay glared at her friend.

"We need a teacher in the worst way." Hassie gazed at her, eyes bright with hope.

Move to Buffalo Valley? *Her?* As a teacher? It was enough to make Lindsay choke on her drink.

Three

Gage Sinclair had spent the morning riding the field cultivator down the long rows of maturing corn. He had nearly a thousand acres planted in corn, two hundred less than the previous year. If the weather held, he could expect to clear a hundred bushels per acre, but if there was one thing he'd learned in his years of farming, it was not to count his bushels before the harvest.

His mother was waiting for him when he parked the cultivator and climbed down. Days like this he had a thirst that wouldn't quit. He'd taken a half gallon of iced tea with him, but that had disappeared quickly.

"Lunch is ready," she called when she saw him.

"I'll be there in a minute," he called back, looking around for his half brother.

Gage hadn't seen Kevin all morning, and he suspected the boy had stolen away to be with Jessica again.

Gage washed up, then walked into the kitchen, inhaling the mouthwatering aroma of freshly baked bread. His mother routinely baked bread and cinnamon rolls on Saturday mornings.

"Where's Kevin?" he asked, pulling out a chair.

Leta glanced up, surprised. "I thought he was with you."

"I told him to change the oil in the pick-up when he finished his chores," he said between enormous bites of his sandwich. It'd been eight hours since he'd last eaten and he felt hollow inside. It was going to take more than a couple of roasted chicken sandwiches to fill him up.

"He did that a couple of hours ago." Leta turned her back to him and busied herself with something he couldn't see, but Gage wasn't fooled.

"You talked to anyone in town lately?" he asked. He didn't need to elaborate; they both knew he was referring to the crisis with the school.

"No," Leta mumbled. "Don't worry, Gage. Everything will work out."

Her optimism and faith had become an irritation to him, although he should be accustomed to both by now. Hassie Knight wasn't any better. They seemed to believe that, somehow or other, a new teacher would be found to replace Eloise Patten. As if hiring a replacement was a simple, everyday occurrence. Gage knew it wasn't going to happen. "Mom, it would be doing Kevin a disservice to send him away to finish high school. It's time he accepted responsibility for the farm."

"I agree."

"Then you'll consider letting him home-school?" Gage was well aware of all the problems with that solution. He knew it wasn't ideal, especially for Kevin. But it was the best he'd come up with.

His mother sighed. "We've already gone over this countless times, and my position hasn't changed."

"You can't keep ignoring the realties." Gage wolfed down the second sandwich before the discussion ruined his

appetite. Moving Kevin in with his aunt and uncle wasn't the right solution. He should be learning more about the everyday operation of the farm. True, the boy deserved a decent education, and Gage was willing to see him through high school—some college, if possible—but this land technically belonged to Kevin, not Gage. Unfortunately, his half brother had some difficult lessons to learn. The land didn't hold his heart, not the way it should. At this point in his life, Kevin thought about only two things: Jessica and his sketchbook. He did what was asked of him, but with little pride and less joy.

Gage, on the other hand, couldn't imagine doing anything else. Farming was his life and like generations before him, he felt most alive when his eyes were filled with grit, his lips chapped and his neck red with sunburn. The land sustained his soul. If he never left North Dakota again, it would suit him just fine. He knew plenty of farmers who'd lived their entire lives without ever traveling outside the state. Whether you raised crops or livestock, the land meant responsibility, day in, day out. A man didn't leave behind what was most important to him.

"Kevin's probably drawing up in the hayloft," Leta said.

"Not in this heat." Drawing was all well and good, but it wasn't *serious,* not for them. Not like farming. But Gage couldn't force Kevin to care about something he obviously didn't. He lived with the hope that eventually the boy would appreciate the rhythm of life played out each year on the farm. That he'd learn to see the particular beauty that was so much a part of his inheritance.

"I need to drive into town this afternoon," his mother told him when he'd finished lunch. She hesitated, then added, "You could use a haircut."

Gage ran his hand through his hair, knowing she was

right. Cutting hair wasn't something she especially liked; she'd do it, but preferred if he had Hassie take a pair of scissors to his thick head.

"I've got things to do."

"Whatever it is can wait."

His mother didn't disagree with him often. Suggesting he drive her into town was her way of telling him he'd been working too many hours, and it was time for a break.

"Fine." She was generally right about matters such as this, and he'd learned to heed her wisdom.

She patted him on the shoulder as she walked into the bedroom to gather her things.

Grumbling under his breath, Gage washed, changed his shirt and dragged a brush through his hair. It was nearly a month since he'd last been to town, not that there was much to see these days. He'd have Hassie cut his hair, if she had time, and then share a beer or two and some conversation with whoever was over at Buffalo Bob's.

"I left a note for Kevin," his mother told him when he joined her. She had a basket of eggs over her arm, her purse and a vase full of flowers. The eggs and flowers were for Hassie in exchange for the haircut. Like him, Leta never expected anything without payment. As a farmer, Gage often skimped on luxuries, but he'd never run short on pride.

Gage turned on the car radio as he drove into Buffalo Valley. KFGO, "the Mighty 790" AM radio station in Fargo, played country music, which Gage and Leta both enjoyed. Working out in the fields, Gage rarely listened to the radio. He didn't need music when he could hear a melody in the wind. Besides, the radio distracted him. The time he spent on the tractor helped him sort out the answers to life, answers he found in silence.

It was a thirty-minute ride into town.

"You recognize that car?" His mother motioned toward the new Bronco parked in front of the pharmacy.

"Can't say I do." A new car would have been cause for celebration in Buffalo Valley. The only person he could think of with enough money to squander on a car would be Heath Quantrill, but the banker wasn't likely to park outside Hassie's.

"My!" his mother exclaimed, "look how clean it is."

Most folks didn't bother to wash their vehicles more than once or twice a year, if that. No need to show off the rust. In any case, it was a waste of time, since a vehicle parked near a barn would be caked in mud again as soon as it was driven out of the yard.

Gage parked a few spaces away, not wanting to emphasize the contrast between his battered green truck and the shiny new Bronco. His diesel truck had turned over two hundred thousand miles last month. John had bought it shortly before Kevin was born, Gage remembered. It'd been used ever since.

Gage had hoped to replace it last autumn, but grain prices had been down, just like the year before and the year before that. He'd eke another six or eight months out of this old truck. He'd been holding on for the past ten years, so one more wasn't going to make much difference. Thus far, whatever had failed he'd been able to repair, but that wasn't always going to be the case.

Gage could hear Hassie talking up a storm even before they entered the pharmacy. One glance at the two women sitting at the soda fountain told him they were from the city. Some Southern city, he guessed, judging by the slight—and very attractive—drawl. Atlanta? New Orleans? Their skin was pale as winter wheat, and their clothes looked like they

came out of a fashion magazine. Gage didn't know anyone from Buffalo Valley who dressed in such bright colors. Both were young and pretty, and he couldn't imagine what would bring them to Buffalo Valley.

"Leta…Gage." Hassie greeted them both with enthusiastic fondness. "Come meet Lindsay Snyder and her friend Maddy Washburn. They're visiting here from Savannah—imagine that! Lindsay is Anton and Gina's granddaughter."

Savannah. Yep, he'd guessed right. Close enough, anyway. Gage touched the rim of his cap and nodded in their direction. His mother reacted with characteristic pleasure and started chatting about old times and what a dear person Gina Snyder had been.

Seeing that he'd walked in on a hen party, Gage was eager to make his escape. He would have left immediately if not for Lindsay Snyder. He'd given her a perfunctory glance but noticed the way her gaze stayed on him. Their eyes met again and held. Seemingly embarrassed, she offered him a small, apologetic smile and looked away.

Gage quickly excused himself. "I'll be over at Buffalo Bob's," he said as he hurried out the door. Getting his hair cut could wait; his mother could do it that night if it truly bothered her.

"Tell Bob he's going to have guests tonight," Hassie shouted after him, looking pleased with herself.

Gage didn't think the two visitors would be eager to linger in this town, but he'd pass the word on to Buffalo Bob and leave it at that.

Brandon Wyatt sat in the bar off the restaurant in the 3 OF A KIND, and Gage climbed onto the stool next to his friend and neighbor. The place was dim and mercifully cool, and he could hear Garth Brooks in the background.

"Get you a beer?" Buffalo Bob asked him.

Gage nodded. Bob—ex-biker and now the owner of this establishment—was the only man Gage knew who wore his hair in a ponytail. For that matter, he wore a black leather vest year-round. Still had a Harley, too.

"Howdy, neighbor," Gage said to Brandon.

Brandon glanced over at him. "Good to see you."

"You, too," Gage said. He'd known Brandon his entire life. Their properties adjoined each other and they'd shared just about everything farmers do over the years.

"How're Joanie and the kids?" Gage asked, raising the cold beer bottle to his lips. He hadn't seen Brandon for some time. Joanie used to stop at the farmhouse once a week or so, but come to think of it, Gage hadn't seen her in a while, either.

"Everyone's fine."

It was the clipped way Brandon said it that alerted Gage to trouble. He stared at his friend and wondered if he should ask. He decided against it. Brandon would come to him if he wanted advice, which he seldom did. That wasn't how they did things. They were independent men who mostly kept their own counsel. As far as friends went, Brandon was about the closest one Gage had, but they rarely spoke, rarely spent time together. If he needed anything, though, he could count on Brandon, just like his neighbor could count on him.

They'd gotten together more often before Brandon married Joanie, but that had been eight or nine years ago. Brandon had gone to Fargo to buy a new tractor and the following weekend had found an excuse to return to the city. Soon he was spending as much time there as he was on his own farm. It didn't take a rocket scientist to figure out there was a woman involved. Within the year, Joanie

and Brandon were married. A daughter and son followed soon after, a little more than two years apart. They were eight and six if he remembered right. Cute kids.

Gage didn't know Joanie all that well, but from remarks his mother let drop, he suspected she hadn't made the transition to farm life as easily as the couple had hoped. Life on a North Dakota farm could get desperately lonely for women, especially in the winter months when it wasn't unheard-of to go two or three weeks without even leaving the house. Women, especially women not born to this life, seemed to think that sounded romantic until they experienced it themselves.

Gage's mind wandered away from Brandon and Joanie to the two women visiting at Hassie's. Both seemed vibrant and full of energy. He'd have to be a dead man not to notice. Over the years, Gage had given some thought to marriage but time and opportunity had worked against him. It wasn't like single women were exactly plentiful around here.

He had to be realistic, and his chances of meeting someone in Buffalo Valley were slim to none. All that meant was that he had to venture farther afield. He had to be realistic in other ways, too. He wasn't going to appear on any of those he-man calendars, but he was fairly good-looking. He possessed a strong work ethic and had a powerful sense of what was important. True, he was responsible for his mother and Kevin, but if he did find a woman willing to marry him, he'd take the necessary steps to care for their needs and see to his own and his wife's, as well.

As far as he knew, there were only three eligible women in the vicinity and he'd known them his entire life. Sarah Stern—used to be McKenna—was one, but she had something going with Dennis Urlacher and that put her off-limits.

Margaret Clemens was the second possibility. She was a rancher, and she worked the land with her father. The Clemens family had one of the most prosperous herds in the state on their Triple C spread.

Margaret was complicated, though. She might be a woman, but she'd never dressed or acted like one. He wouldn't be surprised to find out that she cursed and chewed right along with the hired hands.

The last was Rachel Fischer, a widow with a ten-year-old son. He'd given some serious thought to asking her out, but while he liked her—admired her, even—he didn't feel any strong attraction toward her. Of the three women, he liked Rachel best and respected her for staying in Buffalo Valley when her parents had closed down their restaurant and moved south. Her husband had died of leukemia when the boy was about six. Her parents had helped as much as they could, but money had been tight and gotten tighter. Gage knew she'd been tempted to leave with them, but for the sake of her son, she'd remained in town, thinking he'd had enough trauma and disruption in his young life without being uprooted from everything familiar. A decision that took courage.

The fact was, not one of those women really appealed to him physically, and if he was going to all the effort of seeking one out, he should feel *something*.

He believed that when he did meet the right woman he'd know, but at thirty-five, Gage suspected it might be too late.

"Who's that over at Hassie's?" Buffalo Bob asked. He'd tossed a dish towel over his shoulder and eyed the Bronco parked across the street.

"Anton and Gina Snyder's granddaughter. She's in town with a friend," Gage told him. "They used to live here, the Snyders. Hassie seems to think the ladies'll put up here for the night."

That information cheered Buffalo Bob. "Great, I could use the business."

Gage suspected they'd be among the few guests the hotel had all summer. "She going to be the new teacher?" Buffalo Bob asked next.

The thought hadn't occurred to Gage. "I doubt it."

With a morose and uncommunicative Brandon Wyatt sitting next to him, Gage finished off his beer and ordered a second. Again and again, his gaze was drawn across the street.

A couple of times he thought he heard the sound of women's laughter coming from Hassie's, but he could have imagined it. His imagination seemed to have shifted into overdrive, and his head was filled with thoughts of Lindsay Snyder. He couldn't recall the other woman's name now.

Lindsay's blue eyes had sparkled with laughter and during those few seconds they'd stared at each other, he could almost feel the joy bubbling just beneath the surface. Within those few seconds he'd recognized that she was someone he'd like to know better. But there was no reason for her to stay; by morning she'd be back on the road.

A deep loneliness came over him. Gage had experienced it before; and life had taught him that, given time, it would pass. Life had taught him something else, too. The land demanded a farmer's first allegiance and wouldn't lightly accept his sharing that love and loyalty with another. This was a lesson Brandon was only now beginning to understand, and Gage intended to learn from his neighbor's mistakes.

Joanie Wyatt sat alone in the darkened room. She hadn't meant to fight with her husband. The truth was, she'd been hoping for a romantic afternoon—just the two of them. The grandfather clock chimed midnight, the sound as bleak as her thoughts. It was useless to try to sleep. Not that their

disagreement seemed to bother Brandon, who'd been asleep for nearly two hours.

She'd asked him to come into town with her. It was a small thing, but they had almost no time alone these days. Sage and Stevie were attending Billy Nobel's birthday party in Bellmont, which gave them a rare free afternoon. She'd been the one to suggest they buy groceries and then stop at Buffalo Bob's for a beer.

All either of them did these days was work. Joanie had planted a huge, ambitious garden, and found herself spending hours every day looking after it. What had started as an experiment, a pleasure, had developed over the years into a necessity and now a chore. It made sense to raise as much of their own food as possible, seeing that they had the land. Then there was Princess to milk and chickens to feed and in the past year they'd added pigs. Thankfully Brandon did the butchering, but the care of the animals had become part of her duties.

The animals tied them to the farm, so it was unusual to get away for more than a few hours. In the last four or five years, Joanie had come to feel isolated, to doubt her own sanity and lately her femininity, her attractiveness. It'd been weeks since they'd last made love, weeks since they'd done anything but fall into bed at the end of the day, too exhausted to even kiss. Whatever romance had existed in their marriage now seemed dead.

Their argument that afternoon had started out as an innocent conversation on the drive into town, a mere mention of the washing machine, which was about to give up the ghost.

"We can't afford a new one," Brandon had snapped.

Her mistake, Joanie realized, was mentioning the two-hundred-thousand-dollar combine Brandon had purchased

two years earlier. They couldn't afford an eight-hundred-dollar washing machine, but forking over six figures for a combine was done without blinking twice.

That remark had sent their afternoon on a downward spiral. By the time they reached town, she'd walked over to Hansen's Grocery on her own while Brandon headed for Buffalo Bob's. He'd had three beers before she joined him.

Despite his sullen demeanor, Joanie had tried to make the best of the situation. Hoping to put the argument behind them, she'd asked Buffalo Bob about the karaoke machine he'd recently purchased. He'd been eager to have someone try it out and so, with everyone watching, Joanie had gotten up to sing an old Beatles song. Her singing voice was halfway decent and she'd earned a hearty round of applause. Soon others, their inhibitions no doubt loosened by several beers, were taking their turns, and Buffalo Bob had thanked her for getting things rolling.

Then, on the drive home, Brandon had accused her of flirting.

"With whom?" she'd cried.

He'd been silent for a long moment before he said, "Buffalo Bob."

The idea was ludicrous and she didn't know whether to laugh or act insulted. Instead of doing either, she said nothing. When they got home, Brandon had stormed off to the barn and she'd left almost immediately to pick up the kids.

Her appetite was dismal and the kids were filled up on excitement and birthday cake, so she'd just made a chef's salad for dinner. Brandon had taken one look at it and claimed he wasn't hungry. Joanie had sat at the dinner table alone with her children.

"Is Daddy mad?" Sage asked. Her daughter had always been sensitive to her parents' moods.

"Of course not, sweetheart," she'd assured her, wanting to lay the eight-year-old's fears to rest.

"How come he isn't eating dinner with us?"

"Well, because…" Joanie groped for a believable excuse. "Because we went into town while you were at the birthday party and had a little party of our own."

The excuse satisfied their son, who'd shown only minor concern over Brandon's absence from the dinner table, but Sage didn't look convinced. "Maybe I should make Daddy a sandwich and take it out to him."

"If he wants something to eat, he'll say so," Joanie insisted. She wasn't going to pander to Brandon's moods, and she wasn't about to let their daughter fall into that trap, either. Joanie felt she'd put together a perfectly good salad, and if he wanted something else, he could damn well cook it himself.

After dinner, the kids watched a favorite Disney video. By nine they were ready for bed, tired out from the day's activity. Joanie tucked them in, listened to their prayers and came back downstairs.

Brandon sat in front of the television. His gaze didn't waver from the screen when she entered the room. The show was a rerun of *Walker, Texas Ranger* and she didn't want to waste her evening sitting with an embittered husband watching a show she'd already seen.

Without a word she'd set up her sewing machine on the kitchen table, intent on making her daughter a new dress for church. It was a hundred-mile round trip to the closest church. A priest came to Buffalo once every two weeks to say Mass, but Joanie wasn't Catholic. Brandon had stopped attending services with her three years earlier, so she made the long drive alone with the kids. Her husband had given up doing a lot of the things she

considered important, another sign of the growing discontent in their marriage.

As she worked, Joanie had brooded, alternating between resentment and despair. She deftly ran the flowery fabric beneath the frantic needle, but the task didn't calm her, the way it usually did. This sewing machine had once belonged to her mother. Joanie had inherited it when her mother purchased a newer model, but God help her if she were to hint at buying a new sewing machine. Look what had happened when she'd asked about a washer.

At ten, Brandon had wandered into the kitchen, glanced around, said nothing, then gone up to bed. It didn't take Joanie long to follow. She waited until the room was dark before she climbed beneath the sheets.

Brandon lay next to her, as cold and silent as a corpse.

"I'm sorry about this afternoon," she whispered, staring up at the ceiling.

He didn't say anything for long minutes, then finally, "Me, too."

"What's happening to us?" she asked, her heart breaking. At one time they'd been so much in love. Neither of them would have allowed anything—a disagreement, a misunderstanding—to come between them. But these days they almost seemed to invent excuses to argue.

Their courtship had been wildly romantic, but even then her mother had seen problems looming. When Joanie announced that she wanted to marry Brandon, her parents had advised against it. As a result, Brandon had never gotten on well with her family. Her parents didn't dislike him, but he chose to believe otherwise. If she wanted to spend holidays with her mother and father, she and the children went alone.

"I guess your parents were right," he mumbled in the dark.

"What do you mean by that?" she demanded, angered by the comment. She wanted to end this tension, not heighten it. Brandon couldn't seem to let their disagreement drop, and it annoyed her.

"You'd have done better marrying Stan Simmons, like your mother wanted. He could buy you ten washing machines if you asked. Hell, he'd take them off the showroom floor and not miss a single one."

"I wasn't in love with him. As it happens, I fell in love with you. As for those washing machines, I don't need ten. Five will do." She expected Brandon would chuckle, roll over and hug her, but he didn't. "That was a joke," she said.

"I know."

"Then why didn't you laugh?"

Brandon sighed. "The answer should be obvious."

"Apparently not."

"Okay, if I have to say it, I will. I didn't happen to find your little joke all that amusing."

Joanie swallowed a groan, wondering why she even tried. "You're impossible."

"Yeah—and not only that, I drive a two-hundred-thousand-dollar combine." He abruptly rolled onto his side and jerked the covers over his shoulder.

Joanie waited until she was sure he'd fallen asleep before she slipped out of the bedroom and walked into the living room. For two hours she sat alone in the dark and listened to the chime of the grandfather clock every fifteen minutes. Eleven. Quarter after eleven. Eleven-thirty. This was her life, she told herself. Her life that was disappearing.

Joanie had gone into this marriage because she loved Brandon. It had seemed so right, despite her parents' concerns. Brandon was responsible and hardworking, kind, gentle...

They'd met, of all places, at a theater. She'd gone with a girlfriend who'd deserted her when she'd run into her latest heartthrob. Joanie had been about to leave when she saw Brandon and liked what she saw. So she'd purchased a ticket, anyway, and hoped against hope that he was attending the same movie.

He was, and they'd sat not far from each other. Only later did he confess that he'd purchased the ticket for a different movie, but had followed her, hoping for the opportunity to get to know her. Joanie had gone from feeling flattered to infatuated all in one evening.

After the movie, they'd had coffee together and talked for hours. They saw each other again the next weekend, and by then she'd broken up with Stan Simmons, much to her parents' disappointment. Stan's father owned a huge appliance store that did a lot of advertising; Stan-the-Man's television ads were often humorous, and he'd become a local celebrity. Stan Jr. was in line to take over the family business. Marrying him would have guaranteed her a life free of financial worries. Instead, Joanie had followed her heart. Not once had she regretted that decision.

She still didn't regret it—unhappy though she was right now. Despite their problems, Joanie deeply loved her husband. What she had to do was find a way to recapture what they'd lost. She couldn't do it all on her own, though; Brandon had to want it, too.

"Joanie?" Her husband stood silhouetted in the dim moonlight. "What are you doing up?"

"I…I couldn't sleep."

"Because of what I said?"

She nodded.

"Let's not fight, baby."

"I don't want to, either," she whispered.

He held his arms open to her and she went to him, savoring the feel of his embrace. "I woke up and found you gone," he murmured against her hair. Then with a deep, shuddering sigh, he told her, "We'll find a way to buy you that new washer. The corn's good this year. Come harvest, we'll buy you a washer—and a dryer, too. I promise."

"It's all right. I can make do for a while. Joshua can keep the washer going for me. And the dryer should last until next year."

Her husband kissed the top of her head and his lips lingered there, giving Joanie the impression that he was either immersed in thought or still half-asleep. "Come to bed," he urged a moment later. He slid his arm around her waist and led her back to their bedroom. She moved into his arms and pressed her head against his shoulder. He didn't reach for her to make love, and she didn't indicate that she was interested. The physical aspect of their marriage had always been strong—except for the past few months. When all else failed, this was an area where communication had remained healthy. But it'd been a month since the last time he'd wanted her...and a month, more than a month, since she'd wanted him.

It wasn't a good sign and Joanie drifted into an uneasy sleep, worried that her marriage was in more serious trouble than she'd suspected.

Refreshed and rejuvenated from her two-week vacation, Lindsay hadn't been home an hour—hadn't even picked up the dogs from her parents yet—when Monte showed up at her apartment door, holding a huge bouquet of long-stemmed red roses. The flowers were beautiful; even more beautiful was the look on Monte's face. Without a word it told her how much he'd missed her, how bereft he'd felt while she was

away. That look alone was worth every miserable moment they'd been apart. It was a mistake to be this happy, to feel such undiluted joy, but she couldn't help herself.

"Welcome home," he said at last.

"Oh, Monte." She covered her mouth with one hand, hardly able to believe he'd come.

Before another moment passed, she was in his arms. "I've been lost without you," he whispered between kisses. "Never again," he insisted, clasping her by the shoulders and gazing intensely into her eyes.

The roses were clutched in Lindsay's arms, the thorns biting into her skin, but she barely felt the pain. "Who told you I was home?" she asked breathlessly, once they broke apart.

"No one. I overheard your uncle say you'd be back sometime today."

Not knowing how to react, Lindsay stared down at the flowers. She loved him, she'd missed him—but she wasn't ready for a confrontation. Especially now, with her heart so hungry for the sight of him. Again and again she tried to remind herself that they'd covered this ground before. Nothing was going to change. And as she acknowledged this, her joy at seeing him began to dissolve.

"I know you said you wanted to break things off, but I'm hoping you've come to your senses. Tell me you have," he pleaded. When she didn't immediately respond, Monte answered for her. "Your kisses say you've been missing me," he whispered.

"I did miss you." She couldn't lie, but the truth was more than she wanted to confess. In an effort to diminish the growing intimacy, she carried the roses into the kitchen.

"I've done nothing but think about you," Monte told her.

Lindsay brought out the stepladder to reach for the vase

stored above the refrigerator. She'd done a lot of thinking, too. But during her trip, on the road with Maddy, everything had seemed much clearer than it did now.

Monte leaned against the counter, gazing steadily at her. "You've had two weeks. Surely you realize we belong together."

Lindsay set down the vase. It seemed ridiculous that they should be having the most important—and perhaps the final—discussion of their relationship while standing in the middle of her tiny kitchen. There was so much she'd wanted to tell him, about her trip and her visit to Buffalo Valley. She yearned to share the things she'd learned, the places she'd seen—the Badlands, Yellowstone Park, Mount Rushmore. He was her friend, too, and that aspect of their relationship was as difficult to relinquish as the rest.

"You've come to your senses, haven't you?"

"Yes, I suppose I have." She sounded so…weak, so unsure. She *was* weak, but her resolve was growing stronger. She refused to let him talk her out of the very things that were most important to her.

Monte sighed. "Thank heaven for that."

It took him a moment to realize she was still standing on the other side of the room. "Come here, sweetheart," he murmured. "Let me show you how much I've missed you."

"I don't think you understand." Her voice was emotionless.

"You said you'd come to your senses."

"I have—and it's over, Monte. Unless you've changed your mind about marriage and a family. And I don't think you have."

He stared at her as if he didn't believe her. "You don't mean that," he said, shaking his head impatiently.

"I do mean it."

"I've heard that before, Lindsay, and it's foolishness. We belong together, we always have. You know it, and I do, too. We're good together."

"That's true, Monte, but I want more. I want a husband and children. Is that so difficult to understand?"

His mouth thinned. "For the love of God, does it always have to go back to what *you* want?"

"In this case, yes. It's my life."

He pounded his fist against the counter, then seemed to regret the outburst. "Lindsay, would you listen to reason? I *can't* marry you. I just can't do it. Marriage ruins everything—I know that from experience. You—"

"Don't, please."

He advanced toward her, then stopped. "Fine," he said, his voice cold, "if that's the way you want it."

"I'm afraid it is."

"You'll be back," he said. "Until then, all I can do is wait." He slammed the door on his way out of her apartment.

Afterward Lindsay sat, mulling over their conversation, her arms wrapped around her knees. A chill spread down her arms that had nothing to do with the air-conditioned room. His bitter words about marriage echoed in her ears; so did his claim that she'd change her mind, that she'd come back. He seemed to think she'd eventually be willing to accept him on his terms, willing to give up her own dreams.

Lindsay bit into her lower lip, and hugged her legs all the harder.

It did no good to relive the same old arguments. The furniture in her uncle's showroom might come with a guarantee, but life didn't. Neither did marriage. But Monte's divorce had destroyed any possibility of his taking a second chance on commitment. Nothing she could say or do would be enough to reassure him.

For two years, Lindsay had believed that Monte would see the light and realize that she wasn't his ex-wife. Because she was stubborn, and because she loved him, she'd refused to accept defeat. His marriage, brief as it was, had forever marked him. Monte was incapable of giving her anything more than he already had.

Maddy had said it on their vacation. Either she take what he was offering or end the relationship.

Lindsay had made her decision. One thing was certain; she had to stay away from him. Her love for him made her too vulnerable. He would fight to preserve their relationship, and he'd work at wearing her down, the same way he had before.

Leaning back, she closed her eyes and reviewed her options. A new career, returning to college, starting her own business…. Unexpectedly she remembered her visit to Buffalo Valley—and her conversation with Hassie Knight. She smiled. Hassie hadn't come right out and said it, but without a teacher Buffalo Valley was doomed. That was the answer Lindsay sought. She would take the job; obviously, the town needed her…and perhaps she needed it.

Lindsay had minored in education and could apply for a teaching certificate in North Dakota. She had an opportunity to make a difference. A year—she'd give Buffalo Valley a year of her life. In a twelve-month period, they could locate and hire a permanent replacement for the high-school position. She'd fill in, and those twelve months would give her the distance she needed from Monte.

A chance like this didn't happen every day. Her roots were in this dying town—her family's heritage—and it was within her power to help. At the same time, she'd be saving herself from the agony of a dead-end relationship.

And, she thought with growing excitement, she could

move into her grandparents' home. It was pretty dilapidated—no wonder it hadn't sold. She recalled the peeling
paint, the broken porch steps and falling-down fence. But
she could get it fixed up, and she'd have a free place to live
if she took the job. The house would be a connection to her
past, while teaching school could be her future.

She'd do it. Decision made, she dug through her purse
for Hassie's phone number. Funny, she mused as she
reached for the telephone, she'd somehow known when she
left Buffalo Valley that she was destined to return. She just
hadn't realized it would be this soon.

Four

The word that a high-school teacher had been found traveled faster than a dust storm through Buffalo Valley. Gage heard about it from Leta late one afternoon, two weeks after Lindsay's visit. His day had been spent doing the second summer cutting of alfalfa. He smelled of grass and sweat and was hungrier than a bear in spring.

"You remember meeting her, don't you?" his mother said, excitedly.

"There were two women in Hassie's that Saturday," he commented as he poured himself a glass of iced tea. He remembered, all right. And he knew without his mother's telling him that it was Lindsay who was coming back.

For two weeks now, the woman had been on his mind, crowding into his thoughts when she was least welcome. In the time since her visit, he'd thought of her far too much, and he didn't like it. He distrusted the feeling that had come after their brief introduction. It was too close to hope.

Gage didn't want to feel anything for her. He couldn't *afford* to feel anything—not for a city woman who'd be leaving after a year.

A darkening mass of clouds gathered on his horizon, a sure sign a storm was brewing. Only this storm was of his own making, and Gage wasn't going to let himself get caught in it.

"The Snyder granddaughter's the one who's coming back," Leta told him.

He nodded. "I can't imagine why she agreed to teach here," he said casually.

"She's got roots in Buffalo Valley. You remember Anton and Gina Snyder, don't you?"

Gage nodded again. Anton Snyder had sold his farm before the bottom fell out. He'd lived in an era when it was possible to make a decent living off the land. In the thirty years since the Snyders had sold, the reality of farming had changed.

"Aren't you going to say anything?" his mother asked.

Gage drank half the glass of tea in huge gulps.

"Well?"

"She won't last." He said it because *he* needed to hear it, needed to remind himself that he shouldn't put any stock in her coming. Or her going.

"Don't be such a pessimist."

"She *won't* last," he said again. "Mark my words." Lindsay Snyder had been born and raised in the South. One month of a Dakota winter, and this magnolia blossom would hightail it back to Savannah faster than he could spell blizzard.

"I don't care what you say," his mother chided, "we're lucky to get her."

If it was luck that had brought Lindsay Snyder to Buffalo Valley, then it was bad luck and he wanted no part of it. He didn't know her, had barely even seen her, and he was already attracted to her. Attracted—to a woman who wasn't going to stay.

Kevin stormed into the kitchen, the screen door slamming in his wake. "Calla said we got a teacher. Is it true?" His excitement rang through the room.

"Hassie phoned with the news," Leta said. "Didn't I tell you we'd find a teacher? Didn't I?"

Kevin nodded as if he, too, had shared their mother's faith from the first. The boy was all legs and arms yet, as tall as Gage and fifty pounds lighter. Gage had looked much the same at seventeen, but had filled out over time. A stint in the Army after graduation had helped firm his muscles, and given him the confidence to tackle the world. After two years at an agricultural college, he'd come home and farmed with his stepfather, intending to buy his own section of land, but then John had collapsed with a heart attack one July morning. He was dead ten minutes later, despite Gage's frantic efforts to revive him.

"A bunch of us kids are going over to clean up the school." Kevin looked toward Gage. "We're gonna need help."

The implication was clear. Kevin wanted Gage to volunteer his services.

"Everyone's doing something," Leta put in.

Gage ignored the dig. "Where's the new teacher going to live?" He avoided saying her name because he found he liked the sound of it too much.

"Hassie told her a house came with the teaching contract, but Miss Snyder says she wants to live in her grandparents' old place," Leta answered, frowning a little. "The house is going to need work—but I suppose she already knows that, since she looked it over while she was here. Still, she probably doesn't realize how *much* work…."

His brother and mother were watching Gage as if preparing the house *and* the school was entirely up to him. "What are you looking at me for?" he demanded.

Kevin's gaze widened. "*Someone's* got to get the place ready for her to move in."

"You're a member of the council, aren't you?" his mother added.

"Yes." Gage rolled his eyes. For the sake of his sanity, he planned to keep his distance from this Southern belle. Worse, a Southern belle who was all keen to discover her "roots." A woman who probably had sentimental ideas and foolish illusions about this place and these people. Nope, he thought again, she wouldn't last until Christmas.

He'd had a perfectly good day and wasn't about to let his family ruin it by loading unwanted obligations on his overburdened shoulders. He'd just opened his mouth to say that when the phone rang.

Kevin raced for it as if someone might beat him to it. "Hello." A moment later, he turned and thrust the receiver at Gage. "It's for you."

"Who is it?"

"Heath Quantrill."

Gage wasn't excessively fond of the banker, but then his aversion was toward all bankers and not just Quantrill. In truth, he—along with just about everyone else in town—owed a great deal to Heath's grandparents, who'd founded Buffalo County Bank. The original bank had been in Buffalo Valley, and by the end of the sixties, there were branches in ten other towns and cities. While the other branches appeared to be thriving, the one in Buffalo Valley had to be operating at a loss. Gage suspected Lily Quantrill kept it open for nostalgic reasons. Her grandson had been managing it since last year, driving in from Grand Forks three days a week.

Rumor had it that Heath Quantrill wasn't happy in the banking business. It was his brother, Max, who'd been slated to take over the operation. Until recently Heath, the

younger of the Quantrill grandsons, had spent his time gallivanting around the world, rushing from one thrill to the next. Heath had the reputation of a daredevil who took crazy chances with his life, but it was his brother, his staid older brother, who'd died.

"Hello, Heath," Gage said.

"Glad I caught you," Heath said, sounding anything but. "Did you hear about the teacher?"

"I heard. When does she arrive?"

"Three weeks."

So soon? Gage could feel his gut tightening. It wouldn't be long before every unattached male within a fifty-mile radius would find an excuse to drop by the high school, hoping for a chance with the new teacher.

Let them, Gage decided abruptly. *He* wasn't interested. *He* had better things to do.

"Hassie asked me to contact the members of the council for an emergency meeting."

"When?"

"Tonight at seven. Can you be there?"

Gage didn't feel he had a choice since he'd missed the last one. "Yes." He didn't need to attend the meeting to know what it was about; Leta and Kevin had already told him. The entire town was going to turn itself inside out to welcome a woman who wouldn't last three months.

When he'd finished talking to Heath, Gage took a quick shower and changed his clothes.

"Dinner's ready," his mother told him when he came downstairs.

The three of them sat down at the table, and after his mother had said grace she passed him the platter of fried chicken, one of his favorites. He hadn't taken his first bite before Kevin began to talk about school.

"Did you repair the chicken coop like I asked?" Gage broke in before the entire meal was ruined with talk of Lindsay Snyder.

"I did it this morning." Kevin immediately returned to the subject of school. "Jessica and her friends are going to ask Miss Snyder about holding a dance. It's been years since the last one."

Gage started to tell his brother exactly what he thought of that, when his mother interrupted him.

"I think it's a wonderful idea, Kevin."

The boy glanced at Gage. "Before you ask, I mucked out Ranger's stall, too. And I've already fed the dogs."

Gage nodded.

"Speaking of dogs, I heard the new teacher's got two of 'em."

Gage nearly groaned. It didn't matter what the subject, his brother and mother would find a way to turn it back to Lindsay.

"What's for dessert?" Gage asked in one final attempt to talk about something else.

"Peach pie."

Another of Gage's favorites. "Is this my birthday and someone forgot to tell me?" he asked. Fried chicken, mashed potatoes and peach pie were what his mother generally made for special occasions.

"Not your birthday." His mother blushed with happiness. "But certainly a day for celebration. Oh, Gage, why can't you be happy? We have a teacher, and she's going to bring a breath of fresh air to this community!"

Buffalo Bob Carr knew his luck had changed when he won the 3 OF A KIND in a poker game two years ago. He'd inherited five thousand dollars from his mother's estate;

he'd been looking for a way to invest it and prove to himself, and his father, that he was more than a bum on a motorcycle. Then he'd won the entire business.

He'd been rolling through Buffalo Valley on his second-hand Harley when he met Dave Ertz, who was trying to sell the hotel, bar and restaurant, at that time known as The Prairie Palace. With no buyers in sight, Dave had held a poker game, charging a one-thousand-dollar entry fee. Winner take all. Four men had played, and Bob had won with three of a kind, hence the new name of the establishment.

The way Bob figured it, his momma would be real pleased to see him as a businessman. His old man had always claimed he'd never amount to much, and up to this point, he'd been right. But not anymore. Buffalo Bob, as he'd taken to calling himself, was a dignified entrepreneur.

Bob had taken the four thousand bucks left of his inheritance, ordered a brand-new neon sign, reupholstered the restaurant chairs, spruced up a few of the hotel rooms and opened his doors for business. It didn't take him long to discover why Dave Ertz had wanted out. Money was tight in the farming community, and folks didn't have a lot to spare. A night in town was considered a luxury. The truth was, he sold more beer than anything else. Thus far he was making ends meet, but only because he knew how to pinch his pennies. If nothing else, his years on the road had taught him frugality.

He didn't need a master's degree from a fancy business college to figure out that if the high school closed because they lacked a teacher, he might as well board up the place and ride out of town the same way he'd rolled in.

Then, the day before, the word had come. One of the women who'd been his guests two weeks ago had decided to take the job. God bless her!

Jokingly, Buffalo Bob had said he deserved the credit for Lindsay's decision to return to Buffalo Valley. Well, he figured he *was* partially responsible for this sudden reversal in the town's fortunes. He'd put the two women up in his best room and served them his special all-you-can-eat spaghetti dinner.

That Saturday night had been one of his best financially. He'd recently picked up the karaoke machine from a restaurant in Cando that was going out of business. With Joshua McKenna's help, he'd managed to get it working. That was the day Joanie Wyatt had stopped in and gotten things started with a song from the Beatles' "Sgt. Pepper" album. Bob had sold more beer that one afternoon than the entire previous week. He'd sell more this coming weekend, too, now that folks around town had a reason to celebrate.

"What's the special tonight?" Merrily Benson asked, breaking into his thoughts. She was his one and only Buffalo Gal. He'd considered that a nice touch, calling his waitresses "Buffalo Gals." Granted, Merrily was it, as far as staff went.

Buffalo Bob looked up from his desk and smiled at her. He'd come into his tiny, makeshift office first thing this morning to pay bills; now it was almost noon. Paying bills usually meant juggling bills—his suppliers, electricity, water. Taxes. And maintenance. He'd had Joshua over to fix the refrigerator unit the day before and the repair had eaten up most of the profit he'd made in the last couple of weeks. But he'd get by; he had before and he would again.

Dressed in her uniform with the rawhide fringe skirt and matching vest, Merrily looked like the real thing. Yup, his one and only Buffalo Gal—in every sense. Merrily and Bob were soul mates. He'd recognized it the minute she'd come into town and approached him about a job. He hadn't

been any better off then. He was barely making ends meet, but he found he couldn't refuse Merrily. Even if it meant tightening his already uncomfortably tight belt.

"What's with the smile?" Merrily asked. "I thought you were all bent out of shape about the refrigerator going on the blink?"

"Joshua McKenna came by to tell me a teacher's been hired."

Merrily's eyes lit up, and she threw her arms around his neck. Her kisses were the sweetest Bob had ever tasted, but he knew better than to let himself get accustomed to their flavor.

Merrily had a bad habit of disappearing.

He was finally beginning to see a pattern with her. Just when they started to get emotionally as well as physically involved, his Buffalo Gal would pack her bags and quietly vanish.

The first time it'd happened, he'd been devastated. He'd awakened one morning and been shocked to find her gone. She'd hit the road without so much as a note goodbye. The only reason he'd known she'd left of her own free will was that she'd told Hassie Knight.

On her way out of town, Merrily had dropped in at Dennis Urlacher's gas station to fill up her old wreck of a car. While she was there, she'd casually announced that it was time for her to move on. Just that abruptly, she'd left him, bewildered and sick at heart.

Three months later, she was back.

Buffalo Bob never knew from one day to the next if Merrily would be staying, but he'd grown to accept the uncertainty. He didn't know if she'd always return to him, but he realized there wasn't a thing he could do about it. Merrily had her own rules. The fact was, he loved her.

She knew he was good for a job, a room and a small salary. But she'd only let him so close to her heart, and no closer. The moment it looked like she was in danger of falling in love with him, she'd take off, like a canary fleeing its cage. Only this pretty little canary always flew back. So far, anyway. Bob had learned to keep the door open for her.

"A teacher. That's great news." Merrily continued to hug him, then broke away. "I need to know what the special is," she said and stepped back, tucking her fingertips in the waist of her skirt.

Buffalo Bob shuffled through the pages on his desk. He planned the menus two weeks in advance, but couldn't recall what was scheduled for that night. To his surprise, Bob had discovered he was a reasonably talented cook, but folks around here weren't looking for anything fancy. He served meat and potatoes with an occasional venture into the unusual. Well, unusual for Buffalo Valley. His spaghetti on Saturday nights sold well, chicken Caesar salad had done okay, but his Polynesian sweet and sour meatballs had been a dismal failure. And his Thai noodles—forget it.

"How about pot roast?" Merrily suggested. "With mashed potatoes and gravy."

"Pot roast?"

"That's what my mother always served the first day of school."

Merrily had never mentioned her mother before. That was interesting, but he wasn't entirely sure he followed her line of thinking. "It's weeks before school starts."

"Yeah, I know, but you got a teacher so school *is* going to start. It'd be kind of a celebration."

"Sounds good to me." Just about anything she suggested would get a favorable response from him. He had a couple of roasts in the freezer, lots of potatoes… Why not?

Merrily sat down on the chair beside his desk and fingered the edges of a book, riffling the pages with her thumb. "Bob," she said, not looking at him.

He glanced up. Generally Merrily didn't hang around the office much. If she wasn't tending bar or filling in as a waitress, she stayed in her room. Some days he barely saw her.

"I…" She didn't meet his eyes. "Listen, I know you aren't exactly rolling in dough."

She wanted a loan. He could feel it coming even before she said the words. Because of the refrigerator unit, money was tight, but he didn't have the heart to refuse Merrily.

"How much?" he murmured, saving her the trouble of asking.

"How much?" she repeated with a frown. "Do you think I was coming to you for money?"

He didn't answer and wanted to kick himself at her look of pain. "I don't need a loan, Bob. In fact, I don't need anything." She was out of the chair and his office faster than he could stop her.

"Merrily," he called, following her as she dashed up the stairs to her room at the farthest end of the hotel. "Merrily!"

She whirled around and would have slammed the door, but he wedged it open with his foot. "What did I say?" he asked. He thought she'd come to him for money, and he'd give it to her, as much as he could, because he loved her. Because there was damn little in this world he *wouldn't* give her.

"You think I want money."

He didn't know what to say when he saw the tears on her cheeks. "Don't you?"

"Well, sure, everyone wants money, but that wasn't what I was going to talk to you about."

"What *were* you going to say then?" he asked patiently.

"I…I was just going to tell you that you didn't have to pay me this week."

"Not pay you?" He wasn't sure he understood. "Why not?"

"Because!" she cried, angry all over again. "You're worried about what that repair on the refrigerator cost, and you might not have enough."

His heart melted at her words. "You'd do that for me?"

"Yes, you idiot."

"Oh." For once he found himself speechless.

"Forget I offered, okay?"

Buffalo Bob shook his head. He wasn't going to forget; in fact, he was going to remember it for a very long time.

Merrily swiped the back of her hand across her face and offered him a feeble smile. "Go back to paying your bills and I'll start thawing those pot roasts." She hurried past him on her way to the kitchen, but he reached out a hand to stop her.

Merrily glanced over her shoulder.

"Thanks," he said.

She smiled, kissed him briefly on the lips, then ran lightly down the stairs.

Lindsay was delighted that her parents had decided to accompany her to Buffalo Valley. Her dad drove his truck, pulling the U-Haul trailer, while Lindsay followed behind in her own car, Mutt and Jeff, her dogs, traveling with her. They were mixed breeds, poodle and spaniel, easygoing dogs who loved car rides.

Leaving Savannah hadn't been easy for a lot of reasons, but particularly because of Monte. It'd taken several confrontations before he'd accept that he wasn't going to be able to cajole her into staying. As she prepared for her departure, he'd become angry, insisting she'd be back.

He was right, of course, but when she did return, he would be completely and totally out of her life.

Maddy had cheered her decision and even helped her pack. Lindsay knew she could count on her friend's support and encouragement during the next year. They'd parted with promises to keep in touch.

Traveling with two dogs and all her worldly possessions made for a much slower trip this time around. Six days after they left Savannah, the Snyders pulled into Buffalo Valley and parked in front of Knight's Pharmacy.

Her father climbed down from the truck and looked around as if seeing the town for the first time. His last visit had been three years earlier, when he'd come to move his father to Savannah. The trip had been quick and made in the middle of winter. Lindsay wondered just how much he'd noticed.

Hands on his hips, he stood there for a long moment. When their eyes met, Lindsay saw his doubts and worries, and she tried to reassure him with a smile. She knew what she was doing. He needn't worry about her.

Lindsay attached the leashes to Mutt and Jeff before she opened the car door. She, too, studied the town that was to be her home for the next year. It did look bleak and sad. Ever the optimist, she'd convinced herself it wasn't as shabby as she remembered. But it was. Worse, even. Still, she didn't let that dissuade her.

"Lindsay, look!" her mother said, pointing to a banner strung between Hansen's Grocery and Knight's Pharmacy.

Someone had taken an old white sheet and painted WELCOME, MISS SNYDER in bright red paint across it.

This simple greeting completely changed the grim reality of Buffalo Valley.

"Lindsay." Hassie stepped out of the pharmacy and threw open her arms. "Welcome back."

After hugging the older woman, Lindsay introduced her parents. "You remember my dad, don't you? This is Brian and my mother, Kathleen."

"Brian, of course. Oh my, you do look good. Come in, come in. The whole town's been waiting for you. You made good time." Chattering happily, Hassie ushered them inside.

Lindsay and her parents had just sat down at the soda fountain when others started to arrive. Jacob Hansen was the first. He came in from the grocery store across the street.

"We got your cupboards stocked with a few of the necessities," he told Lindsay.

"My cupboards?"

"At the house," he explained. "That's our way of thanking you."

"Oh…thank *you*." Lindsay hadn't expected anyone to do that.

"It wasn't only me and Marta," Jacob was quick to tell her. "We had a pounding last Monday night. Practically everyone in town contributed something."

Lindsay had never heard of such a thing and turned to her mother, who explained, "Everyone brings a pound of something to stock the kitchen."

"How thoughtful!"

"The high-school kids repainted the inside of the house," Hassie told her. "Did a good job, too."

"Your grandmother had the wallpaper stripped off years ago," her mother said. "Most homes this age were wallpapered, but your grandmother Gina liked a more modern look."

"Joshua McKenna contributed the paint," the grocer leaned forward to say. "You remember Joshua, don't you? He's the president of the town council."

"But the kids picked out the color." A tall, rather attractive brunette approached her and held out her hand. "I'm

Sarah Stern, Joshua's daughter, and my Calla's going to be one of your students."

"Hi, I'm Lindsay." More and more people filled the pharmacy, and she raised her voice. "Like I told Hassie when I phoned to ask about the job, I've never taught school before and I'm going to need a lot of help."

"You got it," Buffalo Bob shouted, giving her a thumbs-up sign. "We got all-you-can-eat spaghetti tonight, and Lindsay and her folks eat for free."

A cheer went up, and Lindsay exchanged smiles with her parents, although she couldn't help noting the hesitation in her mother's eyes when she looked at the restaurant owner.

"You need help unloading that trailer?" Lindsay's gaze fell on a man wearing a uniform shirt advertising a brand-name gasoline. He stepped forward and offered his hand. "Dennis Urlacher," he said. "From this welcome, you can guess we're pleased to see you."

Lindsay laughed at his comment. "Is one of your children going to be in my class, too?"

He shook his head. "I'm not married."

Lindsay saw the way he looked at Sarah and guessed the two of them were probably an item. Romance, however, was the last thing on her mind. She'd come to recover from one unhappy episode and wasn't planning to complicate her life with another.

"We're serious about helping you unpack the trailer," Joshua McKenna said, glancing around at his friends and neighbors. "Might as well say yes, seeing you've got this many volunteers."

Lindsay would've preferred to relax for a few minutes before tackling that project, but her father answered for her. "We'd appreciate as much help as we can get," he told them.

Her grandparents' house was two blocks off Main, and Lindsay walked over, leading her dogs and half the town; her father drove the truck and U-Haul, while her mother brought Lindsay's car.

"This is the closest thing we've had to a parade in years," Hassie joked, planting herself beside Lindsay.

Rounding the corner, Lindsay saw her grandparents' house. She gasped, hardly able to believe her eyes.

The yard had been cleaned and the flower boxes planted. A row of bright red geraniums brought a flash of color to the white house. The windows sparkled, and a wicker rocker had been placed on the front porch, with a large welcome mat in front of the door.

"It was one of your grandmother's favorite spots," Hassie whispered, sounding almost emotional.

"This is too much," she protested.

"We wanted you to know we appreciate what you're doing," Joshua McKenna said as he passed her, carrying the first load from the trailer.

"The fence has been repaired, too," Lindsay said in wonder. "And it's painted and everything…"

"We didn't want your dogs to get lost," Hassie said. "You can thank Gage Sinclair for that."

Gage was someone Lindsay hadn't forgotten. They'd met during those few moments when he'd come into the pharmacy with his mother. Lindsay didn't think she'd ever seen such depth and character in a man's face. He was in his thirties, she'd guess, but the years couldn't have been easy ones. The tracery of fine lines at the corners of his eyes told her that. His hair, a coffee-brown, had been in need of a cut. He was deeply tanned, but this wasn't the kind of tan one got from sitting under a lamp. His tan had been baked on by long hours in the sun. It was his eyes, though, that

had struck her most. They were the most incredible blue, verging on gray.

Before they'd had a chance to exchange more than a word or two, he'd made his excuses and left. Later, Hassie had told her Gage had a younger brother who'd be attending the high school. In those few moments, Lindsay had keenly felt his appraisal, but whatever he thought he'd kept to himself.

"If you like what we did to the outside, just wait till you see the interior." Her face bright with joy, Hassie grabbed Lindsay's hand and led her into the house.

Inside, Lindsay paused. The place was virtually unrecognizable. The living room was a bright white and when she moved into the kitchen she found it to be a cheery shade of lemon-yellow. Her bathroom was a robin's egg-blue, and her bedroom a pale lavender.

What hadn't been repainted had been scrubbed until it glistened. The floors shone with wax, and the entire place smelled fresh and clean.

"I can't *believe* anyone would do all this." Lindsay had wondered how she was going to make the house liveable and still manage to get everything ready for the first day of school. She'd had no idea that the entire town of Buffalo Valley had foreseen her dilemma and taken action.

With so many people helping, it didn't take more than thirty minutes to completely unload the trailer and the truck. By the time Lindsay had finished thanking everyone, her mother was in the kitchen putting away pots and pans and filling up cupboards and drawers.

Lindsay leaned against the doorway. "I'm exhausted."

Her mother laughed. "My goodness, Lindsay, you're their hero."

"I wonder if they'll feel the same way at the end of the

school year?" her father teased, digging into the stacks of cardboard boxes for her CD player.

Lindsay headed toward the largest bedroom, which faced the front of the house. Her bed had already been assembled, thanks to Dennis Urlacher and Joshua McKenna. She found the box that held the sheets and then, with her dogs patiently waiting, she made the bed. Mutt and Jeff immediately hopped up, making themselves comfortable. She'd barely been in town an hour and already her clothes were hung in the closet and her kitchen cupboards were stocked. This old house, which had felt so stark and empty only a few weeks earlier, had been scrubbed clean, repainted and repaired, until now it looked and felt like home.

In two days, her parents would return to Savannah and Lindsay would be alone for the first time since her arrival. Her gaze fell on the fireplace and she recalled the memory of her grandmother and the moving brick.

She would find that brick, she decided, and discover what her grandmother had slipped inside all those years ago.

Five

Minutes for the August 21st meeting of the
Buffalo Valley Town Council

As recorded by Hassie Knight, Secretary and Treasurer, duly elected.

The meeting was opened by council president Joshua McKenna with the Pledge of Allegiance to the American flag. Council members attending: Joshua McKenna, Dennis Urlacher, Jacob Hansen, Hassie Knight, Heath Quantrill. Marta Hansen and Buffalo Bob Carr sat in as observers. Absent: Gage Sinclair.

In regard to old business: Joshua McKenna commended everyone on the hard work and effort that went into cleaning up the school and yard. He also mentioned the work done to the old Snyder place to welcome the new schoolteacher. In refurbishing the house, the council spent two hundred dollars to supplement what wasn't donated by the community businesses. Hassie Knight read a thank-you letter written to the town council by Lindsay Snyder.

In the matter of new business: council president Joshua

McKenna reminded the council of Lindsay Snyder's request for guest speakers at the school on Friday afternoons. In an effort to set a good example, he volunteered to be the first speaker. Heath Quantrill offered to speak on banking practices and Hassie Knight promised a chemistry lesson. Dennis Urlacher declined to participate but volunteered Gage Sinclair, seeing that he was absent due to harvesting pressures.

It was brought to the council's attention by Marta Hansen (who is not an official member of the council) that because Miss Snyder is from the South and unaccustomed to the harsh North Dakota winters, the search for a permanent replacement for Eloise Patten should continue. The council is taking her suggestion under advisement. Hassie Knight recommended the town give Lindsay Snyder a chance to prove herself first.

It was reported that Rachel Fischer is looking into opening a pizza parlor on weekends, using her parents' restaurant, which has been closed for three years.

The meeting was adjourned at precisely noon.

Respectfully submitted,
Hassie Knight

Heath Quantrill had found the summons from his grandmother when he reached the Buffalo Valley bank bright and early Wednesday morning. The fact that she hadn't phoned him at home told him she wanted to see him regarding a bank matter. He couldn't even guess what he'd done to incur the old woman's wrath *this* time.

Sitting down at his desk, Heath looked over the application from Brandon Wyatt, a local farmer applying for a fifteen-hundred-dollar loan to buy a new washer and dryer.

Brandon had been into the bank late last week for the application and returned it Tuesday afternoon by mail. It wasn't the first time he'd seen Heath regarding a small loan. Brandon had one large outstanding debt—a loan on a combine, with a balance of over a hundred thousand dollars. He'd purchased it at a Fargo dealership, with financing arranged at a local bank by the dealership itself. Heath figured Brandon's wife must really need this washer and dryer for the farmer to approach him before harvest time. Because he knew and trusted Wyatt, Heath approved the loan after giving it little more than a cursory read.

Despite the fact that he'd lived with bankers his entire life, Heath was learning the banking business from the ground up, compliments of his cantankerous grandmother, Lily Quantrill. He'd known from childhood that one day he'd be an important part of the family business, but he hadn't been in any hurry to assume that responsibility. Not when his big brother appeared to be the financial whiz kid.

In college, Heath had taken all the right classes, graduated with an acceptable grade-point average and then left to spend the summer in Europe. Except that his summer had lasted eight years. He'd skied the Alps, climbed a few mountains, crossed the Sahara Desert on a camel and sailed the Mediterranean. He'd fallen in love with Greece and two or three women along the way. His sense of adventure knew no bounds.

Without a thought, without considering the consequences, he'd blatantly risked his sorry neck in a series of insane quests. It never occurred to him that while he was involved in one extreme game after another, his brother Max would be killed in a freak highway accident.

Heath had been called home for the funeral; his grandmother had tracked him down in Austria. He'd always

loved the stubborn old woman, although unfortunately the two of them had never gotten along. Everyone else in the family had kowtowed to her for years. But not Heath. After his initial three months in Europe, she'd demanded he come home and accept his rightful place in the family business. He'd ignored her summons and managed quite nicely even after she'd cut off his healthy allowance.

Max's death had shaken him badly, even more than his own parents' premature deaths. It had also angered him. Had Max survived, Heath would have punched him out for risking his life. If he was seeking a dangerous thrill, there were far better ways than trying to avoid a deer in the middle of a snowstorm.

His grandmother, however, had gotten her revenge. Upon Heath's return to Grand Forks, she'd promptly sent him to the old bank in Buffalo Valley. She fully intended to shape him into a banking executive, no matter how unsuited she felt he was for the job. She'd started him at the bottom, working him at each position until he'd satisfactorily proven himself.

The first time Heath saw Buffalo Valley, he'd thought it was a joke. Surely there'd been some mistake. The old woman couldn't possibly expect him to commute three days a week to this godforsaken place! But that was exactly what she'd expected. For twelve months now, he'd been doing his penance.

The town was in the last throes of death, a death that would have been inevitable if the Snyder woman hadn't agreed to step in as teacher. When he'd heard the news, Heath hadn't known whether to cheer or weep.

The message from his grandmother weighed heavily on Heath's mind as the day progressed. He found himself second-guessing the reason. He reviewed his files, wonder-

ing what he'd done now to displease her. He couldn't come up with any questionable decisions he'd made, any meetings he'd forgotten or deadlines he'd missed. He might not *want* to be a banker, but he was perfectly adequate. His skills were instinctive, and he'd proven himself at every turn. Or so he thought.

His grandparents had founded Buffalo County Bank, and his father had taken over the leadership, joining his grandmother after his grandfather's death. Then, during Heath's last year of college, his parents had died within six months of each other. His father had suffered a heart attack, and his mother, who'd battled cancer for years, succumbed to it a few months later. With the highway accident that had claimed Max, Heath and his grandmother were all that remained of the Quantrill family.

Traffic inside the bank had been slow all day, but then it was most days. He called Brandon Wyatt to tell him he could stop in to sign the papers later that week. By four, he was on the road toward Grand Forks and the retirement center where his grandmother lived.

"It's about time you got here," she muttered from her wheelchair the minute he walked into her suite.

"I'm happy to see you, too, Grandma." Grinning, he bent down to kiss her cheek. Lily was eighty-five, and Heath swore she'd outlive him.

"Sit down," she ordered.

Another day he might have stood and enjoyed the breathtaking view of the Red River from her tenth-floor apartment, just to spite her. But he was curious about her mood and complied rather than press the issue. He trained his gaze on the water, mentally preparing himself for a tongue-lashing.

"Do you remember Rachel Fischer?"

Heath had to stop and think. The name was vaguely familiar.

"She came into the bank for a loan recently," his grandmother added.

"Oh, yes." Heath nodded. He did remember. "The widow. She wanted twenty-five hundred dollars for a pizza oven."

"That's correct."

"Her parents owned the old café." As he recalled from the paperwork, the Morningside Café had been closed for three years. The place, now boarded up, was an eyesore on Main Street—one of many.

"Do you happen to remember what Rachel intended to do with that pizza oven?"

He raised an eyebrow at her question.

"She told me she wanted to start a pizza restaurant that'd be open on weekends for pick-up and in-town delivery." He recalled that, at the council meeting, Joshua had mentioned the possibility of Rachel's new business. Naturally he couldn't say anything about rejecting the loan.

"A pizza restaurant," Lily repeated.

Heath studied his grandmother. Her voice was calm, as if she were laying a trap for him. But he knew he'd made the right decision in rejecting Rachel Fischer's application. The woman, a widow with a ten-year-old son, had nothing in the way of collateral. Twenty-five hundred dollars might not sound like a lot of money, but to the people in Buffalo Valley it was a fortune.

"You turned her down."

"I did." He would again, too, without hesitation.

His grandmother wheeled her chair closer to him. "Why?"

He found it ludicrous that she'd even ask.

"Because any new business in Buffalo Valley is doomed," he finally answered.

"Is that a fact?" The old woman's face darkened. "My understanding is they found a teacher."

"Yes, but I still would've rejected the loan."

"Tell me your reasoning." She folded her hands on her lap, patient as ever. Once again, Heath had the feeling she was lying in ambush.

"First, she had no collateral—"

"That's not what I hear."

Heath frowned. Come to think of it, Rachel had offered to have him hold her wedding ring, but the plain gold band was worth a hundred dollars, if that.

"A hundred-dollar ring?" He made it sound like a joke.

"The wedding ring her dead husband gave her." His grandmother's gaze seared holes straight through him. "This man was her *husband* and the father of her child. Do you think she'd willingly surrender her wedding band and not walk over hot coals to get it back?"

"I—"

"She has a job, doesn't she?"

"For minimum wage. Driving the school bus." Nine months of the year she was responsible for delivering Buffalo Valley's grade-school age children to the Bellmont school thirty-five miles west of town.

"You didn't feel she could repay the loan with that?"

"No." How she managed to survive on these meager wages plus what she received from Social Security was beyond him. From the loan application he'd learned that there'd been very little insurance money after her husband's death.

His grandmother's stare intensified, and she hit him with another sharp question. "Have you taken a look around Buffalo Valley recently?"

Considering that he drove into town three days a week

and was a member of the council, Heath presumed she already knew the answer.

"Well?" she demanded in that deep voice of hers.

"I'm aware of what's happening in town, if that's what you're asking. Without a new teacher, it would have died in a year. With one, it'll take two years, maybe three." It wasn't what his grandmother wanted to hear but it was the truth.

"Dying, you say. That being the case, I'd say the town was badly in need of people willing to invest in the future."

"That's true, but—"

"Don't *but* me," his grandmother snapped.

Heath flinched. He held his breath for a moment in an effort to keep from arguing with her. "Grandma, listen, I did everything by the book," he began quietly.

"Exactly."

He blinked in confusion. "Then what's your point?"

"My point, young man, is that you've failed both me and Buffalo Valley. I sent you to this branch not as punishment, which is what you seem to believe, but to provide you with a training ground for all future banking decisions."

Heath clenched his hands at his sides. He'd heard all this before and he didn't buy it. It seemed to him that he could've learned everything he needed to know at the slick new bank in downtown Grand Forks.

"Buffalo Valley holds a special place in my heart." She relaxed and some of the anger left her eyes. "William chose Buffalo Valley for our first bank."

"I know." All this was ancient history. As far as Heath could see, the only reason the bank remained open was Lily Quantrill's nostalgia for her past. Even the most in-experienced accounting student could figure out that they'd been operating at a loss for several years. The

minute his grandmother died, he intended on cutting his losses and moving out.

"You aren't telling me you want to give her the loan, are you?" He'd do it if ordered, but Rachel Fischer wasn't a better risk now than when she'd originally applied.

His grandmother shook her head sadly.

"You *don't* want me to give her the loan?" There was no satisfying the old woman.

Her eyes closed. "The woman offered you the most precious item she possesses. You couldn't ask for better collateral. And she already has the building."

"She wants to run a pizza restaurant. Just how many pizzas do you seriously think she's going to sell in a town the size of Buffalo Valley—especially in winter?"

"She won't have rent, won't have high overhead, won't have anything but her supplies and the loan on her pizza oven."

"Yes." He'd already heard all that and still felt the widow was a poor risk.

His grandmother shook her head again. "What I want to teach you is that looking at the bottom line can only tell you so much. A real banker makes decision with his head *and* his heart. You have an overabundance of one and are completely lacking in the other."

Heath looked away.

"Give the widow her loan, Max."

He straightened. "I'm Heath, Grandma. Max is dead."

"Don't I know it," she grumbled. "Now go," she said, gesturing with her hand. "Go before I say something I'll regret."

Gage had been cutting wheat all morning under a darkening sky. Most of the six hundred acres planted were already harvested. With the threat of rain in the air and the

wind picking up speed, he decided to get the combine out of the fields before it got stuck in the mud.

He'd worked sixteen hours the day before and he'd been up before the sun that morning, hoping to beat the storm.

Not until he pulled into the yard did he notice Lindsay's car. He was instantly angry, but he understood his reaction. He didn't want to see her, had taken pains to avoid contact with her. He wasn't a man who ran away from many things, and he barely knew this woman, but she dominated his thoughts to an unprecedented—and disturbing—degree. He'd wondered what it would feel like to kiss her, to hold her, to have her as part of his life. At night when he stumbled into bed, exhausted, he couldn't close his eyes without her image filling his mind. It made him damn mad because he knew he was setting himself up for trouble. Most everyone agreed she wouldn't stay. Marta Hansen thought it prudent that they continue to search for a permanent replacement. Gage agreed. Lindsay had signed a one-year contract and in his opinion, it'd be a miracle if she lasted that long.

As bad luck would have it, Lindsay and his mother stepped out of the house at the precise moment he'd decided to head for the barn.

"Gage." His mother raised her hand and called to him.

Briefly he considered pretending he hadn't heard her, but knew it would do no good, especially when one of the dogs came running after him, barking like crazy. He removed his hat and drew his forearm across his brow, then bent down to scratch Tramp's ears, cursing under his breath. With the border collie leaping beside him, he walked slowly toward the women.

"You remember Lindsay, don't you?" his mother asked as he approached.

"Yeah." He nodded once, aware that he could have been more polite.

"Hello, Gage."

"Lindsay's visiting every family that has a high-school student," his mother explained.

"I'm new to teaching," she said, apparently for his benefit, "and I'm going to need help from the community. Leta and Hassie have been wonderful already." She smiled fondly at his mother.

"What kind of help are you looking for?" Gage asked, his voice gruff and unfriendly.

She ignored his lack of welcome. "I was hoping you could tell me something about yourself, something you could share with my students."

"That's why she's here, Gage," his mother said, frowning at him. "Lindsay wants to get to know everyone, and I was telling her about your bees."

"I've been meaning to thank you for the jar of honey," Lindsay added. "It's delicious."

"It didn't come from me. My mother's the one who sent it."

"Gage!" Leta chastised. The phone rang inside the house and she glanced over her shoulder. "I'd better answer that," she said reluctantly. She took a couple of steps toward the door, then hesitated, looking from Lindsay to Gage. She seemed almost afraid to leave the two of them alone.

"You go on. I'll walk Miss Snyder to her car," Gage told her.

His mother hurried to the house, leaving the two of them standing in the yard with the wind whirling dust devils about them.

"Would you be willing to talk to the class about your

beehives?" Lindsay asked. She gazed up at him, eyebrows drawn together.

He was framing his refusal, but she didn't give him the opportunity. "Joshua McKenna said he'd come and talk about the history of North Dakota," she went on in a rush. "He's apparently quite knowledgeable in that area, plus he's read quite a bit about the Lewis and Clark expedition. I'm hoping to convince Jeb McKenna to talk about buffalo—I mean bison."

"Jeb said he would?" That surprised Gage. His neighbor to the south had lost a leg a few years back and become something of a recluse. He'd quit farming and taken up raising bison, surprising everyone with his success. But since the accident, he rarely ventured into town. Gage knew Joshua worried about his son, and Sarah had bent over backward to help her brother, but to no avail.

"Joshua's talking to him for me."

That explained it. And it also gave him a diplomatic way of avoiding this. He already knew that her students couldn't care less about his bees. Kevin had been around them all his life and showed zero interest.

"If Jeb agrees, then so will I."

Lindsay frowned, clearly puzzled. "Have I done something to offend you?"

So she liked the direct approach. Fine, so did he. "As a matter of fact you have. You came back."

She scowled fiercely at him. "Do you mean to tell me you'd rather the high school just closed?"

"No. It's nothing personal, Miss Snyder, but I don't want you here." His words were carried off by the wind, but anger flared in her eyes, and Gage knew she'd heard him.

"Why should you care one way or the other? You don't know me."

"I don't *want* to know you."

She blinked as if he'd so utterly baffled her, she no longer knew what to say. The storm broke just then, and she turned around and ran straight for her car. Thunder crashed overhead, and the rain fell in fat, thick drops that beaded on the dry, dusty soil.

Her car door slammed. She was dry and safe, but Gage stood in the downpour and watched as she drove out of his yard. By the time he dashed into the house, he was drenched to the skin.

He hadn't even removed his hat before his mother laid into him. "I want to know what you said to Lindsay."

Unaccustomed to that tone of voice from his soft-spoken mother, Gage just stared at her.

The rain pounded against the roof, and Leta raised her voice. "Answer me, young man."

"I'm thirty-five, Mother, and could hardly be considered a young man."

"Then quit acting like a nineteen-year-old."

Gage hadn't fought with his mother in years, and would prefer to keep the peace now. As far as he was concerned, what he had or hadn't said to Lindsay Snyder was none of her business. "I didn't say anything."

"Yes, you did. I saw the way Lindsay raced to her car. You insulted her, didn't you?"

"If she took exception to—"

"I won't have it! You were rude to her, and I won't have it. Do you hear me?"

Gage had hardly ever seen his mother this angry. Her face was red, her eyes blazing and she held herself ramrod straight.

"Mom—"

"You'll apologize."

"The hell I will." Gage wasn't going to let his mother dictate his actions.

Before their disagreement could turn into a full-fledged argument, he left the house. He'd rather stand in the pouring rain than fight with his mother over a woman like Lindsay Snyder.

By dinnertime her mood hadn't improved. She didn't speak to him while she placed their meal on the table, then pointedly stalked out of the room when Gage and Kevin sat down to eat.

"What'd you do to make Mom so mad?" Kevin asked as he pulled out a kitchen chair.

"Nothing," he barked at his younger brother.

Kevin raised both hands as if to protect himself. "Sorry I asked."

Gage reached for a biscuit, then froze as his mother marched back into the kitchen with a bouquet of purple prairie wildflowers she'd cut that morning. "Take these with you."

Gage's eyes narrowed. "I'm not going anywhere."

She left the room again and, relieved, Gage returned to his meal. He hadn't taken more than two bites when his mother was back, carrying her purse and the flowers.

"Kevin," she said, "would you kindly drive me into town so I can apologize for my son's rudeness?"

"Ah…" Kevin looked helplessly from his mother to Gage. "I was hoping to drive over to—" He stopped in mid-sentence when Leta glared at him. "All right," he agreed, grabbing a last bite of biscuit and standing up.

Gage could only imagine what his mother would say to Lindsay. Furious, he bolted to his feet and threw his napkin onto his plate. "Dammit all to hell." Leta was going to make his life miserable until he gave in and did what she asked.

He stomped out of the house, pausing only long enough

to grab the truck keys from the peg by the door. At least the rain had stopped.

His mother hurried after him, slogging through the mud. "Take the flowers with you."

He didn't look back as he marched across the yard. "The hell with the flowers."

His anger sustained him all the way into town. Even when he'd parked outside the teacher's house, he had to draw several deep breaths in an effort to cool his temper.

What annoyed him the most was knowing that his mother was right. He owed Lindsay an apology, and given the opportunity he would've offered her one. He resented being pressured into it.

Climbing out of the truck, he walked up her porch steps and leaned on the doorbell. The dogs barked wildly—sounded like useless little critters. He moved his hat and stabbed his fingers through the tangled mass of hair, determined to make the best of this. He'd say his piece, then leave.

The door opened and Lindsay stood on the other side wearing shorts and work boots, with her ash-blond hair tied up in a kerchief, and a hammer and chisel in her hand. She seemed as shocked to see him as he was to find her looking like…like a construction worker.

"Gage?"

He stiffened. "I'm here to apologize."

Her face relaxed, and she opened the screen door for him. "Come in."

He stepped inside and the dogs greeted him as though he were a long-lost relative. He decided they might be useless—sure weren't much protection—but they *were* kind of cute. Petting them gave him the opportunity to look the house over. He was impressed; what had, a few weeks earlier, been a decrepit old house was now a home.

Her curtains and furniture, a dark-green rug, some lamps, photographs and prints on the clean white walls—it all made an incredible difference.

Frowning, he noticed the fireplace. Apparently she'd been hammering away at it. "Something wrong with your fireplace?"

"No."

"Then why—"

"No reason."

"If you're dismantling the fireplace, there's got to be a reason."

She set the hammer and chisel aside. "Are you here to apologize or to question my remodeling efforts?"

Remodeling? Gage sincerely doubted that, but she had made one good point. He wasn't there to chitchat. "As I explained, I came to…apologize." The words didn't come easy, nor did he mention that it had been at his mother's insistence. "I was rude to you earlier this afternoon."

"Yes, you were."

She certainly wasn't cutting him any slack.

"Why?" she asked. "What have I ever done to you?"

He didn't know how to answer. He couldn't find a way to tell her that every time he saw her or thought about her, he got angry. So, instead, he told her what he suspected. "You aren't going to last. All you're doing is raising everyone's hopes. Once reality hits, you'll move on. You'll abandon the community."

"I signed a contract for one year and I intend to honor that."

"Like hell you will." He was angry again, so angry he couldn't keep from raising his voice. "You won't make it past the first snowfall."

"Like hell I won't." She was yelling now, too. "I'm a woman of my word."

"Why'd you come in the first place? What's Buffalo Valley got that you can't find in Savannah?"

"None of your business." She stood only a few inches away from him, her eyes spitting fire, her lips moist and shining. The top two buttons of her sleeveless blouse were unfastened, leading his gaze to the promise of her breasts. Her legs were long and slender and— Then he knew. It was obvious.

"You're running away, aren't you?" She'd accepted the piddling teacher's salary the town had offered because she wanted out of an unhappy situation. She was escaping a love affair gone bad.

It was the only thing he could think of to explain why she'd move to a town as desperate as Buffalo Valley. At the thought of her in the arms of another man, his gut tightened with a wave of jealousy.

"What's the matter?" he taunted. "Did you find out he was married?"

"I think you should leave." She clomped over to the door in her heavy boots and held it open. Her dogs trotted behind her, sat on their haunches and stared at him.

He hesitated at the door, where she stood with her arms crossed and her eyes narrowed. With a nonchalant shrug, Gage did as she requested, recognizing that once again, he'd screwed up. God help him if his mother heard about *this*.

In no mood to return to the ranch and answer her questions, Gage headed for Buffalo Bob's, badly in need of a beer.

The bar had two or three patrons, but Gage didn't feel like company and made his way to a table in the back, preferring to sit in the shadows.

Dressed in her Buffalo Gal outfit, Merrily walked over to him. "What can I get you, Gage?"

"A draft beer." He watched her return to the bar—and

watched as Buffalo Bob's eyes followed her every move. Another farmer, Steve Baylor, was in town, too, with some gal Gage didn't recognize. They were whispering to each other. At that moment Gage would have given anything to be enjoying his beer with Lindsay. But instead of acting like a gentleman, instead of apologizing properly, bringing her flowers the way his mother had suggested, instead of inviting her to dinner, talking and getting to know her, he'd sneered at her. Insulted her. He knew the reason, too. She scared the hell out of him.

Merrily brought his beer in a frosty mug and he paid her, grateful that she didn't attempt to strike up a conversation. He needed a beer and solitude, in that order. It took another beer to find the courage to do what he knew was right.

Lindsay was furious. So furious she could barely stand still. When she'd arrived in Buffalo Valley it had all seemed so wonderful. The house had been readied for her, the cupboards filled and the welcome mat placed on her front porch. In the weeks since, she'd confronted reality.

The one-room school was wholly inadequate. The only computer available was the laptop she'd brought with her. The school district could barely afford textbooks, let alone computers.

Lindsay wanted to do a good job, give her students a basic education and supply them with everything they needed to face the world after graduation. To do that she was going to need help. Lots of it.

The first time she'd met Gage that Saturday at Hassie's, she'd liked him. When she thought about returning to Buffalo Valley, he was someone who'd come to mind, someone she'd instinctively assumed would be a friend. Instead, he'd been rude and arrogant, insisting she wouldn't

last. His attitude, she'd discovered, was unfortunately typical. While everyone was friendly and welcoming, the town seemed divided on the issue of how long she'd stay. Some seemed to feel she'd serve out her contract, others that she'd leave halfway through. Nobody thought she'd stay a day longer than one year. Although she had roots in Buffalo Valley, she wasn't considered one of them. The prevailing attitude didn't upset her, and in truth, she'd been expecting it. She knew she had to prove herself, and that was something she was prepared to do. Something she felt she *could* do.

But after today's confrontations with Gage, Lindsay wasn't sure anymore. His hostility had come as a shock. It discouraged her and made her question her own ability to succeed at this. She sighed heavily and glanced around. More discouragement. She'd practically dismantled the entire fireplace and hadn't found any hollow brick.

The doorbell chimed, and barking crazily, Mutt and Jeff raced to the front door. A surreptitious look through the window revealed Gage Sinclair. Again? She hadn't recovered from his last verbal bout.

"Open up, Lindsay, I know you're in there," he called when she didn't immediately open the door.

"Go away!" she shouted back. "Whatever you have to say doesn't interest me."

"The least you can do is hear me out."

"If you've come to apologize again, save it. I'm still bleeding from the last one."

She found it ridiculous and embarrassing to be yelling at someone through the door. Before long they were bound to attract attention.

Gage pounded on the door again. "All I want is to talk to you."

Exasperated, Lindsay threw open the door and folded her arms, leaving the screen door between them. "All right. Say what you have to say and then kindly *go!*"

Now that they stood face-to-face, Gage couldn't seem to get the words out. "Well, I…I was thinking, maybe you…" He paused, squared his shoulders and continued. "Would you like to have a beer with me?"

"You came back to ask me out for a beer?"

He hesitated. "Well…yes."

If she hadn't been so astounded, she would have laughed. He'd been rude and insulting, then showed up on her porch and practically broke down her door because he was looking for a drinking companion?

"It isn't a trick question," he muttered.

"Thank you, but no."

"That's what I thought you'd say." He turned to leave.

"Gage, wait." She stopped him. She'd rather have him as her friend than her enemy. Opening the screen door, she stepped onto the porch and touched his arm. "It was…sweet of you to ask."

His reaction to her touch was immediate, and he shocked her by taking hold of her shoulders. He stared down at her with his incredible blue-gray eyes, immobilizing her.

She recognized what was about to happen. She became aware that he was going to kiss her at the same moment she decided it was what she wanted. He pulled her into his arms with none of the finesse to which she was accustomed. When he kissed her, it felt wild and dangerous. Intense. He kissed her with an urgency that had her clinging to him with both hands.

Lindsay had done her share of kissing, but had never experienced anything like this. Gage kissed her as if…as if he'd been waiting to kiss her his whole life.

What astounded her more was the realization that one kiss wasn't enough. He stopped for a moment to catch his breath, then kissed her again, with the same abandon, until her knees threatened to go out from under her.

When he released her, Lindsay stumbled backward. She caught herself on the porch railing, clutching it with one hand while heaving in deep breaths. Hardly believing what he'd done, what she'd allowed—no, *wanted*—she placed the back of her hand against her lips and stared at him.

"When you change your mind about having that beer," he said, "let me know." Then he turned and walked over to his truck, parked in front of her house.

Six

Brandon hadn't mentioned their anniversary all day. They'd been married ten years, and he'd apparently forgotten. That hurt. Joanie did her best to pretend it didn't matter, but it did. She didn't want to fight. Not today. Not when it seemed that all they did anymore was fight.

They didn't usually have loud arguments the way some couples did, with angry words and slamming doors. Instead they ignored each other. They were infinitely polite when they did have to speak, and both made an effort to avoid doing or saying anything that would distress their children. Sage, at eight, seemed the most perceptive of the undercurrents. Joanie wanted to spare her daughter and son their parents' unhappiness.

Actually, Brandon's forgetting their anniversary shouldn't have surprised her. He hadn't remembered her birthday last March, either. At Christmas he'd given her a token bottle of cologne, the same scent he'd bought the year before. She half suspected he'd purchased two bottles at a discount and saved the second for the following Christmas.

With the kids anxious for the start of school on Monday

morning, Joanie spent the day in town picking up the necessary supplies of paper and crayons and lunch bags and a thermos for Stevie. When she returned home, she started dinner, determined to make it a special evening despite her husband's forgetfulness.

At six that evening, Brandon came in from the fields. "What's for dinner?" he asked.

"Steak."

"We celebrating anything special?"

"It's our anniversary," she said, putting on a brave smile. "I baked your favorite coconut cake this morning and picked up a couple of frozen entrées for the kids. I thought we might have dinner together tonight, just the two of us."

"How long we been married now?" Brandon asked, opening the refrigerator and pulling out a jug of iced tea. Despite years of her complaining, he drank directly from the pitcher, guzzling the liquid.

"Ten years," she told him. The fact that he had to ask was indicative of the problems in their marriage, she thought wryly. "Your parents mailed us a card. I put it on the buffet." The Wyatts had retired to Arizona, in the same town—a suburb of Phoenix—as Rachel's parents. The payments Brandon made on the land were the bulk of their retirement income.

She didn't mention that they'd gotten a card from her parents, too, because any mention of them could lead to a disagreement. If he looked at the one card, he'd see the other for himself.

"Ten years?" Brandon repeated. "Has it really been that long?"

Busy tossing the salad greens, picked fresh from the garden, Joanie answered with a nod. The most profound

years of her life, she mused. In some ways the happiest, in others the hardest. In retrospect she realized she'd romanticized life on a farm and had come into this marriage an innocent. Completely naive. It didn't help that she'd married a man who was as stubborn as they came. When she grew discouraged and depressed, Brandon threw the fact that she was a city girl in her face, as if to discount her years with him. Lately, she had to force herself to remember why she'd fallen in love with Brandon, and search for ways to recapture what they'd lost. But she seemed to be the only one who was trying....

Microwave dinners were a rare treat for Sage and Stevie, and they wolfed them down, then ran outside to play. While Brandon showered, Joanie set the kitchen table with their best china and silverware. Her husband might not appreciate her efforts, but she was determined to make this evening as special as she could.

Brandon didn't comment when he saw the table, but he lit the candles without her having to suggest it.

"Would you open the wine?" she asked, carrying the salad to the table.

"We have wine?"

She handed him the bottle she'd picked up in town from Buffalo Bob. He sold a small supply of wine and bottled liquor and had helped her choose a nice mellow merlot.

"I guess I should've taken you out to dinner," Brandon said as she began to fry the two steaks. Their barbecue had broken last summer and hadn't been replaced. "But why pay good money when you cook better than anyone?"

It was a compliment, she supposed, although she would have relished a night away from the kitchen.

Dinner went well. They tried to celebrate, make the

most of an intimate romantic dinner. Three times the kids raced into the house for one reason or another, but Brandon shooed them back outside with a gruff command.

When they'd finished eating, Joanie took the dirty dishes to the sink and Brandon wandered out to the yard. Clutching the edge of the sink, Joanie closed her eyes and tried not to cry. They'd lost something vital and she didn't know how to get it back. When she tried to talk to him about it, Brandon told her he was perfectly happy and if she wasn't, then the problem was hers.

"Joanie," Brandon called her from outside.

She brushed her hand across her cheeks and walked to the door.

"Joanie, could you come here a minute?" Brandon called again. "In the barn."

She hesitated, then opened the screen door and headed across the yard, unable to fathom what was so important in the barn.

The kids were there with Brandon, standing by the pickup, jumping up and down. Sage had her hands over her mouth and Stevie was smiling like there was no tomorrow. Brandon, too.

"Happy Anniversary, sweetheart," her husband told her and stepped aside.

There, in all their glory on the bed of his truck, were a brand-new washer and dryer. Joanie stared at those beautiful white appliances and was stunned into speechlessness.

"Say something, Mom," Sage cried.

"Oh, Brandon." She fell into her husband's arms, sobbing with happiness.

Brandon wrapped his arms around her and hugged her, whispering how much he loved her.

Joanie didn't think one person could hold this much joy.

Moments earlier, she'd been feeling sorry for herself, convinced that she was unloved and unappreciated. Then Brandon did something this wonderful.

"Why's Mom crying?" Stevie asked his sister.

"Because she's happy, stupid," Sage answered.

"Don't call your brother stupid," Brandon scolded her.

Laughing and crying at the same time, Joanie spread light, watery kisses over her husband's face. It seemed impossible that he'd been able to keep the gift a secret.

"We knew last week," Sage told her, then smugly added, "And we didn't say a word."

"I'm proud of you both." Joanie broke away from Brandon long enough to hug both her children.

"While you were shopping this afternoon, I drove over to Grand Forks and picked them up," he explained before she could ask when and how.

"They're beautiful." She ran her hand over the shiny new surfaces. "A dryer, too?"

"Figured I might as well go for broke. We were gonna need a new one soon enough."

"Oh, Brandon." She kissed him again. "It's the most beautiful washer and dryer I've ever seen."

"Top of the line, too."

"Oh, honey, I can't believe it, I just can't believe it."

"Gage said he'd come over one day next week to help me hook them up."

She wiped the tears from her cheeks and offered him a teary smile. "I thought you'd forgotten our anniversary."

Grinning, he brought her back into his arms. "I love you, Joanie."

"And I love you."

"Are you and Mom going to get all mushy again?" Stevie asked, covering his eyes.

Brandon laughed. "You two did good," he told the kids, and they raced out of the barn.

With his arm around her, Brandon walked Joanie to the house. When he reached the porch steps, he paused and jiggled his eyebrows, a long-ago signal that he was in the mood for lovemaking. She threw her arms around his neck and aimed her lips toward his ear to whisper. "Hold on, fellow, because you know what? It's going to be worth waiting for."

Brandon laughed boisterously, and taking her by the waist, swung her around.

The rest of the night reminded her of the way it was when they were first married. The anticipation. That simmering excitement. Several times they exchanged knowing looks and Brandon did his best to steer the kids to bed early but with little success. At nine, both Sage and Stevie were finally upstairs and the noise level dropped considerably.

"Alone at last," Brandon whispered from behind her while she finished the last of the dishes. He slid his arms around her waist and moved his hands up inside her blouse. His sigh was audible when he encountered her bare breasts. Their weight filled his hands. Brandon had always loved her breasts and she loved the way his hands fit over them, the way her nipples responded to his touch.

"When did you take off your bra?" he whispered close to her ear, sounding almost drunk with desire.

"When I got home from town. I was too hot." She often did these days, especially in the hottest part of the afternoon. Until now he hadn't noticed or cared.

"Oh, baby," he whispered. She could feel his arousal and sighed with longing. It'd been more than six weeks since they'd last made love. It seemed like a lifetime ago and she'd missed the intimacy, missed the closeness.

"I love you so much," he crooned, turning her in his arms.

Their kiss was explosive and it didn't take them long to move from the kitchen, turning off the lights as they progressed into the bedroom.

"Now, what was that you mentioned earlier," Brandon teased. "About something worth waiting for…"

Joanie giggled and crawled onto the bed. "Come over here, and I'll show you." She didn't need to issue a second invitation. Brandon slipped out of his clothes in record time.

Like their kisses had been earlier, their lovemaking was volatile. And wonderful. Afterward, Joanie lay in his arms, too happy to sleep, her head on her husband's shoulder.

"If I'd known this was my reward, I'd have bought you that washer and dryer a whole lot sooner."

"Oh, Brandon." Twisting her head, she nibbled on his earlobe. "You don't need to buy me anything in order to make love to me. I'm your wife."

His arm tightened across her back. "It's going to get better, baby, I promise. Both kids are going to be in school full-time this year, and you won't be so tied to the house."

Joanie had thought about that a lot. "Would you mind if I took a part-time job?" She knew Peggy Stablehaus was looking for shorter hours at the bank, and Joanie had some banking experience. When she met Brandon she'd been working as a teller.

"You can do whatever you like. All I want is for you to be happy."

"I am happy." And she was. She loved her husband, and her children, and despite what Brandon assumed, she loved the farm. Their life together wasn't what she'd expected, but as long as they had each other, she could cope. As long as they had this love, this passion, she could survive the tough times. Living from year to year, praying for good prices for

their crops was an emotional drain. As was watching her husband pour his life's blood into the land, each year making less and less profit from his backbreaking labor. Yet despite the hardships and the uncertainty, she was content to be his wife and the mother of his children.

"I love you," she whispered sleepily, kissing his jaw, "and I'm proud to be your wife."

He rubbed his chin against her hair and covered her with the thin, cotton sheet. Joanie had rarely known such love and contentment as she did right that moment.

Lindsay knew she was in over her head the minute her twelve students filed into the one-room schoolhouse. The first to walk in was Calla Stern. If Lindsay hadn't known better, she would've thought she'd taken over an inner-city class. Calla wore black army boots and black everything else. She had her nose pierced and her hair spiked. Everything about her spoke of attitude, most of it bad.

Gage's brother, Kevin, followed Calla with his arm tightly wrapped around a girl who was even blonder than he was and a head shorter. They selected their desks across from each other and shoved them close together.

Two boys roared in behind the lovebirds, arguing heatedly as they elbowed each other at the door. These were the infamous Loomis twins, Larry and Bert. Lindsay had met them soon after her arrival and heard horror stories about them from almost everyone in Buffalo Valley. The twins lived in Bellmont and rode the school bus into town. She was grateful they were fraternal twins and not identical. That, at least, diminished the potential for confusion—and mischief.

Since Larry and Bert couldn't agree on anything, Lindsay foolishly suggested they sit at opposite sides of the

room. The boys vehemently disagreed. They'd sat next to each other their entire school lives and weren't about to let an upstart city teacher separate them now.

Her day had gone downhill after that. By three-thirty, when school was dismissed, Lindsay was so tired she barely had the energy to walk home. Her first inclination was just to fall into bed and cuddle up with her dogs at her feet and sleep until morning. She'd had no idea teaching would be this physically and mentally exhausting. One day in the classroom, and she was convinced America's teaching professionals were grossly underappreciated, not to mention underpaid.

Instead of barricading herself inside her house, she decided to visit Hassie at the pharmacy. Lindsay was badly in need of some inspiration. Gage Sinclair had predicted she wouldn't last beyond the first snowstorm; the way she felt just then, she wouldn't last till the end of the week.

"Looks like you could use one of my extra-thick, extra-rich chocolate sodas," Hassie said immediately.

"What I need is a hot toddy and a bottle of aspirin."

Hassie laughed amiably and made her way to the counter. She automatically reached for the ice-cream scoop while Lindsay climbed onto a stool and slouched forward.

"That rough, was it?"

"Worse."

"The Loomis twins are a handful."

That was the understatement of the century. "I've arrived at one profound conclusion," Lindsay said, propping her elbows on the counter and, with an effort, lifting her head. "The classroom is not meant to be a democracy. After today, it's a dictatorship. I don't know what I was thinking. Hassie, I feel as though I'm drowning, and it's either sink or swim."

"You'll do just fine. If you want, I'll stop by tomorrow

and give those little hellions a chemistry lesson they won't soon forget."

"I've got you scheduled for next week. Joshua McKenna agreed to speak this Friday. And I *think* his son Jeb will come in a couple of weeks—although Sarah said not to count on him." She hadn't heard from Gage, but had taken the liberty of putting his name down for a lecture on honeybees later in the quarter.

"Anyone else volunteered?"

"Gage—well, sort of."

Hassie set the fizzing soda in front of her. "Speaking of Gage, it seems the two of you are getting along famously."

Lindsay went still, wondering if Hassie had seen her and Gage kissing on her front porch Saturday night. "He stopped by—"

"I saw his truck parked outside your place—not once but twice."

"He…came to apologize."

Hassie chuckled. "That boy has more style than I gave him credit for."

"You—saw?" Heat rushed to her cheeks. Lindsay had no reason to be embarrassed, but Hassie was the only person in town who knew about Monte.

"My goodness, Gage had you practically bent in half. I had no idea the boy could kiss like that."

Lindsay would rather not discuss the incident, but now that Hassie had brought up the subject, she couldn't ignore it. "I know what you saw, Hassie, but it wasn't the way it looked."

Striking a relaxed pose, Hassie leaned forward on her crossed arms. "You don't have to explain a thing to me. Gage is a fine man. You're both young and if you were to become romantically involved—"

"We're *not* romantically involved." That was definitely

a path Lindsay intended to avoid. She was healing from one relationship and wouldn't immediately immerse herself in another.

"Gage Sinclair is a good man."

"I'm sure he is, but I'm not interested."

Doing a poor job of disguising a smile, Hassie grabbed a rag and wiped down the counter. "Don't be so quick to make a decision," she said. "I don't know what would have happened to Leta and Kevin if Gage hadn't taken over the farm after John died. Nice man, John Betts, but not much with finances. He was up to his neck in debt when he passed on. So instead of buying and working his own land, Gage took over the farm and he's the sole support of his mother and half brother."

Despite what she'd said, Lindsay was curious about Gage. "He was born here?"

Hassie nodded. "Leta was a widow for almost ten years before she met and married John. Gage was about thirteen or fourteen at the time. He went into the Army as soon as he graduated from high school. The military seeks out farm boys, figuring they know how to work hard and don't have a problem following orders. He stayed in the Army for several years, then he went away to school for a while. When he returned, he started working the farm with John. He was looking for acreage of his own when John died."

"He's never been—" Lindsay stopped, unsure she should be asking these questions. Not that she was afraid of what Hassie thought, but because she herself might start thinking of Gage in terms that wouldn't be good for either of them. Despite her claim that their kisses meant nothing, Lindsay had trouble suppressing the memory. In her entire life, she'd never been kissed like that.

"Gage Sinclair would make you one hell of a husband."

"Hassie! The kiss was nothing. He—came to apologize."

"Twice?"

"Yes. We seemed to have started off on the wrong foot and—"

"You two were doin' some pretty fancy footwork when I saw you." Hassie laughed, looking pleased.

Lindsay could see it would do no good to argue. This tendency to discuss everyone else's business was part of living in a small town—something her father had warned her about. People felt they had the right to know and comment on whatever you did; there wasn't a lot of privacy. It'd been foolish to let Gage kiss her on the front porch where someone was likely to see them.

"Here," Hassie said, stepping out from behind the counter and reaching for an aspirin bottle. "Take two of these and call me in the morning."

After one last sip of the rich chocolate soda, Lindsay headed home, stopping at the small post office on her way. Inside her mail box was a thick letter from Maddy, which she read right there, hungry for news of home.

Monte had written her twice so far, his first letter asking bluntly if she'd changed her mind yet and was she ready to move back to Savannah? Lindsay had read the letter and tossed it. His second had arrived ten days later, and in it he expressed his annoyance at not having heard from her. That letter ended up in the same place as the first. As far as she was concerned, everything had already been said.

That night, after a quick salad for dinner and with the dogs at her feet, Lindsay sat down and wrote a long reply to her friend, telling Maddy about her first day as a teacher, about Calla Stern and the Loomis twins. She wrote about the people she'd met since arriving—without going into detail

about Gage—and how her first day in the classroom had shattered her illusions.

Her frustration with the fireplace didn't help, although she didn't tell Maddy about that. Lindsay had done everything other than dismantle the entire structure and all to no avail. Somewhere in this fireplace was a hollow brick, and inside it was something her grandmother had placed there all those years ago. She might have only been ten at the time, but she knew what she'd seen. Now, what had started as mere curiosity had turned into a mission. Lindsay was determined to find that brick, or tear down the house trying.

Once she'd poured out her feelings to her best friend, Lindsay felt much better. It'd only been her first day of teaching. Things were bound to get better. This was a period of adjustment for them all, she told herself, teacher as well as students.

The phone rang just as she'd finished sealing the envelope. Lindsay stared at it—almost afraid to answer in case it was a parent who disapproved of the way she'd handled her class. If so, Lindsay wasn't sure she'd disagree.

"Hello," she said, trying to sound professional and confident.

"It's Gage."

He was the last person she'd expected to hear from. "Oh—I'm glad you phoned."

"You are?"

"Hassie saw you kissing me," she blurted out. She was still unfamiliar with life in a small town and she had an uncomfortable suspicion that the news was all over Buffalo Valley by now. She could count on Hassie to be discreet, but there might well have been others….

His soft laughter annoyed her. "If it doesn't bother you, it doesn't bother me."

"As a matter of fact, it *does* bother me," she said curtly. Leave it to a man to make light of the situation. She had no interest in being the subject of gossip, especially this soon after her arrival.

"You don't need to worry. Hassie isn't one to talk out of turn."

Figuring he'd only be amused, she didn't mention her fear that the incident might have been noticed by others. "Just make sure it doesn't happen again."

"What? Kissing you?"

What else did he think she was talking about? "Yes."

"You liked it that much?"

Lindsay fumed silently. After the day she'd had, she was in no mood to deal with the likes of Gage Sinclair. "I suppose there's a reason you phoned me?"

"Two reasons, actually," Gage answered.

Lindsay could hear the smug cheerfulness in his voice, and it irritated her all the more.

"I'll come and talk to the high-school class about honeybees, if you want."

Gratitude cooled her irritation. "That would be wonderful. Does two weeks from Friday work for you?"

"October would be better."

"Great. I'll put you down for the first Friday in October." They chatted a bit about what she was looking for in the way of a science lesson—and then Gage broached the second reason for his call.

"I was wondering if you'd like to have a beer with me Saturday night at Buffalo Bob's."

Lindsay hesitated, weighing the decision. She was tempted to say yes. The man's kisses could buckle her knees. But she'd just met him and they were already the subject of local gossip. "Um, I don't think that would be a good idea."

His own pause was lengthy. "What I said about you getting over someone back in Savannah—that's right, isn't it?"

She hesitated again, then admitted the truth. "Yes." It was best to be aboveboard with Gage. "I…I'm giving myself a year to heal. It isn't you, Gage, it's me. I don't want to leap from one relationship into another…."

"I asked you out for a beer. It wasn't a marriage proposal."

"I know, but I thought…you know."

"As a matter of fact, I do. I won't ask you again."

A man and his pride were a frightful combination. "That's probably for the best."

"The way I see it," Gage told her, "you'll have to ask *me* the next time around."

Rachel Fischer knew good pizza when she tasted it. And her own, baked with a thin homemade crust and topped with sauce made from the tomatoes grown in her garden, was excellent. Now that she had the small pizza oven, she was in business.

The past four years had been difficult, and she was only now beginning to feel optimistic about the future. First her husband, Ken, had died after a long bout with leukemia. By the time of his death, the farm had been mortgaged to the hilt and two weeks after the funeral, the bank in Fargo had repossessed the land and the equipment and even their pick-up truck.

Not long after she'd buried Ken, her parents, who owned the Morningside Café, decided to close the restaurant and move south. Her mother had urged Rachel to join them. Buffalo Valley was dying and there was little to keep her there.

The decision had been wrenching, but in the end, she'd felt that Mark had already endured enough upheaval in his life. Then the job driving the school bus had become available and

she'd accepted that. She moved into her parents' old house and had managed to hold on, like everyone else in town.

In Rachel's view the tide had begun to turn when Hassie found a replacement for the high-school teacher. The fact that Lindsay Snyder had signed a one-year contract was exactly what the town needed. Everyone seemed more hopeful. If ever there was a time to start her business, Rachel sensed it was now.

An offhand comment from her son was what had suggested the idea. He'd gone to Grand Forks with a friend for a birthday party at a pizza parlor, and returned to tell her she made *much* better pizza. When Mark's birthday came around, she invited the same set of friends to the house and served her own pizza. Mark's friends agreed with him. She made the best pizza of anyone.

Rachel thought so, too.

"Mom. Mom!" Ten-year-old Mark raced into the restaurant Friday night, the first official day of business. He was as excited about this venture as Rachel was. "I delivered the flyers to everyone in town. When will the orders start coming?"

"I'm ready any time," Calla told her, following Mark inside.

Rachel had an arrangement with the girl. Since she couldn't afford to actually pay Calla wages to deliver the pizza—not yet, anyway—the teenager had agreed to take on the job for any tips she might collect, plus a free pizza for every night worked. Rachel had talked over the terms of employment with Sarah, Calla's mother, who'd given the project her approval.

Soon, Rachel sincerely hoped, she'd be running a profitable enterprise. She knew how to make good pizza, but she was only now learning what it meant to be a good

business person. Starting small was essential. Her pizza service was open only on weekends. If it grew the way she hoped it would, she could expand later. As it was now, other than for pick-up, the restaurant wasn't officially open. When she'd paid off the pizza oven, she'd save for new tables and chairs and other equipment she needed. Eventually she hoped to add to the menu and open the restaurant full-time.

"What are we going to do if no one orders any pizza?" Mark asked.

Calla had slouched down in a chair to read a magazine. She glanced up at Mark's question.

"People will order," Rachel said with all the confidence she could muster. She was determined to make a go of this venture. Driving the school bus paid barely enough for them to live on and kept her employed only nine months of the year. Hassie had her do the weekly bookkeeping for the pharmacy and that helped some, but not enough.

The pizza business was her dream, and she'd invested far more than her tomato crop in this venture. She'd invested her heart.

"Mom," Mark said, interrupting her thoughts. "Remember when we were in Grand Forks last summer at the big grocery store?"

"Yes." She replied absently as she reread the flyer she'd had printed. It was expensive, but the flyers, along with a large cardboard sign in the window, were the fastest way she could think of to get word out in the community. Every kid on the school bus had gotten the bright yellow sheet that week, and Mark had delivered the rest to everyone who lived in town.

"A lady in the store was handing out cookie samples, remember?"

Rachel nodded.

"Couldn't we hand out samples, too?"

Rachel stared at her son. He didn't look like a marketing genius, but that was exactly what he was.

"That's a fabulous idea!"

Her son beamed her a proud smile. "Bake a pepperoni pizza, Mom, that's your best."

She nodded. It *was* good, but then anything she baked tasted worlds better than the frozen variety Buffalo Bob served, and he charged two dollars more than she did.

"Do you want me to help?" Mark asked as he followed her into the kitchen.

"You and Calla can take orders," Rachel instructed, pointing to the old-fashioned black telephone on the counter.

"Okay." His eagerness to be a part of the business was a real blessing, although Rachel often worried that he was growing up too fast.

The pepperoni pizza was hot from the oven. She sliced it into small squares, loaded them in a cardboard container and handed it to Mark. "This was your idea, so I think you should be the one to do the honors."

"Me?" Mark's eyes grew huge with delight.

"I want you and Calla to walk up and down Main Street and offer a sample to everyone you see." It was five o'clock, and there would still be light for hours.

Calla tossed aside the magazine and trotted out the door with Mark.

Rachel didn't need to wait long for her first customer, although his identity surprised her. Heath Quantrill wasn't exactly her favorite person. She didn't know what to think of him. Naturally she'd heard the rumors about his exploits around the globe. The majority of them couldn't possibly be true, she figured, but all the speculation concerning

Heath Quantrill certainly made life interesting. He was handsome and she couldn't help wondering if he was involved with someone; she suspected he was. Women didn't let a man that good-looking slip through their fingers. But mostly he intimidated Rachel.

He'd turned down her loan the first time, and then apparently had a change of heart. She wasn't sure why and didn't ask. Fearing he might change his mind again, she'd ordered the pizza oven the same day he approved her loan.

"Hello, Rachel." He paused, glancing around at the stark furnishings. "I see you're open for business."

"I am." She set the cheese grater aside before she sliced her finger. His coming into the restaurant flustered her and she tried to hide her nervousness.

"I was just given a sample of your pizza," Heath told her. "It's damn good."

"Don't sound so surprised." She smiled to take the sting from her words.

"The price on this flyer is correct?" He held up the yellow sheet.

"Yes." She'd specifically chosen a low price to attract customers away from Buffalo Bob's. Her pizza was better *and* cheaper.

"You aren't charging enough."

"It's two dollars a pizza less than Bob's." She didn't like Quantrill's attitude. He'd had money all his life and didn't understand that this business venture was everything to her.

"You're not allowing yourself a large enough profit margin."

Rachel frowned. She'd given this some serious consideration and charging less than Buffalo Bob was the best strategy she could think of.

"If you'd like to come into the bank one day next week,

I'd be happy to show you how to figure out a price that's competitive but will allow you a reasonable profit margin."

"I can't do that now. I've already got the flyers printed."

"Tell them that was an introductory price and you'll honor it this time."

"I can do that?"

"Of course, and once they taste your pizza they'll order again."

He was sincere, she realized, about liking her pizza.

"I will," she said, grateful for his advice. "Thank you."

"Good." He set the flyer on the counter. "Now, I'd like to order a pepperoni pizza, and I'd like the introductory price."

Seven

School had been in session about a month and Lindsay was beginning to feel her way as a teacher. Each day was better. It wasn't easy instructing all four years of high school at one time, but she'd made contacts with other teachers in the area and she had help from the community. Most everyone was eager to get to know her and to assist where they could. Thus far, it seemed the community remained pretty evenly split when it came to their expectations of her. Still, everyone seemed grateful she'd agreed to take the teaching job and Lindsay supposed their reserve was only natural. After all, this was a small, rural community, one that was not only conservative and probably resistant to change but experiencing hard times.

She did feel disappointed that she hadn't made more friends by now. Hassie was her confidant and mentor, but she'd barely exchanged more than a few words with Sarah Stern or Rachel Fischer. She wasn't sure about Sarah, but Rachel seemed friendly enough, just preoccupied with her pizza business. Lindsay suspected that given time, things would take care of themselves. She was still new, untried.

And Hassie told her that she herself had encountered a similar reception when she'd arrived in Buffalo Valley as a young bride shortly after World War II.

More important, she'd struck a truce with her students. Once the ground rules had been established, she'd discovered they were eager to learn. She was new, young, and the kids considered her "cool." They were all impressed by what they saw as her urban sophistication, especially when she asked to be called *Ms.* Snyder. No one used "Ms." though, no matter how many times she mentioned it. After a while, Lindsay simply gave up. She'd never thought of herself as sophisticated, but to her students she seemed to represent big-city excitement. Lindsay cashed in on their goodwill and reintroduced programs that had long been abandoned from lack of funds, often using her own savings, meager as they were.

She brought in her camera when she learned they didn't have a yearbook and soon had a staff willing to put one together. Jessica and Calla volunteered to write a town newspaper; soon the entire class was involved.

One afternoon, quite by accident, she found Kevin Betts's sketching tablet and discovered that Gage's brother was an undeniably talented artist. He was shy about letting others see his work. After some cajoling, he'd volunteered, along with Joe and Mark Lammermann, to paint a mural on one wall of the classroom.

The guest speakers from the community added a whole new dimension to their Friday afternoons. She had a number of volunteers already and was drumming up more. Several times she'd run up against that small-town reserve, that reluctance. She didn't push, didn't pressure.

Joshua McKenna had been the first volunteer, and Lindsay was grateful. His family had settled in North

Dakota in 1888, a year before it achieved statehood. He'd brought in the original homestead papers his great-grand-father had been given, as well as stories that had been handed down through the years. Stories of grasshopper in-festations, drought and tornados. The session, for which Lindsay had scheduled an hour, went three, and her students talked about it for days afterward, adding tidbits of their own families' histories in the area. She felt their pride and strong sense of family, and encouraged both. In doing so, she experienced a surge of longing to know more about her own grandparents and what their lives had been like on the farm. Unfortunately she'd been too young to remember anything about the old homestead. By the time she was six, her grandparents had sold the land and moved into town. There was no one she could ask, since all the relatives on both sides had either died or moved away. Her own father had left right after high school, and she'd already heard all his stories about prairie storms and family gatherings.

Lindsay was just beginning to feel good about the way classroom life was developing when she experienced a new sort of crisis. It was a Thursday morning, the last week of September. Kevin walked silently into the class-room with an equally taciturn Jessica. Both slipped into their seats, looking sullen and uncommunicative.

At first, Lindsay thought they'd had a lovers' spat, but then the normally boisterous Loomis twins arrived, their demeanor just as serious. Calla frowned and slumped onto her desk, holding it with both arms as if she defied anyone to pry her loose.

"Hey, what's going on?" Lindsay asked, wondering at the strange mood. "Everyone's acting like it's the end of the world."

"You don't know?" Kevin asked, looking surprised.

She shook her head.

"You didn't listen to the farm report this morning?" Calla challenged, as if it were understood that everyone did.

Lindsay shrugged. "I heard it was a bumper year for corn." When she did turn on the radio, she noticed that the conversation generally centered on crops. There was a lot of talk about options and pork bellies and other subjects that didn't affect her one way or another. At least that was what she'd naively assumed.

"A bumper corn crop is right. Problem is, no one's willing to pay a man a decent wage for his efforts." This came from Stan Muller, a freshman who was obviously parroting his father's comment.

"My mom was crying when I left for school," Jessica said. "She didn't want us kids to know, but it wasn't like she could hide it. It means another year of doing without, and we need so much." She sounded close to tears herself. "My dad said I can forget about college when I graduate."

"It was bad enough that the wheat prices were lower than expected, but corn, too. It just isn't fair."

"Gage was pretty upset," Kevin volunteered. "Mom told him the Lord would provide and Gage said he didn't think the Lord was listening. We're going to need all the help we can get if we're going to make it through the year."

One by one, her students relayed the effects the devastating news was having on their families. Even the kids who lived in town took the news hard, and so did those involved with ranching, although there were more farms in the vicinity than cattle ranches. Lindsay supposed that was what community meant—you cared what happened to your neighbors.

She ran into Gage in town that afternoon. She'd seen

him only once since the kissing episode on her front porch. That had been a week earlier, when they'd met on the sidewalk outside the post office. Gage had taken delight in getting a rise out of her, telling Lindsay that he was waiting for her to invite him for a beer. Flustered, she'd hurried on, certain that at least four people had overheard the comment. The sound of his laughter had followed her.

Thursday afternoon she caught sight of him outside Buffalo Bob's. This time, she was the one to seek him out. "Gage," she called, raising her hand to get his attention.

He waited while she crossed the street. He wasn't smiling. "I wanted to remind you about the sixth," she said.

His stare was blank.

"I have you down to talk to the high-schoolers about honeybees."

"Right."

His eyes, which she'd thought of as beautiful, seemed cold and lifeless just then. Lindsay didn't know what to say or how to say it, but she couldn't let the moment pass without some word of encouragement.

"The kids told me about the corn and grain prices. I'm so sorry, Gage." She placed her hand on his forearm and he stared at it for a moment.

"So am I," he said, and with that he headed into Buffalo Bob's, as though standing on the sidewalk making polite conversation was beyond him. Lindsay felt Gage's barely restrained anger and suspected that his frustration had reached a breaking point. She fought the urge to follow, to sit and talk with him. If nothing else, she could listen, but he wasn't looking for someone to share his worries and he'd made it plain that he didn't welcome her company.

The next person Lindsay talked to was Rachel Fischer inside Hansen's Grocery. She'd dropped in to pick up a few

necessities for the week. "You heard?" Rachel asked when they saw each other at the produce counter.

Lindsay nodded. "I didn't realize how important... It was naive of me, I suppose."

"You can't know until you've lived it."

"Are you worried?" Lindsay asked. Rachel had wagered her future on her fledgling pizza business, and it would be a shame if it went under without having had a chance to get off the ground.

"Damn straight I'm worried," Rachel confessed. "Pizza's a luxury item and farmers around here were counting on grain prices being good this year. It's a blow to everyone."

"Is there anything anyone can do?"

"That hasn't already been tried, you mean?"

"But the government—"

Rachel shook her head. "Farmers feel like the government's sold them down the river. It's tragic—America's small farmers are being destroyed. A lot of people won't make it through the winter now."

Lindsay realized she still had a great deal to learn. "What's going to happen?"

Rachel looked away, as though even speaking the words brought her pain. "The bank won't have any option but to foreclose on mortgages and debts. Some people will be lucky enough to sell their land, and others—others will simply walk away with nothing to show for their blood, sweat and tears. Nothing but crippling debt.

"Some of the farming families in this area have held on to the land for three and four generations, only to lose it all now. It breaks my heart. Imagine—to survive the Great Depression, the dust bowl years and everything else and have to sell out now." She paused. "It does something to a

man's pride when he can't support his family. He feels cheated and angry. People here have always had a strong work ethic."

Lindsay nodded; she'd certainly noticed that. "I wish there was something I could do." For years, she'd heard about the plight of America's farmers but she'd never fully understood their problems.

"We're going to lose more people this year, and the town's already half the size it was while I was growing up."

Marta Hansen saw them talking and walked over to join them. "This is the final straw," she announced. "I told Jacob this morning that we should sell out while we can."

"Mrs. Hansen," Rachel said gently, "things will get better."

Marta shook her head. "People have been saying that for years, and it only gets worse."

"You're not leaving Buffalo Valley, are you?" Lindsay asked.

"Jacob doesn't like to listen to my talk about leaving, but this morning when he heard the corn prices, after what happened with the wheat, he just shook his head. He agrees we can't stay any longer."

"You're not going to close the store, are you?" Alarm made Lindsay's voice unnaturally high.

"It's for sale," Marta said. "We're getting out while we can."

Dinner was miserable for Joanie. The grain prices had been released that morning, and Brandon had disappeared for most of the afternoon. She almost always knew where to find him, but not today. It was as if her husband had wanted to hide from the world. And from his family. He'd closed himself off, didn't want to talk to anyone, not even Joanie.

The kids sat around the dinner table, barely touching their meal, while Joanie made an effort at conversation.

"How was school today?" she asked Sage.

"Fine."

"It was okay," Stevie said with a shrug. Joanie wasn't sure her six-year-old son understood the significance of what was taking place, but he appeared to realize that whatever had happened was bad.

Brandon picked at his dinner, despite the trouble Joanie had taken to make lasagna, one of his favorite dishes. She wished he'd talk to her. They were partners in the farm, a team. She felt hurt that he'd shut her out now, especially since they'd made some real progress lately.

After dinner, the kids went up to their rooms to do their homework, and Brandon sat in front of the television, staring at the set. He hadn't spoken more than a few words all day.

"I talked to Heath Quantrill this afternoon," she said, joining her husband.

That got Brandon's attention. "About what?"

"A part-time job, remember?"

Brandon's eyes flared with anger. "Forget it, Joanie. You call him back first thing tomorrow morning and tell him the whole thing is off."

Joanie's heart stopped at the hard edge in his voice. It took great strength of character and her love for her husband not to react with anger herself. "We talked about my getting a part-time job a few weeks back. Don't you remember?"

"And you chose today of all days to apply?"

Actually she'd submitted her application earlier in the week. "Why does it matter what day I spoke to Heath?"

His gaze narrowed. "It matters."

"But—"

"I support this family."

"Brandon, it doesn't have anything to do with that. We already discussed this, remember?"

He didn't answer her. Instead, he bolted up from his chair and headed out the door. Joanie wasn't going to let him walk away from her. Not this time. Too often in the past she'd sat by and silently swallowed her pride, but no more.

"Brandon, wait up!" She raced out of the house after him.

Halfway across the yard he came to an abrupt halt. "What?" he demanded.

She wanted to remind him that the grain prices were as much a disappointment to her as they were to him. What happened to him, happened to her. She drew in a deep breath and said, "We're going to be all right."

The distant look in his eyes told her he didn't want to hear any cheerful optimism. Nevertheless, she continued, "We've made it through hard times before and we will again."

"That's what our marriage is to you, isn't it? Hard times."

Sometimes he made everything so difficult. "You know that isn't true."

"But you've suffered," he said with heavy sarcasm.

"Stop it. I know you're disappointed, but so am I. Is lashing out at me going to make you feel better?" She clenched her fists at her sides. "I'm only trying to help."

"By applying for a job at the bank?"

"Yes—no. I'm trying to support the family because *you* can't." It wasn't what she'd meant to say and she could tell that her careless words were like throwing gasoline on a lit fire.

"This wouldn't be happening if it wasn't for you," he shouted.

"Now you're saying this is *my* fault?" Her husband had lost all reason. "You're blaming *me* for the low price of

grain?" Her voice cracked. How could he even suggest such a thing? "Do you have any idea how ludicrous that sounds?"

"Not the grain prices, dammit! That washing machine you couldn't live without."

"What does the washing machine have to do with anything?"

"I got a loan to buy the damned thing, figuring I'd be able to pay it off once we sold the corn."

It made sense to Joanie now. He'd taken out a loan for the appliances, adding the dryer when all she'd asked for was a new washer. With the payments to his parents, taxes, payments on the combine and health insurance premiums—plus living expenses—they were always strapped for cash. Now he'd added another payment they couldn't afford.

"I should've known," he spat. "I should've known."

Joanie felt as if she'd been kicked in the stomach. "I didn't realize—"

He stabbed his fingers through his hair. "Now you do."

"It's only been a month. Maybe we could take them back. Maybe we could talk to—"

"No."

Her lower lip trembled with the effort to hold back tears. "Do you have any other brilliant ideas?"

Joanie had nothing to say and ran back to the house. Sitting at the kitchen table, she buried her face in her hands. She knew Brandon wasn't really angry with her. He was reacting to the unfairness of their lives, everything he'd invested of himself in his fields. He'd lashed out at her because she was there. That was what her head told her, but her heart hurt too much to listen.

A few weeks ago Joanie would have expected this, but since the night of their anniversary, things had been much better. They seemed to have recaptured the closeness they

used to share. The first day the kids were both in school, Brandon had taken her with him on the tractor and they'd ridden across the fields, laughing and teasing one another, like in the old days.

The following Sunday, he'd attended church with her and the children for the first time in months. Since their anniversary they'd both made an effort to establish time for intimacy and lovemaking, refusing to put it off with a list of excuses.

Today the low grain prices had hit, and now Joanie wondered if they'd ever recover.

"Mommy."

At the soft whisper, she glanced up to find Sage standing next to the table, frowning. "Are you crying?"

Joanie answered with a weak smile and brushed the tears from her cheeks, unwilling to lie to her daughter.

"Did you and Daddy have another fight?"

Wrapping her arms around Sage's small shoulders, Joanie tried to explain. "Daddy's worried, and we both said some things we didn't mean."

"I'm worried, too. Are we going to lose the farm?"

"Of course not, sweetheart."

"At school today, Danny Hoffman said his family was going to sell their farm."

Joanie pressed Sage's head against her shoulder. "We won't have to sell, sweetheart."

"Danny doesn't want to move to the city."

"I know." It had to be heartbreaking for the Hoffmans. "You don't need to worry, sweetheart. Everything's fine with us."

"With you and Daddy, too?"

Joanie held her daughter close. "With me and Daddy, too," she said.

Sage relaxed. "Good. I don't want you to get a divorce."

"We aren't going to get a divorce."

"You promise?"

"I promised to love your daddy all my life, and I will. Now, are you finished with your homework?"

Sage nodded. "Stevie's playing with his trucks, but I read like you said I should."

"Good for you." Joanie managed a small smile.

It was almost midnight before Brandon finally returned to the house. Joanie lay in bed, unable to sleep, worrying about her husband. Yet when she heard the door open and he crept into their bedroom, she didn't reveal that she was still awake.

His silent undressing in the dark told her he didn't want to wake her. He didn't want to talk to her and, as she so often had before, Joanie pretended to be asleep.

The mattress dipped as Brandon got into bed beside her. Even with her back turned, Joanie could smell the liquor on his breath.

"Joanie," he whispered, his voice husky and slurred, "are you asleep?"

She swallowed around the lump in her throat. "No."

Brandon slipped behind her, cuddling her spoon fashion. His hands found her breasts.

"Where were you?" she asked.

"In the barn."

"You have a bottle out there?"

"Don't start, baby."

"Start what?" He couldn't possibly believe he could steal into the house in the middle of the night and make love to her after the way he'd behaved.

"Another fight."

"I suppose that would be my fault, too."

"Baby, don't. Not tonight. Just once can't you give me what I want without an argument?"

The unfairness of what he said was more than she could take. "Give you what you want? And what exactly do you want from me?"

He pressed his erection against her backside. "Should be obvious. Come on, honey, I'm sorry. Let's put it behind us, all right? We've been doing so well lately."

"You said some horrible things to me."

"I know."

"You want to abuse me with your words and then use my body to relieve your frustrations. I love you, Brandon, and I'm your wife, but I won't be used in that way."

He went still for an instant, then turned over with such violence that he nearly ripped the sheets off the bed. "Fine. Forget I asked. Trust me, it'll be a hell of a long time before I do that again."

"Since I seem to be entirely responsible for the depression in farm prices, I'm shocked you even want to touch me."

Apparently he was either too drunk or too angry to get comfortable, and bunched up the pillow. "Listen, if you want to get a job with the bank, that's okay with me. If you feel you can support this family better than I can, go right ahead."

"Fine."

"Maybe Quantrill can deduct the loan payments from your wages."

"You don't need to worry about me working at the bank." She told him what he hadn't taken time to listen to earlier. "Heath said he isn't planning to hire another teller."

Brandon sounded downright cheered by the information. "Pity."

Whatever closeness they'd gained since their anniversary had been destroyed, she realized. And something

else—Joanie's hope of making her marriage what she'd always dreamed it would be. That, too, had been lost.

Saturday night, Gage sat alone in Buffalo Bob's, nursing a beer. He hadn't driven into town looking for company, but he'd expected the bar to have a little more activity than this.

"Where is everyone?" he asked when Bob delivered his second draft.

"Not in here," he muttered.

It went without saying that the farmers would be tight-fisted after the devastating news earlier in the week. Generally, Gage was careful with a dollar himself, but he couldn't stand being in the house with his mother and brother, pretending everything was okay when it wasn't. Neither of them seemed to appreciate the gravity of the situation. Then again, perhaps they did, and it worried them too much to dwell on what the future held. Either way, Gage needed an escape, so he'd driven into town.

And naturally there was Lindsay Snyder. Without being obvious about it, he'd hoped they might run into each other again, as they had on Thursday afternoon.

She couldn't have any idea how that brief meeting had helped him. The concerned look in her eyes had touched him, and when she'd gently placed her hand on his arm, it'd demanded every shred of restraint not to haul her into his embrace. He'd wanted to shut out the world, use her warmth and caring as a shield. In that moment, he'd *needed* Lindsay.

Unfortunately, she'd made it plain she wasn't interested, which was fine by him. Well, not fine, but acceptable. He wasn't going to press any unwanted advances on her.

Gage wished to hell he'd never kissed her. Those kisses had been a mistake. The feel of her, the taste of her, had imprinted themselves on his subconscious. At

the most inopportune moments, he found himself sub-
merged by swells of desire, wishing he could block her
from his overactive mind. It'd been like this from the
minute they'd met. Thoughts of her tormented him, especially at night....

Her honesty had come as a surprise. She'd admitted that
she'd taken the teaching position to escape an unhappy relationship. He didn't want to think of Lindsay with another
man. He didn't want to think of her at all, and yet she was
constantly on his mind.

"Where's Merrily?" he asked in an effort to turn his
thoughts away from Lindsay.

Buffalo Bob shook his head sadly. "Gone."

"Again?"

His friend nodded and got himself a beer. "She left me
a note this time."

"Did she say where she was going?"

"I doubt she knows herself."

"I'll miss her." Merrily had a soothing manner, almost as
if she'd seen people at their worst and accepted them anyway.
She never tried to force conversation, never pried, but was
friendly and open. Stopping at Buffalo Bob's for a beer was
sure to mean a laugh or two whenever she was around.

"I'll miss her, too," Bob said, his look sober.

"She coming back?" Gage knew it was her pattern to leave
every now and then, but in the past she'd always returned.

"I don't know," Bob told him. He took a deep swig
from his glass of beer. "Can't see why she should."

"Why wouldn't she?"

"Look around you," Buffalo Bob muttered, with a
sweeping gesture of his arm. "I'm not exactly in need of
crowd control, am I?"

Gage had to admit that was true.

"I won't be able to stay open much longer if this keeps up."

Gage nodded. "I heard the Hansens put the grocery up for sale."

"I know. If it'd been up to Marta, they would've left years ago. You staying?"

The question took Gage by surprise. "Of course I am."

Buffalo Bob grinned crookedly. "That's what I figured. You're like me. Too damn stubborn to know when you're beat."

Until that moment Gage hadn't thought of himself in those terms, but perhaps his friend was right.

"How're you gettin' along with the new teacher?"

"What do you mean?" Gage demanded, not liking the turn of the conversation.

"I heard you were—you know, sweet on her."

Gage frowned. And lied. "You heard wrong."

Buffalo Bob arched his brows as if to say otherwise. "Well, speak of the very devil. Look who's here."

Gage swiveled around in his chair and watched Lindsay stalk into the bar. She was dressed in jeans and a dark blue sweatshirt and covered with fine white powder. Must've been working on that fireplace again.

"Welcome," Buffalo Bob greeted her.

She blinked hard and stared at Gage.

"Can I get you a beer?" Bob asked.

She hesitated. "No, thanks. I came looking for some help at the house."

"You got it," he told her. "Gage here will be happy to lend you a hand." He winked in Gage's direction.

"Would you mind?" Lindsay asked Gage.

"I'll do what I can," he told her. This was what he'd wanted, what he'd hoped would happen, but he suspected he was getting in deeper than he should.

She left with the same sense of purpose that had taken her into the bar.

"Well, go on," Buffalo Bob urged. "I mean, I hate to send away customers, but don't look a gift horse in the mouth."

Gage gulped down the last of his beer and hurried after Lindsay.

She waited until they were inside the house before she gestured weakly toward the fireplace. She'd managed to pry quite a few bricks loose, with no apparent rhyme or reason.

"Your…remodeling project?" he said, curious about what she was doing.

Lindsay brushed the hair away from her face. "I'm so frustrated I could scream."

"Don't you think it's time you told me what's going on?"

She groaned and fell onto the sofa. "There's a moving brick in this fireplace. I saw it when I was a kid and I want to find it."

"A moving brick?"

"Well, I didn't actually *see* it move, but I heard it. It made a scraping sound."

"How old were you?"

"Does it matter?" she asked curtly.

"No, but sometimes we allow things to grow in our minds and—"

"I *know* what I saw."

"I believe you, so don't get all bent out of shape." He wasn't going to argue. "Did you think to ask your father where it might be?" he asked, figuring that might be a helpful suggestion.

"Yes, and he doesn't know anything about it."

"But—"

"As far as I can tell, only one other person knows, and that person is dead."

"Okay." He tried to think of another question.

"I probably shouldn't be talking to you about this, but I'm so damned frustrated. I know it's there, Gage! I know it."

"Do you remember roughly where?"

"If I remembered that, do you think I'd go through all this, digging out one brick at a time? I've been at it for weeks and I don't have a damn thing to show for it except a bunch of broken nails." She splayed her fingers as evidence.

"What would you like me to do?"

She inhaled sharply. "Get a sledgehammer and tear down the whole damn thing."

"Ah." Gage hesitated. "Have you considered the structural damage that might do to the house?"

"No," she said, "but I don't care anymore." She sounded tired and angry. "As it is, I'm going to have to bring someone in to repair what I've already done."

Gage glanced at the fireplace and then at her. "Have you had dinner yet?" he asked.

"No."

"Me, neither and if we're going to tear down a whole fireplace and risk having a wall collapse on us, I'd prefer to do it on a full stomach."

She shrugged as if it didn't matter to her one way or the other. "I'm not much of a cook."

"We could take our business over to Buffalo Bob's."

Once again, she made a halfhearted gesture. "I suppose that'd be all right—but it's not a date."

"Most definitely not." He found it difficult to hide his amusement. "If you insist, we could sit at separate tables."

"Don't be ridiculous."

He gave up trying to suppress his smile. "I just want to save you from any unwanted gossip."

"I appreciate the effort, but it isn't necessary."

When they walked into the restaurant, Buffalo Bob looked pathetically grateful for the business. He brought out menus, then proceeded to explain each entrée in far more detail than necessary. An hour later—after roast beef and tomato sandwiches and glasses of beer—Gage walked Lindsay back to the house.

"I have a confession to make," she said as she opened the front door.

"Should I phone for a priest?"

"Don't mock me, I'm serious."

"All right, I apologize." He forced a solemn look.

"When I went over to Buffalo Bob's tonight, I knew you were there."

"You did?"

She nodded.

Well, yeah. He'd *told* her he'd be there, hadn't he? And Lindsay had come to him for a date. Because she was a woman, she had to be clever about it and a little understated, but Gage didn't mind. In fact, he was pleased.

"You aren't going to say *I told you so?*" she asked.

"Is that what you want?"

"No."

"Good. Then let's see if we can find that brick."

for his family. That was one mistake he wasn't willing to make a second time.

"Brandon—" She struggled not to cry, which seemed to make it impossible for her to talk.

"Are you so happy here in Fargo?" he asked.

She sniffled. "Miserable. I told you that. I miss you and my friends and…my life."

"Would it help if we slept in separate bedrooms?"

"No—because it wouldn't be long before we were sleeping together again and then everything would be back the way it was before."

"Was that so bad?"

"Yes. You were always angry and it was me you blamed." Her fingers tightened around his.

Having exhausted everything else, Brandon knew he had no other option. There was only one way left to prove himself. Prove his love. "All right, Joanie, I'll do it. First thing next week I'll put the farm up for sale."

"Oh, Brandon, no! That isn't what I want, either. I thought it was, but I was wrong. You'd be even more miserable in the city than you are now."

Brandon knew that, too, but he was willing to sacrifice everything if it meant holding on to his family. The farm meant nothing without Joanie and his children. He'd just spent four of the unhappiest months of his life, and two thousand acres of prime farmland had been damn little consolation.

"You could move back to Buffalo Valley," he said, thinking out loud.

Joanie frowned.

"There's plenty of empty houses, any one of which we could rent," he added, the idea gaining momentum in his mind. "You don't want to move back to the farm—okay,

I can understand that. Maybe later you'll want to, or during the summer. Right now that doesn't matter. Give me a chance to prove myself to you and the kids. If you're sincere about not wanting a divorce, then at least give me a chance to show you I am, too."

"Move into town," Joanie repeated slowly, seeming to test the idea by saying the words.

He squeezed her fingers again. "We can go out on dates the way we used to."

A hint of a smile touched her beautiful eyes. "I have a good doctor here. I want to continue living in Fargo until after the baby's born—and the school year's finished."

"All right." He could stand another two months. That would give him the opportunity to find a decent house for Joanie and the kids and work out some kind of rental agreement.

"I'd like us to see a marriage counselor, too," she said. "I know Father McGrath is officially retired, but he might be willing…"

He hesitated, although it wasn't because he refused to attend counseling sessions. Other than Father McGrath, the closest thing Buffalo Valley had to a marriage counselor was Buffalo Bob, and somehow he didn't think Joanie would be keen on discussing their marital difficulties in a bar. "Maybe someone in Grand Forks?" he suggested.

She nodded. "We'll probably have to go that far."

He could tell from the way she said it that she expected him to disagree. On the contrary. He was serious when he said he wanted to save their marriage, and in the next few months he was going to show her.

May 1st
Dear Maddy,
I just made the most difficult decision of my life. I'm

leaving Buffalo Valley. How anyone could mess up as much as I have in the last few months is beyond me. All I can say in my own defense is that my intentions were good.

Perhaps Marta Hansen, the grocer's wife, said it best. Last week she told me I was an outsider and would always be an outsider. No matter how long I lived in Buffalo Valley, I'd never think the same as they do. Never understand their ways, despite the fact that my father was born and raised in this town. Marta wasn't insulting me, she was merely stating the truth. Her one fault was that she was insensitive to my feelings, but what can I say? She was right.

I haven't spoken to Gage since our last big blow-out. By contrast, Monte phones me every day. He's serious about marrying me and can't accept that I'm no longer interested. Frankly, I thank God every day that I left him when I did. He seems like a stranger to me now, and I can't make myself care. A year ago, I would have leaped at his marriage proposal.

You asked about Hassie and, yes, her health has improved, but her spirits are low. This stay in the nursing home hasn't been easy for her. The last time I spoke with her cardiologist, he said he'd like to wait a week or two before scheduling her surgery. I haven't told her I'm leaving yet, and I dread doing it.

Kevin Betts, Gage's brother, went through a rough period while he wrestled with rejecting the scholarship from the San Francisco Art Institute. I don't know who it was harder on—him or me. In the end, all I did was give him false hope. He was born with the understanding that he would be a farmer. It's tied to duty and family and responsibility and it's part of

what makes me an outsider. I simply and truly don't understand. For Kevin's sake, I wish I did.

No, I'm sorry I can't tell you what happened in Bismarck. Perhaps one day, but not right now. It was a misunderstanding and a painful lesson. Another incident proving that if I lived here for the next fifty years, I still wouldn't think the same way these people do. I didn't realize one had to be born in the Dakotas to be accepted.

Several of the friends I've made here have tried to get me to change my mind. That's what made deciding to leave so damned difficult. If Gage had said one word, one small word, I would have stayed, gladly signed my name to the contract for another year. His silence said it all.

If I sound miserable, it's because I am.

The last day of school is May 29th, and Joshua McKenna told me he's been in touch with two women who are interested in the teaching position. He hugged me and said how grateful he was that I filled in during this transition time. Anyway, back to the 29th. I'll have everything packed up and ready to go. My dad's flying out and we'll caravan it back to Georgia the same way as I arrived last summer. A little older and a whole lot wiser.

I'll see you soon.

Love,
Lindsay

Rachel sat in the middle of a stack of boxes in Lindsay's living room. Both dogs were asleep by the fireplace, as though life was completely unchanged.

"I can't believe you're actually going to leave," Rachel complained. "We were only getting to know you."

The outcry that had come when her students learned she wouldn't be returning had been a balm to her badly injured pride. Almost every family had voiced regret. Even Marta Hansen, after her cruel and heartless comment, had said she was sorry to see her go.

As she'd told Maddy, the one person who hadn't asked her to stay was Gage. Without saying a word, he'd been the one who'd made it plain she should go.

That willful, stubborn farmer had stood by and said nothing.

She really had a talent, Lindsay thought sardonically, a gift for falling in love with the wrong man. First Monte and now Gage. She'd taken all the lessons she wanted to learn on the care and upkeep of a broken heart. She'd survived the last time around, and she would again. But it wouldn't be easy.

"Sarah wanted me to thank you for everything you did for Calla," Rachel told her. "She said that for the first time in her life Calla thought school was fun." Impulsively the two women hugged, and Lindsay went out to the porch and watched her friend walk away. It saddened her that Rachel had been the one to tell her that and not Sarah.

The months had flown by so quickly, far too quickly. Had she stayed, Lindsay liked to think she might have become good friends, not only with Rachel but with Sarah Stern and the others.

Her father's plane was landing in Grand Forks the following morning and Dennis Urlacher had volunteered to meet his flight, then help him arrange for the moving van. The high-school students were throwing her a party that night and then early the next morning, after stopping by the nursing home, Lindsay and her father would head back to Savannah.

It all seemed straightforward. Decided. But she didn't know how she was going to leave Buffalo Valley and do it with a smile. Not when her heart ached and she had so many regrets.

Gage knew very well that it was Lindsay's car that had passed the country road bordering his land. He sat on the tractor, the tiller churning up the dark, rich earth in preparation for flax, beans and millet.

He stared straight ahead, not wanting to look, pretending it didn't matter. Her leaving was for the best. He'd told himself that so often, he almost believed it. The choice to stay or go had been up to her, and she'd come to her decision without any help from him.

From what Kevin had said, he knew that Lindsay was driving out first thing tomorrow morning. Her father was flying in later today. Apparently she was coming to make her farewells. Anger whirled inside him. He wished to hell she'd just go and be done with it. All she'd done since she got here was stir up trouble. She delved into issues that were none of her concern, got involved with other people's business that was better left alone. He thought about his grandfather and what he'd learned about the man he barely remembered. Gage had a new respect for Jerome Sinclair, but he wondered how his grandfather would have reacted to having his secret revealed. Then there was the matter of Kevin.

With these thoughts came others, flooding into his mind, saturating his memory. The feelings of pride and community Lindsay had restored to Buffalo Valley. The Christmas play that had brought ranchers and farmers together for a celebration of the season. She'd organized a dance that was the closest thing to a prom these teenagers were likely to get. And there was the graduation

ceremony held at the theater only a few days earlier. A high-school graduating class of four. And the quarterly school newspaper. The yearbook, complete with photos.

What Lindsay had done for Buffalo Valley was one thing, but how she'd touched *him* was another. Almost from the moment they'd met, he'd tried to push her out of his mind. He recalled the first time they'd kissed and how his heart had nearly leaped from his body. He'd known then what was going to happen and been powerless to stop it.

Throughout the school year he'd been cautious, careful. He hadn't wanted to fall in love with Lindsay Snyder—but he had. The irony of their grandparents' situation didn't escape him. His grandfather had denied his heart out of love for Gina. It couldn't have been easy, no easier than it was for him to let Lindsay walk out of his life. There'd been no other honorable choice for Jerome, but for Gage—

All at once, he knew. He couldn't do it, couldn't stand by and let her return to Savannah. The instant he saw her car, he knew for a fact that if he let her leave, he would regret it the rest of his life.

She was the window that allowed the light into his world.

With a sense of urgency, he shifted gears, and the tractor belched thick black smoke. He was fifteen minutes from the house, and he raced across tilled, planted land, criss-crossing rows, afraid he'd be too late.

When the farmhouse came into view, he knew he'd arrived in the nick of time. The tractor roared toward the barn. He cut the engine and with one powerful bound, jumped down.

Lindsay stood next to her car, and her gaze held him prisoner. He kept his eyes on her as he approached.

"Lindsay came to say goodbye," his mother told him sadly.

He was about to tell his mother he was sure she had

something in the kitchen that needed tending, but before he could say a word, Kevin appeared.

He was in one hell of a hurry, judging by the way he barrelled into the yard, tires spewing loose dirt like rooster tails. He sprang down from the cab and raced toward Gage.

"You aren't going to let her go, are you?"

"I—"

"Dennis Urlacher just phoned Sarah Stern, and Calla told me it isn't Lindsay's father who's going to drive her home."

"My father wasn't on the flight?" Lindsay turned toward Kevin.

"Well, yeah, he was." The boy looked over his shoulder, then back at Gage. "But there's also some guy named Monte who claims he's going to marry Lindsay."

Gage's jaw tightened. "You're getting married?" he demanded, the shock of it making his voice gruff. He wanted it understood right now that he wasn't going to politely step aside.

Lindsay blinked. She seemed to be in as much shock as Gage himself. "No, of course not…" She glanced out over the fields at the crazy zigzag way he'd crossed the plowed rows. "You were coming for me?"

"Before Gage answers that, I'd like to talk to all of you," Kevin said, standing to his full height and meeting their eyes.

"I want to answer her," Gage said, his heart burning with the need to tell Lindsay he loved her.

"In a minute, Gage," Kevin said forcefully. "All right?"

Gage studied his half brother and saw that whatever he had to say was important. "All right," he agreed.

Kevin thanked him with a courteous nod. "Miss Snyder, first off, I don't mean any disrespect, but I know you don't want to leave Buffalo Valley."

"Kevin…" she began.

"Please, if you'd just let me finish." He turned to Gage and for the first time, he had the face of a man, strong and determined. "And you, big brother, don't want her to go, either."

"No, I don't," he admitted. If his brother had given him the opportunity, he would have told her so himself.

"Okay," Kevin said, "this is the deal."

The deal? Gage arched his brows. His brother had never sounded this firm or confident before.

"Gage, you're marrying Miss Snyder, and Miss Snyder, you're staying right here in Buffalo Valley. It's where you belong. Some of the adults might be old fuddy-duddies, but there isn't a one of us high-schoolers who want you to go. You're the best thing that ever happened to our school. And my brother's been crazy about you for months."

Gage took a step forward. This had gone on long enough. "If you don't mind, I prefer to do my own talking."

"Son," Leta said, holding out her arm and stopping him. "Let Kevin finish."

"Thanks, Mom." The teenager's grin was enormous. "Okay—I'm going to art school."

"But you refused the scholarship," Lindsay said, and Gage heard the utter defeat in her voice.

"Here's the best part," Kevin said, his eyes bright. He pulled an envelope from his shirt pocket. "I was offered *another* full ride—from the school in Chicago. Two scholarships."

"But that's the top school in the country!" Lindsay pressed her fingertips to her lips.

"Gage, you're planning to buy your own land, which is crazy. You have it already. I hereby bequeath this farm to you." He made a sweeping gesture with his arms. "It's yours, it's always been yours. Mom," he said, nodding in her direction, "you're moving to town."

"I am?" Leta's eyes rounded with shock.

"You can stay in Lindsay's house. It's about to be vacated."

Lindsay's mouth fell open.

"Mom, Gage and Lindsay love you, but they're going to be newlyweds. Three's a crowd. Besides, Hassie's going to need help at the pharmacy now."

"You seem to have everything worked out," Gage said, feeling both amused and oddly respectful. "But about the farm, you don't just hand over land this valuable…"

"Don't fight me on this, Gage. I know, I know, you refuse it as a gift. Well, big brother, this is one argument you aren't going to win. You want to pay me for the farm, then fine, you can pick up my college living expenses."

"Oh, Kevin," Leta said with a sigh.

"Two scholarship offers. It was meant to be," Kevin announced. "Now, I suspect Lindsay and Gage need a few minutes in private, so, Mom, why don't you and I just disappear into the house?"

Gage stood before Lindsay, his heart full of feeling. Full of love. Her beautiful blue eyes were brimming with tears.

"Don't cry, darling."

Sniffling, she rubbed the back of her hand across the high arch of her cheek. "You were willing to break my heart, but you can't stand to see me cry?"

Gage had to hold her. He closed the space between them and gently took her in his arms. She threw her own arms around his neck and clung to him.

Gage relished the feel of her, breathed in her unique, delightful scent. He placed his hands on either side of her tear-streaked face and kissed her just like he had that first time. Kissed her as if this was the last kiss granted him on earth; kissed her with all the hunger and love stored in his heart. He

didn't have the words to say what he was feeling. All he had was his heart, open-wide, exposed, vulnerable. And hers.

Lindsay responded to his kiss in a way that told him she was his, would always be his. Her body moved against him and he groaned.

"I was coming to ask you to stay in Buffalo Valley. I was coming to tell you I love you," he told her, their arms around each other, holding on tight.

"I'm an outsider."

"Yes." He wasn't going to argue with her. "Foolish and stubborn, too, but along with that, you're honest and honorable. It wasn't just Kevin and those schoolkids you taught to dream. It was me, too."

"You?"

He lifted his head enough so she could see the truth in his eyes. "I'd given up the hope of marrying, of having a family. I don't have a lot to offer you, Lindsay."

"You have a double portion of everything that's important to me, but it's enough to know I have your heart."

Gage's chest expanded with a sharp intake of breath. It seemed inconceivable that she loved him, and yet the look on her face told him she did. He kissed her again because it was impossible not to.

"Will you marry me, Lindsay?"

She nodded. The tears were back, shining in her eyes. "Oh, Gage," she whispered, smiling up at him, and then it seemed she was crying too hard to speak and she merely nodded.

Rising on her tiptoes, she kissed him. Wrapping his arms about her waist, their mouths joined, Gage swung her around, his joy overflowing, unrestrained.

The wind came up then, whirling around them, singing in his ears. He understood his grandfather's love and the sacrifices Jerome had made for Lindsay's grandmother.

Life had come full circle and had brought him a priceless gift in Lindsay. He was going to accept this gift and love her the rest of his life.

And beyond.

Epilogue

Buffalo Bob's face brightened when this morning's first customer walked into the restaurant. A tourist, he guessed, his first since Gage Sinclair had married the schoolteacher, Miss Snyder, in mid-July, when the hotel had been full of guests for the wedding.

"Good morning!" He greeted the woman, who was attractive, well-dressed, probably in her fifties. He handed her a menu when she pulled out a chair and took a seat at the table. "We've got a great breakfast special this morning. Eggs, bacon and hash browns for a buck fifty."

"Actually, all I want is coffee."

"Coming right up," he returned cheerfully.

The good mood was a facade to hide his disappointment over Merrily. She'd left again, vanishing in the middle of the night. On the bright side, she'd stayed longer than any previous time. She'd be back, Bob knew, when she was ready, and as always he'd be waiting for her. He didn't know why she felt the need to disappear like this. He'd gotten comfortable having her around and had thought she seemed less on edge than she used to be. Maybe next time she'd stay.

"This is a nice town, isn't it?" the woman asked, looking down Main Street.

"Real nice." He poured her coffee, and seeing that she wanted to chat, set the glass pot on the table. "A year ago, it looked different than it does now."

"How's that?"

"Well, there used to be a lot of closed businesses. There still are some, but not near as many. The new high-school teacher got the movie house all cleaned up for a school play and afterward, the owner—a farmer over in Devils Lake—decided to reopen it. That's been a real plus, to have a movie house in town again."

"I'll bet it is. Not many towns this far from any major city have a theater."

"You're right. Last week, Jacob and Marta Hansen announced that they'd sold the grocery store. A friend of the high-school teacher's bought it. Funny name, too, something like Mason or Madison. No…Madeline. She wants us to call her Maddy. She flew out for the wedding, and I saw her talking to Jacob and Marta and then, next thing I heard, she'd bought the grocery. Apparently she's got some great ideas. Lindsay's thrilled."

"Lindsay? You don't happen to mean Lindsay Snyder, do you?" The tourist perked up.

"It's Lindsay Sinclair now. You know her?"

The woman hesitated. "We met once, briefly."

"Terrific teacher. She's been a real bonus to this community. It looked for a while like we might lose her, but Gage Sinclair put an end to that idea when he proposed. They were married last month. The whole town showed up, even Hassie Knight, who owns the pharmacy. She suffered a heart attack not long ago, but it looks like she's going to be fine now that she's had bypass surgery."

"I'm glad to hear Lindsay's happy."

"You should've been here when her old boyfriend from Savannah—some guy named Monte, if you can believe it—showed up with her dad and found out Lindsay decided to marry a local farmer. I thought he was gonna have a conniption. Lindsay's dad was so disgusted with the guy, he walked off and left him. Folks around here are still laughing at the temper tantrum ol' Monte threw right in the middle of Main Street."

The woman smiled. "Buffalo Valley seems to be growing."

"We got a full-time pizza restaurant now. Rachel Fischer took over her parents' old place. I had to give up selling the frozen variety, seeing that no one wanted mine when Rachel's selling the real thing."

"I can imagine."

"Sarah Stern rented one of the storefronts for her quilting shop. Do you know Sarah?"

"I can't say I've had the pleasure."

"She sews really fabulous quilts. They seem to be catching on, too. And from what I understand, she recently hired Joanie Wyatt." He paused and scratched his head in puzzlement over the living arrangements the Wyatts had set up. "Joanie and the three kids moved into town. It's the funniest thing I've ever heard of. The wife living in town and the husband out on the ranch. Brandon visits once or twice a week, but he doesn't spend the night. Whatever works, I guess."

Her smile was friendly as she reached for her purse.

"I didn't mean to talk your ear off."

"You didn't. I enjoyed it."

Buffalo Bob was relieved. Some folks liked it when he talked about the community, but there were others who preferred to be left alone. Jeb McKenna, for example.

"I don't suppose you could tell me where the cemetery is."

"Oh, sure. It's outside town. You take Main Street to Division Street, just past the grain elevator and go left."

"Thanks."

Not wanting to make a pest of himself, Buffalo Bob returned the glass pot to the burner.

The woman took one last sip of her coffee, then stood and placed a dollar bill on the table.

"Do you want change?" He only charged fifty cents for a cup of coffee.

"That won't be necessary."

"Thanks. And come again."

"I'm sure I will," she said.

"Listen, seeing that you know Lindsay, would you like me to tell her you stopped by?"

She hesitated. "All right."

"Who should I say?"

"Tell Lindsay her aunt was briefly in town and will be getting in touch with her later."

"Sure thing."

"Her aunt Angela Kirkpatrick."

* * * * *

Dakota
BORN

Also by Debbie Macomber

To Shirley Adler
My cousin and cherished friend

SHIPMENT FIVE

Belonging to Bandera by Tina Leonard
Court Me, Cowboy by Barbara White Daille
His Best Friend's Bride by Jodi O'Donnell
The Cowboy's Return by Linda Warren
Baby Be Mine by Victoria Pade
The Cattle Baron by Margaret Way

SHIPMENT SIX

Crockett's Seduction by Tina Leonard
Coming Home to the Cattleman by Judy Christenberry
Almost Perfect by Judy Duarte
Cowboy Dad by Cathy McDavid
Real Cowboys by Roz Denny Fox
The Rancher Wore Suits by Rita Herron
Falling for the Texas Tycoon by Karen Rose Smith

SHIPMENT SEVEN

Last's Temptation by Tina Leonard
Daddy by Choice by Marin Thomas
The Cowboy, the Baby and the Bride-to-Be by Cara Colter
Luke's Proposal by Lois Faye Dyer
The Truth About Cowboys by Margot Early
The Other Side of Paradise by Laurie Paige

SHIPMENT EIGHT

Mason's Marriage by Tina Leonard
Bride at Briar's Ridge by Margaret Way
Texas Bluff by Linda Warren
Cupid and the Cowboy by Carol Finch
The Horseman's Son by Delores Fossen
Cattleman's Bride-to-Be by Lois Faye Dyer

The rugged, masculine and independent men
of America's West know the value of hard work,
honor and family. They may be ranchers, tycoons
or the guy next door, but they're all cowboys at heart.
Don't miss any of the books in this collection!

ARCHER'S ANGELS

TINA
LEONARD

USA TODAY Bestselling Author

ⒽHARLEQUIN® COWBOY AT HEART

Recycling programs
for this product may
not exist in your area.

ISBN-13: 978-0-373-82621-6

ARCHER'S ANGELS

Copyright © 2005 by Tina Leonard

All rights reserved. Except for use in any review, the reproduction or
utilization of this work in whole or in part in any form by any electronic,
mechanical or other means, now known or hereafter invented, including
xerography, photocopying and recording, or in any information storage
or retrieval system, is forbidden without the written permission of the
publisher, Harlequin Enterprises Limited, 225 Duncan Mill Road,
Don Mills, Ontario M3B 3K9, Canada.

This is a work of fiction. Names, characters, places and incidents are
either the product of the author's imagination or are used fictitiously,
and any resemblance to actual persons, living or dead, business
establishments, events or locales is entirely coincidental.

This edition published by arrangement with Harlequin Books S.A.

For questions and comments about the quality of this book,
please contact us at CustomerService@Harlequin.com.

® and TM are trademarks of Harlequin Enterprises Limited or its
corporate affiliates. Trademarks indicated with ® are registered in the
United States Patent and Trademark Office, the Canadian Trade Marks
Office and in other countries.

Printed in U.S.A.

www.Harlequin.com

TINA LEONARD

is a *USA TODAY* bestselling and award-winning author of more than fifty projects, including several popular miniseries for Harlequin American Romance. Known for bad-boy heroes and smart, adventurous heroines, her books have made the *USA TODAY*, Waldenbooks, Ingram and Nielsen BookScan bestseller lists. Born on a military base, Tina lived in many states before eventually marrying the boy who did her crayon printing for her in the first grade. You can visit her at www.tinaleonard.com, at www.facebook.com/tinaleonardbooks and www.twitter.com/tina_leonard.

To Nicki and Jason Flockton, for kindly sharing their love and their excitement over their children with me and our friends, the Gal Pals. Your joy was inspiring.

Much love to my children, Lisa and Dean. Don't leave me too soon—I'm enjoying you too much.

And heartfelt gratitude to my editors on this book, Paula Eykelhof and Stacy Boyd, whose belief in this series has meant so much to me.

Prologue

Love at first sight? Yes. Love over time?
Yes. But there are no shortcuts to the
heart.
—Maverick to his sons one night, after
their mother had passed, when they wondered how a man ever knew he'd found
the one woman for him

From: TexasArcher
To: AussieClove
Howdy, AussieClove. What's shaking Down
Under? I just got home from riding a bull at
the rodeo in Lonely Hearts Station. After the
events me and some of my bros decided
to drink some of the wildest concoction
on the planet. We ended up baying at the
moon beside Barmaid's Creek, with some
crazy gals for company. You should have
seen me ride that bull—if he hadn't come
back around to the left, I would have been

the first brother in my family to stay on that cursed piece of cowhide, Bloodthirsty Black.

From: AussieClove
To: TexasArcher
G'day, TexasArcher. Nothing shaking here except maybe my head. My older sister, Lucy, is devastated tonight. She and her husband have learned they can probably never have children. So I threw myself into work, hoping to stay positive.

The stunt tonight involved a boat, some fire, a shark and two guys wearing what I would call thongs. I think guys should never wear swim clothes that are smaller than their...well, you know. What do cowboys wear under those Wrangler jeans?

From: TexasArcher
To: AussieClove
Man alive, AussieClove. Sorry to hear about your sister—that's too bad. Around our ranch, we're having a population explosion. We've got babies popping out all over the place. I'm never having kids. In fact, I'm never getting married. Too complicated.

One time, I was stuck in a truck with my twin brother, Ranger, and his now-wife, Hannah, and they griped at each other for days.

I finally escaped, but Ranger wasn't so lucky. He rolled down an arroyo and demanded that a medicine man marry him and Hannah because he was convinced he had to get married to live. My twin's weird. By the way, I wear briefs and sometimes nothing. What do Aussie girls wear under their clothes? (I can tell you right now, floss-size drawers would never hold everything of mine.)

From: AussieClove
To: TexasArcher
I'm sure. J

Chapter One

Clove Penmire's heart pounded as she got off the bus in Lonely Hearts Station, Texas, suitcase in hand. For all her fascination with cowboys and the lure of the dusty state she'd read so much about, she had to admit small-town Texas was nothing like her homeland of Australia.

A horse broke free from the barn across the street, walking itself nonchalantly between the two sides of the old-time town. A cowboy sprinted out of the barn and ran up the street after his horse, laughing as he caught up to it.

Clove smiled. From the back she couldn't tell if the man was handsome, but he was dressed in Wrangler jeans and a hat, and, as far as she could tell, the cowboy was the real thing.

That's what she had traveled to Texas for: the real thing.

That sentiment would have sounded shallow, even to Clove, just a month ago. But having learned that her sister, Lucy, could not have a child, Clove's thought processes had taken a new course, one that included fantasies of tossing her brother-in-law into the Australian ocean.

All over the world there were people who couldn't conceive when they wished. They adopted, or pursued other means of happiness. She hadn't been overly worried, until Lucy confessed that she thought her husband might leave her for a woman who could bear children.

Lucy had laughed a little sadly and said that perhaps she was only imagining things. Clove had murmured something reassuring, but inside, fear struck her. Lucy loved her physician husband. He'd always seemed to adore her. Men didn't leave women because they couldn't bear children, did they? Robert was a wonderful man; Clove had been surprised, and distressed, at the turn of events.

So she'd taken drastic measures. She'd come to America for Archer Jefferson.

The cowboy hauled his horse around, leading it back toward the barn. Clove could hear him lightly remonstrating his wayward beast, but the horse didn't seem too concerned.

The cowboy caught her interested gaze, holding it for a second before he looked back at his horse. The man was extremely handsome. Breathtakingly so. Not the cowboy for her, considering her mission, and the fact that she was what people politely referred to as... the girl with the good personality.

The girl everybody loved like a sister.

The girl men liked to be friends with.

And the worst, the Nerdy Penmire.

She sighed. If Lucy had gotten all the beauty, their mother always said with a gentle smile, then Clove had gotten all the bravery. Which was likely how she'd ended up as a stuntwoman.

A stuntwoman with thick glasses.

Had she the face of other Australian exports like Nicole Kidman, for example, she might have been in front of the camera. But instead, she was a stunt double. Lucy said Clove had the life other people dreamed of.

Maybe.

Clove watched the cowboy brush his horse's back with his hand and fan a fly away from its spot-marked face. He was still talking to the animal; she could hear low murmuring that sounded very sexy to her ears, especially since she'd never heard a man murmur in a husky voice to her.

"Archer Jefferson!" someone yelled from inside the barn. "Get that cotton-pickin', apple-stealin', dog-faced Appaloosa in here!"

"Insult the man but not the sexy beast!" he yelled back.

Clove gasped. Archer Jefferson! The man she'd traveled several time zones to see! Her TexasArcher of two years' worth of email correspondence!

He was all cowboy, she realized, more cowboy than she'd come mentally prepared to corral. "Whoa," she murmured to herself.

Okay, a man that droolworthy must not lack for female friends. So why had he been writing her for two years? She wrinkled her nose, pushed her thick glasses back and studied him further. Tight jeans, dirty boots. Long, black, unkempt hair under the black felt hat—he'd never mentioned long hair in their correspondence. Deep voice. Piercing eyes, she noted as he swung around, catching her still staring at him. She jumped, he laughed, and then tipped his hat to her as he swung up onto the "dog-faced" Appaloosa, riding it into the barn in a manner the stunt-woman in her appreciated.

Just how difficult would it be to entice that cowboy into her bed? Archer had put the thoughts in her mind about his virility, with his Texas-size bragging about his manliness and the babies popping out all over their Union Junction ranch—affectionately known as Malfunction Junction.

Seeing him, however, made her think that perhaps he hadn't been bragging as much as stating fact. Her heart beat faster. He had said he wasn't in the market for a relationship.

But a baby, just one baby…one stolen seed from a family tree that bore many…from a man she trusted more than a stranger from a sperm bank.

Maybe she *wasn't* brave.

"Howdy!"

She jumped as Archer strode across the street to where she stood.

"Are you lost?" he asked.

"No," she said, her gaze taking in every inch of him with nervous admiration. "Yes."

He grinned. "My name's Archer Jefferson."

She wished he wouldn't smile at her that way. Her heart simply melted, despite the cold chill of February. He made her dream of a blazing fireplace, soft blankets and naked him holding naked her tight.

"Can I help you?" he asked. "If you're looking for a job, the cafeteria is that way. If you're looking for a hair-do," he said, eyeing her braided hair momentarily, "I'd choose that salon over there. The Lonely Hearts Salon. Owner's a friend of mine. Salon owner across the street, of the Never Lonely Cut-n-Gurls, isn't."

She felt him studying her glasses, the cursed thick things that gave her clear vision when she was doing stunts. Contacts made her eyes itch and burn.

Lucy said Clove hid behind her glasses. Clove blinked, thinking that right now a curtain was the only thing she'd feel truly hidden behind.

"You sure are a quiet little thing," Archer said. "Don't be scared. We're all real friendly here."

Scared! She was a daredevil!

But if she told him that, in her lilting Aussie accent, he would know who she was right off. And he would think she was nuts for coming all the way to Texas without telling him. He would know it was no accident that she was standing outside the rodeo he had told her he was participating in.

"I'm not scared," she said, trying to disguise her accent. "Thank you for your concern."

"Ah, she speaks," Archer said. "I've got to run, but if you need anything, just grab someone off the street to help you. This is a friendly town, if you bypass the Cut-n-Gurls."

"I'll do that."

He tipped his hat, and with a flash of long-legged denim glory, he disappeared into the arena building.

Her breath slowly left the cage it was bound in.

No doubt his genes were as sexy as his jeans. He was far hotter than the thong-wearing models she'd last worked with.

Now she just had to get those jeans off of him.

He hadn't seemed particularly inclined to strip down to the "briefs or nothing" of which he'd boasted. Not even a flash of male attraction had lit his eye. "I don't know if I can do this," she murmured, suddenly doubtful about her mission.

He was terribly manly. And she had very little experience with men. Lucy had always been the one who warmed to hearth and home.

Clove took a deep breath. For Lucy's sake, she had to be brave.

She went into the walkway where Archer had disappeared. He was leaning against a rail, looking at his Appaloosa. Seeing her, he grinned. "Glad you came in. I was just thinking you might need a hotel."

Her throat gulped of its own accord. "Ah," she said, "I was wondering…"

"Yes?" he said, smiling down at her.

He was so tall. "Would you care to go to dinner with me?" she asked, her voice barely a whisper.

The friendly smile slipped from his face. His gaze touched her glasses. Then a forced veneer of friendliness came back to his expression. "I'm sorry. I can't."

She blinked, knowing her face was bright red.

"Okay. Thanks, anyway."

Backing away, she saw sympathy in his gaze.

She turned and tried to walk away with as much dignity as possible. He was not remotely interested. How humiliating!

This was not going to be easy. In fact, it likely was impossible.

On the other hand, she was a stuntwoman known for her never-fail nerves. And she hadn't paid for a round-trip airline ticket to wind up going back home without a Texas-bred souvenir.

For Lucy's sake, she would bring out the daredevil residing inside her and let it loose all over that cowboy.

ARCHER JEFFERSON watched the little fraidy-cat walk away with some regret. My goodness, she was a shy one! Traveling by herself required some bravery, though.

If he had a rule—and usually he didn't—it was that most women were to be avoided. He'd learned from watching his brothers fall that women came in exciting, colorful packages; some fun to open, some not. But a shy woman didn't hold much threat to his well-being. And that one, with her oversize specs and timid little voice couldn't put fear into a flea.

Scratching his head, he thought about her dinner invitation. Much as he might have enjoyed showing a newcomer the town, he had to get his horse ready for the show. Honky-Tonk was a tricky Appaloosa. She thought she knew things she didn't, and they'd had more than one disagreement between them about who was boss.

"You're just a bit sassy," he said to Tonk.

"You think you're entitled to your own opinions. But we both know better, don't we?"

She pinned an ear back and gave him a sidelong stare.

"Females and opinions go together like butter and bread," he continued.

And it often seemed as if his Appaloosa had her fair share of womanly arts, conniving and one-upping being some of them. He knew quite well that females had a spectrum of tricks up their dainty sleeves. He'd watched seven brothers before him fall prey to the wedding-ring chase.

The last brother who'd fallen was Calhoun. He'd settled at the ranch, the first married brother to do so. Calhoun had brought his wife's family—two children, Minnie and Kenny, and a grandfather, Barley—with him.

And Calhoun's success had generated some brotherly angst around the ranch. Calhoun had the kids, the father-in-law, the occasional roadshow participation as a rodeo clown— for which his wife, Olivia, adored him—but Calhoun had also became a hit with his paintings. Though he'd started out painting nudes, he had switched to family portraits and had a waiting list of people who wanted him to commit their children to canvas.

He was that good.

Unfortunately, Crockett, the family's first and best artist, had taken umbrage at this. Crockett felt Calhoun had one-upped him in the creative department. Archer frowned as he worked his way through the mud in Tonk's hoof. Usually, the brothers were happy for each other. But ever since the youngest brother, Last, had brought a new baby to the ranch, along with the baby's unmarried mother, Valentine, no one had been happy.

Or maybe the trouble had started when Mason left. Oldest brother, and patriarch of the Jefferson clan, he'd taken his wandering feet onto the road. He'd said he wanted to find out what had happened to their father, Maverick. But the brothers knew that was a lie; Mason had been nearly knocked to his knees when Mimi Cannady, their next-door neighbor, married another man and had a baby.

But that had been more than a year ago. Mimi and Brian were divorced now, a friendly divorce. And Mason had returned and was now very fond of one-year-old Nanette.

Archer sighed. Maybe all the craziness around Malfunction Junction was just the result of twelve brothers growing up together with no female touch to soften them.

Last was never going to settle down with Valentine, though he seemed to be receiving better marks for his daddy skills.

Mason was never going to get his head straight about Mimi. All the brothers *except* Mason knew Mimi was putting her ranch up for sale in order to move into town.

Bandera never shut up about poetry. He wrote it, he sang it, he reviewed it and recited it, and if he didn't shut his face, Archer was going to smother him in his sleep.

Crockett needed to just shut his yap and paint. There was room for two artists in the family tree.

"I'm the only brother who keeps my pipe shut," Archer told Tonk. "My insanity is on the down-low. I write a woman who is far away and who will never bother me. As far as I can see, I add no turbulence to this family ship. Why can't the rest of my brothers be more suave? Debonair?"

It sounded as if Tonk groaned. He gave her a tap on the fanny. "Hey," he said, "no comments from you. Or maybe I won't defend you the next time my brothers call you dog-faced." He frowned, looking at the pretty colors of his spotted equine. She was beautiful! What was it about her that they didn't get?

So Tonk was a little unusual. Archer liked unusual things.

She reached out with her back hoof, not really kicking at him but giving him a little goose. He stepped back, eyeing her warily. *"Tonk,"* he said, his tone warning.

She flipped her mane at him.

"Excuse me," he heard.

Archer glanced up to see the little plain newcomer looking at him. "Yes?"

"I was just offered employment at the Never Lonely Cut-n-Gurls Salon."

"You were?" Straightening, he stared at her.

Marvella, the owner of the Never Lonely Cut-n-Gurls, was always on the lookout for fresh stylists, and Marvella's stylists were known far and wide to be babes—and if they weren't babes, then they were possessed of supernatural talents. If you were a man, the Cut-n-Gurls could *always* help you out.

"Yes." She nodded. "But I knew you said they weren't your friends."

"They're not, that's true. What is it that you do?" he asked, staring at her speculatively. Maybe there was more to her than he'd first thought. Marvella had a pretty good eye for these things.

"I—I'm not doing anything right now," she said. "I'm on vacation."

"So, what did you tell her?" Archer felt worry assail him. Employment with Marvella included hassles, so many she'd soon dream of giving back her wages.

"I told her, no, thank you. You said to avoid her."

"I think it would be best. Not that I'm always right."

She nodded. "Even your horse knows that."

Archer frowned. "What do you mean?"

She shrugged. "She doesn't like you."

He was outraged. "She likes me fine!"

She shook her head. "No, see how she distances herself from you? She thinks you're bossy. Trying to enforce yourself upon her."

His jaw dropped. "She's a horse. I'm *supposed* to enforce myself upon her."

"She doesn't like it. She's trying to tell you that you're annoying."

Well, that was it. He didn't have to listen to some half-baked claptrap like that. Tonk and he had a special relationship.

"How long have you had her?"

"Tonk and I have been together six months," Archer said defensively. "And Tonk thinks I'm—"

"Bossy." She reached a hand over the stall, and Tonk slid her nose under the woman's fingers. "I understand, girl. Men can be very trying."

"Are you trying to do that horse-talking thing?" Archer asked. "I don't use horse psychology. I mean, I talk to Tonk, but I'm really just amusing myself. I don't believe we're actually *communicating*—"

Her eyebrows raised. She stared at him, her gaze challenging. Disbelieving?

Something about that attitude caught Archer's attention. He looked at her more closely, finally seeing behind the specs.

"Those are beautiful eyes you're hiding."

Chapter Two

"Thank you," Clove said, "I think."

He looked at her. "No, really. You have lovely eyes. Very unique color."

She was torn between feeling flattered, giving in to worry, or pulling out her tricks. He was, after all, the key player in her plan.

"What's your name, stranger?" he asked.

"Clover," she said, thinking quickly, not yet ready to reveal her identity.

"Clover? Is that a real name or are you making one up just to keep your distance?"

"It's a real name." Just not hers.

He frowned. "You don't look like a Clover."

"I'd ask you what I do look like, but I don't want to know." She leaned over into the stall. "Oh, Tonk has blue hooves," she said. "I think blue hooves on a horse are so pretty."

He narrowed his gaze on her. "Know a little something about horses, do you?"

"A little. My family owns a farm." Clove glanced up at him. "We raise horses."

"Oh? Where's the farm? The Jeffersons know just about everyone in the business."

"Well, you wouldn't know us," Clove said. "Our farm is not doing as well as one might hope."

"Sorry to hear that." He turned his attention back to Tonk, who was still nuzzling at Clove's fingers.

"Oh, Archer!" Feminine voices floated into the stall.

Clove turned to see four beautiful girls walk by with flirtatious glances for Archer. She turned back around in time to see Archer's chest puff out about four inches.

"Hey, ladies," he called. "Nice winter weather, huh?"

They giggled. "We've got some hot cocoa when you feel like warming up," one girl said.

Another nodded. "And some of our special potion tastes good on a freezing night. Madame Mystery's—"

"Yes, yes," Archer said hurriedly. He waved them on. "You girls behave. Get inside before you all catch colds."

Laughing, they waved mittened fingers at

him and moved on after casting him one last alluring glance.

Clove blinked. "They practically undressed you en masse."

He laughed. "Yeah. They're good at that."

And he had no shame! Clove quickly reviewed her position. Maybe *mano a mano* she could get his attention, but groupie corralling put the odds against her. Not to mention that those women were gorgeous.

"They mean no harm," he said easily, "as long as they get no closer than about ten feet."

"How do you know?"

He winked at her. "Women are not hard to figure out."

She held back a gasp at his cockiness. "You haven't figured out your horse."

"And that's why I love only her." He gave Tonk an affectionate pat on the shoulder, and she tried to nail him with a hoof. Swiftly jumping forward, he dodged the hoof, but Tonk's head snaked around, her teeth barely missing his shoulder.

"I guess you'd call that a love peck," Clove said.

"Aw, Tonk wouldn't really bite me. She just knows I like a little sauce to my women."

"Women?"

He grinned, pushing his hat back with a finger.

He was annoying, and much sexier than he'd come across in his emails. She needed a shower to freshen up after her travels, and time to regroup. "I think I'll be going now," she said, retreating from his confident smile.

"Thanks for the dinner offer," he said, "But Tonk and I have work to do."

Now that she'd seen him turn down the quartet of country lovelies, her feelings weren't quite so hurt, so she was able to flip him a shrug. "About that hotel you were going to recommend?"

"There's no hotel in Lonely Hearts Station, but both beauty salons welcome travelers. Head over to the Lonely Hearts Salon. The owner, Delilah, has rooms for rent. You'll be safe over there." His gaze settled on Clove for a moment, then he put the horse's hoof down and came over to the rail, leaning on it to stare down at her. "Do not take a room at the Never Lonely Cut-n-Gurls salon. Even though you will see a big sign out front proclaiming that theirs are the cheapest, cleanest, most comfortable rooms in town."

She backed away from his intensity. "You are quite forceful, sir."

"Yeah, well, someone's gotta be around here." He turned back to his horse. "Otherwise we'd all be love candy for women and ending up at the gooey altar of marriage."

Whew! He was simply brewing in misery when it came to women, Clove realized. In their emails, he'd always made everything sound so wonderful, so carefree, so…fairy tale. But in person, the story was quite different.

"Good luck," she said, backing away, "with your rodeo. Or whatever it is that you're after."

He waved a hand absently.

Clove waved a hand back, mimicking him, but he never noticed. She went out onto the pavement, crossing her arms against the chill.

It was true what Archer said. There was a large sign out in front of the Never Lonely salon. In fact, the whole building was lit up with white lights, like icing on a gingerbread house. Laughter floated from inside, and a piano gaily played ragtime.

She glanced across the street at the Lonely Hearts Salon. A lamp glowed in the window, and it was mostly dark and very quiet, as if no one ever stayed there.

She turned back to the Never Lonely salon.

Four really pretty, lively women who knew how to get Archer's attention lived inside. And hadn't those flirty girls said something about hot cocoa?

Clove shivered. She wasn't used to this kind of cold.

The cocoa—and the chance to get some advice on how to seduce her man—won out. She headed toward the Never Lonely Cut-n-Gurls Salon.

ARCHER WAITED until he heard Clover walking away, then he turned to stealthily watch her leave. Nice fanny, for a girl with a plain face and wacky glasses. She was packing her jeans just fine. He liked her voice, too, he had to admit. It was very sweet, with a slight accent.

"You embarrassed me, Tonk," he said. "Could you at least go easy on me in front of girls? You make me look like I'm the hoss and you're the rider."

Tonk ignored him.

"Hey!" Bandera came and leaned his elbows over the rail. "Let's eat. I'm hungry. Hey, what's up with Dogface? Someone feed her a sour apple?"

"Shut up." Archer put away the hoof pick

and other tack. "There was a girl here a second ago—"

"Oh, is that your problem?"

"And she went to find a room, I think."

"Ah." Bandera nodded knowingly. "And you want the key."

"No! She's not…my type." He glanced at his brother. "I told her to go over to Delilah's."

"Yeah?" Bandera laughed. "If she was that girl in glasses I just saw, then she's just like your horse."

Archer straightened. "Meaning?"

"Meaning she doesn't mind very well. She went straight to Marvella's."

"What? I specifically told her—"

Bandera grinned. "Archer, if you had a Dear Abby column, you'd go broke. No one listens to you."

Archer ignored him. "That crazy girl has no idea what she's getting herself into!"

"Well, don't get too worried about it."

Archer settled his hat on his head. "Someone has to look out for the misfits in life. And if there ever was a misfit, Clover is her."

"Whoa. Color me *impressed*."

Archer slapped his brother upside the head. "Come on. We've got to catch her before she gets too far into the dragon's den!"

CLOVE COULD NOT IMAGINE why Archer had steered her away from surely the nicest girls on the planet. Taking pity on her plight—poor, tired traveler!—they'd treated her to a wonderful array of services.

They'd coaxed her glasses from her, leaving her nearly blind. They'd teased and washed her hair. Perfumed her. Stuck some heels on her feet. Given her a knockout dress to wear, the type of thing one saw on elegant ladies.

She'd been a bit embarrassed, but they'd waved aside her worries. It was all part of the service, Marvella said. Besides, Clove was renting a room, and that more than covered the expense. And gave her girls some practice with a lady's hair, since they mostly had male clients.

"Can I have my glasses for just one sec?"

Marvella handed them to her. Clove put them on so she could peer in the mirror. "Oh, my," she said. "I had no idea I could look like this."

"It was all there," Marvella said. "Hidden charms. The best kind, I always say. I had another girl, once upon a time. You remind me of her. By the time I got done with her, she was a golden charm. She left me," Marvella said bitterly. "Ah well, that's in the past."

"What was her name?" Clove asked, out of politeness more than curiosity. It was clear Marvella wanted to draw out the girl chat a bit more.

"Cissy. Cissy…Kisserton. Now Jefferson."

"Jefferson?"

Marvella nodded. "Those damn Jeffersons get all my girls. They've got Valentine right now, and not one of them has any intention of marrying her."

Clove sucked in her breath. "What do you mean, *they've got her?*"

"One of the brothers impregnated her, another took her to their ranch, and they've kept her there. After she gave birth they put her to work in a bakery."

Clove's eyes were huge. "That sounds *terrible.*"

"It is. If you ever meet a Jefferson man, my best advice to you is *run.*"

Clove blinked. That was the same thing Archer had said about the Never Lonely Cut-n-Gurls! "I'm still confused about the plural," she said.

"Oh, you'd find quick enough that the Jeffersons do everything as a gang, a fixture upon our good and tidy landscape that can't be overlooked, an eyesore, if you will. They approach you in a group. If one of them is alone, soon enough they'll have backup. Before you know it, you're theirs."

Clove could hardly take this in. She thought about Archer's hot, lean physique and felt her breath catch in her chest. "It sounds…"

"Scary, I know."

Clove had been working the adjective "romantic" over in her mind. Hot. Sexy. Fantastic…

Marvella clucked with sympathy. "Don't you worry about a thing. I have my dealings with the Jeffersons as necessary, but one thing is certain—they will never, ever take one of my girls from me again. And right now, you're one of *my* girls."

"Thank you." Now was the wrong time to mention that she'd actually come to town to shanghai some Jefferson genes.

"How can I ever thank you for all you've done for me?" she quietly asked Marvella.

"You sit here," Marvella said, "right up front, my precious, and just smile for the customers who come in the door. Just an hour," she said, "will be repayment enough."

"YOU COULD NOT HAVE possibly seen Clover go into Marvella's," Archer told Bandera. "I have seven-eight brother syndrome, which means I'm so far down on the family tree that I have to be observant or I get run over by my own beloved brothers. And I distinctly saw Clover turn left as she left the pens."

"She may have," Bandera said agreeably. "You may have seven-eight brother syndrome, but I have eleventh-brother syndrome, which means I was so close to becoming Last that I make certain everything is proven fact before I talk about it. And I saw a lady who looked a little hesitant, with big ugly glasses, go into Marvella's."

Archer's boots moved faster as he headed to the door of the salon. "You're crazy. She said she would listen to me. Good evening, miss," he said, tipping his hat to the gorgeous woman seated on a bar stool just inside the doorway.

She stared at him, not inclined to say much, he guessed. Glancing around for Clover, he turned back to the bar-stool babe. "Did you happen to see a woman come in here, one who was lost, wearing glasses as thick as the tires on a truck?"

She looked perplexed, then she shook her head. He glanced over her big hair and her superbly applied makeup. The wooden bar stool only served to enhance her hourglass shape, keeping the focus on her curves as she sat straight for balance.

"You see," he told Bandera, "Clover would stick out in here like a barn owl amongst peacocks. Let's go check with Delilah." He tipped his hat to the babelicious door greeter and headed out.

"Man alive, she was hot as a smokin' pistol!" Bandera exclaimed. "Have you noticed that Marvella's girls just keep getting hotter and hotter? Whooee! I feel like someone just lit a firecracker in my jeans!"

"She was all right," Archer said. "Actually, she reminded me of Cissy. And you know, I love our sister-in-law, but remember, I was stuck in a truck once upon a time with her and Hannah, and I'm telling you, girls who look like that are *misfired* pistols in the wrong hands."

"My hands would be just right," Bandera said. "Oh, how quickly I would volunteer to be her bar stool the next time she needed a place to park that fanny!"

"Dunce," Archer told him. "Get a grip. We've got a tourist to rescue." They went across the street to Delilah's, quietly tapping on the door because of the hour. The Jeffersons had their own keys for the back door, where they could go up the stairs and commandeer a special set of rooms Delilah kept just for them. But right now, Archer was hoping for intel on his lost farm girl.

"Why are you so worried about her, anyway?" Bandera demanded. "Let's go back over to Marvella's and spark a fire with the damsels."

"No hunting for trouble tonight," Archer stated. "If we bring home any more bad news related to Marvella, Mason'll probably run us out of town for good. He still can't believe Last got one of her girls pregnant while Mason was gone."

They peered through the curtained window of the front door. Only a quaint lamp burned on the table. "Guess she and Jerry called it an early night," Archer said. "Darn."

"That means your little friend isn't here. Delilah would be bustling around in the kitchen, making her welcome."

"That's true." Now Archer was extremely worried.

"Could I be mistaken?" Bandera asked. "Perhaps I didn't see her go into Marvella's, and in fact, she has left town."

Archer wheeled to look at him. "*Are* you mistaken?"

"If I say I am, can we go hit on Miss February over at Marvella's?"

"No!" Archer was good and put out with his brother. "How can you think of women at a time like this! There is a poor girl somewhere in this town who has no place to go, and all you can think about is your…you know." He wished it didn't bother him so much that Clover might have left town. Certainly he had not been very friendly. "Just so long as she didn't go to Marvella's, I really don't care where she went. That's all I'm doing, trying to keep an innocent traveler from getting fleeced."

"That's right." Bandera nodded. "That's all that's on your mind. And I'm not thinking about that beauty on the bar stool at all!"

CLOVE COULDN'T BELIEVE that Archer had left without recognizing her. It was so exciting! She felt like a different girl.

She was completely new.

The thought made her bite her lip. Clove felt her puffed-up big hair and her mascaraed lashes. The look really wasn't her, though it was fun. But in a while, her eyes would start to itch from the makeup, and anyway, her scalp felt tight from all the hair spray lacquered onto her head.

She was glad he didn't know she'd run counter to his suggestion and come to Marvella's.

One hour had passed, the allotted time Marvella had asked her to sit out front. Longing for a shower, Clove went upstairs to her new room, closing the door. The feminine side of her wished Archer had noticed the big change in her—and the practical side remembered that he'd noticed her less as Cinderella than he had when she'd been Plain Jane.

It was time to let the inner stuntwoman in her throw caution to the wind.

Surely it couldn't be that hard to attract a man.

"Yoo-hoo!" a voice called.

"Come in!"

One of the stylists walked into her room, leaving a small bottle on the table. "Marvella wants you to have some of her delicious home brew as a welcome gift."

"That's so kind. She's already done too much."

The stylist smiled. "She must like you."

Clove looked at the bottle. "Hey, a cowboy

came in here tonight. His name was Archer Jefferson. Do you know him?"

"Know him?" The woman laughed. "We know *all* the Malfunction Junction boys. Why?"

"Just wondering."

"If you're thinking he's cute, so does every woman in this place. But don't spend too much time thinking about him. That one is impossible. All he cares about is his horse, ugly dog that she is."

Clove frowned. Tonk was beautiful in her own way.

"But if you just can't live without him, you'll probably find him at Delilah's. I'd head up the back stairs if I were you, because Delilah won't welcome you if she knows you're staying here. Tap on the door, say 'room service,' and see if he's hungry."

"You make it sound so easy," Clove murmured.

"Trust me, it's not. Good luck, though." She laughed again and left the room.

Clove stared at the closed door, then at the bottle on the nightstand. The stylist's words ran through her brain, a mockery of her intentions.

One thing was for certain, she wasn't going

to use alcohol to lure a man into her bed. And right now, she was going to shower all this hair spray and makeup off her body. She felt like a doll.

And then, if a shower hadn't washed all the thoughts of Archer out of her mind, surely it wouldn't hurt to go across the street and take a look at the back door the stylist had mentioned.

Not that she would go in, of course. But curiosity had her, and she wouldn't be a stuntwoman if she wasn't up for a dare.

Chapter Three

Archer couldn't sleep, though Bandera was sawing logs like a frontiersman. "I just need to walk it off," he muttered to himself. "I've got nerves before the big show, and I'm worrying about Clover so I don't worry about Tonk."

Neither of the females on his mind obeyed worth a flip, not that he would admit that to Bandera. One thing he did know about Clover—if she was the sort of girl who understood that a man knew best, she'd be under Delilah's roof right now.

Where he could keep an eye on her.

So he took a few laps up and down the main street of Lonely Hearts Station, his gaze darting, ever-watchful, for the traveler who knew about blue hooves. Tonk sure had seemed to like Clover, which was strange, because Tonk didn't like anyone, a fact his brothers were quick to point out, and which Archer was quicker to deny.

He was certain Tonk held affection for him somewhere in her equine heart. She just didn't know how to show it. He'd been told by plenty of women that he didn't know how to show affection to a woman, either, so that made he and Tonk a perfect pair.

Archer was so busy ruminating on the canny females in his life that he nearly got too close to the one peering in the back window of the Lonely Hearts Salon. It was Clover!

She was spying, the little peeping Tomasina.

Or maybe she didn't know how to get in. Perhaps she'd decided to take his advice.

He watched her carefully turn the doorknob and open the door. She appeared to think about something for a second, then closed the door. She opened the door, and closed it again.

Spying. Which meant, he knew with certain chauvinism, that she wanted to spy on *him*.

He grinned, knowing exactly what to do with her now. Sneaking up on her, he reached out and grabbed her around the waist. "Gotcha!" he roared.

She screamed, kicking back with her feet—just like Tonk, dammit—giving him a crotch-kick that left him clutching for air. She pounced, knocking him back onto the ground. Like a helpless puppy he lay there, focusing on the stars in the black-velour sky above, wondering if he was ever going to be able to draw breath again.

"Archer!" she cried. "I didn't know it was you!"

Groaning, he rolled onto his side.

"Are you all right?" she asked. "Here, lie on your back so you can get your breath."

"Uh-huh," he said on a strangled moan. "Don't move an injured man."

"I didn't hurt your back," she said reasonably. "Or your neck. You'll be all right in a minute. You just need to relax. Relax, Archer."

"Lucky for me I didn't want kids," Archer said, "because you just kicked in any chance I ever had of dispatching 'em."

"What?"

He rolled his eyes at her tone. Maybe he shouldn't speak so in front of a lady, but she needed to quit trying to roll him over. He wanted to curl up and think about tomorrow—surely the pain would be gone by then.

"You just made me the first Jefferson male who won't need birth control."

"Oh, no. Archer, don't even joke about that! You sit right up, catch your breath and… maybe we should take your jeans off. Would that help? I read somewhere that jeans cut down on a man's, uh, sperm motility, due to the warmth and constricting nature of the fabric."

She was crazy, he'd admit that. "Thank you, I'm fine. Though I didn't want to end my child-giving days quite that way, I'll admit one swift kick was probably as good as paying some doctor quack to do it."

"You want to have as many children as you possibly can!"

"Don't think I will now that my factory's gone crooked. Help me to my feet."

"I will not. You lie there while I go for help."

"No!" That was the last thing he wanted—everyone in Lonely Hearts and Union Junction knowing that a woman had disarmed him. "Hey, where'd you go tonight?"

"Shh," she told him. "Don't talk. Just think happy thoughts. Happy, healing, healthy thoughts. Big, Jefferson-male-testosterone thoughts."

"There's nothing wrong with my testosterone," he grumbled, "just the delivery system. Move, okay? You're treating me like an invalid."

"I do think you should see a doctor. I kicked you with all my might. I thought you were some kind of crazed freak when you grabbed me."

"You were spying," he said, "I had a right to throw a little excitement into the mix."

"Well, you certainly did that."

Archer painfully gained his feet. "You have a very unusual accent that I can't place. And sometime, when there aren't birds singing in my head, you'll have to tell me how you learned to toss a big man like that. But right now, I'm moving toward my warm bed."

"I would say I'm sorry, but you really shouldn't have startled me."

"To think I worried about you, too," Archer said, not about to admit he'd been out looking for her. "Did you want something specific when you were peering in the window, or has maiming me satisfied you temporarily?" He sighed dramatically. "I need a whiskey."

"Marvella gave me some of her special concoction," Clover offered.

Archer suddenly towered above her. "Marvella!"

She nodded.

"Didn't I tell you not to go over there?"

Clover bristled right before his eyes, just like Tonk before she threw a low-down, scurvy hoof. "You can't order me around, Archer Jefferson. I do as I please. I can take care of myself."

"So I see," he said grumpily. "Now, you go over to Marvella's, get your things and come right over here with me. This side of the street is where girls like you belong."

"Girls like me?" She put her hands on her hips. "What kind of girl do you think I am?"

"Innocent. Travel-weary. Unused to the ways of the world. You came here without a room or any reservations of any kind. Clearly, you didn't have a plan. That's how nice girls end up on the wrong side of the street. Listen, I know what I'm talking about. Marvella preys on girls who have no plan."

She stared at him. "She said the *Jeffersons* preyed on girls without plans. In fact, she said you Jeffersons had impregnated one recently."

"*We* impregnated? No, believe me, that's not exactly what happened."

"But it's close to true?"

He took a second look at Clover. She sounded so hopeful, as if she wanted to believe he was some kind of big bad wolf. Maybe he was, but not for this girl. She was not the type of girl he'd jump on in the woods as she traveled to grandma's. He liked his women spicy. If he had a dream woman, she'd be just the opposite of this lady. "You're very safe with me," he assured her.

He thought she looked doubtful, or maybe puzzled, so he realized this point needed to be outlined in teacher-red ink. "Do I *look* like the kind of man who feasts on innocent girls who can't see very well?"

Just then Bandera opened the door, peering out at them. "What's happening, friends?"

"Nothing. What are you doing up?"

"Can't sleep. Keep waking up, thinking about that lady on the bar stool. Think I'll go try to round her up."

Archer thought Clover gasped, but when he glanced at her, she was looking at her feet. Maybe a bug had crawled across her shoe. He figured her for the kind of girl who spooked easily. "Good luck," he said to Bandera.

"Whatever," Bandera answered. "I'm off."

His brother loped away. Archer met Clover's gaze. "So, *do* I look like the kind of man who preys on perfectly nice girls with strange accents? I'm trying to help you, traveler."

Clover didn't reply for a moment. Then she sighed. "Hope you feel better soon. I'm going to bed."

He watched as she walked away. What had that been about?

"Hey," he said, catching up to her in the middle of the street. Turning her to where he could see her in the bright lights from Marvella's, he said, "Don't go off mad. You kicked me, remember?"

"Yes. But harder than I meant to. Clearly I put you out of commission."

"Well, for a moment or two, but..." He looked at her, trying to see her eyes behind the thick lenses. "I mean, you didn't damage me for *life*."

She shook her head. "It's probably like a party balloon. Once popped, the air is gone."

He straightened. "Sister, there is *nothing* wrong with my party balloon! I am the *life* of the party when I want to be. That's *when* I want to be, and I just don't want to be. With... you know...you."

She looked at him. "Why not?"

He wasn't sure he heard her right. "Are you propositioning me?"

"I might be." She put her hands on her hips and a mulish expression on her face. "Scared?"

"Well, I'm not sure." He rubbed his chin. "It's just that you don't strike me as the kind of girl for casual charades."

"Well, maybe I am." She turned toward Marvella's. "You're not allowed to come in here unless you're a client," she said. "Good night, Archer."

There was definitely air in his party balloon, Archer realized. He liked her straightforward approach. "Wait a minute," he said. "Let's talk about this some more."

"No, thank you," she said. "I've discovered you're full of nothing but hot air, and I want a man who can have fun and then go home after the party is over."

"Isn't that supposed to be my line? I want a woman who goes home after the party?"

"If you had known your lines," Clover said, "you'd be getting a party favor right now. Good night."

She closed the door in his face.

His jaw dropped.

That crazy girl! She'd kicked him. She'd made his wounded soldier rise to the battlefield with all that talk about sex—sex with her—and then she'd shut the door on him.

The only door in town he shouldn't touch.

"DAMN," BANDERA SAID a couple seconds later, walking out the door to find his brother still standing there, hands on hips.

"Damn is right," Archer agreed. "What did Clover do once she went inside?"

Bandera laughed. "She went upstairs. You don't have the hots for her, do you?"

"No. I just hate to see a nice girl like her staying in a place like this."

Bandera shrugged. "She seems pretty confident."

"She does not! She needs direction."

"Dude, are you ever ignorant." Bandera stared up at the windows. "Never tell a woman she needs direction. You'll get a swift kick."

"I know." Archer sighed. "I already did, and strangely, I found it compelling."

"I can't worry about your love life."

"It has nothing to do with love. Merely concern for a stranger in town."

"That's what I'm concerned about, too."

"Your bar-stool lady not interested?"

"Not available," Bandera said. "She's not

cutting hair or taking customers, according to the receptionist."

"Interesting. And too bad, as well."

"Yeah. Not too many women take a man's breath away like that one."

"Yeah." But Archer was still worrying about Clover. "That crazy Clover girl doesn't belong here. She should be at Delilah's."

"You may have figured her wrong," Bandera said. "She might be the kind of lady who can take care of herself."

"Yeah. I guess. Okay, I should git then."

Clover's exit to Marvella's still didn't seem right.

"Well, come on, then," Bandera said impatiently. "We don't need to hold down the porch all night."

"I know." Archer frowned.

"Look, if she puts the sizzle on your griddle, then go inside and talk to her. But if you're just being misguided and friendly, forget about it and let's get some shut-eye. She's fine."

"I think she wanted to sleep with me," Archer said.

Bandera laughed. "That shy, quiet girl? Nah. Besides, she's not your type."

"I changed my mind. I don't have *a* type,"

Archer said. "I have many types, as long as they don't come looking for a ring."

"You misread her," Bandera said. "Remember how we used to say that there were girls for fun, and girls for nun? That one would give you none, bro."

"I don't want anything from her," Archer said, turning to walk toward the Lonely Hearts Salon. "She has an attitude reminiscent of Tonk."

"And we call Tonk dog-faced. Think it over, bro."

"Clover's not unattractive," Archer said. He realized what Bandera had said. "And neither is Tonk!"

His brother laughed. "I pick the girl on the bar stool," he said. "I like a lady who's easy on the eyes."

"Looks aren't everything," Archer said stubbornly.

"But they are the first ticket to my heart, followed by my stomach being fed, my muscles being admired, my laundry being done, and my sex—"

"That's enough," Archer interrupted, getting crosser by the moment. "Glandular responses will remain undiscussed."

A window opened above them. "Archer!"

"What?" He wondered what his glasses-wearing newcomer wanted now.

"Where's the best place in town for drinks and dancing?"

Archer blinked. "Two-Bits."

"Thanks." She shut the window.

Bandera slapped him heartily on the back. "And you were worried about her being lonely. Sad. Homesick. A tragic heroine in a black governess dress right out of *Jane Eyre*."

Archer turned toward Delilah's. "I can't picture Clover dancing." He didn't want to, either.

"It's the quiet ones who'll surprise you."

Archer shook his head. "I reckon."

"Night's still young," Bandera said. "If the wild girls are going dancing, maybe we should provide some partners."

"Now, that idea has some merit," Archer said cheerfully. He'd be willing to bet Clover's idea of dancing was standing by a plastic banana tree, watching everybody else shake a leg.

Finding out that she was an unwatered wallflower would make him feel a whole lot better.

Chapter Four

Clove realized there was a problem with The Plan after spending the early part of the evening getting to know Archer better. Though his email conversations had been Texas tall tale, in person he was Texas short story, she thought, annoyed. All bark, definitely no bite. Not even a nibble.

Apparently, the hook was not properly baited. Bandera had really gone for her as the bar-stool babe. If Archer had, he'd tried to conceal it.

He concealed a lot, this cowboy she'd come to romance. Somewhat rude at times, and definitely in need of a manners injection. Not as kind and poetic as he'd been in cyberspace.

She felt a bit betrayed. He was not going to ravish her; in fact, she doubted he'd ravish any woman. He was more a chauvinistic protector. How dare he tell her she couldn't stay at Marvella's! Breathing deeply to get past the memory of his pigheadedness, Clove told herself to remember the bundles of babies his family had produced. Twelve brothers, for starters, and miscellaneous progeny.

"I just want one," she said longingly. "One."

John Wayne had had his good side, mixed in with his arrogance, she remembered. Still, Archer seemed to be more arrogant than cowboy gentleman.

"Well, at least my heart won't be in jeopardy where he's concerned," she told herself. A good stuntwoman always saw to her safety first, and after getting to know Archer better, she knew her heart was totally, completely safe.

"Maybe safer than I want it to be." She gazed in the mirror. When she'd yelled down to ask him about a place to go dancing, she had hoped he would offer to escort her.

He hadn't—and she had to admit that this cowboy was going to be tough to catch. The most bothersome part was that Archer wasn't remotely attracted to her.

Picking up a curling iron, she absently pressed a curl into her hair. It bounced when she released it—and The Plan took on a modification. She began to do her hair the way Marvella's girls had styled it earlier, Texas big and poufy. Tousled. Sexy. She applied the makeup the way they'd had it earlier, and then she shimmied into a tube-top dress she found in the closet. High heels completed her outfit.

"The revenge of the nerdy girl," she told herself, laying her glasses on the cosmetics tray. "Revenge is supposed to be so sweet."

The girls knocked on her door. "Ready?" they called. "Going out with us, Clover?"

"I'm ready!" Fluffing her hair one last time, she saw the woman Bandera had admired gazing back at her. "I'm definitely going to Marvella's school to learn Hot-Babe Style 101. Then I'm going to get my cowboy," she said with satisfaction to her reflection. "Archer Jefferson, you're not going to know what hit you!"

"THERE SHE IS!" Bandera said as they walked inside Two-Bits bar. "The bar-stool babe!"

Archer peered through the smoky atmosphere and clinging partners. In the light from a neon beer sign, he saw her moving, laughing and snapping her fingers. Dressed in a dress practically painted on her lush body, she danced in a circle with a group of men and Marvella's stylists. "They're having fun," Archer observed.

"They sure are, and I'm on my way to do the same." Bandera took off to include himself in the circle, perilously close to the woman he fancied.

She was hot, Archer conceded. He liked a full-figured lady, and especially one with such nice skin. The breasts were nothing to ignore as they lightly jiggled under the tight material. Idly, he wondered if she was wearing a bra. Strapless dresses just begged to be tugged right off a woman, in his opinion. She had nice legs, and to be honest, he was a madman for high heels.

Checking the door, he wondered when Clover would arrive. He intended to keep an eye on her, because heaven only knew she could get in trouble in a place like this.

"You should dance with me," Bandera's beauty said.

He stared at her, then glanced at his brother. Bandera was surrounded by three Never Lonely Cut-n-Gurls, and the evening looked to be going strong from his perspective. Bandera wasn't even glancing their way.

"I'm waiting on someone," he said.

She looked so disappointed, almost crushed. His bravado, which Clover and Tonk seemed to have teamed up to kick to smithereens, rose a bit.

"Now, don't take it too hard," he said. "You're beautiful, no question. I would dance with you anywhere, anytime."

"But?" she prompted.

"But I'm waiting on this crazy little girl to show up. She's new to town and real unsophisticated. You know what I mean? The kind who'd get lost on a sunny day."

Her eyebrows rose. She had clear, pretty blue eyes, and the just-teased tangle of her silvery-blond hair was appealing. Made a man's fingers want to wander there.

He glanced toward the door again. "She probably got lost on her way here," he said. "I should have offered to escort her."

"That would have been chivalrous," she agreed, "but you didn't, and so now you and I are stuck waiting for a mystery person to show up." She pulled him by the hand, though he didn't fight too hard. Once on the dance floor, he'd shift her over to Bandera, and go back to watching out for Clover. He shot a quick glance toward the potted banana tree strung with white lights, to make certain she wasn't hiding over there.

Cool skin slid into his arms, and he was

jerked into the present predicament. "Gosh," he said. "You feel good."

"So do you, cowboy." She smiled at him, happy that she'd managed to disguise her accent completely.

They moved well together, Archer acknowledged. Bandera was glowering at him, but Archer shrugged. It had been ages since he'd held a soft woman, and this one was firm and ripe, and her lips were glossy—

"Once upon a time I dreamed of a cowboy like you," she said. "He was strong and powerful, and he knew how to romance a woman."

"I know how to romance a woman," Archer said. He could feel his arms warming from the heat her body was beginning to give off. Glowing embers turning to a sexual fire he hadn't felt in a long time—maybe ever. Frowning, he stared down at her, wondering if she knew she was working over his testosterone.

"You could show me," she suggested. "I like romance."

She was definitely coming on to him.

He glanced toward the door, watching for Clover.

The woman in his arms pressed lightly into

his body, a full-length hint of the wonders available.

Taking a deep breath, Archer decided that opportunity only dropped sporadically into a man's life, and when it did, it needed to be seized by the throat.

"Think my brother had his eye on you," he said gruffly, his energy now captured by the fantasy of tugging the dress off of her.

"He may have," she said lightly, "but he doesn't know me like you do."

"Really?"

She looked at him with guileless eyes. Then she lowered her head onto his chest, in a gesture he would have to call gentle surrender. "Really," he heard her murmur.

That was it. Female-led seduction, his favorite pastime.

He dragged her off by the hand.

CLOVE HELD HER BREATH as Archer led her to his truck. She got in when he held the door open for her, and then she stared out the passenger-side window, hoping he wouldn't look beneath the hair and curls to find plain ol' Clove. Unsophisticated, he'd called her. Thought he had to watch out for her, a touch of pity in his voice.

His hand snaked around her wrist, surprising her as he pulled her across the bench seat toward him. Then he kissed her hot and fast and hard, and in that moment, Clove knew she'd underestimated her man.

He was everything he'd bragged about in his emails.

He just wasn't showing it to "Clover."

The way she was now brought out the beast in him. She had rattled the cage.

Pulling back to look at her, Archer said, "Are you okay?"

She nodded.

"You went quiet on me."

It was too quiet in his truck. In the bar, it had been loud and they hadn't talked enough for him to recognize her. He'd also been scoping the door, not paying attention to her until she'd fairly propositioned him.

Switching the radio on to turn his mind from chivalry, she kissed him, reminding him of why they were in the truck.

"All right, then," he said a moment later. "I take it that means yes. I'm in the mood for a swim. Hope you are, too."

In February? Not likely, but if it meant getting him down to his boxers, then she would swim with polar bears in the Arctic.

He put his hand around hers, driving with his other hand. Clove closed her eyes, thinking about Lucy.

Just one baby.

A few minutes later, Archer parked the truck at a creek wooded with trees. He shone the headlights of the truck into the darkness for a few moments, then switched them to low. Putting the radio on a sexy jazz station, he said, "Now let's dance properly."

She went out the driver's side behind him, sliding into his arms.

"God, I never realized a woman could feel this good," he said. "You're like satin."

They danced together wordlessly after that, until the station went to commercial. Then he took Clove by the hand, leading her toward the water. "I was teasing about swimming," he said.

"I'm brave," she said softly. "I can handle it if you can."

"Skinny-dipping in February? No, my plan is to keep you warm."

She thought he would find a grassy spot for them to lie, but instead he walked with her, their fingers interlaced.

"This is one of my favorite places on earth.

My brothers and I used to come here to swim after rodeos."

He ran a hand across her bare shoulders. Clove shivered at the caress, her breath held nervously.

"You're cold," he said. "Come back to the truck."

She wasn't cold, but she followed him, anyway, enjoying his concern for her. He let down the gate of the truck bed, spreading a blanket for them. Turning off the truck lights, he crawled into the bed, pulling her up to join him. Then he covered them with another blanket and rested her head on his chest.

"You're prepared for everything," she whispered.

"No, I'm not. If I was, I'd have a bottle of champagne cooling in an ice chest," he said. "See those stars?"

"Mmm," she said, loving the feel of his chest and hearing his heart beat fast.

"One of those stars has your name on it," he said. "What is the name of that star?"

"It's a secret," she whispered into his ear, straddling him to kiss his face.

"I like secrets," he said, pushing his hands underneath her dress to run his hands over her bare bottom. "You have on no underwear," he said with surprise. "You little daredevil!"

THERE WERE SECRETS and then there were secrets, Clove thought, quietly getting down out of the truck three hours later. She knew the town wasn't far, and she wanted to be long gone before her cowboy awakened.

It had been a night she'd never forget. They'd made the truck rock like mad, and she'd learned that giving up one's virginity was easy when the pleasure was that intense. They'd made love over and over again, hungry for each other. When he'd asked about birth control and offered a condom, she'd said she was fine.

At the final second, she'd confessed her virginity, hoping he wouldn't hop out of the truck.

He hadn't. He'd been quite tender and considerate of her.

She hurried, knowing Archer could wake up any minute and realize she'd left. It was a good thing she knew the real Archer, the grouchy one, or she would definitely have lost her heart to him tonight. What a tender lover! So romantic, yet so masterful. She got chill bumps thinking about it.

Thirty minutes later, she quietly let herself into her bedroom, closing the door. She took a shower, glad to be rid of the curls and the makeup. Snuggling into her covers, she smiled, thinking about Archer.

It was good to be herself again.

Only, tonight he'd changed her, made her feel beautiful. Given her appreciation of her woman's body.

She would never forget him.

Chapter Five

Three months later

In Delilah's kitchen, Clove straightened, her back sore. Cooking at Delilah's was nice, especially because Delilah was so kind. So was Jerry, Delilah's trucker boyfriend. Delilah hadn't really needed another employee, but the fact that Clove was only in town for a short while, until her visa ran out, was a plus.

Clove didn't really need a job, but she wanted to keep busy and make friends. All the ladies at the Lonely Hearts Salon were very eager to make her feel at home. In fact, she liked it here much better than at Marvella's, as Archer had said she would.

Marvella had been nice to her, but Clove had begun to feel uneasy about the male clientele who came to the salon.

"Triplets," the young, pretty doctor had told her at the last appointment. "Congratulations. You hit the jackpot! The first triplets ever to be born in Lonely Hearts Station, I do believe."

Clove had staggered out of the doctor's office, and she was still reeling. Triplets! She might have known that Archer Jefferson was capable of not only impregnating a woman, but doing it in an embarrassingly huge way!

She'd moved out of Marvella's the second she got home from the doctor's office, telling Marvella she felt she'd overstayed her welcome. The truth was, if Archer had felt strongly about Clove not staying at Marvella's when he barely knew her, she knew he'd really freak if he ever accidentally found out his progeny was gestating there.

"I've really done it now," Clove told Delilah, who was putting some plastic wrap over peanut-butter cookies Clove had baked.

"Don't worry," Delilah told her. "You're among friends here."

She was, but for the first time in her life, she was frightened.

"Have you thought of telling the father?" Delilah asked.

Archer had said, on many occasions, he didn't want children. "He wouldn't be happy. I'm skipping that conversation for now."

Besides which, she was already gaining weight. Her face was puffy and her breasts had swelled. If he'd thought her plain and unsophisticated before, now she was downright, well, more plain.

"The thing is," she told Delilah, "triplets are intimidating."

"You'd better believe it," Delilah said. "Pregnancy can be intimidating. You're doing it times three." She looked at her kindly. "If you ever want to talk about the father, you can trust me to be silent."

Clove lowered her eyes. "I'm afraid you'd be surprised. It's not anything I can share. But thank you."

Delilah nodded. "I'm going to my room now." She patted her hand. "Have a cookie and a cup of hot blackberry tea. Go to bed soon, too."

Clove smiled at the older woman. "Thank you so much. For everything."

Delilah smiled and left the room. Clove sat at the table, with only the lamp lit, rubbing her stomach absently. She wore dresses now, with expanding waistlines. Normally, a pregnancy wouldn't show at this juncture, but her three babies seemed to be thriving.

If they were destined to be Archer's size,

she was in for a rocky road. She felt as if she was in the middle of going down a slide, and couldn't stop, no matter how much she wanted to. There was no body double who could perform this stunt for her.

Sighing, she pushed her oversize glasses up on her nose.

"Hey," a masculine voice said suddenly, making her gasp with fright. "What are you doing here, Clover?"

She stood, her heart pounding, her gaze drinking in Archer as he walked into the kitchen. She'd managed to avoid him while staying at Marvella's. She should have known she couldn't hide from him now that she was at the Lonely Hearts Salon. "What are *you* doing here?"

"Looking for cookies and milk. Came in the back way, as I always do, and a pit stop in the kitchen before bed is a necessity." He glanced at the cookies on the tray in front of her, then his gaze caught on her stomach. She watched with some horror as his attention traveled to her swelled breasts, then back to her stomach.

His eyes wide, he met her gaze.

"Oh, you poor thing," he said. "If you want me to kill the jerk, I swear I'll bring an army of Jeffersons down on his head. He'll wish he'd *never* done you this way."

"Archer," she began uncomfortably. "I'm all right."

"You're not all right," he said. "If you were, you wouldn't be unmarried, pregnant and living in a salon."

She swallowed. "I wasn't seduced and then left, if that's what you're thinking."

He looked at her doubtfully. "Clover, listen. You're a nice girl. Very trusting. But that's just what a man can be capable of. Making a woman love him and then leaving her."

She blinked. "It was the other way around. Not that you love me, but…"

He looked at her funny for a moment, as if someone had told a bad joke he didn't get. A muscle near his eye twitched. Slowly, his hand unsteady, he reached to pull her glasses from her face. He pulled her ponytail down, his fingers trembling.

She sensed him pulling away from her.

"Oh my God," he murmured. "Oh, no."

Clove's heart sank.

"This can't be," Archer said. "You can't be her. You can't be pregnant." To say that he was horrified would be putting it mildly. She could see in his face that he still didn't want to be a father. He was not in love with her. In fact, he hadn't known she was who she was. "Tell me I'm dreaming," he said. "A big, huge, ugly nightmare."

She blinked at his harshness.

"I'm sorry," he said. "I mean, we went looking for you that night at Two-Bits. Well, Bandera was trolling for the bar-stool babe, and he took off with three stylists he met dancing that night. I was hanging around waiting for you to show up, thinking you needed a guardian eye. But *you* were the bar-stool babe." He frowned. "I really thought you might need my protection."

"I was fine."

"That's what you said that night when I asked you about birth control." Archer told himself his heart wasn't going to bust a valve; taking a deep breath, he made himself calm down. "You said you were *fine*."

She sank into a chair. "I was fine."

"Not if you're pregnant!" he yelled. "Clover, that is not the definition of *fine!*"

They stared at each other.

Archer couldn't believe his bad luck. One more Jefferson to add to the mix of booties and diapers at the ranch. Mason was going to explode. Hell, *he* was going to explode.

"I suppose you want me to marry you. That's what you're hanging around Lonely Hearts Station for."

"No." She shook her head. "I'm hanging around because I didn't expect to get pregnant this fast, and my plane ticket isn't for another two weeks."

His eyes went wide. "This fast? You didn't expect it this fast?"

"Yes. I have a four-month visa from Australia."

"Australia?"

"Yes," she said softly. "TexasArcher, I'm Clove Penmire. AussieClove, from Down Under."

"AussieClove," he repeated stupidly. "No wonder you haven't been answering my emails. You've been here."

"Yes."

"You came here to meet me."

She nodded.

He thought hard, realizing by her tame responses that he was digging to the bottom of a very deep well. "You came here to get pregnant by me."

"I hoped so."

"You came here to marry an American."

"No. That was never my intention."

"So you just wanted a baby?"

"Yes." She looked away for a moment, then met his gaze defiantly. "Only The Plan went a bit awry."

"I'll say," he said bitterly.

"I'm having three."

The world seemed to drop away from his feet. He stared at her, his gaze narrowed. *"What?"*

She never flinched. "I'm having three babies."

Archer's ears rang, his stomach pitched, his eyes burned. Anger made his body tighten, his guts a pinched cord of disbelief. "Congratulations," he finally said, stalking from the room.

He stood in the hall, gasping for breath, waiting for the stars of fury to leave his vision. AussieClove the stuntwoman had come here to get pregnant by him. The babe at Marvella's and plain ol' Clover were the same person. Whoa. She'd laid a trap and he'd fallen into it like a dope. Amazing what makeup and some curls and high heels could do to turn a man's brain to mush!

This made no sense, though. After their night together, she'd made no effort to contact him, not even under the AussieClove email address—and he would never have put two and two together—so was she done with him? It sure appeared that way. He reached for the one thing he could fight about, even if it wasn't likely.

He stalked back into the room. "This is about money."

She glared at him. "Could you step one foot closer, please, so I can slap you? I really don't want to chase you to do it, because you're not worth it."

"I'm not worth it? Who is the brain behind the lying, cheating plan, Clover? *Clove?*"

"Do you want these cookies or not? I'm going to put them away." She picked up the tray of assorted cookies, tightened the plastic, and put them next to the coffeepot for visitors to find. "I've been baking all day, and now I'm going to bed."

"You're staying here?"

"Yes, I am." She moved past him, and Archer itched to grab her and make her stop bustling around as if his world hadn't come to a bull-stomped halt. He followed her down the hall. "When did that change?"

"When I found out I was pregnant. I moved over here. Because you had wanted me at Delilah's in the first place."

She went up the stairs, and he followed her, carefully avoiding watching her fanny, though it was a Herculean effort. "You got pregnant, and *then* you started taking my advice?"

"Yes."

Nothing about this moment made any sense. "Maybe I should find a stud for Tonk. If all a woman needs to mind is to become preg—"

She whirled on the stairs in front of him. "I didn't take your advice so much as make a decision for the good of my children. Cool it with the cowboy macho, Archer."

"Now just a minute." He followed her into her bedroom. "I am macho. I am somewhat chauvinistic, hardheaded and generally not a role model for young children. You knew all this. And still you came all the way to Texas to get pregnant by me."

She jerked a nightgown from a drawer. "Yes, I did."

"Aren't there any real men in Australia?"

"Plenty. But you were less complicated. Plus, you bragged all the time about your potency and it was just too tempting. Excuse me."

He sank into a chair as she went into the

connecting bathroom and closed the door. "Triplets, damn it. Triplets!"

"Okay, so you weren't bragging," she said through the bathroom door. "Give yourself a gold medal." She came out of the bathroom in a white nightgown that went to her neck, touched her wrists with lace, and hovered at her ankles with more frothy lace. It billowed about her body, leaving everything to the imagination.

"Jeez," he said with some horror. "You're either trying to be a frilly ghost or a gothic heroine. Where's your candle and lantern?"

"The nightgown's practical, it's expandable for three, and it's modest enough for a home like this. So sorry it's not your idea of sexy."

"I'll say." He gulped.

She turned off the light. "Shut the door on your way out, please."

Man, she was a bossy one. She might not like being compared to Tonk, but his Appaloosa and his Australian had some mighty tight tempers on them. It made him want to jerk on the reins hard, but what he'd learned was that the more attitude a woman gave him, the softer his hands had to be.

"Hey." He reached over, switching the lamp back on. "Betty Crocker, you're going to be a little late for your baking tomorrow. We've got to talk this out."

She sighed and shoved a pillow behind her back so that she was sitting up. "I think we should not talk ever again."

"I'm confused."

"That's your problem."

"Maybe, but it would be best for the children if we talked." The three children, he thought, his heart pounding with fear.

A scratching in the hall made Clove jump from the bed in a billow of white and fling open the door. She scooped a cat from the floor, closed the door and got back into the white-sheeted bed. "The four children."

"Four?"

She smiled. "Four children. This is my new baby, Tink." The gray-and-white cat observed him from its secure place in Clove's lap, its large, clear-water green eyes seeming to laugh at his plight. "I named her Tink after Tonk. Because she's tricky like your Appaloosa. Plus, she has lots of spots, just like Tonk. Of course, she doesn't have spotted nostrils like Tonk, but—"

"Okay. Let's stick with human babies conceived by me," Archer said crossly. "Ones without bobbed tails."

"Oh," Clove said, sympathizing with her cat. "It's only half-bobbed. And she's still beautiful, in my eyes."

Archer glared at the feline. "I do not like cats."

"What man does?" She smiled at him. "Well, some do. Very secure men do."

"Pregnant women aren't supposed to have cats. They carry diseases," he opined majestically.

"And I can't take you back to Australia with me," she said to the purring cat. "But Delilah says she'll give you a good home once I'm gone."

"Back up," he said. "I think we overlooked something in the conversation. You're not going back to Australia."

"Yes, I am," Clove said. "I don't like it here. The air is all wrong, for one thing. It doesn't smell right. It sort of smells like an old train depot. And—"

"Which it is, Clove," he said, certain his brain was going to stroke out from his rising temper, "you are not taking my children to a continent affectionately called Down Under."

"You're suggesting that I take them to a ranch affectionately called Malfunction Junction? *That* sounds like it would be good for the children."

She was making him crazy with her defiance. Strangely, he couldn't stop thinking about the pleasure her body had made him feel, and all the sassing he was receiving was giving him a fair-size urge to one-up her with some silencing kisses.

"Anyway, it's not like you were completely innocent in this," she told him. "You told me I'd bent your baby-making delivery system. Ruined the pipes for good. Put the factory out of commission. How was I supposed to know you were better?"

He frowned at the memory of her kicking him. Funny how the sexual pleasure they'd shared had wiped out his memories of the first time she'd had him flat on his back, gasping for breath. "Hey!" He sat up suddenly. "You hurt me. You really hurt me!"

She blinked. "It's in the past, Archer. I really think that, since you got me pregnant with triplets, the factory was only on a fifteen-minute shutdown."

"But I may have overlooked a really bad sign. What if the Curse of the Broken Body Parts hit me?"

"No, I hit you." Clove shook her head. "I

may have been cursing you, but you did scare me and—"

"You don't understand." He scratched his head, shoving his hat back. "You really kicked me *hard*."

"Yes, and still you managed to send three healthy sperm to do their job." She glared at him. "Don't tell me you're a hypochondriac. That would be so unappealing."

She didn't understand. The Curse of the Broken Body Parts had hit all of his brothers—right before they got married. Everything was moving too fast. "I find it somewhat ironic and downright hilarious that you nearly kicked in the holy grail of your quest. You should be gentler around the goods, specifically if you've come twenty-four hours and bought an expensive plane ticket to enjoy them." He sighed. "I suppose you're going to want money eventually. Support payments."

"A hypochondriac and a chauvinist. And I crossed a big ocean to be with you." Clove sniffed disdainfully.

"You're a sperm-stealer wearing a Thanksgiving-dinner tablecloth," he said. "Looks like we're going to be the proud parents of triplets. Please put the cat on the floor. It's making me nervous."

She sighed. "Tink, off you go. Big strong cowboy is afraid of you."

"No, I just need someplace to lay my pounding head." Kicking off his boots and tossing his hat into the chair, he got up into the bed next to Clove. "We need to sleep on this and see if we still like each other in the morning."

"We don't like each other right now!"

He flipped off the bedside lamp. "I know. We've got a lot of hard work ahead of us. Right now, I've got to get over the migraine you've given me."

"You cannot sleep in my bed."

"I sure as hell am not leaving you, Miss Defiance. As soon as I turn my back, you'd probably give me the slip. I am here to mess up your plan, Clove Penmire from Down Under. Consider us wearing golden hand-cuffs. Mmm," he said thoughtfully, "that actually sounds fun. Consider us wearing golden balls and chains, which are connected forever at the ankle. Awkward," he mused. "Make that one ball, two chains and three baby-size ankle weights."

"I get the picture," Clove said, annoyed. "You're not leaving."

"That's right. You invited me into your life

by being so devious. And believe me, I know just how to handle devious."

She sighed and inched her pillow down next to his. But he could feel her hanging on to the edge of the bed, in order to keep as much room as possible between them.

"We're going to have to get a bigger bed," he said, "because I have a feeling you're going to get as big as a house. That voluminous nightgown is only a precursor of more awkward things to come."

"Archer!"

He closed his eyes. Black spots of tiredness danced behind his lids, reminding him of Tonk and the low-down, scurvy hoof she liked to throw every once in a while to keep him honest.

He'd be watching out for Clove's attempts to kick him when he wasn't looking—because the first kick she'd thrown had been breathtaking.

Chapter Six

Clove awakened early the next morning, shifted Archer off her back where he'd settled comfortably and took his hand out from underneath her gown, where, to her dismay, it had come to rest quite proprietorially on her stomach.

He slept like the dead, his face buried in her hair.

Having never had a man in her bed before, this presented a dilemma. She liked having him sleep with her. Too much. He was loud and ornery and thought he knew everything, but when he wasn't expounding opinions and his eyes were shut, he was quite pleasant. Warm. Strong. Sexy.

How could she be strict of will when she really admired his possessiveness toward his children?

She was just going to have to stick to the original plan, for Lucy's sake. In fact, she needed to call Lucy—right now. It was just about the right time in Australia to drop a major bombshell.

She left the sleeping cowboy, closing the door softly. Tink slept in Archer's upturned hat where he'd tossed it in the chair; the feline was curled up just as contentedly as Archer in Clove's bed.

Someone's fur was going to fly when Archer awakened to find his hat taken over—Clove didn't want to be around when he discovered Tink's newfound bed. Quietly moving down the hall, Clove went downstairs into the kitchen. Luckily there was no one there yet, as only Clove rose this early to begin baking.

She picked up the kitchen phone, placed the call, and the next sound she heard was Lucy's voice accepting the charges.

"Clove!" Lucy exclaimed. "I thought we'd hear from you sooner!"

"I'm sorry," Clove said. "I miss you. So much!"

"We miss you! How is your trip?"

"I'm enjoying it. Ready to come home, though. How are you?"

"Good, darling. Good."

"And Robert?"

There was silence for a moment. Then Lucy said, "Good as well. Everything is just fine."

Clove closed her eyes, hearing what Lucy didn't want her to know. "And the farm?"

"Well, the horses are good—miss you, of course—but we're still looking for the right situation to fix all."

Clove nodded. Taking a deep breath, she said, "I have a bit of news, actually."

"Do tell! I hope it's wonderful."

"It is. I'm pregnant."

"Pregnant!" Lucy gasped. "Clove! No wonder you haven't called. You met a man!"

"Well, he isn't the reason I haven't called. I should have called sooner, but—"

"But you've been having too much fun. I'm so happy for you."

"Well, truthfully, this isn't about fun. I'm not in love or anything." Strong like, maybe. Overwhelming attraction, admittedly. But love? Neither she nor Archer would claim that. "Neither one of us are in love."

"I guess your…the father knows?"

"Yes." Clove closed her eyes.

"And what does he say?"

He says a lot, Clove thought. *He says too*

much. "He's still a bit shocked. I'm having triplets."

"Triplets!" Lucy gasped again, then started laughing with excitement. "Triplets! Please come home at once so I can shower you with love and affection and presents. I'll be an aunt!"

"Maybe more a mother," Clove said.

"Mother?" Lucy stopped laughing. *"Mother?"*

"I could use the help," Clove said. "It would be really hard for me to do stunt work and take care of three babies."

"You should stay home and take care of them," Lucy said.

"And pay bills with what?" Clove asked.

"Of course, we would help you—" Lucy began.

"Lucy, I do not want to be supported by my older sister. I don't want to be supported by anyone. And just think how much you'd enjoy having three little ones in the house."

"I would," Lucy said, her voice filled with longing. "It's a dream for me."

"And you really can't imagine me being as good a mother as you," Clove said. "The truth is, you're suited to be a mother, and I'm not. Oh, maybe for one, but three? It would be a disaster."

"I—I'll have to talk to Robert, naturally. He did mention adoption at one point, then sort of lost interest in that idea…and they are your children. Your angels. You would forever be the true mum. And I don't know about Robert, dear. He sort of…sort of loses interest in things these days."

Sort of losing interest in Lucy. Clove didn't have to hear the words to know them to be the worry on Lucy's mind. "It's okay, Lucy. I'll be home soon."

"I'll start decorating the nursery!" Lucy began sobbing. "Clove, this is wonderful, a dream come true. I mean, I hope you're happy. You're quite sure this man doesn't love you? I will be quite happy to come over there and exert sisterly pressure on him if you would like me to. He should know that you are not some alone-in-the-world girl he can take advantage of."

"He does not love me, and I do not love him," Clove said with authority. "Trust me on this. We both understand that it was a one-night thing." It wasn't worth mentioning that Archer was asleep in her bed right now, determined to throw a wrench into The Plan. He didn't understand. He couldn't understand. Lucy and Clove had been there for each other when there was no one else. The sisterly bond between them was stronger than everything. She wasn't about to let Lucy down. "I love you," she told her older sister.

"You can never love me as much as I love you," Lucy replied, just as she always did. "Call me if you need anything. I'll be right there."

"I will."

They said their goodbyes and then Clove hung up, her heart feeling lighter than it had in a long time. She closed her eyes and put a hand on her stomach. "You are the luckiest children in the world," she whispered. "You angels are going to have a beautiful mother, a physician father, a lovely home, and me devoted to your every smile, your every tear."

"Those angels will also have me," Archer interrupted.

Clove's eyes flew open. Archer walked into the kitchen, crossing his arms as he stared down at her. "Let's review the roll call. I think I heard some errors in the lineup."

Clove stared at him, her heart pounding.

"Let's see," he said, holding up a finger,

"first there's the beautiful mother, which naturally is you."

She blinked.

"Then there's the physician father. I'm not a physician. I'm a cowboy, third generation, Texas-born. So one of us is confused. You never mentioned that those were not my children, so that leaves us with a gap in the family history. When did I become a doctor? And what's my specialty?"

Her throat closed. She couldn't speak.

"What is my little Aussie stuntwoman up to now?" He pulled her into his arms, giving her a deep kiss. "Just as good as I remembered the first time," he said when he pulled away.

"Don't," she said sharply, whirling away from him.

"We should kiss more often," he said, "since we're getting to know each other for the sake of the children."

"No, we shouldn't," she said, going to open a bag of flour.

"Clove." He turned her toward him, trying to take the flour from her. "If I understood what you were saying on the phone, the answer is no. You are not giving my children to your sister."

She tugged the flour proprietorially and it dropped to the floor, sending a great white pouf into the air. For a reason she would never understand, Clove burst into tears.

"Yegods," Archer said, "it's only flour, baby."

Wiping her eyes, she managed to get flour everywhere. "You don't understand."

"I understand you have flour on your face, and that you've got three buns in the oven. My recommendation is that you give this job up and come home to the ranch with me where you belong."

Hands on hips, she said, "Archer, I do not need to be rescued. Stop trying to ride in here and toss me over your saddle."

He sighed. "You're very confused. But we'll soon fix that." Gently, he wiped the flour from her face. To her surprise, Clove liked the feel of his fingers stroking her. She stood very still, letting him touch her skin, telling herself it was just the flour he was after, but secretly impressed by his steadfastness despite her tears.

"Let's get back to whatever you're baking. Then you need to turn in your resignation to Delilah."

There was a vast difference between steadfast and stubborn. Clove turned away. "Grab the recipe for the snickerdoodles out of the recipe box. That's what Delilah wants for her guests. She has a family of three from Wichita coming in, and she says that their email reservation indicated that the little boy has never had a snickerdoodle. Delilah has a questionnaire for her guests as to what their favorite foods and desserts are, which I think is awesome for customer service." She turned to face him. "And I'm not turning in my resignation, thank you. I'm more than happy here."

"Here," he said. "The recipe for snickerdoodles, whatever they may be."

Handing her the card, their fingers touched, startling her because she hadn't expected it. Her thoughts suddenly were elsewhere. "I wonder what they'll be," she murmured, looking up at Archer in wonder.

"What?"

She blushed. "The babies."

He smiled at her. "Boys, of course. Boys who will always have the benefits of eating snickerdoodles."

Her eyebrows raised. "You think so? That they'll be boys?"

"Sure. And boys need to grow up around their uncles. Excellent role models."

She turned away.

"Not that your sister wouldn't be a good role model," he said softly, turning her back toward him. "Clove, I remember the email you sent me mentioning that your sister couldn't have children. I could feel your pain and worry."

Her gaze lowered, hiding her thoughts from him.

"I reread those emails while I was home," he told her.

"You kept them?"

"Every one. And it's clear to me what happened. You practically mapped it out in your notes to me. I was always talking about myself, and you talked a lot about your stunt work, but throughout our correspondence, there were hints about your concern for your sister. It was a pretty common theme. Are you sure there's not more wrong in her life than not being able to have children?"

She frowned at him, not liking his thought process. "They've tried for years to conceive. With her husband, Robert, being a doctor, they've had access to advanced knowledge and opportunities. It should have happened."

"Maybe some things don't happen for a reason."

"I refuse to accept that."

"Obviously." He looked at her. "Part of me is flattered that you spent the money on a plane ticket, gave up your virginity and thought I could get the job done for you."

She raised an eyebrow. "And the other part?"

"The other part of me is ticked that you've changed my life without me having a say in it."

"You weren't supposed to find out, and—"

"But I did." He took her chin in his fingers. "And that means that Lucy, as much as I feel for her plight, is now going to have to figure out a different way to have children."

Clove jerked away from his hand. "No."

"Yes. Those children are mine, and they are staying in America." He smiled at her gently, running a hand down her arm. "We may even have to figure out a way to like each other. It would be in the children's best interests."

"You didn't want me, Archer," Clover said defiantly. "Not the first day, when I asked you to dinner. You weren't interested. The only way I got you into bed was through the Never

Lonely Cut-n-Gurls total makeover. But you didn't want *me*."

"True," he said cheerfully, "and blast those Never Lonely Gurls. I told you they were trouble, warned you to stay away from them. But you didn't listen, and now look at the pickle you're in."

She gave him a sour look and began scooping flour into a dustpan. "I don't want you to like me just because I'm pregnant with your children."

He got down to help her. "It wasn't that I didn't want you. I was busy with Tonk when you asked me out. And I sort of sensed you were the kind of unsophisticated girl who would require a lot of time and effort. A needy type, if you will."

She gasped.

"And my intuition was proven correct," he continued, ignoring her outrage. "You have turned out to be quite needy, a veritable time sink."

Standing, she washed her hands. "You are despicable, and full of yourself. I never saw that in your emails. I always wondered why a man who supposedly had so much going for him was content to chat with a woman for two years without ever seeing her face. It seemed odd."

"I like my freedom," he said happily. "All us Jeffersons do. But you have now snared me, and you will have to deal with the consequences of marrying a cowboy."

All her breath went right out of Clove's chest. "You're crazy."

"Then we'll get along, my sweet stuntwoman. By the way, you have let your stuntwork employers know you won't be coming back to work? Far too dangerous a job for a new mother."

"I am not marrying you. I am not listening to you. I think you are insane. You owe me nothing, and I owe you nothing, and that's the way we're going to leave it. Now get out, before I return to Marvella's." She gave him a pointed stare. "Where I know I'll be safe from *you*."

"I don't think so," Archer said, "for a thousand reasons I could share with you, but for right now, it's enough to say that you've invited me into your life, AussieClove, and this father will be sticking very close to his offspring."

Chapter Seven

"Mason can I talk to you?" Archer asked, three hours after he'd left Clove to her baking. He'd figured it was best to give her some time to chew on what he'd had to say.

"Sure." Mason glanced up from the paperwork he was writing on. "What's up?"

"I'd like to talk to everybody, if you can round up just the boys for dinner tonight. I need some advice, and I'd like to do it privately."

Mason rose. "Tell Helga we're going to have a sit-down, then." Their housekeeper would need to prepare enough food. "Leave a note on the kitchen board for the boys that you'd like everybody present."

Archer nodded. "Thanks."

"Are you all right?"

"I'm fine. I just need to air some things out. Need some guidance." He smiled, but it was tense. "Had a bit of a surprise today, and a family consult's the way I'd like to bring it up."

One thing was for certain, he was going about this differently than Last had. He felt Last had waited too long to talk to Mason about his baby. He'd avoided the problem. A man, in Archer's opinion, faced everything with his eyes on the horns. Last was the youngest, of course, and he had a lot of baggage being the Family Philosophe. They'd relied on him over the years, when they'd had their wild stages, to be the family compass. No one had wanted to let the baby of the family, with his incisive opinions of what a family should be, down. Consequently, Archer felt Last was so burdened by their need for him to be the strong one that when he faltered, it was tough for him to face it. Last had changed a lot lately, though, and Archer was proud of the strides he was making. Last sure liked baby Annette, and he and Valentine had turned out to be pretty good at routing visitation hours.

But my goal is to do things my way.

Either way, it wasn't going to be easy.

MASON, BANDERA, LAST, Crockett and Archer gathered at the family table, their plates piled high with barbecued chicken, red beans and rice, rolls and steamed broccoli. Though Calhoun lived nearby, oftentimes he and Olivia ate with Minnie and Kenny and Barley as a family. Two or three times a week, they joined the brothers at the main ranch house, particularly on the weekends, when Helga wasn't as overburdened by their presence, Olivia said. Helga loved Kenny and Minnie, though, and always claimed meals were better when as much family was around as possible.

With time, the brothers had begun to appreciate their housekeeper's genuine love for their family. Besides, they couldn't not love Helga after her daughter Kelly had married Fannin.

"Group's getting smaller," Mason observed.

"Yes, it was even smaller when you were gone so long," Last said.

Mason put down his roll. "Well, you didn't have any trouble enlarging the family tree in my absence."

The rest of the brothers groaned at the continuing warfare and focused on their food. It was, Archer decided, not one reason but many that the moodiness around the ranch was so pervasive.

"Not tonight," he said on a sigh. "We're going to have to leave our war drums silent and cogitate on the newest issue at hand. I need your advice and not to be given several refrains of grief."

"What's up?" Bandera asked.

"Well," Archer said slowly, "I, too, will be enlarging the family tree."

Every brother stopped what he was doing, whether in midbite or mid-dig to stare at him.

"Go on," Last said with obvious interest. "Don't leave us in suspense."

"I'm going to be a father," Archer said.

"You don't even have a girlfriend," Crockett said, dumbstruck. "Don't you have to have a female for that?"

"Apparently not," Bandera said. "Let him finish."

At the head of the table, Mason had turned into a concrete gargoyle, his mouth open, his roll dripping butter onto his plate and the tablecloth.

"I'm going to be a father," Archer repeated. "To triplets."

So loud a gasp went up from the brothers that it was amazing the plates didn't jump an inch from the *whoosh*. Mason leaped to his feet, tossing his roll to the table. It bounced on the floor, to the delight of the dog.

"That is the last straw! What is the matter with you dunderheads! I taught you the condom song. I put condoms in the stockings at Christmas! And all you do is fornicate and populate! Every last one of you is irresponsible, immature and careless about the ranch's future!"

The dog, fearing she was being yelled at, grabbed her treasure and exited the dining room in a blur.

"Hello," Mimi Cannady said, sticking her head around the corner. "Am I interrupting anything?"

"Yes!" Mason roared at their next-door neighbor, and the only woman he'd ever cared about, though he was Johnny-come-lately to figure it out.

If he'd *ever* figured it out, Archer thought. "Mason," Archer said sharply.

"Sorry." Mason sighed. "Mimi, please. Would you care to have a seat and join us?"

"I think not. I just stopped by to let you know that I am putting the ranch on the market next week."

Mason sank into his chair, staring at her.

"Hate to eat without you, Mimi," Bandera

said. "Grab a plate. Join the Addams Family as we dine. Lurch is speechless, as you can see, so it might be a pleasant meal for a change."

"No, thanks. I've upset Mason's digestion, so I think I'll head on off. Bye, guys." She went around the corner, then poked her head around the door frame. "You know, it doesn't look the same with just you five sitting there." Her blue eyes were wide with sentimental tears. "We really had some good times," she said softly. "I wish my baby was going to get to grow up on the ranch the way I did. But I guess that was a unique childhood."

Mason stared at the doorway Mimi had left empty. He glanced around at his brothers, his throat working, his face distressed and somehow older. "Dammit to hell and back," he said, throwing his napkin onto the table. "This place is a freaking zoo. I'm going out."

He left the room in the opposite direction Mimi had gone.

"Excellent," Archer said. "So far everything is normal."

"Oh, yeah," Crockett said sarcastically. "I think that went very well. Every night should be so warm and cozy. Next thing you know, we'll have our own reality show, just like the Brady Bunch."

"That wasn't a reality show," Bandera pointed out. "And Helga really isn't like Alice, do you think?"

The brothers glared at him. Bandera looked at each of them, then picked up his fork and began to chew forlornly.

"So…back to your announcement," Last said with a grin. "Triplets, eh? I cede the trophy for family error to you, bro."

"Who is she?" Crockett asked. "Anyone we know?"

"Even I don't really know her," Archer said. "She's an Australian stuntwoman."

"Dang," Bandera said, his tone admiring. "Hang ten, brother!"

"We need a woman who can put a little juice back into this family," Crockett said. "She sounds fun! An Aussie stuntwoman bearing triplets! Does she have an accent? Does she say, 'G'day, mate'?"

"Jeez." Archer ran a hand through his hair. "She's not what I would classify as fun. She has a slight accent. She's never called me mate, and we don't even come close to being friends. As far as the stuntwoman thing goes, as exciting as it might be, I'm making her quit her job. Too dangerous."

"You're making her quit her job." Bandera chewed and thought about that. "How did she take that?"

"Very well for a first mention, I thought."

"Which means he talked, she ignored him or possibly laughed in his face, and he plans to revisit the subject. So, are you moving Down Under?" Last asked. He looked thoughtful. "And…when's the wedding date?"

His brothers stared at him. Uncomfortable tickling began along his neck and continued up over his skull. Archer cleared his throat nervously. "Too many questions to be answered tonight. Let's eat this grub."

Crockett's eyes were round. "You *are* marrying the mother of your triplets, aren't you? We Jeffersons are going to start getting a bad reputation if the seed doesn't stop getting scattered with such enthusiasm."

Last glared at Crockett. "I know you're referencing me, and, in case it's any of your business, which it isn't, Valentine isn't interested in marrying me. Nor am I interested in marrying her. What happened, happened. We're happy with our baby, and we've worked it out just fine."

"I guess I have to know, Archer, in the spirit of family history and precedent," Crockett said, "did the Curse of the Broken Body Parts factor in? Did she hurt you?"

"Yes and no," Archer said crossly. "She kicked me."

"Kicked you?" Last asked.

"In the family jewels," Archer elaborated.

They stared at him.

"And you *still* eked out triplets," Last said, his tone admiring. "Had she not disturbed the House of Archer, you could be expecting quads or quints!"

"I don't know if that qualifies for The Curse," Archer said. "I saw stars and maybe a galaxy far, far away. But nothing broke, although it certainly felt crippled at the time."

"I think that means you're safe," Last opined. "The Curse is a precursor to courtship the hard way, but clearly she didn't kick you as hard as you thought she did. Although there is probably a story," he added thoughtfully, "that we need to hear about how a lucky brother goes from receiving a kick in the zipper to unzipping *her* zipper. Even a stallion usually treads carefully around a filly with aim."

"Did you ask this woman to marry you?"

Bandera wanted to know. "Did you give her an option?"

"He doesn't have to answer that," Crockett interrupted. "I agree with Archer—let's just eat."

"You don't want to hear about marrying mothers, Crockett," Bandera said, "because you've got the hots for Valentine."

Everyone gawked at Crockett now that the secret was out. The silence was stiff and somehow heavy. Uncomfortable. Embarrassed. He pushed back his chair, tipping it over, and left the dining room.

Last vacated as well, throwing his napkin onto his plate with fervor.

Bandera shrugged, got up and left.

Archer blinked as he sat alone. "Congratulations, Archer," he said to himself. "So happy for you, Archer. Fatherhood will suit you, Archer. Aren't you the lucky dog, Archer?"

Leaning back in his chair, he closed his eyes. "It doesn't matter." He had his own ideas about family and responsibility, and now that tricky Miss Clove had shanghaied him into being a father, everything—most importantly, her—would go by his set of standards.

Three little boys. They would grow up to be just like his brothers and him. Jefferson males. Hardworking, hard-loving. Hardheaded.

Just like Clove.

One of them was going to have to bend, because he had no intention of ending up without his woman, like Mason, or having custodial arrangements, like Last.

Clove was due a compromise, and he was excellent at the skill of convincing.

"ARCHER," CLOVE SAID when he returned late that evening with flowers, "you do not need to romance me. I understand you have an ornery need to try to change my mind, but that just shows me you don't understand how important this is to me. There is not going to be a compromise."

He grinned at her, slow and sexy. "Yes, ma'am." Handing her the flowers, he sat at the kitchen table. "I looked forward to your cookies all day long."

She looked at him suspiciously.

"Did I mention I like the new curves on your figure?"

"Flattery isn't going to work." She put her glasses on and gave him a look of disdain. "You passed me up when I was wearing these."

"And any man would," he said reasonably. "I can't even see your pretty eyes. Why do you wear those things?"

"Because I can't see."

"Obviously, or the salesperson would never have sold them to you. Here, let me help you." He slid them from her face. "Now, the real you. You shouldn't hide behind those things."

Clove blinked. "Hide? *Hide?* I never hide. I'm a stuntwoman. I'm brave, no different than you when you're on a bull or a bronc or your Appaloosa."

"I knew we had something in common. Bravery," Archer said with satisfaction. "This isn't going to hurt as much as we think it will."

"What won't hurt?" Clove gave him another suspicious look as she placed a glass of milk in front of him. "I can't bear to see you eat cookies without milk, but I am not serving you, for the record. I'm only complementing my baking."

He grinned, making her heart flutter. "Thank you," he said. "Even if you're not serving me. The cookies are delicious, and it won't hurt much to fall in love with you."

"What?"

He shrugged. "We're going to have to, you know. For the sake of the children."

"We're going to have to fall in love?"

"Yes. These are the best chocolate-chip cookies I've ever eaten. Do you stand in this kitchen all day and bake these wonderful morsels?"

"Yes. It's the trade-off Delilah and I made. She wouldn't charge me, though I said I wanted to pay her. But she said no woman related to the Jeffersons ever owed her a dime. No matter how many times I try to explain that I'm not related to the Jeffersons, she seems to think I am."

"Delilah doesn't know I'm the father?"

"No. I haven't told anyone. Remember, I didn't want you to know."

"And that makes me quite wary of you, AussieClove. Secretive wasn't something I saw in your email persona."

"Guess we were both in for some surprises."

"Yes." He sniffed a snickerdoodle, his face wreathed with pleasure. "Definitely worth the wait. So how did Delilah know you were related to me?"

"I told her that you recommended I stay here—and I am *not* related to you."

"We are related by baby, and I'll pay your bill while you're here, at least until I move you to the ranch. You don't have to stay on your feet all day."

She ground her teeth. "Back to the have-to-fall-in-love part, I don't think that's how it works."

"I've done a survey of my family, and between those who have a working relationship with the mother of their child, and those who have fallen in love, Cupid is definitely preferable." He looked at her. "You have your reasons for doing things, and I have mine. We should work together on this—for the sake of our children."

He sounded so smug she wanted to argue. Wanted to throw a wall of denial at him, maybe even a cookie jar.

She had a feeling he'd throw it right back and call it fun.

Chapter Eight

"I came here to find you, by the way," Archer said, eating his cookie and reaching for another. He settled himself comfortably into a kitchen chair.

"Well, here I am."

He grinned at her curt tone of voice. "No, I meant, before I knew you were pregnant yesterday. I had returned here to start hunting for you. I was going to start by asking over at the Never Lonely if you had left a forwarding address."

She used a spatula to move some cookies onto a baking sheet, then put it down to come stand in front of him. Manfully, he resisted the urge to sweep her into his lap and give her a Texas-size smooching, starting with her earlobes and ending up at her toes. He'd done a lot of thinking now that he'd gotten his predicament off his chest to his brothers, and he'd decided this new family was going to go all his way.

He was going to be an excellent father, just as Maverick had been to him and his brothers.

"Were you looking for the plain me or the dolled-up me you made love to?" she asked.

He winked. "Wouldn't you like to know. But I believe in leaving a woman guessing."

She looked so sweet and so forlorn standing there, hoping he'd say the right thing. Archer grinned. She thought she was a tough girl, but she was sweet as a snickerdoodle. Her half-tailed cat wound around her ankles, meowing for attention. Clove's hair was silvery and chin-length blond—recently cut. He liked the style on her. It brought out the blue in her eyes and gave her a well-cared-for look. "So who cut your hair?"

"Delilah."

He nodded. "I should have known. The style is simple and attractive. I like it better than the bar-stool-babe style you had before." He looked at her for a moment, his thoughts flying. "You're pretty," he finally said softly. "And pregnancy agrees with you."

"You're avoiding the question."

"No, I'm not." He stood, taking her gently by the arms, which sent Tink scurrying to the hallway. Lifting Clove, he sat her on top of the counter. "I was merely looking for Clover, Clove, any way you look. I told you, I don't have a type. I like ladies in general. And all the girls like me."

Her lips parted in astonishment. He laughed. "But if you won't serve me, then you must feed me."

"I will not." She drew back a bit, but her eyes were on him, watching. He noticed she didn't push him away or hop down from her perch.

"I wanted to find you," he said, breaking a cookie into quarters as he moved between her legs, "because I couldn't forget you. Eat." He put the cookie into her mouth. As she chewed, he kissed her fingertips.

She swallowed. "Yes, but—"

"You talk too much. That's your problem. We liked each other better when we wrote and didn't speak." He fed her another piece of cookie and kissed the inner crook of her arm. "You smell like homemade treats," he said. "I find that strangely erotic."

"I wouldn't be surprised by anything about you that's strange."

He laughed, putting another cookie into her mouth. "What do you expect from a cowboy? I like my woman in the kitchen." He kissed her palm. "I like my woman in the bedroom." He ran a hand under the skirt of her dress, pulling her toward him and nearly off the counter. "I'm going to like my woman in every room of the house. And outside the house, wherever I can get you."

He slid her onto his waist so that he could kiss her above the sweetheart neckline of her dress. Her legs stayed wrapped around him. Archer groaned. "You stay sexy like this, and I'm going to have to make love to you, little mama."

"And when I'm not sexy? When I get huge? And can't see my feet?"

"I'll suck your toes," he whispered. "I promise you'll always be able to feel those little piggies just fine."

That made her slide down from his waist. He didn't stop her.

They stared at each other for a long moment.

"It's not going to work," she said.

"Why not?"

"I know you're doing this for the children. And while I appreciate your feeling responsible, I don't want a man that way. I've always been independent."

"You need to come to the ranch. See the real me before you decide what you want. I've seen the real you. I've seen several real yous. Now it's your turn."

She moved away. "I don't want to."

"For the children, you should."

She began putting away cutlery in a drawer. "We can't make something out of nothing. And that's what it would be. I did this for Lucy, and in my mind, my motivation is clear. Maybe not right or pretty, but clear."

He sighed. "If you don't want to go to the ranch with me, then let's take a weekend away where we can talk."

"If you talk, I might give in. That's what you want." She turned to look into his eyes. "You don't know what it would be like to be childless. You wanted to be that way for always. My sister did not. She loves her husband and wants him to be happy. This is the closest to real motherhood she will ever have, Archer. I can't let you sway me, and even if I could, I would always know you did it because of your sense of masculine pride. You ignored me both before and after the Cut-n-Gurls fixed me up. Suddenly, my pregnancy has you beating your chest like a caveman. But since you went back and read our emails, surely you saw your desire to always stay single and footloose. I have no desire to change that."

He sat down. "I understand about your sister. I sympathize. And no, this wasn't how I saw my life. But I'd be a cold human being if my heart didn't warm to the thought of three little babies with my blood, my genes and maybe my mother's and father's characteristics."

She looked away.

"You want me around," he said. "You want your babies to know their father. There's nobody like me. I'm rough-and-ready and a little wild, but I know how to take care of the people I love. And I am the kind of man who will love his children."

"Lucy and Robert will," Clove said, her voice trembling and not so sure of itself.

"Only in the capacity of aunt and uncle. I'm sorry, Clove," he said. "You had a good game and you pulled a good stunt, but I'm no fool. My children stay here, and if I have to make it a legal issue, I will do that."

Her eyes widened. "There's no way you can!"

"I can. Marry me, stay here, and bear my children on Texas soil. I'll take very good care of you. But if you fight me on this, I won't lose. Mason has suggested that, given your orneriness, the only way to make you see the light is with a custodial lawsuit. However, that didn't work very well in Last's case. I prefer to do things without lawyers. Especially since you and I are well suited to each other." He smiled. "I can't forget the little woman who got me all fired up in my own truck bed."

"You can't treat me the way you do Tonk. You can't just badger me until I do your wishes."

"I'd rather go about this like rational adults. It would be best for all if you quit acting like a savior for your sister and let us go about our business."

She gasped. "How dare you?"

"How dare you do what you've done? It's sneaky and wrong and quite possibly the most heartless thing I've ever known a woman to do. You and I are quickly going to get sideways on this matter—"

"We already are. Good night."

Clove left the kitchen. Archer watched her go, his lips flat and drawn. What a dilemma he'd gotten himself into! She was so stubborn and truculent, like a mule in a garden patch.

Then she could be all sweetly melting in his arms, driving him mad thinking about her body. His babies inside her body.

He wished she'd let him romance her so that they could capture something real before the babies arrived. From the way they'd made love, he knew there could be something between them. She'd been so innocent that night that the memory of it made him want to cry. She'd turned his heart to jelly with her intent to give away his children. He deserved the chance to prove himself a good husband, a good father, a good lover.

Now all they were going to see of each other, he supposed, was their bad sides.

He heard her bedroom door close upstairs. His jaw tight, he shook his head.

She was his virgin. She was going to stay his.

He headed up the stairs.

Walking into her room, he planted himself on the floor. "I plan on you and I getting along, Clove. We simply have to. I know we're on opposite ends of a very long spectrum, but you can't take my children, and you can't leave Texas."

She didn't say anything. She sat silently on the edge of her bed, not looking at him.

He frowned. "Clove, I sincerely believe something good could happen between us if you'll let it. I know I'm willing to try."

When she didn't move, retort or flinch, he went over and bent down in front of her. "Clove?" She seemed suddenly so pale. Brushing her hair behind one of her ears, he stroked her cheek. "Just because you're silent doesn't mean you've suddenly decided to agree with me, does it?"

She met his gaze. What he saw there frightened him.

"I have cramps," she said.

"Cramps?" He puckered his forehead. "Like, stomach cramps from something you ate?"

"I think…cramps." Sweat broke out along her upper lip.

"I don't think you're supposed to do that." Archer dabbed away the sweat and felt her palm. Cold. She was frightened. "Do you want to lie down?"

"I don't think so." Her eyes widened as she gazed at him. "I'm scared."

"Okay. Let's put in a call to the doc." Pulling his cell phone from his pocket, he said, "You know the doc, right? Pretty little thing? Makes no time for us Jeffersons except medically speaking," he babbled. "Hello, Doctor," he said, running a hand over Clove's shoulders to comfort her. "You've been seeing Clove… Great Scott, did you tell me your last name, AussieClove?" he asked.

"Clove Penmire," she reminded him.

"Clove Penmire, soon to be Jefferson," he said, drawing a groan from Clove. "But we'll take care of the particulars later," he said hastily. "Clove mentioned she's cramping in her tummy. I don't think she's eaten much today, maybe a cookie or two, and we've been bickering a bit, though I don't think I upset her bad enough to cramp…oh, all right. We'll be right there."

He hung up. "Clove, the doctor says for you to come on, sweetie. Those were her words, not mine. I mean, she was saying it to you, not me—"

"You're rambling," Clove said. "Do you always do this when you get nervous? From your email correspondence, you never struck me as excitable. I always thought you sounded so brave and devil-may-care."

"Well, whatever gave you that impression was wrong. I am brave, but right now, as the father of these triplets, I am exercising my right to ramble. Let's take these stairs slowly, sweetie."

"I wouldn't want you to lose your footing," she told him.

"No, you wouldn't. It would be an ugly sight, me rolling down the stairs, boots over head." He was rattling, and it was helping him feel better. Cramps! That didn't sound good. He didn't want anything to happen to Clove—or the pregnancy she'd come so far to conceive. "Maybe my sperm weren't as robust as I thought they were," he muttered.

"That's just as likely as me saying perhaps I shouldn't bake so many cookies."

He appreciated her attempt at humor because he'd broken out in a sweat. "The truth is, now that I know I'm going to be a father, I'd like to stay in my exciting position. I'm going to have three boys! Here, sit here," he said, helping her slide into his truck. "Calm down, everything is going to be just fine."

She gave him a glare. "Archer, I am calm."

"Oh. Okay." He ran around the vehicle, hopped inside, turned the engine and accidentally gunned it. "Sorry."

Her face was so pale. His fingers tightened on the wheel. "Everything's going to be fine," he repeated, more to reassure himself than her.

TWO HOURS LATER, Clove let Archer lead her from the doctor's office. She was tired, but mostly relieved.

And not surprised. "It would make sense that you and I have completely incompatible Rh factors."

"Isn't that odd? I never knew my blood type until today."

"As irresponsible as it seems, I didn't, either. I'm twenty-six, and I didn't even know there was such a thing as an Rh factor. And I'm one of the fifteen percent who is negative," Clove said.

"It seems the doc should have checked you for this before."

Clove sighed. "I didn't ask you your blood type, Archer. You would have spooked, I'm sure."

"I probably would have. No matter," he said cheerfully. "A little injection to your rump was the answer. I hope," he said, sounding worried again. "I mean, I know it's all good. And that crazy little doc even managed to get a blood donation out of me."

Clove giggled. "You looked so perplexed when she told you that big boys give blood quarterly." She glanced over at his bandaged arm. "You never told me you were afraid of the sight of blood."

"I'm not. I've seen plenty."

She outright laughed at his growl. "Everyone's but your own, I guess. Dr. Fern said she figured taking blood out of you would keep you from being so antsy for a while."

"In all this time, we have never known that doctor's name. Who would have ever thought that gorgeous doc's first name was Edna? My brothers are going to have heart failure. No one can marry a girl named Edna Fern!"

"She says she doesn't want to marry or even have a boyfriend. Dr. Fern says all the men around here convinced her that she's better off single for now. Patching them up and hearing them wail after rodeo injuries made her think she was better off with her cat, dog and bird. And I think she said she lives with her elderly grandma."

"Well, there you have it," Archer said. "No one will risk her wrath anymore by trying to ask her out. Luckily for me, I'm spoken for."

Clove knew he was teasing her, but at the same time, she didn't want to start feeling comfortable with him. "Did you ever try to ask her out?"

"Nah. She's too smart for me."

Clove gasped. "I'm very smart!"

He laughed. "And jealous, too. Glad you're feeling possessive of me."

She crossed her arms and looked out the window. "I hate the idea of being house-bound for the next few days."

"I think it sounds like fun. We're going to watch videos, read great literature... Did I ever tell you my father was a huge fan of Brit lit? We went to public school, but my parents were big on home—"

"Wait," Clove said. "*I'm* confined to bed. You're not."

"Where you are, I am. You have no family here, and it's up to me to take care of you. Lucy would want that," he said logically, clearly pleased with his argument.

"Archer, you are smug, self-assured, over-confident and—"

"And those were all the reasons why you bought a plane ticket, my dear. You wanted me, you got me. And you're going to love reading the paper in bed with me every morning. I'll read the financial section and the fun-nies, and you can have 'Hints from Heloise.'"

She had no reply for that. Part of her wanted him around because as loony as he was, he was fun, and he kept her mind off her problem. She'd been so frightened of miscarrying! The fear that had washed over her at the thought of losing these babies still sat inside her. They were becoming so real to her; her pregnancy was bringing her a joy she'd never expected.

Besides, being bed-bound with Archer was something many women would dream. The con was that they would get on each other's nerves; the pro was that she fully remembered how sexy and considerate he could be. They couldn't make love again, and probably never would, but he was outrageous company, something her daredevil heart enjoyed. Even when he was playing the irascible, wayward cowboy hunk.

Yet she could not allow him to take over her life the way he wanted to. He was bossy and stubborn. Even his horse rebelled.

"The only question left for us to answer, I guess is," Archer said, "my bed or yours?"

Chapter Nine

"Never mind," Archer said suddenly as he pulled up to Delilah's salon. "I don't think it's a good idea for you to walk upstairs. I'm thinking stairs are verboten. You stay here, and I'll go pack for you."

"No!" Clove moved to open the door.

He reached out and caught her fingers. "Clove, I know you want to rebel about everything, but stairs cannot be a good thing for a woman who's been given orders to rest. I will pack your things."

"You can't pack my things!"

Her eyes were so tired, he thought, though even the dark circles were attractive.

She made him want to protect her, he realized. For all her blowing in the wind about how independent she was, he knew she needed him. And that made her more attractive.

"I think I really like you," he said slowly. "I

know you won't believe that, but you're doing something funny to my heart."

"I don't know why," Clove said.

"I don't, either, because heaven knows, all you do is rile me." He shook his head in wonder. "I'm pretty sure I was meant to have a brunette who likes to fish. Fishing is comfortable for the soul. I think she should like fishing, sex and pool."

"Fishing comes before sex?"

"Yeah, but only because I dream of making love in a boat, out in the middle of a lake, where no one is around, just me and my gal and the night sky overhead—"

She sighed. "In Australia, we would make love on an ocean."

"Yeah. I can see that," Archer said enthusiastically. "You see why fishing is so critical. After we make love, we'll have a finned creature or two to toss on the barbie." He winked. "Did you notice me trying to incorporate some Aussie slang?"

She wrinkled her nose. "You may call it that, pardner. I'm getting out of this truck now, and I'm going to giddyup to my bed, where I am staying till this storm blows over."

"Very nice on the slang part, but you're staying put, and I'm fetching."

"Is that slang?"

"It's fact," he said. "Don't move."

He got out of the truck. She slowly got out on her side.

"No, Clove," he said. "You have to stay here. No stairs. Dr. Fern did not okay you for stairs."

"I'm going to the top of the staircase, and then I won't come down for two weeks. That's my plan."

Gently, he helped her sit back down in her seat. "Clove, I have a ranch to help run. I cannot leave you here alone. Those are my children, and I'm going to see to their safety and your well-being. Delilah can't take care of an invalid for two weeks. She has a business to run." He touched his fingers to her cheek. "It's time to say, 'Yes, Archer.'"

"That's what got me into this predicament," she told him.

"No, what got us into this predicament was me saying yes to you. You and I are still going to have a talk about that one day, because you pulled a Tonk on me, and if you weren't so much my kind of girl, I'd be madder than heck."

"Your kind of girl?" Her look of surprise caught at his heart.

"Yes. I think you must be. We had two years' worth of email correspondence between us, and I know we both had separate reasons for writing, but I know I enjoyed having an Aussie pen pal, despite the fact my brothers thought I needed more in my life than a cyber-gal. I thought you were one of the most interesting women I'd ever talked to, and I have clearly been proven correct. But despite that, the saying goes that we must be careful of the seeds we sow. You sowed three seeds, and I'm going to harvest those little bundles of joy in about six months. Sit. I'll be right back."

She seemed to do as he asked, so he headed up the stairs. Of course, she was liable to disobey or disappear on him, so he had to pack fast. She'd come to town, he recalled, with one tiny suitcase, so he grabbed that from her closet and shoveled undies and other drawer contents into the suitcase.

He cleaned out her makeup drawer in the bathroom without hesitation. Grabbed shoes and clothes from the closet, cramming them into the suitcase. He wasn't doing a very good job, but they were only going to be in the case for about two hours. The bottle of perfume on the dresser, he figured, should go on top so it wouldn't break.

It was then that the picture on the mirror caught his eyes. Clove and another woman hugged each other, each laughing for the camera, clearly having the time of their lives. Turning the picture over, he read the inscription. "To the best sister in the world. The only one I trust and can run to at any time. If it wasn't for my brave sister, I wouldn't be alive today. There is no one like you, Clove. I love you. Lucy."

Frowning, he blinked, rereading the inscription. His heart hammered, felt as if it was knocking on a piece of his soul with a bad omen. Restless worry came over him as he read it a third time.

Then he quietly laid the photo in the suitcase, closing it tight.

ARCHER WAS QUIET on the drive to his ranch, so Clove fell asleep. When she awakened, he was listening to soft country music, his face was grim, and he was pulling into the driveway of a very large ranch.

"Wow," she said. "Did you mention in any of your emails to me that you lived on a real ranch?"

He frowned. "What do you mean?"

"I mean that this is beautiful, and seems to go on and on, except for that cute house on the hill."

"That's Mimi's house, at least for another week. She's selling out, which has my brother, Mason, in an uproar. Try to ignore him."

"All right." She got out and Archer came around to take her arm.

"How are you feeling?"

"I'm fine! Just tired." She pulled her arm away.

Several big men came out onto the front porch, waving at them. Archer took a deep breath. "Welcome to the family," he said. "The very diluted version."

She was nervous. They were obviously more nervous, which surprised her, because she wouldn't have expected such big men to be that way about anything.

"Clove," Archer said, "these are my brothers. Mason, Last, Bandera and Crockett. I have more, but they're sort of dispersed for the moment. Bros, this is Clove Penmire. You may recall that I had an Australian pen pal. This is she."

They solemnly shook her hand. Her face burned with embarrassment. Of course, they knew she was pregnant, she realized as they all slipped surreptitious glances at her stomach. Which meant they also knew that she had shanghaied Archer's sperm.

They had to think she was an opportunist and very likely after money. For the first time the result of her actions hit her. She'd been so busy thinking about Lucy, she hadn't considered Archer's brothers. If Archer had done what she had done, Lucy would be very angry and would probably never like him.

She put her head down.

"Welcome to the family," Mason said gruffly. "You need to get inside. Archer, can I talk to you privately?"

"Sure. Will you guys introduce Clove to Helga—our and Mimi's housekeeper—and if Calhoun's around, his gang, too. Help her get settled."

With a pang, she watched Mason and Archer walk away.

"Let me get your stuff," Last said kindly. "I'm sure you'd like something to eat, so let me show you to the kitchen. Helga always has something tasty sitting out for us. You fellows go on. I can handle settling Clove in."

They nodded to her, apparently happy to let Last be in charge of her, and moved away.

"Sometimes we talk a lot," Last said, "and sometimes we don't. Today we seem to be a taciturn bunch."

"I'm sure I'm unexpected," Clove said faintly.

"Yes, you are, but if you only knew how much happens around here that's unexpected, you wouldn't worry a bit. Besides, you'd be surprised at how much of our unexpected happenings turn out to be blessings."

She blushed. "I guess you know I'm expecting."

He grinned. "We may be taciturn, but we don't keep many secrets. Congratulations, by the way. We like babies around here."

"Oh, I won't be staying here," she said hurriedly. "After I get through with this period of rest, I must return to Australia."

He looked at her, settling his hat back on his head. "How about you don't owe me any explanations, and how about I find you a cookie and some tea in Helga's kitchen?" Gesturing for her to follow, he carried Clove's bag into the kitchen. "We didn't like Helga's cooking when she first came here, but now we consider it a good thing. Most especially when it's cold outside. She can cook a cabbage soup that would make you cry with joy, believe it or not. And her poppyseed cake will take your breath away."

She smiled at Helga, who gave her a broad wink.

"More babies," Helga said. "Good!"

Last chuckled. "We don't have secrets, as I said. Sit right here and let Helga fix you up. I'm going to head out for the moment, and figure out where you're sleeping tonight. We have three houses on the ranch, and we want you where you can rest comfortably."

"Thank you." Clove sat silently, appreciating the warm cup of steaming tea Helga put in front of her. Two banana-nut muffins joined the tea, a pretty gingham napkin was put beside her hand and a nosegay of cinnamon sticks tied with straw was laid in front of her china plate for decoration.

Though she was tired physically and mentally, Clove realized she felt at home and welcome.

"Eat," Helga said in her German accent. "For babies."

Clove nodded, and as Helga draped a crocheted shawl over her shoulders, she knew Archer had—again—not been bragging in his emails.

This really was a special family. A special place.

"You are first girl Archer brings home," Helga said.

Clove started. "Ever?"

"Yes. While I've lived here. The brothers say he is too much afraid to like a girl."

"Why?"

"Because." Helga looked at her. "His mother died when he was very young. All he knew was that she went away and never came back. They say he is always afraid of that."

"Oh." Clove blinked.

"So you won't leave."

It was a question couched in a statement. Clove's skin prickled as Helga's worried gaze searched hers.

After a moment, Helga turned back to stir something on the stove. And Clove looked out the big kitchen window, seeing the spring, still-unawakened landscape, and the two big men standing outside talking more with their hands than with their mouths.

They weren't so taciturn—and they weren't so unruly, either. Right now, Archer seemed to be on the receiving end of whatever Mason was saying.

Clove turned away, knowing that she was

the topic of their conversation. Unexpected and not yet considered a blessing, she figured she was about as trusted as Tonk.

"THERE'S JUST NO WAY around it," Mason said sternly. "You have to marry her."

"Mason, trust me, it's just not going to happen," Archer replied. "She'd yell so loud if you said that to her they'd hear her in the next county."

"How do I have two brothers get women pregnant out of wedlock," Mason roared. "Both with women who do not want them? Is there a chance that I've done something wrong? Did I miss a concept? You should be in love to make babies! It works better that way!"

"Admittedly. But I'm working on her."

"Working on marrying her?"

"No. Working on getting her to fall in love with me."

Mason stared at him. "Can I ask you why you got her pregnant if you knew you weren't in love with each other?"

"I thought she was fine."

"Well, clearly," Mason said with disgust. "She is fine. But that's no reason to knock someone up. Consensual sex with a lady who is fine is no reason to just uncork the—"

"Mason. I thought she was 'fine' as in 'on birth control.' She said she was fine, and clearly we have two different meanings of that word."

"That's what happens when you meet people who are not from your background," Mason said. "You have to overcome a host of communication issues, and one of them is language differences. So you didn't ask her to elaborate on her 'fineness.' You just dived right in."

Archer frowned. "Mason, it's all irrelevant now."

"Except that she won't marry you. That makes it pathetic. We are not having three children out of wedlock!"

"One is better than three?"

"Well, don't you think it's a bit odd?" Mason demanded. "It's like, here's my mistake, times three!"

"I really don't feel like it's a mistake."

"Oh, it's not a mistake to be having children by someone you've just met."

"Not everybody takes their whole lifetime to acknowledge a good woman, Mason," Archer said stiffly.

Mason blinked. "I'm going to overlook that," he said, his voice low.

"Well, you overlook a lot. Now, for the moment, you and I need to agree that we're not on the same page about my marital status. Clove has been to the doctor today, and she's tired. I'd like to go make her feel at home."

Mason raised his eyebrows. "And where do you expect to take her?"

"To one of the houses. I don't care which."

"Has it ever occurred to you that Miss Penmire might prefer to be married? Have you asked her?"

"I've mentioned it, but I told you, she's not interested in staying here. I'm going to try to change her mind, but she's a decisive little thing."

"Three babies," Mason said. "I can't believe it."

"Neither can I. Or Clove."

Mason shook his head. "All right. I have a plan."

Archer's eyes widened. "What do you mean?"

"You're clearly out of options with this gal. You want her?"

"Of course," Archer said without hesitation. "In my heart, I know she is right for me.

You learn a lot when you write someone for two years. Despite the fact that she came here on a mission, I'd like to give her more than just babies. I'd like to give her my name."

"Then what I propose is this. I'll discuss it with the boys later, but for now, my first thought is that we buy Mimi's house and land."

Archer looked at Mason, astonished. "We already have five thousand acres, and we only have six of twelve brothers working the ranch. Not to mention, I mean…" *Are you giving Mimi up that easily?* he wanted to shout.

"You're wanting a way to stay here, and Clove and you have three babies on the way. We'll need land for future generations."

Archer slowly took in what his older brother was saying. "Are you saying we buy Mimi's place for Clove?"

"For our babies," Mason said. "The way we're popping out all over here, this ranch isn't big enough for all of us. I have to think of the economics of future generations. How will we send them to college? What will we buy their wedding dresses with?

"I ran a forward proposal the other night on the costs this ranch is running, with wedding gowns, educations, braces, college—

these are just the basics for each child in the family—and we're going to have to expand. Tighten up.

"Mimi's place is ideal for two reasons. One, we know it's a good property. The sheriff kept that place right. Also, we know ranch land here will appreciate. We'll have more space to branch out, and I haven't decided yet if that means cattle or agriculture, or something entirely different. For the moment, I think we buy it, keep strangers from moving in who may give us trouble over the pond, and offer the house to Clove. I don't see her and three babies fitting into any of our available scenarios. But Mimi's place is just right."

"Clove said they already have a farm of some type in Australia," Archer said.

"Yes, but this is Texas land, next to her Texas family, where the Texas man she wanted so bad lives."

"True, but her ties to her home are pretty strong," Archer said, thinking of the inscription on the back of the picture. "She and her sister are very close."

"As her husband, you'll be closer," Mason said.

"I don't know. She was pretty desperate to have children for Lucy."

Mason's eyebrows shot into his hair. "What are you talking about?"

"Clove claims she's giving the children to her sister to raise."

"Have you gone stark raving mad?" Mason demanded.

"I didn't say I like it—"

"I know you don't! Well, figure out a way to make her change her mind. Those children are staying here. There's no other way for it to be. Their Jefferson birthright is on this ranch."

Archer shook his head. "I completely agree. I just don't know how to get Clove to see it that way, and I'm not sure that a house is what would make her look favorably on me. Clove's extremely independent."

"And you're an extreme wuss. Get back to her and win her heart. Surely you are not going to be the only brother in this family who can't get his girl."

"No, I'm not." Archer glared. "I'm looking at the other brother who can't."

He strode away to find Clove.

She was morosely eating a muffin, looking as if she'd lost her best friend. She stood when he walked into the kitchen.

"Earlier you asked me a question," Clove said.

Archer blinked. "I'm kind of lost on the question. There's been so much drama. Could you refresh me?"

She took a deep breath. "You asked me, your bed or mine?"

Archer perked up at the mention of beds. "So I did. Yes, I did. Do you have an answer?"

She nodded. "I do. I'd like to stay in a hotel in Union Junction. I called my sister, Lucy, and she will be here tomorrow to stay with me until my visa runs out."

He looked down for a moment, thinking about Mason's words. Mason could not win his woman, and he was willing to give her house to Clove and the babies they were expecting. Frankly, he had not expected Mason to back him to this extent, given the reaction he'd had to Last's baby.

Of course, this situation was entirely different from anything the brothers had experienced so far.

"I'm glad your sister is coming to be with you," he said carefully, "but I'd feel bad for the two of you to be in a strange town with no one you know. There's plenty of room here for the two of you to have time alone."

She looked at him for a long moment. He

saw something in her eyes change. "Are you sure?"

"Absolutely," he said, feeling hopeful that he might be targeting what was bothering her. "But right now, I'm going to tuck you into bed."

Chapter Ten

"We have three houses, and Calhoun built his own on the property," Archer said. "We juggle houses when necessary. Right now, Valentine, Last's ex-girlfriend, is living in one of them with their child. Valentine would be glad to let you stay there. Knowing you might feel awkward about that, and figuring you might like a very quiet place to completely relax, I would also like to propose the foreman's shack. Well, we call it a shack, but it's a modest bungalow. Very homey."

"Where will the foreman go?" Clove asked.

"Oh, we don't have one anymore. I mean, we're about to hire some extra help, since we're down so many brothers, but no one's living there now. Every once in a while, Shoeshine Johnson comes out to give us a hand, and he likes staying in the bungalow. He's a real good farmer, and bus driver, and knows bulls. So we use him when he's available. But he's not here now. As I say, the place is simple, but I like it. There's a VCR and a video collection. Nothing on DVD yet, but…"

She smiled at him. "I'd feel very comfortable there. Thank you."

"I thought so. It's probably hard to be around strangers."

"Archer…you and your family are being very kind, considering…everything."

He nodded. "Let's get you resting."

She walked behind him as he took her bag. He reached back and put his arm around her shoulder, guiding her down the porch toward the truck.

"I'm all right," she said.

"I know, but something about becoming a father to three makes me feel protective." He grinned, opening the truck door for her. "I don't think my brothers thought I had it in me. For fatherhood, that is. How are you feeling, by the way?"

"A bit tired, actually."

"Well, you're about to feel a lot better. You're going to rest a lot, just like Dr. Edna Fern said." He shuddered and started the truck. "I still can't get over that name."

"Archer isn't the world's most common name."

"Nor is Clove, when you think about it. Or Clover." He frowned. "What would you have done if your plan hadn't worked?"

"Truthfully, I don't know. Now that the consequences have come home to me, I wish I hadn't done it at all." She looked down at her hands. "I changed your life and I didn't mean to. I think I would go to a sperm bank. That's what I would do."

He stared at her. "And miss out on all that fun?"

"It's not fun for you or your family."

"Actually, I meant the making love part. That was fun."

"But over so quickly. You know what I mean?" She looked at him, her eyes wide.

He couldn't believe his ears. "I was trying to be gentle since it was your first time."

"Oh." She blinked. "You mean it gets better?"

"Well, yes." He wasn't sure if his pride was hurt or not, and he decided he needed to overlook his ego screaming at the insult. "I'll give you the chance to try to wear me out in a few days. When you're feeling better."

She shook her head at him. "My sister will be here."

"Did you ever consider that I might have some restraint?" he asked.

"No," she said.

"Don't tell me you're one of those women who believe that men are solely interested in their own sexual pleasure?"

"Well, yes," Clove said. "You know, you did share an awful lot about yours and your brother's exploits."

"Yeah." He frowned at her. "I am mad at you, just for the record. Personally, I think it's wrong to make love to a man, get pregnant and not tell him. I know a lot of single guys would debate that with me. They'd love it if a woman kept that news to herself. Kind of spoils the routine, you see."

"Yes, I do," she said dryly.

"But not me. I always want to be right in the thick of things. Here we are." He shut off the engine. "Simple, but peaceful. Just what Dr. Edna would recommend."

She looked at the serene bungalow, then at him. "Thank you so much," she said, "for everything."

"You're welcome."

"I just don't understand why you're so nice about it all."

He sighed and pushed his hat back on his

head. "Look. I'm kind of a floater. I'm too far down in the family food chain to understand huge pressure. I watched my twin, Ranger, fall in love with a saucy young lady, and he had a helluva good time doing it. You might say it was an adventure for all of us. Now, I guess I'm on my own adventure. You hit me between the eyes—"

"Legs," she reminded him. "But it was an accident."

"That's right! I'm still mad at you about that, too!" But he shrugged at her. "The fact is, if this is my adventure, then I want to enjoy mine as much as he did his. Well, some days it looked like Ranger was having fun, and other days he looked like he was pretty confused. My twin is happy now, though. You and I are bound together forever by three little bundles of joy, and I want us to get off on the right foot. If our feet don't end up at the altar, so be it. But let's have fun together." He thought about that for a minute. "I'm sure it's best for the children if we're laughing instead of bickering."

She nodded. "Okay."

"So, on to movie watching. Let's get you tucked up in bed, and then we're going to watch *Batman!*"

He saw her pucker.

"The one with Michael Keaton? Lots of stunt work," he said hopefully.

She got out of the truck and walked toward the bungalow. Grabbing her case, he hurried after her. "My second choice would be *The Adventures of Mr. Bean*. Not dangerous stunt work, but I do love economical humor. How about that?"

She smiled and followed him inside after he unlocked the door. "Oh, it's so homey," she said. "I love the fireplace! And the plaid blankets, and the deer wallpaper—is that a real armadillo?"

"Yes, it is," he said proudly. "And this is a real deer head, and this is a real squirrel and this is a real mountain lion. We're very proud of him."

She shivered. "It's not very pretty, is it?"

He looked at the mountain lion with some bemusement before taking in her round-eyed expression. "I guess not. You know, I think I'll move these critters into the attic. Make yourself comfy, and pick a movie you want to watch."

Quickly, he put his old friends away and hurried down the stairs. "What did you find?"

She held up a video. "Is this what they call a girlie film?"

"Girlie?" He read the label, feeling himself blush. "Er, it's a guy film. We don't need to watch that."

"But it's *Suzanne and the Gunslingers*. I think that sounds adventurous."

"No." He hid it behind the other fifty videos they had. "This may be a problem," he said. "We moved the VHS machine here when the DVDs came out because we figured we could watch the old stuff when we came here. Sometimes we use this place as a hunting lodge, when Shoeshine's not on the ranch. In fact, I think that's *his* girlie movie!"

She laughed. "It is not. Poor Shoeshine."

"I'm certain he left it here," Archer said innocently. "Now, how about…*Silence of the Lambs?* Or even *Braveheart?* It has stunt work—"

"Here's one." Clove pulled it out and smiled at him. "And look. This one actually does have Shoeshine Johnson's name on it."

Archer took the video from her. "*Driving Miss Daisy*," he said. "Clove, I don't think there's much stunt work in this one."

She nodded. "I know. I'm kind of unplugging from the job right now."

He gulped. "I guess Shoeshine doesn't unplug from his. Wouldn't you know he'd leave behind the one movie about driving somebody. And it doesn't sound like anything explodes, gets naked and or has espionage in it."

"Which makes it perfect for relaxing."

He was pretty certain he'd gnaw his nails off from boredom. But if this movie was what Miss Clove wanted, then that's what she'd get.

A knock sounded on the door. They glanced at each other.

"Are you expecting company?" Archer asked.

"No. Not until tomorrow."

He opened the door. Mason stood there, carrying two sacks. Bandera was carting drinks from the truck, and Crockett carried firewood.

"We figured you needed groceries," Mason said.

"Comfort food," Last said. "Beer, wine, juice, water. Beer and wine for the father-to-be. Water for the little mama." He grinned. "And firewood, in case this place has a chill on it since we don't keep the thermostat turned on when no one is here. Yes, it is a wee bit chilly."

Clove sank onto the sofa.

Archer felt a little overwhelmed by all his brothers' attention. "We're not exactly in the wilderness."

"Still," Bandera said cheerfully, stacking drinks in the fridge, "when there's no sustenance, you might start imagining you're looking for locusts and honey. And we even brought Ben & Jerry's ice cream," he said with a satisfied smile, "and pickles. We figured we'd save you the midnight run to the grocery, Archer."

Archer glanced at Clove. She was torn, it seemed, between amusement and mortification. "They're my family," he said apologetically. "We've always been a bit overwhelming."

"How are you feeling, Miss Clove?" Crockett asked.

"I'm just ready to sit down and watch *Driving Miss Daisy*. That's what Archer chose for us to watch."

"Archer?" Bandera looked at him with surprise. "Our resident nonromantic?"

"Where's Last?" Archer demanded. "Just wondering, since the rest of you rode to our rescue."

"He's talking to Mimi, on behalf of Mason, the emotional chicken," Crockett said.

"Hey!" Mason yelled.

Crockett shrugged. "Last will be right here. Helga made brownies, so we put a plate on the counter for you." He frowned, looking around the room. "Where are all the friendly beasts?"

"Residing in the attic for the moment." Archer gave him the raised eyebrow signifying *discuss later.*

"Can we talk to you for a moment, Clove?" Mason asked. "On a more serious matter. We won't take up much of your time."

"All right."

"Give her time to change," Archer growled. "She's supposed to be resting. Can't this wait until tomorrow?"

"I think we should talk tonight." Mason looked at the brothers, and they all nodded.

"All right. Clove, take your time getting ready. We'll all sit here and drink a beer."

"Thank you." She disappeared into a bedroom, then came back out. "Which bedroom is mine, Archer?"

All the brothers glared at him. Archer blinked. *Wherever mine is,* he thought, but didn't say it. "You choose," he said. "I'm easy."

He wasn't, but for the moment, he would ignore the pounding in his chest. He needed to get his brothers out of here so that he could have time alone with Clove, before Lucy arrived and he lost the chance to bond with the mother of his children.

MASON CLEARED his throat after Clove left the room. "Archer, we'd like to talk to you as a family."

"Go right ahead," Archer said. "I'm listening."

"We want you to work hard at making an honest woman of Clove."

"What the hell do you think I'm trying to do?" Archer demanded. "I'm watching chick flicks. I've hidden our best hunting trophies. I'm working on the situation. I'm sure I have it well in hand."

"We think you could wind up in a dodgy situation, when her sister arrives. Clove told Helga she was returning to Australia with Lucy," Mason said. "That's not the best thing for our babies."

"*Our* babies?" Archer stared at his brother. "Since when did you become the welcome committee for tiny beings wearing diapers?"

"Since you're having three of them, and they're yours," Mason said. "Ours."

"And what was Last's baby?" Archer demanded.

"Well, there were too many questions up front," Mason said. "He wasn't sure about this, and he wasn't certain about that. Made it hard to get excited about the baby when he wasn't paying attention to whether it was his or not. We've rectified that since then, and Last's bundle of joy gets plenty of uncle love. But in your case, you know you're having children with Clove, especially as she set out to lure you to the bassinet." He wrinkled his forehead. "I suppose that would be plural now. Bassinets."

"Okay, okay." Archer rubbed his face. "So what? You're all here to team up with me to convince her that life here is just what she's always dreamed of? Come on, Mason. Life here isn't what anybody dreams of, apparently. Everybody up and left as soon as they found a bride. Except Calhoun, but there were extenuating circumstances there."

"We're more than shorthanded now, Archer," Mason concurred. "We can't have you jetting off to Australia to lie on the golden beaches and chase little joeys. We need you here. You're going to have to make certain you don't mess this up. Last has gone to make an offer on Mimi's house and land. Before it goes on the market to the general public."

"*Last* did? Is there something wrong with *your* mouth?" Archer glanced at his brothers incredulously. Crockett and Bandera shifted uncomfortably, staring out windows as they leaned against walls. "Are you the world's biggest yellowbelly? How can you sit here and lecture me when the best thing that's ever going to happen to you is moving off her family ranch into town where you'll actually have to make an effort to see her, the baby and the sheriff?"

"Archer," Mason said on a growl, "you're mouthing off about stuff you know nothing about."

"Peace, brothers," Crockett interrupted. "Let's get on with the business at hand. Archer, Last is making an offer to Mimi that's fair. As the member of the family who can get the job done with a minimum of wrangling, not to mention hard feelings, we felt Last was the proper one to offer. We want you to make an offer to Clove. Mimi's house for her and her children so that she'll feel comfortable staying here." He took a deep breath. "It's the right thing to do, Archer. You got her into this boat—or vice versa—but she has no choice but to return to Australia, unwed and her children fatherless, unless you act."

"You know," Archer said, "I would like to act. I really, really would. But it's hard when you show up acting like all Clove needs is a roof over her head. I'm telling you, this girl is not that simple. This is not a scheme on her behalf to hook me. She does not want me. She is not acting out of a desire to be with me for the rest of life as we know it. I wish it were that easy. I could have all the gold in the world and she would not be one whit more interested in me than she is at this moment." He frowned. "Hang on. Clove's gotten very quiet."

He strode off to find her. The bedroom door open, she obviously felt no need to act as if she wasn't listening to their conversation. And indeed, she wasn't, he realized, as she was fast asleep in a bed with a set of deer antlers as a canopy. He sighed and closed her door.

Rejoining his brothers, he said, "Everybody out. Thank you for your concern and worry, but my girl has had a very rough day. She can't handle intrigues and house offers. The doctor says she needs rest and that is what she is going to have. You're jumping the gun, anyway. If she doesn't get rest, who knows if she'll carry these children to term. I don't understand enough about pregnancy to know, but my guess is it's a good idea to follow doc's orders. Thank you for the food— I'll take very good care of her. Good night."

After a moment of glancing at each other, his brothers silently filed out, their faces downcast. They meant well, Archer knew, but Clove required the kind of handling they would never understand.

When the house was empty, he turned off the porch lights. Miss Daisy would have to wait for another day, so he put the tape away and returned the sofa pillows to their proper positions. As all the groceries were stored, he headed to Clove's chosen room. Pulling off his boots and stripping to his boxers, he crawled in bed beside her, sighing as his chilly skin was warmed by hers. In her sleep, she rolled over, putting one hand on his chest and her cheek on his shoulder. Closing his eyes, Archer's chest relaxed, all the pressure he'd been feeling melting away.

This was heaven.

But then she stirred against him, tucking herself up under his chin. His eyes widened in the darkness.

"Archer?" she murmured.

"Yes. What is it?" he asked, suddenly worried that she wasn't feeling well.

"Do you ever wonder if…what might happen if it's not just our blood types that are incompatible?"

He blinked. "No."

"Oh."

None of this sounded good. "Do you wonder?" he asked.

"Sort of," she whispered. "I mean, we had sex and that's pretty cut-and-dried. But people have to be really compatible if there's going to be anything else."

So there was a chance. She was thinking about the future, wondering what it held in store for them. He thought about Last and Valentine. No compatibility for the long haul there, so Clove had a good point. "Go to sleep," he said. "We don't have to have all the answers tonight. You're supposed to be resting happily and thinking good thoughts. Not worrying."

"I'm not worrying," she said softly. "I just don't see us being compatible."

Well, she'd been right about everything until now. Gently, he rolled her onto her back.

He stroked her face with his palm. "Can you see me?"

"No."

"I can't see you, either. That means this is a blind compatibility test." Then he kissed her. Softly at first, then more deeply when she didn't resist. When her lips touched his more urgently and he felt her tongue experimentally touch his, he kissed her harder, faster, his mouth moving against hers in a sexual mating dance that had her moaning beneath him.

She cried out, a small, surprised squeal against his lips, her fingers suddenly clutching at his shoulders. He pulled back in alarm. "Are you all right?"

"Yes," she said, her voice astonished in the darkness.

"Are you sure?"

She took a moment to answer, her hands sliding down his arms. "I think so. Give me a couple seconds to figure it out."

He frowned. "Figure what out?"

"I think I just...you know."

He passed a hand across her stomach. "Tell me."

"Had a climax," she whispered, then giggled. Relief swept over him. He rolled over onto his side, saying gruffly, "Go to sleep. The babies probably wish you'd settle down. The doctor said we weren't supposed to have relations, and I assume that means all forms of pleasure."

He felt her turn over. A sigh left his chest, the worry lifting from him. That crazy little giggle floated across his memory, and he grinned to himself in the darkness. "Guess you answered the compatibility question, though."

She gave a little backward kick, her heel lightly grazing his calf, which made him chuckle. "We can run a retest tomorrow, if you'd like."

"Archer!"

He laughed.

ARCHER WAS SLEEPING like a dog until his senses warned him something was different from the easy comfort he'd been enjoying last night. Keeping his eyes closed, he assessed his surroundings. Warm, soft body next to him—check. In fact, Clove's hand lay dangerously close to his maleness, and if not for the sheet, he'd be getting pretty close to happiness. His body acknowledged this fact, slowly stirring up an erection.

But his mind countered his desire. Something was still not right.

His eyes snapped open, to find a stunningly lovely woman staring at him from the foot of the bed. "Hello," she said.

"Crap!" He jumped from the bed, startling Clove. She sat straight up, clutching the sheet.

"Lucy!" Clove jumped from the bed, rushing to hug her sister. "Why didn't you call me? I would have met you at the airport!"

Lucy eyed him over Clove's shoulder as they embraced. Archer stared right back at her, until he realized he was wearing nothing but black boxers and this was no way to meet his children's auntie for the first time. Grabbing his jeans, he jerked them on, never taking his eyes off Lucy. For added composure, he snatched his cowboy hat off the headboard and jammed that on his head.

"My taxi driver knew exactly where the ranch was," Lucy said, in a voice much like Clove's. "And then the man I met at the ranch said I'd find you here. So the taxi driver brought me. The door was unlocked," she said, more to Archer than anyone. "I assumed you were awake and about, but when I called out, no one answered. So I came on in. Of course, I expected you to be alone, Clove," she said, her tone slightly surprised but not necessarily disapproving, Archer noticed.

"I'll get us a cup of joe," he said, retreating. "Clove, can you drink coffee? Or do you have to have water or juice or something healthy?"

"Orange juice, please," Clove replied. "Lucy, this is Archer Jefferson."

The sisters moved out of their embrace so that Lucy could shake Archer's hand. He wasn't certain how he felt about that, since he didn't have a shirt or boots on, and this was Clove's sister. And she was gorgeous like a movie star, though he suspected it was all natural. "Sorry I'm not clean-shaven," he said, trying to be polite.

"It's fine," Lucy replied. "I had visions of Clove being alone. I'm happy to see she's been in good hands."

Uncomfortable, he merely nodded, retreating to the kitchen so the ladies could talk. He fixed coffee, his mind racing. So this was the Lucy who couldn't have children, the sister Clove loved more than anything. She certainly hadn't seemed to be hurting for money, style or manners. Scratching at his chest, he thought about Clove's determination to help her sister. He would help his brothers if they needed him to, but there was something deeper between the two women. Perhaps because there had been so many brothers in his family, they had shared the bonding and emotions equally amongst all of them, so that it seemed less intense. Would he have a child for one of them? He didn't think so.

Of course, it was a little hard to compare, because he didn't hold the key of creation within his body. Other than the sperm donation, the male of the species got off pretty light. He wondered how much heart a woman had to have to use her body to help her sister.

Lucy walked into the kitchen, picking up a coffee mug and pouring herself a cup. She looked at him, her gaze frank.

"Cream? Sugar?" he asked.

"No, thank you." She sipped the coffee, her eyes gauging him over the rim.

"Long flight?" he asked.

"Very long, but not bad. The prospect of visiting my sister kept me from noticing any discomforts."

He nodded. "Where is Clove?"

"Showering. She said she hadn't had a chance to last night."

"It was a long day for her."

Lucy put her mug down. "So what does the doctor say, exactly?"

"That she needs rest. And possibly another round of whatever that injection was to keep our Rh factors compatible. Mostly rest."

Lucy went a bit pale. "Is it likely or unlikely that she'd miscarry?"

"With rest and care, her chances going full term are pretty good." Archer shrugged. "The next couple of days are pretty important for her." He looked at her, his gaze curious. "So. I guess you really wanted to be a mother for Clove to have gotten pregnant."

"This was not my idea," Lucy snapped. "I didn't know Clove was trying to help me like this. When I put her on the plane in Australia, she told me she was coming to America to see the world. She needed to unwind from stunt work. That was it."

"Sorry." Archer took a deep breath. "I know Clove well enough to know that she would take the path she thought best and not consult a soul."

"Clove has always been brave. Very kind and generous." Lucy looked at him. "Not to put too fine a point on it, but the last thing I expected to find was a cowboy in my sister's bed."

The lady was inquiring, he figured, and a man should always be honest. "Fine points don't trouble me," he said mildly. "And, with all due respect, I hope you realize that I'll be doing everything in my power to *stay* in Clove's bed."

Chapter Eleven

"And if she doesn't want you in her bed?" Lucy asked Archer.

He smiled. "We're very, very compatible."

"You're not at all what I expected," Lucy said.

"I could say the same," Archer replied, pouring himself another cup of coffee.

"So you didn't just balk when you found out my sister was pregnant? Have your way with her and then go on?"

He dug around for some bagels his brothers had put away. "No, ma'am. Do I look like that sort to you?"

She sighed and took the plate of bagel and red grapes he offered her. "Thank you. Then I don't understand. If your intentions are to care for my sister, why is she returning to Australia?"

"You'd know the answer to that better than me."

"I meant, without you," Lucy said. "Why is she returning without you?"

"This is my home," Archer said simply. "I'm not planning to leave it. And she hasn't invited me. She wasn't planning to tell me she was pregnant."

Lucy put her plate down, her fingers trembling. "I guess Clove told you that I—"

"She did," Archer said swiftly, his tone kind. "I don't need further details."

She glanced down for a moment. "Did she also tell you that my husband and I—"

"She mentioned something about it."

"I see." Lucy bit her lip, clearly humiliated. "I guess she told you that the farm isn't doing well."

He shook his head.

"It's ours," she said. "Mine and Clove's. My husband is a doctor and doesn't know a lot about such things. We don't ask him for money for the farm. It's ours, and it's all we have left between us. We're adopted," Lucy said quietly. "Did she tell you that, too?"

"No." Archer's mind scrambled to keep up with that information. "Clove and I really haven't had a chance to get to know each other to that extent."

She blushed. "This is very awkward."

"You're telling me." But he was starting to understand Clove's desperation better.

"Good morning," Clove said, walking to stand beside her sister. They hugged each other briefly around the waist, then Clove sighed over the bagel and grapes her sister held. "Would you mind if I have some of that?" she asked Archer.

He grabbed a plate. "Feeding you well was what my brothers had in mind." With two plump stems of red grapes beside a bagel, he handed her the plate.

"Glad to see you with an appetite." After he'd poured a glass of apple juice, he said, "I'm going to head out. You two will enjoy being alone for a while. Lucy, I have work to do. I'm sure you can take over here."

Lucy nodded, her eyes grateful. "I can."

"All right." He went into the bedroom, grabbed his shirt, put on his boots and slipped on his belt before walking back out of the bedroom. "I've got an Appaloosa that wants breakfast, too," he told the women, "and she gets ornery if her food isn't right on time."

Clove looked at him, her gaze a bit nervous. "Say hello to Tonk for me."

He was pleased that she still thought kindly of his horse. "I will. Nice to meet you, Lucy."

Tipping his hat, he left, thinking it was a great time to get out and clear his head.

Between his brothers trying to buy Mimi's house for Clove, and Lucy's small, elegant satchel that foretold her plans for a very short visit to Texas, he had a lot to think about.

He did not want to lose Clove, not when she'd started getting under his skin in the kind of way no other woman ever had.

LUCY TURNED TO CLOVE after Archer left. "So. You left out some important details," she said. "Let's sit on this nice, terribly western sofa and you can fill in the story."

"Starting with?" Clove followed Lucy to the sofa, plate and cup in hand.

"The fact that you just happened to land one of the most handsome men on the planet."

Clove shook her head. "Archer would smirk at both your description of him and the notion that he's been landed."

"I don't know. He seems…interested in you."

"Archer's hard to explain. I wouldn't be overly impressed with his interest."

"And you met him how?"

Clove looked at her sister. "Over the internet. We've corresponded for two years."

Lucy thought about that for a moment. "So, in light of the fact that you came straight to Texas and haven't ventured from your original destination, I can assume that your trip was less about seeing the world than about seeing this cowboy. Those must have been some emails."

Clove shrugged. "They were pretty tame, actually."

"Did he know you were coming to meet him?"

She shook her head. "No. I didn't tell him my real name. I wanted to meet him first."

"Good move. That first meeting must have been impressive."

Clove looked at her sister carefully. "He was more attractive than I thought he'd be, certainly."

"I'll say." Lucy laughed. "And so you met him, gave him a fake name for safety's sake, and he seduced you?"

"I seduced him."

Lucy laughed at her. "Clove. Not you."

"Yes. Me."

The smile slipped from Lucy's face. She stared at her sister for a long moment. "All right. Let me run through this again. You flew around the world to meet this man, and decided to seduce him, and then called me and told me you wanted me to raise your children." She frowned. "It's not like you to act so crazily."

Clove was silent for a moment. "Stunt work."

"No." Lucy shook her head. "Those are calculated risks. You threw yourself out on a huge limb for no reason that I can see. This makes no sense." She stared at Clove for a long moment. "No, wait a moment. You decided to get pregnant and give me the children to save my marriage because I couldn't have any? Is that closer to the real crazy truth? That's the idea that cowboy seems to be peddling."

Clove sighed. "Lucy, as wild as it sounds, it's not unusual for women to use a surrogate mother. That's all I wanted to be."

Tears welled in Lucy's eyes, which she wiped away. "First of all, honey, you can't take advantage of this poor man because of me. You're going to have to tell him the truth. I think he's falling in love with you. Or something. He certainly seems fond of you, and quite concerned for your well-being."

"He knows the truth."

"He does? And he's not angry with you?"

"I would say that his anger is overridden by his determination to make certain his children stay here. Also, his brothers agree with Archer's tactics. They came here to talk to me last night but I fell asleep." She sighed. "It had been a long, scary day. Archer and I have incompatible Rh factors, and I'd had some cramping. Now he's even more determined to protect me and his children."

"I see. Well," Lucy said, "considering that he's had fatherhood sprung on him, he's being damn responsible."

Clove nodded. "Yes."

Lucy took a long drink of coffee. "Secondly, you can't interfere in my life without asking me. I don't want to be a mother this way."

Clove was shocked. "Lucy!"

Lucy shook her head. "It's true. I'm sorry, and it's going to sound mean, but I wanted my own children. Mine and Robert's. But if it's not meant to be, it's not meant to be. I can accept that. I also accept that my husband is going to leave me."

"Don't say that!"

"I can say it because he already has." Lucy's eyes welled up again. "And I can be more honest and say that our problems go deeper than my inability to conceive. Robert says he feels overwhelmed by marriage to me. I don't think bringing triplets into the picture is going to help him."

"I don't understand. Robert loves you. I honestly thought he just wanted to be a father so badly that he—"

"Robert does love me. But the fertility problem lies with him." Lucy swallowed, her eyes full of pain. "I always say that I cannot conceive for his benefit. The truth is, the doctors say—and these are associates of his—there's a problem with his sperm."

Clove put her arms around her sister. "I'm so sorry. Aren't there procedures for that?"

"There are. And we recently tried one. It didn't take. I believe that was a breaking point for Robert." She hugged Clove, burying her face in her hair. "Thank you for trying to make my dreams come true, Clove. But you can't save my marriage, honey. You can't make a man feel things he doesn't, and you can't change what a man feels about himself."

Clove felt tears well in her eyes but she was determined not to let her sister see them. Lucy had already been through enough. "I wish I'd been there for you."

"Actually, it was time for Robert and I to

face this by ourselves. While he loves you, he feels that I pay more attention to you sometimes than I do him." Lucy laughed a little. "Since he works odd hours, it's probably true."

"I didn't know he felt that way."

"Oh, well." Lucy pulled away, leaning her head back against the sofa to look at the ceiling. "I believe at the end he was just angry and saying things. Anything. People lash out when they're hurt. He feels that he's let me down." She rolled her head to look at her sister. "I'm glad I came to visit you. I wanted to tell you in person that Robert had left me, but I also needed to get away. It's so simple and comfortable here."

"It is." Clove sat next to her sister and put her head back on the sofa as well. "There's something very comfortable about Archer. He makes me feel better about everything."

"It's that lordly I've-got-everything-under-control attitude of his."

"Maybe. Although he really doesn't have everything under control, you know? His horse, for example. Tonk is tricky. And he likes that. I know from his emails that he likes rodeo, and there's no control in that. His family life—same thing. They're always out of control."

"It's an inner confidence he has. Very attractive. He has control of himself."

"That's true," Clove said with surprise. "I've never met a man so sure of himself. He just goes for it, with all his heart, when he wants something."

"Something you two have in common," Lucy said. "Heart. Inner confidence."

"I have no inner confidence."

"Right. You just leave home and go around the world to get pregnant so your sister's marriage will be saved. Clove, you're scarily brave. Just like Mom always said."

"Maybe she meant that I was an insane risk taker. I think she was just being polite."

"What are you going to do about him?" Lucy asked. "Now that you've taken this insane risk of trying to catch this cowboy?"

Clove rolled her head to look at her sister. "I am not trying to catch Archer. He wasn't remotely interested when he met me. We were together one night and accidentally hit the big bonanza, and I'm not sure which one of us was more stunned. Now he's determined to keep me here, but it's all about the babies."

"It's a start. Robert and I started our relationship with a rose," Lucy said thoughtfully. "A rose that led to a long courtship without sex. He saw me in a mall one day, gave me a rose and told me I was beautiful. I was still recovering from losing our adopted parents, and I'm afraid I jumped at the attention. Still, we didn't have relations right up until the night before we married. For you and Archer, sex came first. Maybe the love and the marriage will come later.

"Two years of correspondence is a pretty powerful getting-to-know-someone device. People generally write more than they say, especially men. They're tough on verbalizing their feelings sometimes." She blinked.

"One time, a long time ago," she confirmed softly, "Robert wrote me a love poem. It was the most beautiful thing I ever read. When he puts his feelings on paper, it's thrilling." She sat up, snatching the red grapes off her plate. "That was the only time he ever wrote me anything, though."

"I know we've discussed this before, but you're certain adoption isn't an option?" Clove asked, still disbelieving that her sister's marriage could be over.

"At this point, definitely not," Lucy said, "since there's no father in the picture. How-

ever, you and I were adopted, Clove. I…
something in me wanted my very own flesh
and blood. And Robert wasn't keen. I think…
he didn't want to announce to the world that
he couldn't—that we couldn't—get pregnant."

"I see." Clove took her sister's hand in hers,
squeezing it. "I love you, Lucy. Thank you for
coming here. I needed you."

"I needed you, too. I can't believe you're
going to be a little mother!" Putting one hand
on Clove's tummy, she laughed. "You're going
to be the most beautiful mother in the world."

"Not me," Clove said. "That would have
been you. Remember, I'm the dowdy little
sister."

"If you believe that, you haven't looked in
the mirror lately. Pregnancy—or something
else—agrees with you." Lucy gave her a
saucy wink. "Maybe it's Texas air that agrees
with you. Or love."

Clove stood. "I'm going to take a nap. I
don't know why I'm tired, because I slept
hard last night."

"I don't know how you could sleep with
that gorgeous man in your bed! I must admit
I was completely surprised, Clove. My little
sister in bed with a man!"

Clove blushed. "Archer tends to make himself at home."

Lucy laughed. "It's wonderful to be the object of a man's attentions."

Clove wasn't sure about that yet. "Wake me up in an hour, okay? I'm sorry to bug out on you, but I seem to get very—"

Lucy waved her hand. "Go on. I am going to sit here like a lady of leisure and enjoy my vacation by reading a magazine. And maybe cooking a little. The farm keeps me so busy that I never have time to relax."

Clove nodded, feeling guilty. "I shouldn't have left you with all the work."

"Well, it was time for you to get away, Clove. Truthfully, I'm happier about you than I've ever been. You always worked so hard. Always were older than your years. It's great to see you blossoming." Lucy smiled. "We'll figure something out about the farm later. Let's think about the babies first. Triplets, my word!"

Clove swung around. "Lucy! Robert left you when you told him I was having triplets, didn't he?"

Lucy looked at her.

"It's true, isn't it? That was the final straw?"

"Clove, infertility is infertility. He was happy you were pregnant—"

"But three babies. Not just one, but three. That made him feel bad, didn't it?"

She hesitated a second too long for Clove not to know she'd hit the truth. "Well, he may have been a bit hurt. I mean, it's probably hard on a man's self-esteem to know that his sister-in-law can have children but he can't give them to his—"

"So instead of helping your marriage, I ended it," Clove said frankly.

"Now, Clove," Lucy said, "we were already having troubles—"

"But that's when he finally left. I called you and told you about the babies and you were excited for me, and you told him, and he left."

"It doesn't matter, Clove. I really think he would have left eventually. The strains were tearing us apart."

"It matters to me, Lucy," Clove said, her heart breaking. "It matters more than anything to me."

Chapter Twelve

Two hours later, Archer let himself into the little bungalow. "Clove?" he called.

She came out from the bedroom wearing a pretty dress and a frown. "Yes?"

"Oh." He glanced around. "Where's Lucy?"

"Right here." Lucy walked to join her sister. "Hey, Archer."

"Is everything all right?" he asked, wondering why they looked so serious.

"Did you need something?" Clove asked, glancing around. "Did you leave your hat here?"

"No. I've got my hat." He was perplexed by her sad expression. Clearly, the sisters had an issue on their minds. "And I don't need anything. Are you okay?"

"Yes." She sighed. "We've been chatting. That's all."

Well, woman talk probably made women frown sometimes. "Well," he said, "can this little monster chat with y'all?" He pulled his hat from behind his back, and the little kitten Clove had adopted in Lonely Hearts Station popped her head up from inside, meowing.

"Tink!" Clove gasped, running to take the kitten from his hat. "Look, Lucy. This is my little kitty!" She rubbed Tink against her chin. "You're still so soft, Tink!"

Lucy gave Archer a droll look. "Nice, cowboy. Very nice."

He grinned. "Thank you."

"Thank you," Clove said. "I thought you didn't like cats!"

The grin slipped from his face, turning his expression uncomfortable. "I'm going to make a huge effort to like Tink. And she's going to make a huge effort not to be so fond of my hat. Aren't you, Tink?"

Tink cared about nothing except batting at Clove's earrings. She laughed. "I love this little ball of fur."

Lucy was still looking at Archer, he finally realized. "What?" he said to her.

"Just watching you do your thing, cowboy," she said.

"And it's a very good thing, too," he replied. "You two keep bonding. I'm off to haul in some feed."

"Bye, Archer," Clove said.

"How are you feeling, by the way?" he asked as he turned in the doorway. "Do you feel like eating at the big house tonight? I can drive you up and we can make it a quick evening. The boys would understand you couldn't make an all-nighter of it."

"I'd like that," Clove said. "Lucy?"

"It should be interesting," Lucy said, her eyebrow lifting.

Archer laughed. "Wait till you meet my brothers. They're even more interesting than me."

Clove smiled, waving Tink's paw at him. "Can you bring me an extra hat to transport Tink tonight? I think she feels at home in your hat, but I assume you don't always want to share such a conveyance with her."

"Sure." Archer settled a long look on her, taking in her dress and her hair, and last, her lips. "I'll be back around six," he said. "Call if you need anything."

He closed the door behind him.

"Whew," Lucy said. "He warmed the room twenty degrees with the way he looked at you!"

Clove blushed, thinking about the kiss they'd shared last night. He'd warmed her without trying to, in ways she didn't even know a woman could be warmed. "He's just sexy," Clove said. "It's not that he's doing anything extra for me."

Lucy was still staring at the door. "Clove, you've got to get down off your fence."

"What do you mean?"

"Either you want that sexy beast or you don't."

Clove sank onto the sofa and looked at her sister. "Lucy, it's not that simple. I didn't come to America to find a man. I could have found a man in Australia."

"But that hunk is here," Lucy said, "and it's time for you to figure out you've got one devilishly manly fellow trying his best to pay attention to you." She looked at the kitten sitting in Clove's lap, swatting at the buttons on her dress. "Men do not fetch kittens for women they're not interested in."

"It was nice of him."

"It was extraordinary. Makes me wonder what else he has up his sleeve." Lucy smiled. "Kind of fun finding out, isn't it?"

"What do you mean?"

"I got the distinct impression that he intends to woo you until you go over to his side."

Clove's female pride flowered a little. "Did he say that?"

"In so many words, and then a few more. He seemed to think that anything standing in his way was only a flimsy challenge to his right and might. I like that in a man. I really do."

Clove sighed. "Lucy, if you had seen him when he first met me, there was no spark. No ember to burst into flame. It just wasn't there. And I wear baggy nightwear and dresses to hide the fact that I am beginning to lose my waist, and now he finds me attractive? I just don't buy it."

"Well, there are two things at work here that you probably don't understand. Men love babies. They may not tell you this, but they love the look of a woman carrying a baby, specifically when it's his baby. It's a proclamation to the whole world of his manhood. You're carrying three of his, and you can get as big as his barn, and he's just going to find you more attractive. This is how the men who are really worth loving act. There are the losers out there who don't get it. But real men love to see their woman blossoming."

"Eh," Clove said with distaste. "And the second thing at work?"

"Oh. Well, you may not want to let the mirror tell you this, but you are more attractive now. You're filled out, you look happy, rested...content. It just shows. And it makes you more alluring to him. So don't think about what happened when you first met him. Goodness, Clove, not every love is destined to happen in the first instant two people meet. Sometimes it's the ones that take a long time that are the most tested and meaningful."

Lucy looked sad and Clove changed the subject. "So, do we go eat with the boys?"

"Sure!" Lucy's eyes widened. "I'm nearly divorced. I deserve an evening with attractive cowboys!"

"Lucy!"

Her sister laughed. "Oh, my goodness, quit being such a silly. A girl can look and not touch, can't she? What's the harm in that? Besides, I'm not a cowboy sort of girl. I married a doctor who hated our farm. Doesn't that tell you everything?"

Clove shook her head. "I don't know anymore."

"Don't be upset, Clove. There's so much good in your life that I want you to enjoy it. Be happy."

"I'm trying," Clove said. "But right now,

I'm just looking forward to eating dessert to-night."

Lucy laughed. "That's my girl."

ARCHER WAS NERVOUS as he went to pick up Clove and Lucy. He figured it had to do with the fact that tonight felt oddly like a date; Lucy was somewhat parental about Clove, and he and Clove had never truly had a date. The picking-up and eating-with-the-family phase was one they hadn't done before, so this had special meaning. He straightened his bolo, hoping his brothers would behave in this first sit-down meal with his lady.

Just thinking about it made him more nervous. He worried about moving Clove from the bungalow for an hour, but surely eating a delicious meal Helga had prepared constituted resting. Then he wondered if he should take flowers for Clove. He fumbled with his hat and picked up a bucket for Tink that he'd spread a towel in for easy, clean, comfortable transport.

No, flowers would be seen as a sign of wooing on his part, and that would spook Clove. Delivering Tink had been enough. Dinner with his family would be a hurdle they should successfully cross before more was done.

Looking at his teeth, he slicked his hair once more.

"Nervous?" Last said, coming into his room.

Archer grunted.

Last leaned up against the wall. "You like this girl."

"What gives you that impression?" He checked his teeth. White, with maybe a small uneven crook on the side. He was shaven, except that his face always seemed a bit dark with stubble around his chin.

"You and I are the new dads in the family. Unexpected fatherhood is a bit of a jolt, isn't it?"

"I've had bigger jolts." Archer checked his fingernails to make certain no dirt resided beneath. "Should I wear cologne, or is that overdoing it?"

"Overdoing what?"

Archer met his brother's gaze. *"It."*

Last laughed. "Ah, you must mean the eager-swain routine."

"No, I don't mean that," Archer retorted. "I just don't want to be a dope."

Last shook his head. "You're a dope no

matter what, as far as Mason's concerned. You didn't use a condom. Get over it. You cost the ranch money. Blah, blah, blah. You know the routine."

"I don't care," Archer said. "I like her. For the first time in my life, I really like someone."

Last nodded. "I know."

Archer stared at himself in the mirror. "It's as good as it's gonna get."

"I think she likes you fine, bro. By the way, Mimi accepted Mason's offer."

"Offer to what?" Archer frowned, still fiddling with his bolo.

"To buy her house and property."

Archer stopped fiddling and stared at his brother. "Just like that?"

"I guess so. I made the offer, and she said yes."

Archer thought about that. "Mason's letting her leave. Just like that."

"Archer, nothing is just like that. Especially not with Mason."

"Why did you make the offer and not him? I don't understand that."

"Because it's Mimi. Because he can't face her with any big decisions. You know him."

Archer chewed on that. "Something's

fishy here. Mason didn't even blink when he learned Mimi was going to sell her place."

"He did. He threw his napkin down and left. But he knew it wouldn't do any good to steam over it. You know Mimi. When her mind's made up, it's all hell's-bustin'-loose. Mason figured we needed the land now that we're filling out as a family."

"Well, I'm not letting Clove go," Archer said with determination. "Mason may be a wimp, but I'm not. I know how to handle my destination."

"Destiny, Archer," Last said with a sigh.

"Same thing to me. I'm outta here." Archer left, sweeping all thoughts of his family from his mind. As far as he was concerned, he was going to convince Clove that she and the babies belonged right here. With him.

THE LAST THING Clove expected was how handsome Archer was when he came to pick her up. He'd always been attractive, but all dressed up in his best jeans and boots and combed hair, he was downright hot. She glanced at Lucy for confirmation.

Her sister's eyes were huge as she took in Archer's appearance. "Mind the fence," she said to Clove. "I'd be getting down off it if I were you."

"What fence?" Archer asked.

"No fence at all." Clove sent Lucy a warning glance. "Thank you for coming to get us."

"Thank you for joining my family for dinner. This will be a simple, quiet meal. Just what the doctor ordered."

Lucy followed them silently as Archer led the way to his truck. He helped Clove into the cab, then opened the door for Lucy. "Seat belts, ladies," he said.

Clove sat quietly, enjoying seeing the ranch as it went by. "It's very peaceful here."

"Yes. I'm sure Australia is, too. I've always wanted to go to Australia."

"You told me that once," she murmured.

Lucy cleared her throat in the back seat.

"Maybe you'd like to come see my house sometime," Clove said hurriedly.

"I'd like that."

Clove could almost hear her sister exhale with relief. She frowned, thinking it wasn't right to invite Archer to her home just yet. They had too much to figure out, and proffering an invitation gave off meaning she wasn't ready for.

"Here we are," Archer said. "The humble abode."

Clove got out of the truck, and Archer ran around to help her walk up the steps.

"I can do it," she said.

"I know. But you're not supposed to stress or strain anything."

She sighed. "I'm not a doll, Archer."

"That's debatable, Miss Penmire," he said. "Hope you like roast beef and mashed potatoes, because Helga's cooked that and a Yorkshire pudding."

"I'm dying and going to heaven," Lucy murmured behind them. "Real Texas cooking."

They went into the dining room, which was aglow with candelabra. "My," Clove said. "This is very pretty."

"It looks fancy," Archer said, "but don't get the impression we eat like this every night. This is the holiday tablecloth, and these are the special-event candles." He wrinkled his forehead as his brothers filed into the room, taking seats at the table. "If Mimi and the sheriff are moving to town, who gets Helga? Us or them?"

Bandera stared at him. "We don't know."

Mason shrugged. "Haven't thought about

it. Miss Clove, Miss Lucy, forgive my brothers' manners and allow me to reintroduce ourselves to you. Bandera, Last, Crockett, and me, Mason." He lifted a wineglass to Clove. "Congratulations on your pregnancy, and more importantly, welcome to the family."

All the brothers raised a glass to her. Clove blinked, not sure how to take their welcome. "Thank you," she finally murmured, picking up her water glass.

Lucy patted her back. Clove felt so guilty. The Jeffersons seemed so sincere, even though she had enticed one of the brothers under false pretenses.

Helga served her plate, heaped high with aromatic food. She nearly sighed with anticipation. "This looks wonderful."

Helga nodded, filling Lucy's plate. "Heaven," Lucy said.

Clove glanced at Archer. She found his gaze on her, watching her every move. "What?" she whispered.

"You're beautiful," he whispered across the table.

Everyone heard him. Clove felt herself blush, so she looked down at the napkin in her lap. As Mason began to eat, she followed suit, though she'd lost her appetite.

"How are you feeling?" Bandera asked.

"Wonderful, actually. Thank you," Clove replied.

"Good," Mason said. "Because we'd like to discuss some living arrangements with you."

Clove lowered her fork. "Living arrangements?"

"Yes. Now that you're here and expecting children, we'd like to make your life a bit easier. Less complicated."

He paused to look at her.

"Thank you," Clove said, wondering if she should be grateful or worried.

"Next door to us is a house you may have seen on your way up here," Mason continued. "It's the sheriff's house, but he and his daughter and her baby are moving to town."

"I see," Clove murmured.

"We'd like you to consider living there," Mason said. "We'd like for you and your children to have a place to call your own."

Clove's fork fell into her plate. She put her hand in her lap as she glanced at Archer. He was watching her, waiting for an answer. Clearly, he'd been in on this plan, too.

"Careful," Lucy murmured. "Think before you speak."

But Clove couldn't react beyond the angry

astonishment she felt. "No," she said. "We already have a place to call our own. It's my home, and I don't need another one."

What they didn't understand was that she didn't want them to rush in and take care of her. Her feelings would be different if Archer had wanted her—ever wanted her—but he was obviously doing what he had to do to save face in his family. "You don't even know me," she told them all. "And most especially you," she said with a pained look at Archer. "There's just no way I can accept such an... arrangement."

They stared at her, completely buffaloed by what was lacking in their offer. She sighed. Lucy patted her hand. "Look. I'm a practical woman. I want the best for my children. That doesn't mean moving away from the people who love me, away from the land where I'm comfortable."

"I also want the best for my children," Archer said. "And I echo your sentiments."

Lucy and Mason stared at each other. "We've got ourselves some hardheaded ones," Mason said to Lucy.

"Don't look at me," Lucy said. "I may be eldest, but she's always been her own woman."

Mason nodded and bent his head to eat.

The other brothers followed suit. Archer's gaze remained locked on Clove. She stared back, her chin lifted. Clove rose and went to the window. Lucy smiled, going to stand beside her sister.

Mason looked at Archer. "You've got your hands full with that one," he said. "Best of luck to you. You've finally met your match."

Clove turned away from the window. "Archer, would you mind taking me home?"

The men instantly stood.

"Are you all right?" Archer asked.

"I'm fine. Lucy, you stay here and eat. I'm going to go lie down."

"I'll go with you—"

"No," she told her sister. "There is no reason. Please stay and enjoy the wonderful food and company."

Lucy looked from Archer to Clove. "All right," she said, sitting down. "If Archer doesn't mind."

"Happy to be of service. Step out carefully this way. Wear my jacket," he said, laying it across her shoulders.

"I'm sorry to be such a party pooper," Clove told the brothers. "Thank you so much for everything."

"Are you sure you're all right?" Archer asked once they were outside.

Clove looked up at Archer as he once again settled the jacket better over her shoulders. "Archer, could I talk to you, just the two of us?"

Chapter Thirteen

Archer gazed down into Clove's eyes, seeing concern there. "Are you sure you're feeling okay?" he asked. "Maybe we overdid it. I should have made sure you stayed at the bungalow tonight. I didn't know it was going to rain—"

"Archer." She put a hand on his arm. "Relax."

His heart seemed to stop. "You worried me."

Her gaze stayed on him. "I really need to talk to you."

"Let's go." He led her to his truck, his heart pounding nervously. He kept his arm protectively under hers, steadying her on the ground that was beginning to slick with the light rain.

He wanted Clove to grow to trust him. To understand that he wanted to protect her. And he hoped that she could love him.

Because he was pretty certain he was falling in love with Clove. Fallen, more likely, since he'd felt ill when the cramping had started and he'd realized the babies might be at risk. He wanted Clove to be healthy, wanted her to enjoy this pregnancy she'd wanted so badly and which he now wanted as well.

Silently, they drove to the bungalow. Going inside to the den, Clove turned on the lights, keeping them dim. She sat in front of the window, looking out. "It's like a fairyland," she said. "So pretty here in the country."

"Yeah. Unless there's an ice storm. We get some of those. And once, a twister. This is supposed to be Tornado Alley, but luckily, we've only had one wild one come through in all the years we lived here. And one big, big storm, which nearly took out the town with flooding." He went into the kitchen, putting the kettle on for coffee. "What can you drink? What would you like?"

"Hot tea would be wonderful."

He liked her being willing to allow him to fix something for her. "You didn't eat much."

"I have very little appetite right now. I wonder if that's bad or good."

Shrugging, he said, "Probably fine, as long as you're listening to your body. When do you see the doctor again?"

"In a week. But I plan to be at home seeing my own doctor by then."

He dropped a tea bag into the hot water, his shoulders tightening with dread at the sure tone of her voice. "So is that what you wanted to talk to me about?"

"That, and some other things."

He brought the cups over, joining her on the sofa where they both faced the window. "I'm listening."

"I need to go home," she said softly. "I need to think."

"About?"

"About a lot of things, but mostly, what I've done."

He sipped his coffee, put his boots up on the ottoman and watched her intently. Her hair fell over her shoulders. It still held an occasional twinkling droplet of water shining among the strands. "I should make a fire," he said. "Hold that thought. I don't want you getting chilled. It's still nippy, like spring will never fully arrive."

Getting up, he stuck a few pieces of rolled newspaper under the logs that were already in the fireplace. With a long match, he lit the paper and replaced the screen. "I really enjoy this bungalow. More in the winter than in the summer, obviously. It's a great place to come when I want to sit and think." He glanced up at her. "How about I leave you alone so you can think? I know you've got plenty on your mind."

"No." She shook her head. "I'd be better off getting my thoughts out in the open. My conscience is killing me, Archer. I took advantage of you, and you and your family are being so nice to me that the guilt is overwhelming."

"You're overwhelmed because we're nice?"

"I'm overwhelmed," she said softly, "because of what I did. They say no action goes without a reaction, a consequence of some kind. My actions had consequences for you, your family, and even my sister."

He sat beside her again, certain that the fire was going to catch. "What has your sister said?"

Clove's eyelids lowered for an instant. "That her husband left her. About the time he found out I was pregnant."

"I see."

"Archer, I was really desperate and I thought I could make things right, but I made matters worse for everyone. And not only that, but I did it in a super-huge way."

He patted her hand. "I thought our family was fertile, but you're like a peach tree, popping out all over."

A nice peachy blush hit the tops of her cheeks, which he thought was kind of sweet. "Hey, it's a good thing," he said. "I like odd numbers. We're lucky."

"One would have been good," she said dryly.

"But three's something to brag about. It's like Poppin' Fresh Family. All that lovin' in the oven."

"That's exactly it. It's just outrageous!"

He laughed. "Well, I'm excited. You have to do all the work, and I get to be Instant Dad. Why should I complain? I see that my job is to support you and comfort you when you begin to feel like this ottoman has lodged in your tummy."

That earned him an eye roll. She sipped her tea for a second, then said, "Archer, if you hadn't discovered I was pregnant, would you have wanted to see me again?"

He thought about that for a moment. "I suppose not," he said. "You didn't seem too keen on me. I did come looking for you, but I didn't really expect to find you, and it's usually not a good idea to chase a woman who doesn't like you. The rewards just aren't there."

"I don't believe you've ever experienced that."

"No, not me personally, but my brothers have, especially Mason. It's not good when the love wires get crossed." He touched her finger, stroking her skin lightly. "I'm glad you're pregnant," he said. "It gives me a tie to you. A claim on you."

Her eyes widened. "Why would you want it?"

"Because I want a family."

"You could have had one with any woman."

"But you were so cute. And you set your big eyes on me, and I liked that, and then you were sweet in bed, and I liked that even more, and then you turned out to be remarkably fruitful. I can say, this is Clove, she's pregnant with my triplets." He gave his chest a solid thump. "Makes me look very studly. Potent. Quite moved me up in the brotherly food chain. Beat that, brothers!"

"You're crazy," she said, "and you're making all this up."

"No, ma'am. I truly am excited to be a father."

"I was planning to deceive you."

He put his coffee mug down, getting up to look out the window at the rain, which was falling harder. "Quit beating yourself up, Clove. I'm from a family that does things for crazy, sometimes inconceivable, reasons. I've met your sister. I can imagine you'd want her to be happy. It's not that big a deal. It would be if I didn't want to be a father, but I think I always secretly dreamed of being the brother to do something big. It's hard to make a statement in a family of twelve." He turned and grinned at her. "What else do you want to say to me?"

"It's just hard," she said. "Simply put, it upset me that your brother mentioned the house next door for me. Mimi's house? Is that what you call it? I don't feel right about having a house bought for me just because I became pregnant. I just can't accept it."

Archer nodded. "I completely understand. I would feel the same way."

"Really?"

"Yes," he said, coming back to the sofa to stroke her chin once with his finger. "I'd feel the same way."

Her eyes sparkled, and he decided he missed her without her glasses. "Your eyes are beautiful, but I liked you with your glasses. You were spunky like that. Why don't you wear them anymore?"

She looked at him shyly. "I feel more attractive without them. They're very bulky. I'm trying a new kind of contact lens Dr. Fern's friend recommended to me."

"Really?" He looked close into her eyes. "I can't tell you're wearing them."

"I am."

He'd only meant to look into her eyes and see the contacts, but now that he was this close, he could smell her perfume. He could sense her unease, which he found attractive, too, because it meant she felt something around him besides nothing. "I like you," he said softly.

"I think I like you more than you like me," she said.

"You don't act like it," he said.

"Be patient. I'm not very good with men yet," she said.

"You never let on in your emails. I would have thought you were quite the sophisticated Aussie with your stunt work and fun."

"I'm not," she said.

"I'm not sophisticated, either," he said, running one finger lightly over her lips. "But if you hold still a second, we can both practice."

And then he kissed her ever so softly, and he felt so much better just having her lips touch his that it didn't matter that she hadn't fallen for him head over heels the way he wanted her to. All that mattered was that he had her now, and she was letting him kiss her—

"Oh, Tink," Clove said ruefully, moving away when the kitten patted playfully at her leg. "You little minx."

Clove scooped Tink up, her eyes no longer gazing at him. Archer felt a moment's tingling regret, and yet, he knew he shouldn't be pushing the limits right now. "You need to rest."

"I know. I think I'll turn in now." She couldn't look at him, instead she cast a worried eye at the door. "Do you think Lucy is all right?"

"All right?" He chuckled. "She's not that far away, and one of my brothers will bring her home when she's had enough of them. That could be any time now."

"Do you think?"

"Absolutely. Most people have a ten-minute window of patience around us."

"All right." She visibly relaxed. "What are you going to do?"

"I'm going to sit here and sip my coffee.

Make sure the fire dies down and doesn't throw a spark out. Then I may sleep on the sofa until your sister gets here."

"Thank you," Clove said. "I appreciate you...what you're doing for me. In spite of everything."

"We'll answer all the big issues another time. Let's not try to figure them out at once."

"You're right." She smiled, the first time he thought he'd seen her smile in a long time. "Good night."

"'Night." He tipped his hat to her.

She disappeared into the bedroom with Tink. "Lucky cat," he muttered. Still, he was under the same roof with Clove, and for now, he'd be happy with that.

A man never knew when he might have a chance to kiss the mother of his children, and he intended to hang around for the next opportunity. It might arrive sooner than later, if he was patient.

Clove poked her head around the door. "Archer?"

"Yes?"

"What does Tonk do when it rains?"

"She's in the barn with the other horses. We put them up earlier."

"Is she warm?"

"Very. Quite content is that spotted equine."

"You're sure?"

He smiled. "Clove, the horses here are babied like you're babying that kitten."

She raised her chin. "Good. I was only curious." In a second, she'd disappeared, taking her feline with her. Archer grinned to himself. A woman who worried about a man's horse was a very good woman. And he liked her more now than he had even five minutes ago. "You're going to like being married to me," he said to the empty spot where she'd been standing.

CLOVE STOOD INSIDE the doorway with her kitten in her arms, looking at the big bed that wouldn't have Archer in it tonight. She thought about how kind he was and about how nice his brothers were being to her. She and Lucy had never known that type of warm acceptance.

Crossing to the bed, she sat down, putting Tink into the old hat Archer had provided for her. For a moment, she watched the kitten pick at the straw of the hat experimentally, testing her limits and her strengths.

Clove knew about testing her limits and her strengths, too. But now she wondered what would have happened if she'd just come to Texas to meet Archer, without a plan any more involved than simply meeting the man she'd corresponded with for two years. Would they have liked each other? Would he have been this focused on her?

She didn't think so. They probably would have laughed a bit, gotten to know each other better, marveled at each other in person, and then gone their separate ways. He would never have come to Australia to see how she lived.

It bothered her now. Having gotten to know him and having spent time with his family who wanted to buy her a house, she realized she had set the clock on fast-forward for a relationship that would never have happened without her pregnancy. Their pregnancy.

She had changed Archer's life and it didn't feel right. He was being a very good sport about everything.

She walked back out to the den. "Archer?"

"Yes?" He sat up. "Are you all right?"

"Please stop worrying about me." Hovering in the doorway, she looked into the eyes of the man who she was trying desperately hard not to fall for. "In every good romance story, there is usually an evil villain to keep two people apart."

Archer nodded. "I know. I was just thinking how happy I am that Lucy turned out to be so sweet. She could have not liked me, you know."

Clove stared at him. "Lucy! Why would you think of Lucy when you worry about villains?"

"I don't know. I was worried she wouldn't like me, I guess. And that she might sweep you off back to Australia. That she might feel like slapping me for not taking proper precautions with you."

Clove's face scrunched with a frown. "Archer…Lucy knows what I did and why I did it. She's not proud of it, but she knows you had no part in what happened."

"Well, I did. Mason's real big on the condom song he sang to us as kids. You'd have to be part of our family to understand, but it goes something like this, 'Condom, condom, where's my condom? Oh, my gosh, it's gone to London. Without a condom, I can't play. Why oh why did condom go away?'"

He looked at her incredulous face. "The next verse is, 'Here is condom, at the store! Buying it is not a chore! Condom, condom—

any color!—is my friend. Otherwise my freedom I will spend.'"

She stared at him.

He shrugged. "It's ugly, Mason's doggerel,
but effective, believe it or not. The singsong
quality of it sears into the mind so that we
never had a chance to forget it. He said he had
to be creative for thirteen-year-olds, to short-
circuit the raging hormones in our brains."

"You needed condoms when you were thirteen?"

"Nah." Archer sipped his coffee, frowning when it was too cold. He got up to put the
mug in the microwave. "Mason believed in
scaring us to death to keep us in line. When
you're young and impressionable and all you
want to do is kiss Missy Tunstine just once
if you could catch her at her locker at school,
well, that song unnerves a boy so bad he
never makes the first move."

"I don't believe you. You're telling me a
fairy tale, Archer."

He got his coffee out of the microwave
when it dinged, and then held up a hand. "I
am telling you the truth. The condom song
was a deterrent in more ways than one. Hey,
at that age, a guy is trying to summon a little
courage around a girl. When you have to start

thinking about your condom running off to London, you just freeze up."

"So you never kissed Missy Tunstine."

"I didn't say that." He gave her an eyebrow and maybe a bit of a smirk.

She sensed a challenge. "Well?"

"Luckily for me, Missy didn't have hang-ups. She caught me at my locker and smooched me so fast my toes curled in their boots."

Clove felt a momentary dislike for the brave and forward Missy. "And then?"

He shrugged. "And then when we turned fifteen, Mason put condoms in our Christmas stockings. It was all very straightforward as far as he was concerned. As a single parent, his role was to make certain we didn't get ourselves in trouble."

Clove hesitated, trying to decide if she should concentrate on the trouble part—a heading she fell under—or the rest of the Missy story. Sighing, she said, "So back to my point, which you got me off of quite effectively, I am the evil villain in this story, Archer. I've been thinking about it, and I feel we need some time apart to sort this out."

"No," he said, "I've never been more sorted in my life."

She shook her head, looking at his honest face and alarmed eyes. "You're a good man, Archer."

He set his mug down. "What you've done is give me the possibility of three children, Clove. I'm beside myself with joy."

"But with me. If I hadn't been playing the part of the brave and forward Missy, you would not have picked to spend your life with me. You would not have chosen me as the mother of your children. In fact, you would have probably gone off with a girl like Missy, into the sunset, a woman who made your toes curl in your boots and who understood life in Texas."

"I see what you're worried about," Archer said, "but you have to understand I like my ladies a bit forward. I like the fact that you jumped me."

"Well, I think that's a bit strong—"

"There I was," he said, his voice dreamy, "minding my own business, and here comes this little scaredy-cat girl, looking like she just got off the train from Lost and didn't have a ticket to Found."

"Archer!"

"And then she goes and gets dangerous on me, with a 'do and some makeup and heels, courtesy of the Never Lonely Cut-n-Gurls. I have to beat my brother off of her, practically, explaining to him that I got first dibs on the babe, even if she doesn't look like scaredy-cat anymore."

"I have never in my life been a scaredy-cat!"

He caught her by the hand, pulling her close. "You are scared of me, babe."

Chapter Fourteen

Archer and Clove stared at each other for a moment. If he wasn't so handsome, if he wasn't such a tall, well-built specimen, if he wasn't so manly, maybe she would actually believe that this man wanted her forever. But in the nerdy-girl stories she'd read, the woman had to stay beautiful to have her "revenge" by winning the man.

She was about to get very broad and misshapen. Slowly, she pulled her hand away from him. "I'm afraid," she admitted.

"I know," he said, "and I suspect it's about all the wrong things."

"I want to say, let's start over…let's see if you really like me, without the fact that I'm pregnant being part of it." Her heart felt very sad as she said this. "And yet, the babies are the best part. A miracle."

"That's right," Archer said. "And since I

put them there, you should cut me some slack. I should be racking up points for good aim."

She tried not to smile at him. "I can tell that you are the kind of man who moves his way through life by making people feel better. A laugh and a smile are your emotional props."

"Yeah, but I can be serious, too. I'm feeling pretty serious about you."

They stood a foot away from each other, thinking about what was growing between them.

"And you know, I'm not just another pretty face," he said, coaxing a smile from her.

"Another story?"

"Yes, and this one's just as true as the one about the condom song." He pulled his shirt off, pointing to a scar on his upper chest, opposite from his heart. "This is where my twin, Ranger, shot me with a BB gun at close range. It was an accident, but it hurt like a son of a gun and I went boots over ass into the pond. My brothers had to fish me out, and then they had to hold me down so I wouldn't kill Ranger."

Her eyes widened. "That's a terrible story!"

"Yeah. I was lucky it wasn't a rifle or something. Mr. Misfire got grounded for a week by Mason, and we got the lecture of our lives on how firearms were to be properly handled before we put someone's eye out."

"Oh, dear," Clove said. "That tiny little scar does ugly you up a bit."

"Yeah," Archer said, "and take a look at this." He pulled his jeans down to the top of his underwear, where she could see a very shapely ridge of buns. Her throat dried out, and she stepped back.

"I'm looking," she said, "and everything appears to be in its place."

"But roll down the waistband a fraction."

Was he daring her? She darted a glance at him. He was staring ahead, waiting.

With trembling fingers, she pulled the waistband of his boxers down. His skin was smooth and medium brown, as if he'd spent most of his life outdoors without a shirt on. "There's nothing there," she said.

"There's a chicken-pox scar. I had one lingering, festering pox even after all the others were gone. My twin thought he was being funny and pounded it with a magazine. Mason then pounded his head."

"Gross."

"Brothers are gross. Don't you see it?"

She let the waistband snap back. "No." But he'd made her want to see more, and she had to resist temptation. Missy might have been a brave lockermate, but Clove had already thrown herself at him once.

"Huh." Archer craned to look. "I guess it is gone. I have a scar along my collarbone from where—"

She turned away from him. "It's not going to work, Archer. I will always see myself as the villain."

He was silent for a moment. "Will it help if I told you I like bad girls?"

She shook her head.

"All right." He passed her and put his hat on. "If I know one thing, it's that a woman who's made her mind up about something is fairly predictable. Like I said before, I don't want to go hunting where there's no game. Wise men pick the right spots for game if they want to eat." He went to the front door. "You do what you have to do to feel better, Clove."

And then he left.

She stared at the door, realizing that the pain in her chest was the price of her actions.

"I'M SORRY," Lucy said two days later. She and Archer stood in the barn, where he was tossing hay into stalls. "My sister doesn't know what she's thinking right now. She's been through a lot very quickly."

"You have nothing to apologize for." He kept his face averted from Lucy. It was just too painful to think about Clove. Never in his life had he experienced the type of pain he was feeling now. It never left him.

"But I do," Lucy said. "You know, I came here prepared not to like you. I felt that you'd taken advantage of my little sister. But then I met you, and I've spent time with your family, and you really are everything a family should be."

"We have our faults."

"I know. And so do we. That makes us who we are. But deep inside, this is a good family that's done its best. And so have Clove and I. The thing is, she's making decisions based on the past."

"Yeah?"

"Yes. She felt abandoned when our parents died. In her soul, she fully expects to be abandoned by everyone she loves. I've tried very hard to make certain she understood, when I married Robert, that she was part of our family. Of course, Robert's decision to leave is abandonment. But it's not her fault. Nor could she fix it."

"Why are you telling me all this?" He stopped pitching to fix her with a glare.

"Because you need to know. This is not Clove not wanting you. It's Clove not knowing how to get from one side to the other in a relationship."

He put the fork against a stall door. "Some things can't be fixed."

"Not by people," Lucy agreed. "Sometimes only by time."

"I don't have a lot of time," Archer said. "Those are my children your sister is growing. My psyche tells me I should be a father to them. I should take care of their mother during her pregnancy. I should see their first steps. These are not difficult concepts."

"No," Lucy said with a sigh, "but the two of you started off running before you were ready to crawl. Relationships take time. And healing."

"How much time are you suggesting she needs?" Archer asked.

"I can't say that. I don't know if it's five minutes or five years."

"Years!"

Lucy put her palm up. "Wait, Archer. I don't have the answers. I'm only suggesting that my marital difficulties and separation are hard on her. You'll probably be happier in the long term if you allow the dust to settle."

He sat on an old chair in the barn, thinking. "It runs counter to everything I believe."

"I know. You're from a family of fixers. Clove tried to be a fixer, and it blew up in her face. Then when she was feeling guilty, you tried to give her a house."

"That wasn't the smartest move, but Mason's pretty obtuse when it comes to family matters. We'd just been through Last's paternity suit. It all worked out, but the idea that one of the Jefferson children might not be part of the family really tore at him. Hence the overeager offer to put Clove in Mimi's house." He pulled at his jaw for a second. "To be honest, it was a bad idea all the way around."

"Because you wouldn't have wanted to live next door to your family?"

"No," Archer said. "Because Last said it really hurt Mimi's feelings that Mason wanted to buy her house and land."

"Oh, my," Lucy said. "Does she like your brother?"

"There's some history there. No one's really sure what the history is, but it's always there, threatening to bubble up and boil over."

"I see."

Archer sighed. "And now Mimi's accepted the offer, but she told Last she thought Mason was a sap not to propose the deal himself."

"Ah. Sounds unhappy."

"And now Mason's even more miserable. He knew that if Mimi said she was going, then she was, and there was nothing he could do about that. Clove just got caught in his misery."

"Did Mimi want Mason to talk her out of moving?"

"I don't know." Archer stood, tossing more hay into the stalls. "Mason gets so worried about the Family Problem, as he calls it, that he gets tunnel vision. Family first, everybody else last."

"That sounds like Clove," Lucy murmured. "I've relied on her for that over the years." She sat straight, looking at him. "You know, I have a part in this, too. I should have realized that Clove would take my marriage problems as hard as she did. I should have realized from her job choice alone that Clove was trying to maintain control over unpredictable circumstances. Always pushing the limits to prove she could rely upon herself. I haven't been there for her as much as she's been there for me," she said sadly.

"Hey, it's never too late," Archer said. "You're sitting here, aren't you? Bending my ear?"

"Yes," Lucy said, laughing.

"Well, then. You're 'there' for her. She's just got to settle down a bit and realize we're all here for her."

"It's going to be the first time in her life she's had that," Lucy told him. "I've paid more attention to the farm than to Robert or Clove."

"Well, then," Archer said, "we're all just worthless."

Lucy smiled. "No, we're not. We just need to get to know each other more."

"I like you, Lucy from Australia," Archer said honestly. "Even though I was pretty certain you were going to be a big burr under my saddle."

"I like you, too, Archer from Texas, and if you don't try to be too big of a fixer, my sister may come around once she gets through freaking out over the fact that she's going to have three little bassinets in her house."

"I really, really want to be in that house with her," Archer said wistfully. "My boys are going to need me to teach them how to be men."

Lucy looked down at her fingers for a second, and suddenly, Archer realized just how hard it was for her to be having this talk with him. "I'm sorry, Lucy, about…your family."

"It's life," she said slowly. "At least I'll have Clove's babies to love."

He blinked. If his plan for happiness worked out, Lucy would not have Clove's babies nearby to cuddle and love every time her fingers yearned for soft baby skin. Her nephews would be on the other side of the world. "It's chilly out here," he said gruffly. "You'd best go inside and get warm."

Lucy stood, nodding, pretending that he didn't see her wiping away a tear. "Hey, I just came by to let you know we're leaving tomorrow, in case you don't come by the house."

Archer dropped the pitchfork. "Tomorrow? Is that safe?"

"The doctor says it'll be safer for her to travel now than later."

He felt himself starting to shake. A wall of realization hit him like a giant tidal wave he couldn't move away from, threatening to sweep him under and crush him. "I…is there no chance she'll reconsider?"

Lucy shook her head. "For all the reasons we already discussed, this is what Clove feels she has to do."

Archer stood, jamming his hands in his pockets. "I'm destroyed," he said. "Broken-hearted. And for some reason, slightly jealous of you."

She nodded. "I know. I would be of you if Clove was staying here. I would be thrilled if she was comfortable enough to stay and make a home with you, but I would still be partially jealous of all you brothers getting to love my babies."

"And still I think you're awesome," Archer said. "Clove is lucky to have you for a big sister. If you decide you want us to come over there and give Robert a good ol' fashioned sense-whomping, just say the word and we'll load up."

Lucy smiled. "Thanks. Keep your passport updated. For now, I must admit to being the one who needed some sense-whomping. But Clove shouldn't have to pay for my errors."

Archer shrugged. "We all pay. It's family legal tender, emotional when spent and harmful when saved."

"Wow," Lucy said. "You're really deep. Did you ever think of becoming a writer?"

"Believe it or not," Archer said, "my writing is what brought me to this place. Now I can only hope to write a decent ending."

"Goodbye," Lucy said. "Good luck."

"Thanks," Archer said, his heart sunk so low he didn't think it would ever fill his chest again. "I can tell I'm going to need it."

Chapter Fifteen

One week later

Archer stared at the computer screen, realizing he had an email from Clove. He clicked on it swiftly.

Hi, TexasArcher. Actually it feels pretty silly to call you that now, since I know you. Anyway, I just wanted you to know that Lucy and I arrived home safely and everything is fine.

He swallowed, his fingers hovering over the keyboard. Finally, he wrote:

Hey AussieClove. It's fine to call me that since we might as well go back to who we were. Sometimes starting from the beginning is good. Glad your trip went well. Take care of yourself and drop me a line every once in a while.

His fingers trembled as he wrote the words. They were the hardest lines he'd ever written. He meant them, but mostly, he wanted to say, *Please come back. We could work things out.*

But he knew he couldn't type that. Shutting off the computer, he went to find Mason. "Mason," he said when he reached his brother's office, "we go about things south of sensible sometimes."

Mason sighed. "Is that a news flash?"

"No."

"So why are you bringing it to my attention now?" Mason looked over a pair of glasses at Archer.

Archer gaped at his brother. "When did you start wearing glasses?"

"Since I got old," Mason snapped. "And that's not a news flash, either."

Archer shrugged, taking a seat across from Mason's desk. "How's the finances?"

"We're good. We're in the black. In spite of my fears of losing some productivity, being down brothers, we're actually moving forward. Some of our investments panned out nicely. Adding Mimi's farm to our land is going to be a good thing. We need to consider doing some crops on her portion. Maybe a bed-and-breakfast outfit, if we raise Helga's salary and hire her some help. I have lots of ideas for profit that we should discuss later, after I finish going over these projections. With careful planning, our children will have a healthy ranch to run if they're interested."

"Our children?"

Mason colored up his neck. "I consider all children born into this family to be our children. Jefferson children. I am planning for their financial security."

"I see," Archer said. "There for a moment, I thought the new glasses were a symbol of some pending announcement. Since you're getting old and all."

His brother glared at him over the spectacles. "They're only for reading! The computer bothers my eyes."

"Ah." Very sensitive was Mason to his new eye issues.

"So, have you figured out a solution to your problem?" Mason demanded. "I'm not sure it's a good idea to let your woman just up and walk away like that."

Archer glared at his brother. "No more of a good idea than it is to let *your* woman up and walk away."

Mason glared back. "To whom are you referring?"

Whew. Of all the brothers, Mason was the nut least likely to crack. "Never mind. Hey, Last said Mimi's feelings were hurt over your offer on her land. Have you talked to her recently?"

"Hurt? Why would she be hurt? It was a perfectly good offer. Full price, in fact, which was sensible between friends. I'm sure the sheriff was pleased." He blinked at Archer. "I even gave her extra time to move out. I wouldn't want the baby or the sheriff to feel unsettled."

Archer shook his head, wondering if more was changing about Mason than his eyesight. "Last felt Mimi wished *you* had brought the offer. You two used to be pretty close."

Mason leaned back in his desk chair, pondering Archer's words. "I did not want to talk to Mimi about buying her house," he said, his tone measured and deliberate. "I did not want her to leave. But what is a man supposed to do if a woman decides to go?"

Archer stared at him, his heart beginning to race with frustration and realization.

Mason shrugged. "I decided to make it easy for her. That doesn't mean it was easy for *me*."

It took Archer a long time to process what

his brother was saying. When he did, when he realized that he and Mason were in the same boat, their sails turned into the winds of heartbreak, he simply left the room.

One week later

From: Clove
To: Archer

Hey, Archer—I'm starting to get a little potbelly! Well, it's more than a potbelly, it's more like a pot. Lucy says I exaggerate, but since I've always been trim, I feel like it's a pot. I'm thickening up sideways, too, which is kind of funny because I always thought my stomach would go forward. The other day I thought I felt something move. Like little butterflies moving up my stomach. Isn't that crazy? Talk to you soon, Clove

Archer bit his lip, ground his teeth and forced himself to think calmly.

Thanks for the note, Clove. Glad it's all going well. Archer

There. Mason would be proud of him for his coolheaded response. Lucy would be proud of him for allowing Clove time to fig-

ure out her world and how the babies and he
fit into it. He had no molars left from grinding his teeth in his sleep and soon he'd be
gumming his food like an old man, but hey,
if giving a woman space raised the odds in
his favor, then so be it.

Suddenly, another message popped up on
the screen from Clove. It had been only moments since he'd sent his to her. Greedily, he
opened it.

From: Clove
To: Archer

I have to tell you something strange. Remember when you kissed me, and I cli-
maxed? I think about that all the time. Being
pregnant makes me think about you that
way a lot. Though I may have made a giant
mess of how I handled things, I loved making love with you. That was the single most
wonderful experience in my life, besides
finding out I was pregnant. I wish I hadn't
kicked you first—it wasn't very ladylike and
wasn't an indicator of how I really feel about
you. Clove

Archer took that note in for a long time. "I
sense a thaw," he said. "This aloof-male stuff
is rough on me, but Lucy's right. It's work-

ing. So I won't say that I can't wait to be inside her again someday and that I can't wait to hold her and kiss her and sleep with her every night. Instead, I'll say something else."

Well, you sure got my attention. Don't worry about it. Archer

He looked at his typing. The words lay in the box, seeming stark and unemotional. "Oh, well," he said. "Sister knows best." He hit Send and turned the computer off.

CLOVE STARED at Archer's email, her mind racing. She'd sent him such an emotional note, which had been so difficult for her to write! It was borderline internet seduction! And he sounded so distant. As if what they'd shared hadn't meant as much to him.

Maybe it was different for a man.

"What?" Lucy asked, coming into the room.

Clove looked up from the screen. "Sorry. I must have mumbled to myself."

"You didn't mumble. You distinctly said, 'Maybe it was different for a man.'" Lucy looked at her. "Almost everything is different for a man. What's the topic?"

"Making love." Clove pointed to the email. "I poured my feelings out to Archer, and this is the reply I got back."

Lucy read it over. "Huh," she said, getting up and walking to the door. "Some men forget stuff easily," she said as she disappeared from the room.

"Forget easily!" Clove frowned. She hadn't forgotten him. But if he forgot her, then…that sort of proved what she'd thought all along. Archer wouldn't have wanted her, Clove Penmire, for the woman she was. Sort of like Last hadn't wanted Valentine after their one-night incident, which she had gathered from the bits Archer was willing to mention about the situation.

She missed the easygoing email relationship they'd once had. They'd met by accident when she'd written to ask a question about farming, as the Jeffersons had a website advertising stud fees and other services for their Union Junction ranch. Archer had responded with an answer, and they'd found common ground to socialize about. But that was in the past, she realized. "Okay, babies," she whispered, patting her stomach. "I guess it's just us now."

IN AGONY, ARCHER WAITED three weeks to hear from Clove. When he did not, he packed his duffel and checked his passport.

"What are you doing?" Last demanded as he walked into Archer's bedroom.

"Taking a trip," Archer answered.

"Going to hunt some kookaburras and kangaroos?"

"Something like that." He was in no mood to jest.

"Wish I had your focus," Last said.

"There were extenuating circumstances to your situation," Archer said, his voice grim as he tossed a belt into the duffel. "My relationship wouldn't have survived Marvella's interference, either. It may barely survive anyway, and it doesn't even have a heartbeat right now."

"Mason's gonna pop a coronary if you never come back. This place is going from Malfunction Junction to Malfunction Ghost Town."

"Mason has his own dilemmas to stew over."

"That's true. So now what?"

"So now," Archer said, zipping up his bag, "if she won't come to my world, I will go to hers."

Last's eyebrows rose into his hair. "Does Mason know?"

"No. You do. That's sufficient."

"Mason's going to be upset," Last said, "especially since you worked him over about Mimi."

"I did not," Archer said, "work him over about Mimi."

"He's superticked. He told the baby this morning that her mother was stubborn."

"The baby doesn't listen. Nanette only cares that she has her uncle Mason's undivided attention."

"Have you ever thought it strange," Last said slowly, "and I'm reaching here, I know, but just generally speaking, that Nanette sort of sometimes looks like Mason?"

Archer sighed, looking up from his passport. "Last, stop trying to make everything perfect. As you can clearly see, nothing in this family is ever going to be a fairy tale."

"You don't see it in her nose?"

"That tiny chubby piece of skin that won't take on a real shape until she's maybe fourteen? Or do you mean the apoplectic face she makes when she grunts in her diaper? That's when she resembles Mason." He tossed the paperwork into his carry-on. "Gotta go, dude. Wish me luck."

"Yes, but luck for what?" Last called after him.

"It doesn't matter," Archer yelled back as he started his truck. "I just need good luck for a change!"

"Here. Let me drive you to the airport," Last said with a sigh. "You may never come back and then the airport will keep your truck and it'll be a mess. Or you'll come back in two weeks and you'll owe so much in parking you'll have to mortgage the ranch."

"Thanks," Archer said with a grin.

"Never too much trouble among brothers," Last said. "At least not more than usual."

ARCHER HAD BEEN THINKING long and hard about his arrival in Australia. He'd pondered calling Clove and letting her know, and he'd ruminated on phoning Lucy.

In the end, he'd decided turnabout was fair play. Clove had nabbed him almost the moment she'd stepped in to Lonely Hearts Station, complete with her plan.

Today, he was the traveler with the plan. Stepping off the plane, he marveled at the change in the countryside. Tired from his long flight, he was energized by the people and the atmosphere.

A taxi took him and his lone duffel from the airport toward the address he gave the driver.

Two hours later, the taxi dropped him off at Penmire Farms—and a more dilapidated place he'd never seen. Archer's jaw sagged. Of course, he was in a different place and things might be a bit more casual here; not everyone had a Mason to crack the whip.

But this…something wasn't right. In fact, if he didn't know better, he'd think the roof of the white-painted farmhouse was sagging. Squinting, he decided maybe his eyes weren't adjusted from such a long flight—until he realized that the chimney was missing a few bricks.

A window of the two-story farmhouse appeared to be cracked. The fence, which held in a few mares and geldings, was ramshackle. Mason would kick every one of their tails if they ever let the fence at Malfunction Junction get in that shape. And the flower beds that first Tex their brother and then Last so carefully cultivated were lacking here.

He took a deep breath. Okay, it couldn't be that bad. Most of the problems, hopefully, were cosmetic. The livestock and horses, it appeared, were fed and recently brushed.

Yet the farm really did have a run-down appearance. The bushes were tall and the grasses around the wide porch blew in the slight breeze. Perhaps this casual approach to the farm had begun when Robert left. Archer tugged at his hat, thinking. Clove had been very desperate and upset about Robert leaving her sister. Possibly she had known that two women couldn't run this place without a man. Men, actually. It would take a dozen men to whip this place into shape.

And he was willing to bet his little Aussie-Clove didn't know a dozen men. Sighing, he decided there was no reason to delay the shock of his arrival. He went to the wide, white porch and rang the doorbell.

Clove answered the door, her eyes widening when she saw him. "Archer!"

"In the flesh. Returning the favor, as it were."

She stared at him, not glad but not shocked, it seemed, for him to be on her porch.

"Are you surprised?"

"That you're here, yes. But that you'd come here, not really." She looked up at him. "I'm not making sense."

"It's okay," he said. "I understand. None of it does."

She stepped away from the door so he could come inside. He did, his gaze instantly moving around the hallway, noting that, while it was clean, the run-down conditions extended to the house as well.

Clove looked embarrassed. Mortified. He sighed. No point in avoiding it. "So. I guess you and Lucy have been trying to manage by yourselves for a long while. And now that you're pregnant, she's trying to manage a lot more by herself."

She didn't reply.

"Why didn't you tell me?" he asked.

"Why should I?"

"I don't know. So I could help you?"

"You didn't want to come here," she reminded him. "What was I going to say? My sister and I are over our heads in this deal, and Robert hates the farm? We're five inches away from having to give up the one thing we've ever had, that was left to us by the only parents we ever knew?"

He was silent, thinking.

"Archer, this is the reason I knew it wouldn't work between us," she said softly. "You wanted me to stay there, live in the house your brother bought for me, and be happy. But you didn't know me. Not where I came from, not how I live. Not what Lucy and I struggle for, which shapes the person I am. You just wanted me to fit into your life. And while I appreciated everything you wanted to do, it would never have worked because you didn't know *me*. Settling onto your ranch would have been as big a lie as a woman putting on lots of makeup and curling her hair and acting sexy to catch a man." She met his gaze with pain-filled honesty. "Deceit is no foundation for marriage." Her shrug showed her fatigue.

"Is Robert still…"

"Gone? Yes. It's just Lucy and me."

"How are you feeling?"

"Large, strangely enough." She smiled a little. "I suppose it's normal with three. The doctor says everything is progressing and that it's natural to be tired."

"I wish you had told me that you needed help, Clove," Archer said.

"Archer, I wanted many things from you, but help was not one of them. Penmire Farms may not seem like much to you, but it means everything to us."

Chapter Sixteen

Archer looked at her. After a moment, Clove took his hand. "I'm really glad you're here," she finally said. "Welcome to Australia."

Slowly, he pulled his hand away from hers. She lowered her gaze, recognizing distance.

"Thank you," he said simply. "I made a reservation at a hotel in the city."

"That's thirty minutes away, at least," she said, surprised. "Why don't you stay here?"

"With two unattached women? It doesn't seem appropriate."

"No one cares here, Archer. We're too far out in the country."

"I care."

Her eyes went wide. "You didn't at your ranch."

He looked at her, and then she realized what he was trying to say. He'd still been romancing her when they were at the bungalow in Malfunction Junction.

Now romance was not on his mind. She blushed, her feelings hurt in some way she couldn't define. "Can I offer you some food? Something to drink? I'm sure you'd like something after your flight."

"I'd like something cold if you have it. But I'm not particular. Whatever's easy."

She brought him a beer, and he took it gratefully. "Thanks."

Awkwardly, she moved to the patio. "Join me outside. It's nice out here."

He got up, following her outside. Sitting, she watched him look over the pasture that served as their backyard.

"So, how long has it been this way?"

"Since our parents died. We try, we really do, Archer. Lucy and I should probably give up, but the farm is ours. It just seems that the more we do, the farther we slide back."

"I can appreciate that feeling. It's ranch life." Still, he gazed out at the paddock, and she could feel him measuring the work, the money, the effort it would take to get the place in decent shape.

"You're always a surprise," he said finally.

"How is Tonk, by the way?"

He grimaced. "Still keeping me off guard, too. I'm trying to teach her cutting, and seventy-five percent of the time she does everything perfectly. Exactly the way she should. The other twenty-five percent of the time, she's got a mind of her own. We differ on approach, and she's stubborn."

"You'll eventually wear her out of that last twenty-five percent. She knows who's boss. Not that she likes it."

"It's a very slow process."

Clove smiled. "See that Hanoverian out there? Fifteen-point-three hands. I got her when she was just a spindly, argumentative lass. With some love and lots of attention, and teeth grinding on my part, we worked out a training schedule. Go try her out."

"Right now?"

"Sure. Jumper saddle's in the barn. You can try the cross-pole oxer if you're in the mood. If not, the cavaletti will give you a warm-up. Her name's Encino."

"It'll be good to use the muscles I've been sitting on for twenty-four hours," he said. "I know one thing—if I'd known a flight could last so long, I would never have let you return here."

She watched him walk toward the barn. If he didn't want her flying pregnant, then he wasn't expecting to try to talk her into going back to Texas. Her heart folded up like weary bird's wings. Not that it was unexpected. She supposed they'd made their peace with what could, and could not, be between them.

And yet, something inside her must have wistfully been hoping for the magic they'd once felt to steal back over them. The love-making had been fun and hot and exciting—they'd been very interested in each other then.

She went inside to brush her hair. The mirror gave away the toll her pregnancy was taking on her. She didn't want to tell Archer that the doctor had said she'd probably be completely bedridden within a month.

If she told him, he'd be obliged to stay. She spritzed on some light perfume and used concealer on the dark circles under her eyes.

"Why am I doing this?" she asked her reflection.

Because you liked him from the moment he first touched you. Maybe the moment you watched him ride his spotted Appaloosa into the barn. And you fell for him when he made love to you.

"And I've been kidding myself that my heart is not going to be very, very broken," she whispered. With a sigh, she put away her things and went back out to stand on the patio.

Archer had Encino saddled and was now walking her in a large circle to warm her up. In a few moments, he let her slowly navigate the cavelletis. She enjoyed watching him work the horse. One thing he would find, she thought proudly, was that her horse training was perfect. The saddle she used was kept repaired and clean, as was Encino's stall. The horses were cared for like babies, and she was proud of how well she trained them.

A few minutes later, he was soaring over the cross-pole oxer, with Encino showing her best jumps. Archer moved well, and Encino made it look like magic, landing on the ground lightly, almost prancing with the joy of being exercised again since Clove could not do it.

After another jump, he rode up to the patio. "Nice," he said. "You trained her?"

She nodded.

He patted the horse's neck. "I could never get Tonk to do all that."

"Encino's sweet. Perfectly mannered, a technical learner. But you haven't had Tonk long enough to work out all the kinks. Be patient. Give her time."

His eyes lit on Clove suddenly, his gaze

dark with intensity. "I am," he said, "but she's enough to try a saint."

Clove lowered her gaze, knowing that he was talking about her.

"I'm going to jump Encino once or twice more because she seems eager. Then I'll give her a hose-down in the shower I saw in the barn."

"Thank you." Clove turned away, heading inside and shutting the patio door behind her. Her heart pounded and her blood felt on fire. That look made her so hopeful.

Maybe, in spite of everything, he did care about her.

Then again, he hadn't replied with much interest to her attempt to tell him by email how much she'd enjoyed making love with him. He was here, but maybe he'd come here for his children.

For a girl who'd learned that life had tough lessons, it was very hard to hang on to the fairy tale.

It was time to find out.

WHEN ARCHER WALKED BACK inside, Clove simply said, "I'm glad you're here."

He looked at her. "Thank you."

"So you like my horse."

"She's a good jumper. I presume you show her."

"When I have time. We don't do a lot. I get offers on her when I do, but I'm not selling her. I'm sure you're wondering why, considering the shape our farm is in."

"No." He shook his head. "Once you've put time and effort into a horse, you weigh the options of starting over versus keeping what you've got."

She took a deep breath. "I'd like to talk to you about the option of starting over or keeping what we've got."

He sat down across from her, his fingers drumming on the lace tablecloth of the small patio furniture. "I'm listening."

"I figure," she said slowly, "that we're at either an impasse or a crossroads."

"Probably."

"I'd like to call it a crossroads and pull out a new map."

"Go on."

"I'm wondering if we should choose the option of starting over."

He pushed his hat back. "And what's wrong with keeping what we've got?"

Her stomach tucked a little. He didn't seem open to changing their current unstable relationship. Or arrangement. What was it, anyway? "Well, as far as I can see, there's nothing essentially wrong with what we've got, but I think it could be better if we start over. That is, go back to the beginning."

"When we were only writing each other? That doesn't work very well for me."

"No, I meant, back to the beginning when we…when, you know, we had our encounter."

He blinked. "Sexually speaking?"

She forced herself to look into his eyes and say, "Yes. Only this time, I won't kick you."

"Thank heaven for small favors."

Was he laughing at her? Clove felt she'd met him halfway, and maybe he should do a little more than be the stony, questioning rock across the table—if he was interested in their…whatever it was.

"So, are you asking me to make love to you?"

"I'm asking, actually I'm suggesting, that we go back to what we liked about each other, before everything else got us confused."

His gaze narrowed on her. "Your theory is that our best communication is in bed."

"Or a truck. I liked that, actually. It was all very romantic when we were under the stars, before everything got so complicated."

"So we're going to turn the clock back, start over, and rediscover who we might have been together."

"I…it's crossed my mind."

He nodded. "I see."

They stared at each other for a long moment, and Clove thought the silence was the loudest scream she'd ever heard. Or maybe that was her blood pounding in her ears.

"No," Archer said.

She felt herself go light-headed. "No?"

"It doesn't make sense. You'll hop out of bed after we're through and say, 'Oh, that didn't fix it after all. It's just going to be me and my sister and my babies, toughing it out like Scarlett O'Hara.' Well, I didn't come all the way over to try to communicate with you that way. We need to talk, is what I think. And I think we need to talk about how we're going to take care of these babies."

There was nothing for her to say to that. Lowering her eyelids, she waited for him to speak.

When she felt his finger take her chin up, she made herself look at him.

"Okay," he said softly. "I hurt your feelings and that's the last thing I meant to do. Maybe I'm not listening."

She pulled away from his finger, but kept her gaze on him. "Do you remember when I told you that, due to Tonk's posture, I could tell she didn't like you? That she didn't like the fact that you were trying to boss her?"

"Yes." He sat back in his chair.

"That may be your nature," she said carefully. "In trying to order the chaos in your life, you try to rule it. Only, it doesn't really work that well with horses. Or with women."

"So you're saying I'm bossing and not listening."

"It would be better if we had a fresh start, rather than trying to work around our fears. You've met my family and seen my home. I've met your family and seen your home. We know a lot about each other's worlds. We're at a point where we ought to be able to go forward, together. Listening to each other."

"I think I like it," he said. "And I am listening."

She smiled. "Thank you."

"Now let me be sure I have this right. As part of our new listening exercise, you want me to take you back into that bedroom and make love to you."

"Our ears would probably be more receptive to messages from each other after that."

"No kidding," he said. "I have never heard of sex as a hearing aid, but I am a man. I can be open to new ideas. I'm not afraid of alternative methods."

This felt better. They were returning to the easy banter they'd shared in the beginning. Clove felt herself relaxing.

"But I can't do it," Archer said. "And I'm not just being stubborn."

She tensed again. "Then why not?"

"Because…I'm skeptical. Afraid, even, to use a word I don't use often."

"Afraid? Of what? I thought we covered all that."

"I am afraid," he said pointedly, "of hurting you."

"Because of the babies?"

"Precisely." He crossed his arms over his chest. "So while your theory of intimacy as an emotional navigational device appeals to my, um, baser instincts, my intelligence tells me that it's a bad idea."

"You can't hurt me," she said, "unless we did something on the kinky side and that's unlikely today. You've been flying for many hours, and I know you're worn-out—"

"I'm not *that* worn-out," he said. "Do you have your doctor's permission to be intimate?

Because it's not an option unless I know the doctor thinks it's fine. And even then, I'd probably worry that the doctor was a quack, or that he wasn't familiar with triplet cases, or—"

"I talked to Dr. Fern, your favorite doctor," Clove interrupted. "She called here to check on me."

He sighed. "Ever thorough is our Dr. Edna Fern. Still a hideous name, though." He perked up. "Why were you discussing sex with Dr. Fern?"

She laughed at his glower. "In case the topic came up."

"And when would it come up, with me in the States and you here?"

"You see, if we spent more time communicating and being intimate, you wouldn't ask such silly questions," Clove told him. "Dr. Fern told me you were flying over."

"She did?"

"Yes, she did. She didn't know the time, and I thought you'd be here tonight, so you arrived too early for me to have the wonderful cake baked I'd planned. See the mix on the drainboard?"

He glanced away for a second to eye the

laid-out utensils and cake preparations with some regret. "Who told her?"

"Last. He was calling to check on something for Valentine. Or maybe it was Mimi. Anyway, that's how fast the news travels."

"This feels very much like a setup."

She smiled. "Conspiracy theory?"

"I'm not sure who would be conspiring with whom."

"Anyway, Dr. Fern said you probably have about a month to think it over. That coincides with what my OB-GYN here says, too."

"What happens in a month?"

"I'll probably go to bed for the duration."

"Bed!"

She laughed at his expression. "Doesn't sound like much fun, but it is a fact. I'm supposed to keep these babies in here as long as possible for optimum health."

"Then we ought not jolt them about," Archer said.

"I believe you are afraid, and that's just not romantic. I've heard about father fear before. Do you know that men sometimes are afraid the baby will grab their—"

He jumped to his feet. "Clove, I am a rancher and a cowboy, but there's only so much information I can handle. If we're going to make love, then let's break out the…uh, I need to go to the store."

"For what?"

"Chocolates. No champagne for you, obviously. But maybe some body paint and Perrier. Things to romance you with properly, since I really didn't the first time. Roses. Some shrimp. Aren't we supposed to throw shrimp on the barbie in this part of the world?"

"It sounds good to me, but since I can tell you're anxious, and I'm afraid you'll disappear from sight if I let you out the door, I'm going to pull a Missy Tunstine here and lay one on you. How about you just come in here," she said sweetly, "and let me strip off your boxers before you strip a gear? I've never seen a man so worried."

"I wasn't like this before," he said, allowing her to lead him into the bedroom. "I felt in control before."

"Even though I'd kicked you?" She closed the door and began unbuttoning his shirt.

"Well, that was unexpected, but worth it in the end." He stopped her fingers, kissing them one by one. "Clove, I am afraid I'll hurt you or the babies."

"Well, let's try out the doctor's opinion

first. If I hurt you, you can just say, 'Ouch!' All right?"

"Okay," he said as she smoothly removed his shirt. "If you hurt me, I'll just say ouch—wait a minute! Clove, hang on. This doesn't seem like a good idea."

He sat on the bed, a picture of depression.

She looked at him. Then she dropped her dress.

"Well, I *was* worried, but I believe we can work around it," he said, springing up off the bed to pull her down on it with him. "Come here, you," he said. "I am going to kiss you for a month of Sundays."

She pulled at him, tugging him closer, and they rolled over in the bed so that she was on top. His hands slid into her panties, then quickly reached to unsnap her bra. She tugged off his jeans, and they went flying.

"You make me crazy," he said, kissing her face and her eyelids.

"You make me crazier," she said, "and I like it. All those roles of responsibility wear me out. I want you to be the one thing in my life that doesn't demand me to be anything but sexy."

"Sexy as hell," he said on a growl, tearing off her panties. "If you want the bottom, call it, because I'm all good with you on top and I'm ready for duty."

"Shh," she told him. "Cowboy, it's my turn to please you."

Ever so slowly, she slid onto his erection.

"Ah, God," he said, "*thank* you for this woman."

She started to move on him.

His eyes closed for an instant. "I'm dying, of pleasure I waited too long to have."

She moaned, thinking that she'd waited all her life to feel this wonderful. He gently moved her onto her back, and she gazed up at him. "I like your method of communication," he said. "I like it so well I'm hearing what you're thinking."

That made her giggle, which he took as permission that all was well. He moved faster inside her, and the pressure built inside her to where she could only stare into his eyes. The communication they were sharing no longer had anything to do with words, just feelings.

She cried out with pleasure, and he held her tight. When she felt him climax, too, somehow she felt the spasms start all over again.

They lay against each other, spent for a few moments, before he rolled her to lay against his chest as he lay on his back.

"You really like me," she said.

For reply, he gave her a light spank on her bare bottom. "Listen, I'm usually a long-distance runner," he said.

"And I'm usually...oh, I'm usually nothing at all because you're the only man who's loved me." She popped her head up to look down at him. "So. I guess you shared too much."

"Sorry. I meant I'd do better next time."

"Yeah? And who was complaining?"

He chuckled. "Okay. I'm trying to be overly impressive."

"And maybe I like you just the way you are."

"Funny," he said. "I used to think that about you."

"And now?"

"Now I—"

"Yoo-hoo!" Lucy called. "I'm home!"

They tossed the covers up over their chests, lying with little more than their eyes peeking out over the comforter.

"Clove?" Lucy said, coming into the bedroom. "Oh," she said. "Hello, Archer. I see you made it in good shape."

"Hi, Lucy."

"No jet lag, I guess?" Lucy called as she left the room, laughing.

He rolled his head to look at her. "Your sister thinks I'm after your body."

"And my sister better be right," Clove said, getting out of bed to pull on her clothes.

"So now what?" Archer asked, grabbing his clothes, too.

"What what?" Clove replied.

"Now that we're communicating better, when do we get married?"

She turned to look at him. "Married?"

"Yeah. You know. What two people do, sometimes at an altar with a priest before smushing cake on each other's faces?"

"Eww," Clove said. "I'll be forgoing that."

"Well, I'd be careful with the cake," Archer said.

"I think we should talk some more."

"Okay," he said, pulling her backward onto the bed and tugging at her dress. "I *like* the way you converse."

Gently, she moved his hands and got up from the bed. "I mean," she said, worried now, "that we should talk more. I don't see having a two-continent marriage."

"I don't, either."

"Well," Clove said, "then we have to talk.

Real talk. There's Lucy to consider. And this farm. I just can't pick up and leave her to everything with Robert gone. You know how much trouble it is at your place now that your brothers have found wives and left things shorthanded. It's no different for me than for you."

"That's true," Archer said. "This is stickier than I thought it would be. We do need to talk more. But can we talk with you in this bed? I swear I think better when you're naked."

"No," she said. "Right now, I think we'd better leave our clothes on."

He grabbed her, kissing her deeply. "You still make me crazy," he said. "But that's a bonus in your favor, I've come to believe."

"Good," she said, "because there may be bad news looming."

"I figured," he said, following her out of the bedroom.

Chapter Seventeen

"So how did the meeting with Robert go?" Clove asked her sister as they joined Lucy in the kitchen.

Archer listened with interest, perching himself on a bar stool and watching as Lucy and Clove set about preparing the cake.

"It went as well as can be expected when two people realize they can't make something work, in spite of their best efforts."

Archer didn't like the sound of that. He looked at the sandwich and chips Clove put in front of him with appreciation but not much appetite.

"I am so sorry," Clove told her sister. "I wish there was something I could do."

"There's not." Lucy sighed and opened the mix while Clove greased and floured the pans. "He doesn't understand the business here and has lost interest in trying."

"Maybe…we should just sell out," Clove

said, her voice sounding a tad broken to Archer's ears. "I know we said we'd keep our parents' farm forever, but it is true that Robert feels out of his element here, and maybe a promise to our parents isn't worth losing your marriage." She stopped flouring to look at her sister. "I'm trying to picture myself in your shoes. If it was my marriage in danger, I would probably go with my husband."

Archer perked up. That sounded promising.

"I don't think that would help at this point," Lucy said. "Robert wants to live in the city, and I understand that, but he also says that he doesn't want me to give up my family inheritance. That he would feel like he forced me to do it. He says we should accept that our lives are too different."

"Oh dear," Clove said.

Oh dear was right. Archer munched his sandwich, using Lucy's conversation to analyze his and Clove's dilemma. It wasn't hard to see Robert's point. He'd feel the same way, probably.

Yet, his stubborn head wouldn't allow him to accept that Clove and he might not be able to "communicate" their way to marital and familial happiness. Of course, he and Clove were expecting children—many children all at once—and that gave him extra impetus to solve the problem.

He drummed his fingers, thinking about Mason always harping about the Family Problem. There was a lot involved with making things work out between two people, let alone twelve. It made Archer appreciate why Mason always had a crab in his attitude. "This is a really nice farm," he said.

The women stared at him. Clove's eyes were huge in her face as she hesitated in her pan preparation. "It's in disrepair," she said.

"And I can see where that would be frustrating to a man who wasn't born to rural life. But the fact is, it's a nice farm. If I were a buyer, I would buy this place in a second."

"Are you suggesting we sell?" Clove asked.

"I'm not suggesting anything. I'm merely eating this sandwich and dying for that cake," Archer said.

She looked at him uncertainly. Lucy watched him, too, and he saw the pain in her eyes. She really did not want to lose her husband. "So, how much is this about the baby problem and how much is it about feeling lost about the farm?"

"I would call it an even split, one feeding on the other. When you can't make anything work—that's what Robert said—you realize you might better pack it in."

"Jeez," he said, "I'm sorry."

Clove turned away, but not before he saw her glance at her sister in distress. Sighing, he eyed the tea glass Lucy set in front of him, feeling doleful.

He sighed. "I guess there would be no reason to wonder if you might have been better off with just the two of you in the house, in order to be a really intimate, married couple."

Lucy gasped. Clove stared at him, her expression looking as if it might wilt to tears any second.

"I'm only saying that married people could use a little space to grow one on one," he said hastily. "Please, please don't cry. I really don't know what I'm talking about. I was sort of theorizing. At our ranch, we call it talking out of our as—uh, hat. Talking out of turn. I should just sit here and eat if I know what's best for me."

They focused on him as his rambling wound down. Oh, boy. He'd stirred up a hornet's nest, he could tell. Clove was thinking a thought that had clearly never occurred to her before, and Lucy was wondering if she had put Robert second or maybe third in her marriage. It was time to take his own advice and skip the third-wheel routine. "Hey, I think I'll go check on Encino," he said, hurriedly snatching up his plate and glass to take with him. "I'm very good at chatting with mares, so don't even think about me. No worries, mate."

He sidled out the door.

Clove looked at Lucy. "As much as I want to bean him, I think he may have hit on something."

Lucy shook her head, putting the cake in the oven. "What difference would it make now?"

"I don't know. Maybe none. But maybe it's worth suggesting to Robert that Texas is starting to look good to me as a residence."

"Would you go?" Lucy was astonished.

"I'm beginning to look at the reality that it may be best for all concerned," Clove said. "The babies, Robert, you—"

"Archer."

"And Archer." Clove's heart did a funny flip when she said his name.

Lucy sat on the stool Archer had vacated. "How do you really feel about that cowboy?"

"Like he just spelled something out to me that I didn't want to see. He does a lot of spelling, that cowboy, and it's annoying." She took a deep breath. "But when I get past being annoyed, sometimes I think he's got deep thoughts. If I'd been Robert, I don't think I'd want to live here with my wife's sister and her three newborns."

"Robert was happy for you," Lucy said quickly. "As am I."

"Of course," Clove said, "I know you are. But if he was already feeling overwhelmed by the ranch, if he already felt left out because of the relationship between you and I, if he knew that the newborns would come first with you since you wanted children so badly…where did that leave him? I sort of see Archer's point. And, not to mention, I was always here. It's not that the two of you ever felt comfortable walking around nude, or… having private moments in front of the TV."

"Well," Lucy said, "I walked in on you today, so we're even now." She smiled a little sadly. "I want you to be happy. Don't think about what went wrong with Robert and I. There was just too much, I think. Now your focus should be on you and your new family. Trust me, Clove, you should make this work—if you want it."

"It was not my intention to fall in love with

Archer." Clove looked at her sister. "The funny thing was, I did."

"Well, he's just so likable. You know? He's easygoing. He's hunky. He's loyal. He's stubborn. He likes you for you. Where in there is the downside?" Lucy asked. "I know none of that can make you love him if you don't feel all the right emotions. But if you do, you might think twice about letting him board a plane back to America without you."

Clove nodded.

"Well, this cake will be done soon enough," Lucy said. "I'll bring you two out a piece. In the meantime, why don't you go talk to him."

"I wouldn't know where to start. My mind is racing. I'm happy, but I'm afraid. I'm excited, but I'm nervous."

Lucy laughed. "That sounds like love."

"Yes, but what if we can't make it work? What if, in our best efforts, we can't figure out a way to bond our lives together?"

"Well," Lucy said, "there's always email."

CLOVE WALKED into the barn slowly, thinking about her situation. About Archer. How she felt about him. And the babies.

She had to make a decision. Futures were

at stake—everyone's—and they were all at the most important moment of their lives.

"Archer?" she said.

"Yeah?" He poked his head up over Encino's stall.

"What are you doing?"

"Brushing this horse. I like her. Brushing and currying relaxes me. Hoof picking, not so much, but I like it, too."

"Can we talk?"

"Sure. Sorry, Encino. More later."

He came out of the stall, closing it behind him. "That's a great horse. You did an awesome job with her. I'm crazy about Tonk, but she'd just as soon give me a hoof as look at me. Encino's sweet. She knows her manners."

"You were imposing yourself on Tonk because she was yours. You're relaxed and spoiling Encino, so she's responding. But I will admit that Encino has been a love to train."

"I'll bet. When I get home, Tonk and I are going to start off on a new foot. Or hoof."

She didn't know how to take his comment about returning home. "Just remember, you haven't had her as long as I've had Encino. Patience is key."

"You learned a lot about horses being at Penmire Farms, didn't you?"

She sat on a bench that was in the breezeway. "When it's all you've got, you tend to learn it, fast, and try to do it the best you can. I did stunt work to help pay the expenses, but as you can see, Lucy and I didn't do as well as we could have if given more time. When we were left Penmire, it was under some debt our adoptive parents had taken on, fully expecting that they'd be around to use the equipment they'd purchased." Her eyes grew dark with remembering. "They had wonderful plans for Penmire." She looked at Archer. "Once upon a time, it really was a premier place for fine horses. People came first to Penmire when they were looking for the best prospects."

"I'm sorry, Clove."

"It's all right. Thank you, though." She smiled at him. "You know that running a ranch is a make-or-break business. And we were two young girls, not knowing what we should have known about money. About life. About business. We made mistakes."

"Mistakes can be made even by pros. We may butt heads with Mason, he may be tight as a tick and hard as a stone, but he can run the business of the ranch. He does keep it successful. They say that family money generally only lasts two generations. I believe that if Mason weren't in charge of our ranch, we'd not see financial wellness past this generation. Not to mention that the eleven of us make mistakes all the time that don't help our financial status.

"So don't take it too hard, Clove. And I'd say the same thing to Robert, if I knew him. People think running a ranch is all pretty horses and fields of waving grain. It's *ass*-busting. And most of the time, heartbreaking, unless the right things happen."

"Back to those mistakes you mentioned—"

"You're not one of them," he interrupted swiftly.

"Thank you." She ducked her head, then raised her chin to look into his eyes. "I've been thinking about us."

"You have?" He sat down beside her. Together they looked out the breezeway at the beautiful evening, before he turned her face to his. "I'm almost afraid to ask."

"I need to be more aware of the effects of my decisions. I changed your life when I came to Texas, and I was only thinking about myself."

"You had a lot on your mind," Archer said. "Clove, you've been in a difficult situation."

"Yes, but it can get a lot more difficult if I don't stop being so stubborn."

"I am used to stubborn women. You and Tonk. Didn't you tell me to exercise my patience with Tonk because I didn't know her that well? I am willing to do the same with you."

She tried to hold back a small smile but couldn't. His eyes were so warm and deep that it was like looking into dark, welcoming pools. "I may require lots of patience if I am not too emotionally bankrupt the first generation."

"I'm pretty tough," he said. "I think I can handle one little Aussie gal."

"And three babies."

"And three babies."

"So I'm coming to Texas if you'll still have me."

He pulled his hand away from her chin. "I don't think that's the best idea."

"Why?"

"Because you'll always miss your sister. And she's going to be alone now," Archer said.

"It is true…but I don't know what else to

do. I am trying to make responsible decisions! What are you suggesting?" She was almost afraid to ask.

"I don't know yet. It's going to take some pondering." He pulled her up into his lap. "You can't run this farm in the condition you'll be in soon. Bedridden and wearing a nightie. My favorite doctor's order."

"Yes, but," she said, trying not to think about the delicious tickling he was making her feel inside, "that means Lucy won't have anyone to help her. You know, we really are going to have to sell this place."

"I am afraid you're right," he said, his tone reluctant. "It's certainly something you and your sister will have to talk over, but it doesn't look good, I have to be honest."

"This is all my fault," she said, feeling sick.

"This is not all your fault, Clove. We are not a product of our family's mistakes. We are affected by them, but we don't have to let angst rule our lives. Besides, I liked you. I let you jump me. That should tell you that, from the start, I was all over you like a stallion on a filly."

"You were not," she said, laughing. "You didn't even like me. I had to have the Never

Lonely Cut-n-Gurls give me the Revenge of the Nerdy Girl treatment."

"And if you ever do that again, I'll…shave my head and see how you like that," he said, back to nuzzling her neck.

"I would miss your hair for certain."

"And I think you're beautiful just the way you are. When I remember you coming into that barn, with all your scared, cute little nerves and saying, 'Do you want to take me to dinner?' in that tiny little voice of yours, I just get chills."

"Fever?"

"No. Desire." He held her tight, letting his hands start to roam. "Did you ever watch *Grease?*"

"What good Aussie hasn't?" she said, giggling as his hands got more playful.

"My chills are multiplying," he sang.

"You are so silly," she said. "You make me laugh, and I so need that."

"But I'm not being funny," he said. "I'm crazy about you, girl. Let's play alternative personalities. You be Olivia Newton-John from Down Under and I'll be John Travolta from the States."

She slapped lightly at his hands, which were getting too bold. "Goody Olivia or

Black Spandex Olivia? Gosh, I couldn't fit into spandex now if I wanted to."

"Depends on how you want me. Letterman John or Greasy John? I'll let you lead the fantasy."

"Well—" She was just about to answer, when she heard Lucy calling.

"Here I am," Clove called, going to stand in the breezeway. One look at Lucy's face told her something had gone terribly wrong. "What is it?" she asked, heading for her sister. Archer followed close behind.

"Your brother called," Lucy hurriedly told Archer. "Last says Mason's had a tractor accident!"

Chapter Eighteen

"I've got to get home," Archer said after calling the ranch and getting Bandera on the phone. "All hell's going to break loose with Mason down. It appears to be a serious injury, and they've just taken him to the hospital."

He didn't say everything that Bandera told him. One glance at Clove's pretty face, all swelled up with worry and pinched between her eyebrows, told him that less info was a good thing.

Grabbing his duffel and checking for his passport, he said, "I'll stay in town at the hotel where I made reservations. That way I'll be closer to the airport for the earliest flight I can catch."

"I forgot that you'd made reservations," Clove said.

He wasn't really paying attention. "Yeah."

"I wish the cake was finished," Lucy said, "so I could send you off with a piece of it."

"It's all right," Archer said absently, glancing around the room to make certain he had everything. "Okay, you two girls take care of each other, all right?" He gave Lucy a brief hug and Clove a fast kiss on the cheek.

"Let me drive you to the hotel," Lucy said.

"No, thanks. I called the same driver who brought me out here. He'd given me a card in case I needed more transportation. Luckily, he wasn't twenty minutes away from here." He looked at Clove, whose face still seemed fragile with concern. "Take care of yourself," he said. "I'll call soon."

"All right," she replied faintly.

A horn honked outside. "That's my ride. I wish twenty-four hours didn't lay between me and my ranch," he said, worried out of his mind. He was pretty certain Bandera might have parsed some details to keep him from going loco. "Bye," he said, with one last quick kiss for Clove as he ran out the door.

His heart was in his stomach. Mason. If anything serious happened to Mason, they were all going to be in a pot of very hot water.

Mason had been holding their family together for a long time.

"Wow," Lucy said when Archer had swept out the door. "That's a man in a hurry."

"You've been to the ranch," Clove said. "It's just as much to them as Penmire is to us."

"Yeah." Lucy sank onto the sofa, her gaze on her sister.

Clove shook her head, sitting down across from her, thinking that the smell of baking cake would forever be associated with Archer walking out of her life.

"He'll be back," Lucy said.

But Clove knew it was quite far to be apart. Difficult conditions. No real emotional cement between them. Just the babies. "I'm... not so certain."

"He'll call."

Clove's stomach shrank at the thought that it might be a long time before she heard Archer's voice. "I hope so."

"You could go there," Lucy said.

"Not now," Clove replied. "I'm not sure the doctor would clear it. Besides which, Archer as much as said he didn't want me at the ranch."

"Why?"

"Because of everything here."

"Oh." Lucy looked at Clove. "Me."

"And our farm."

"I see." Lucy looked pensive. "He didn't want me to be in Australia by myself."

"He felt like it would be hard on us if…that were to happen. That I would be unhappy if you were alone." Clove was very worried, and she couldn't deny that she wished she could have gone with Archer. "I'd forgotten he'd made reservations to stay in a hotel here. You know, we really didn't have time to grow together as a couple."

"It's unfortunate timing," Lucy agreed. "I should have vacated the premises."

"Don't say that!" Clove shook her head. "No one knew this would happen. And Archer knew you and I lived together. Goodness, when we were in their bungalow, his brothers weren't shy about hanging around us. And the night we had dinner at the ranch, you stayed up there practically all night."

"Now, that was fun," Lucy said. "You don't know this, but Last can balance a beer bottle on his nose."

"Oh, my." Clove rolled her eyes. "Archer is going to be so worried until he gets back to that ranch."

"Yes." Lucy patted her hand. "I'm sorry your visit got cut short."

"We seem doomed to have short bursts of

acquaintance. Almost like email—very abbreviated. And I thought we could go back to the beginning, to when the sparks first flew and we were getting to know each other, but you can never really start over, I guess." Clove went to pull the cake out of the oven as the buzzer went off. The cake, she saw, was perfect. "Once again, the family recipe is perfection. If only relationships were as easy to fix!"

"Tell me about it," Lucy said.

MIMI WAS SITTING in Mason's hospital room when Archer got there two days later. Her eyes were huge as she came to hug Archer. "You look tired," she said.

"You look tired, too. How is the old hoss?" He looked at his brother. Mason's eyes were closed, and he had various tubes hanging out of him.

"He's out of ICU, and that's a good thing. They care-flighted him to the hospital or he probably would have died."

Archer's stomach contracted, feeling as if he'd been delivered a kick by a bull. "What the hell happened?"

"We're not really sure because he was in the fields alone. That's the problem. No one knew when he went down, and so he bled a lot."

Archer glanced at her, worried about the sob he'd heard in her voice. "You should go home and get some rest. Where's Nanette?"

"With Calhoun and Olivia. Minnie and Kenny like to play with Nanette, and Barley loves her, too."

"All right." Archer went to stand beside his brother. There was so much pain etched into Mason's face. Lines he'd never seen before. It was as if age had crept up on Mason when no one was looking. Or maybe staring the Grim Reaper in the face lined one's countenance. "Who found him?"

"Last, thank God."

Archer nodded, putting his hand over Mason's. "Hey, bro," he said.

There was no response. But he really hadn't expected one. "Go home," he told Mimi. "Get some rest."

She came to stand beside him, giving him a hug. "I will. By the way, how is your lady friend in Australia?"

"Good enough." Not really, but it was a long story and he couldn't go into it. Right now, he had to think about Mason. He was beginning to feel quite crazed with his life divided into places so far apart.

"All right." She walked over to Mason and gently stroked his cheek. "Hey, you hard-headed mule."

Then she leaned over and whispered something in Mason's ear that sounded suspiciously to Archer like *Come back to me*.

She stood. "Good night, Archer," Mimi said, leaving the room.

"'Night." He stared at his brother. "Mason, I'm home," he said.

He thought he saw a flicker in Mason's eyelid. He wished Mason would wake up. Of course, the minute he did and was coherent, he was going to want to know if Archer had solved his Family Problem. And Archer was going to have to say no. That maybe it was unsolvable.

It hit him hard, when his mind embraced that thought. Some things were simply impossible.

And no matter how much he might want to change it, maybe he couldn't.

Two weeks later

From: Archer
To: Clove
Sorry I haven't written, but I've been staying

pretty much around the clock at the hospital. Mason is finally looking like he may pull through. Hope you're taking care of yourself. Archer

Clove stared at the screen, blinking at the terse wording. She'd waited in agony to hear from Archer. And he sounded as though he was a world away, which he was, but emotionally just as much as geographically.

It did not feel good. Or right. More was wrong than just his brother. Unfortunately, there wasn't much she could do about it. The doctor had confined her to bed a week early, and a nurse was coming to her house weekly to monitor her and the babies' health.

She was beginning to get scared—about a lot of things. That Archer might never come back. That her babies might not make it. That everything she'd ever wanted might slip through her fingers. This family meant everything to her, and she so wanted Archer to want her, too. So she wrote:

I'm thinking about you daily, Archer. I miss you. Give everyone my thoughts and prayers. And please don't forget that I love you. Clove

THREE MONTHS LATER Archer awoke to his cell phone ringing in his pocket. Sitting up, he grabbed it before Mason awakened. Mason was slowly coming out of the woods, and therapists of all kinds were working with him. Mimi came by often. All the brothers and their wives had been by to visit him. The storm of Mason being down had galvanized the brothers into realizing they needed to work harder at the ranch.

Archer had slept in the chair in Mason's room so often he felt as if he and the chair had become one. "Hello?"

"Archer?"

"Yeah." He rubbed at his stubbly chin.

"It's Lucy Penmire."

He came completely awake. "Hi."

"Um, I thought maybe you'd want to know that Clove has gone into labor."

He jumped to his feet and ran into the hall so he could talk without disturbing Mason. "What? Labor?" Swiftly, he checked the date on his watch. "It's only, wait a minute. How far along is she?"

"In terms of contractions?"

"No. Yes. What month of her pregnancy is this?"

"The fifth. Almost the sixth. Could be the

sixth, depending on the date of conception, which—"

His breath tightened. "Fifth! That's too soon!"

"She did the best she could to keep the babies in. They're just too many and she's so small."

Dizziness swept him. "Did you say something about contractions?"

"Yes, she's having some, but the doctors are worried that's not a real good sign. They're going to perform a cesarean section very soon."

"Crap!" He ran into Mason's room, not realizing his brother was awake and listening intently. "Can they wait until I get there?"

"No. Twenty-four hours, even at the minimum, would be too long. I'm sorry, Archer."

"Crap! I'll be there as soon as I can. Tell her, tell her I got her email."

"Like a while back?"

He heard the gentle reproof in Lucy's tone. But how could he explain he was never at home anymore? And that he was consumed with Mason's care? The ranch, his brothers, life… "Dammit," he said. "I swear, I didn't realize it had been that long."

"It's all right," she said. "But it would mean a lot to Clove if she could hear your voice."

"Well, she's going to hear it very soon." Archer hung up, stuffing his belt through the loops.

"Are we having babies?" Mason asked.

Archer whipped around. "Trust that the very mention of babies would bring the first light of interest to your eyes since your accident."

"You're heading out?" Mason asked, his voice very thin and rusty.

"I am."

Mason nodded. "What are we having?"

"Boys, I'm sure. Hell, I don't even know."

"Archer."

"Yeah." He saw his brother's gaze focus on him tightly.

"You talk about her in your sleep."

"I do?" He was shocked. Often when he slept in the hard old hospital chair, he didn't think he slept at all.

"You do. You yak about her a lot. It's like a nighttime soap opera. I've quite enjoyed it."

Archer shook his head. "And to think I've been trying so hard to make certain you're resting well."

"What else do I have to do but lie in this

damn bed? I might as well listen to you ramble. So this time, fix it."

"Fix it?"

"You love her. Regardless of how this came to be, fix it. Life is short."

Archer swallowed, looking at his brother's face. He would never get used to the shorn patch of skin on Mason's head, where they'd had to go in to reduce some swelling. "Mason, I'm going to call Bandera and have him come stay with you."

"Good luck," Mason said. "Dad."

Archer blinked. "Oh my God," he whispered. "I'll be a father in less than twenty-four hours."

Mason grinned and closed his eyes.

It was the first time Archer had seen his brother smile since his accident. And it was all about becoming a father.

Chapter Nineteen

"Stop right there," Clove said as Archer entered her room three days later. She was sitting up in bed, wearing a pretty jacket. And at least her hair was washed and her face wasn't as swollen as it had been. Soreness was her middle name. But when that cowboy strode into her room, she stopped him with an upturned palm.

She thought she had never seen Archer looking so handsome.

"Do not take one step closer until you hear me out," she said. "This time I'm saying everything on my mind."

"Clove—"

"I am moving to Texas," she said, interrupting him. "You and I and the children are going to be a family when they get out of preemie care."

"Clove—"

"And furthermore," Clove said, "I love you.

I have missed you. It's been torture without you. I know you had to be with your family, but from now on, I intend to be like Tonk. We are sticking to you like a Texas tumbleweed."

"Tumbleweeds don't really stick—"

"Archer, you're supposed to be listening. Those babies want you. I want you. I've changed my mind about Mimi's house. I will live there. I will live anywhere. Just so long as I'm near you."

He grinned at her. "Can I speak?"

"No. I'm certain you still haven't heard me. I know you think the only way we're ever going to communicate is by email—"

She gasped as he opened a velvet box that contained an enormous diamond engagement ring.

"*Now* can I speak?" Archer said, beaming.

"All you want." She gestured to him to come closer. "And you don't have to stand over there any longer."

"Good. Because I didn't want to have to toss this across the room."

"You can bet I would have caught it. Archer, it's stunning!" She stared down at the simple emerald-shaped diamond. There was also a wedding band in the box, of channel-set diamonds. "I have never seen anything so beautiful!"

"I figured I'd better show up with something impressive for the woman who conceives and delivers three babies. It's three carats, one for each baby."

"Slide it on," Clove said. "Although I'm very swollen and it might not fit—"

"Aren't I supposed to ask you a question first?" Archer asked playfully.

"Go ahead." Clove closed her eyes. "I want to hear you say it."

He took her hand. "Open your eyes. I want to see those gorgeous eyes, which I loved even when you wore those crazy specs of yours."

She did, smiling shyly at him, her heart beating happily with joy. "I love you."

"Wait," he said, laughing. "You're making me nervous. I know I'm supposed to make a speech here. A proper proposal."

"You stink at it, so I'm saying yes or we'll be here all night." Throwing her arms around his neck, she hugged him tight. He fell into the hospital bed beside her, careful to avoid her tummy.

"This is still my favorite position with you," he said. "And we're managing to try out so many different locations of being horizontal." He kissed her lips, slowly, softly. "Clove," he said.

"Yes?"

"Clove Penmire, I love you. I want you to consider my proposal. I promise to love, honor and hold you, through good times and bad. I promise to take care of you like a prize among women, because you deserve it. Will you do me the honor of becoming my wife?"

"Yes," she said shyly. "I love you."

"I know. That last email you sent me was the clincher, babe."

She wrinkled her nose at him. "I don't believe you. You never wrote me back."

"I'm sorry. Life was crazy. But I will tell you that when I got that email, and you laid out your feelings like that, I knew no matter what happened, you and I were going to be together forever."

"I do love you." She let him slip the ring on her finger. "It wasn't just about the babies in the end."

"The babies!" He stared at her. "How are they? How are you feeling? Are you all right?"

"Everything is fine." Clove looked at him with that tricky smile he loved. "You can go down to the nursery and see them if you want to. Baby Penmire #1, Baby Penmire #2 and Baby Penmire #3."

"Baby Penmire?" Archer repeated, wrinkling his face. "We're changing that right away! I'll be right back," he said, kissing her nose. "I forgot all about the babies because you look just the same as you did the last time I saw you. Except more beautiful," he said hurriedly.

She laughed. "You're doing good for a new fiancé. Nursery is down the hall."

He tore out of the room. Clove sat very still, a grin on her face, waiting.

A minute later, he ran back into her room, his handsome face stunned. "Clove Penmire almost Jefferson," he said, "those are girls in that nursery!"

The expression on his face was priceless. "Don't you like girls?" she teased.

"Well, I do! But I was expecting boys. Boys I know what to do with. I have brothers, for heaven's sake. But girls—girls are a mystery to me."

She motioned for him to come close, so he did. They kissed for a long moment, then she whispered in his ear, "We ladies are going to enjoy keeping you off balance," she said, "but you miscounted those bald heads, my love.

There are two girls and one boy. You aren't totally outnumbered."

"Oh. Well. I didn't *really* care about having all girls," he said with an embarrassed laugh. "Except for their pink name tags, they all looked the same to me with their caps on their heads and mitten-things on their hands. I'm just thrilled they all have your beauty. I blew them each a kiss and they're all very smart, I can tell. And sweet. And talented. And guaranteed to be successful at whatever they do, due to their mother's intelligent, brave and sexy personality. When can they come home with us?"

"I'm not sure, but whenever it is, it's going to be to *our* home, yours and mine." Clove smiled, her heart full of love and joy for her fiancé who loved her just the way she was. Archer held her tight, and smiled, thinking that this woman, his soon-to-be bride, made him the luckiest man in the world.

It wasn't every man who was fortunate enough to marry a woman who gave him three wonderful children. "You're my angels," he whispered, holding Clove in his arms. "All four of you. As long as I live, my angels are going to be right by my side."

And outside the hospital window the Australian sun glowed golden, sending rays of happiness splashing across their bed.

Epilogue

The wedding was in Australia, and it was everything Clove could ever have wished for. To her astonishment, the entire clan of Jeffersons came down, bringing armloads of gifts, toys and well-wishes. She even met people she didn't know were part of the family, two men named Hawk and Jellyfish. And the first people who had "accepted" her into the Jefferson family, Delilah and Jerry, also arrived for the two-week "wedding vacation" Archer and Clove had arranged. Two weeks, they'd theorized, was the proper length of time for family to get to know each other since it took so long to fly to Australia. Delilah and the Jefferson wives said two weeks was just long enough for them to spoil the babies, since the honeymoon was being put off for a year.

The men helped Robert. They liked him, and they felt that the family farm could be fixed up in no time. Setting about with plans and muscle, they spent their time before and after the informal family wedding repairing fence and tack and teaching Robert those things that he'd never had a chance to learn.

This male tutelage, Clove noted with deep appreciation, seemed to bridge some sort of gap between Lucy and Robert. For the first time in a long time, they touched each other as if they cared. Their gazes lingered on each other.

"It's almost as if they're falling in love," Archer whispered in her ear at the rehearsal dinner. "I would never have believed that they nearly divorced."

"It's strange," Clove murmured. "Robert admitted feeling lost marrying into a situation that he knew nothing about. When we ran into problems, I think he felt powerless to help because he didn't understand the running of a real farm."

"There's a lot to it," Archer agreed. "But he's catching on fast. In fact, he enjoys it." He pressed his lips across Clove's temple as they sat together on the porch. "I think he likes having something to talk to Lucy about. And that he likes having the answers for a change."

"I wish I'd seen that before." Clove turned

to took into her husband's eyes. "Thank you. Thank you for everything."

"I like gratitude," Archer said, "but I'm afraid I didn't do anything."

"You did," Clove said. "You and your brothers, and Jerry, and Hawk and Jellyfish, helped Robert, and gave my sister back her husband."

"Good," Archer said. "I like that kind of gratitude. You worried me when I thought you were going to give her my children to save her marriage."

Clove blushed. "She's my sister."

"And I'm your husband." He grinned. "And I'm never going to let you forget that."

"Good," Clove said. "Because I never want to."

They kissed, each of them in the moment, trusting and in love, and knowing that the family they were sharing was what their hearts had always searched for.

"I love you," Clove said. "Stunt work wasn't half as much fun as falling in love with you."

"I love you," Archer said, "and the three angels you've given me—"

"Are going to keep you hopping for the rest of your life," she said with a smile.

"Just like their mum," he agreed with a grin. "I can honestly say you gave me the adventure that I hoped for, and I couldn't be a happier man."

Twelve months later, in Malfunction Junction

From: Robert
To: Union Junction ranch
Birth Announcement
Robert and Lucy are delighted to announce the arrival of SKYLAR and ZANE ANDREW on Monday 26 July 2004 at 2.00 p.m. Zane, weighing in at 7 lb 1 oz, measuring 51 cm long; Skylar Jayne, 5 lb 8 oz measuring 47.5 cm.

Mum, Dad, Skylar and Zane are all doing really well.

Photos will follow in another email.

Thanks for all your good wishes throughout the pregnancy.

P.S.

I would like to add that Lucy has given me one of the memories that I will cherish for the rest of my life. For anyone who has experienced the miracle of childbirth you will understand what I mean. Zane is just as much a picture of beauty as Skylar. There are no words to describe my feelings for the lady who has given me everything that a man could ever ask for and much more. Well, maybe I'm biased but I think she will do a wonderful job and that most of the babies' wonderful personalities I can already attribute to Lucy. I guess I want everyone to know how proud I am of Lucy, not just because she just gave birth, but for her wonderful qualities as a woman and a mother (hey, I *am* the new father, I can gloat). As a last and very important note, Lucy and I would like to announce that we are going through the final adoption process for two children, two sisters. This farm, thanks to you, is a wonderful place for children to grow up.

Well, I've embarrassed myself enough so I just want to say thank you to all of the "Jefferson Cyber Uncles." You all mean a great deal to Lucy, I know this because she talks about you all the time.

See ya,
Robert

Mason looked at Archer. "Emotional sort, isn't he?"

Archer smiled at Clove and their three babies. She did such a good job with him and the children that his world was complete. Tink scratched at his boot, and through the window, he could see Tonk grazing. Life was very, very sweet. "Emotional is good. You should try it sometime, Mason."

"So, is this the end of the Aussie email correspondence relationship? Clove's happy here, and Lucy's happy there, and you'll split your time between the two ranches, and the children will have dual citzenship?"

Archer's heart filled with love as he watched his wife nurturing their children. "She's happy. And I found the one woman for me."

"Congratulations," Mason said, looking like the strong Mason of old. "I'm really glad to hear it. I remember being very worried about you and your mystery woman." He sighed, and rubbed his chin. "Now, call the rest of the boys in. We need to have a family conference."

"Topic?" Archer asked.

"Mimi," Mason said. "That little gal is driving me nuts with her run for the sheriff's seat! More to the point, she says she wants me to be her deputy!"

* * * * *

YES! Please send me the *Cowboy at Heart* collection in Larger Print. This collection begins with 3 FREE books and 2 FREE gifts in the first shipment, and more free gifts will follow! My books will arrive in 8 monthly shipments until I have the entire 51-book *Cowboy at Heart* collection. I will receive 2 or 3 FREE books in each shipment and I will pay just $4.99 U.S./ $5.89 CDN. for each of the other four books in each shipment, plus $2.99 for shipping and handling.* If I decide to keep the entire collection, I'll have paid for only 32 books because 19 books are FREE! I understand that by accepting the 3 free books and gifts places me under no obligation to buy anything. I can always return a shipment and cancel at any time. My free books and gifts are mine to keep no matter what I decide.

256 HCN 0779   456 HCN 0779

Name	(PLEASE PRINT)	
Address		Apt. #
City	State/Prov.	Zip/Postal Code

Signature (if under 18, a parent or guardian must sign)

Mail to the **Harlequin® Reader Service:**
IN U.S.A.: P.O. Box 1867, Buffalo, NY 14240-1867
IN CANADA: P.O. Box 609, Fort Erie, Ontario L2A 5X3

* Terms and prices subject to change without notice. Prices do not include applicable taxes. Sales tax applicable in N.Y. Canadian residents will be charged applicable taxes. This offer is limited to one order per household. All orders subject to approval. Credit or debit balances in a customer's account(s) may be offset by any other outstanding balance owed by or to the customer. Please allow 4 to 6 weeks for delivery. Offer available while quantities last. Offer not available to Quebec residents.

Your Privacy—The Harlequin® Reader Service is committed to protecting your privacy. Our Privacy Policy is available online at www.ReaderService.com or upon request from the Harlequin Reader Service.

We make a portion of our mailing list available to reputable third parties that offer products we believe may interest you. If you prefer that we not exchange your name with third parties, or if you wish to clarify or modify your communication preferences, please visit us at www.ReaderService.com/consumerchoice or write to us at Harlequin Reader Service Preference Service, P.O. Box 9062, Buffalo, NY 14269. Include your complete name and address.

ReaderService.com

Manage your account online!

- Review your order history
- Manage your payments
- Update your address

***We've designed
the Harlequin® Reader Service
website just for you.***

Enjoy all the features!

- Reader excerpts from any series
- Respond to mailings and
  special monthly offers
- Discover new series available to you
- Browse the Bonus Bucks catalog
- Share your feedback

Visit us at:
ReaderService.com

REQUEST YOUR FREE BOOKS!
2 FREE WHOLESOME ROMANCE NOVELS IN LARGER PRINT
PLUS 2
FREE
MYSTERY GIFTS

++*+*+*+*+*+*+*+*+*+*+*+*+*+*+*+*+*

HEARTWARMING™

++*+*+*+*+*+*+*+*+*+*+*+*+*+*+*+*+*

Wholesome, tender romances

YES! Please send me 2 FREE Harlequin® Heartwarming Larger-Print novels and my 2 FREE mystery gifts (gifts worth about $10). After receiving them, if I don't wish to receive any more books, I can return the shipping statement marked "cancel." If I don't cancel, I will receive 4 brand-new larger-print novels every month and be billed just $4.99 per book in the U.S. or $5.74 per book in Canada. That's a savings of at least 23% off the cover price. It's quite a bargain! Shipping and handling is just 50¢ per book in the U.S. and 75¢ per book in Canada.* I understand that accepting the 2 free books and gifts places me under no obligation to buy anything. I can always return a shipment and cancel at any time. Even if I never buy another book, the two free books and gifts are mine to keep forever.

161/361 IDN F47N

Name _____ (PLEASE PRINT)

Address _____ Apt. #

City _____ State/Prov. _____ Zip/Postal Code

Signature (if under 18, a parent or guardian must sign)

Mail to the **Harlequin® Reader Service:**
IN U.S.A.: P.O. Box 1867, Buffalo, NY 14240-1867
IN CANADA: P.O. Box 609, Fort Erie, Ontario L2A 5X3

* Terms and prices subject to change without notice. Prices do not include applicable taxes. Sales tax applicable in N.Y. Canadian residents will be charged applicable taxes. Offer not valid in Quebec. This offer is limited to one order per household. Not valid for current subscribers to Harlequin Heartwarming larger-print books. All orders subject to credit approval. Credit or debit balances in a customer's account(s) may be offset by any other outstanding balance owed by or to the customer. Please allow 4 to 6 weeks for delivery. Offer available while quantities last.

Your Privacy—The Harlequin® Reader Service is committed to protecting your privacy. Our Privacy Policy is available online at www.ReaderService.com or upon request from the Harlequin Reader Service.

We make a portion of our mailing list available to reputable third parties that offer products we believe may interest you. If you prefer that we not exchange your name with third parties, or if you wish to clarify or modify your communication preferences, please visit us at www.ReaderService.com/consumerschoice or write to us at Harlequin Reader Service Preference Service, P.O. Box 9062, Buffalo, NY 14269. Include your complete name and address.

HWDIR13R